Tom & Lucky
(and George & Cokey Flo)

C. Joseph Greaves

BLOOMSBURY CIRCUS

LONDON · OXFORD · NEW YORK · NEW DELHI · SYDNEY

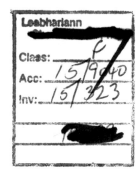
Bloomsbury Circus
An imprint of Bloomsbury Publishing Plc

50 Bedford Square   1385 Broadway
London   New York
WC1B 3DP   NY 10018
UK   USA

www.bloomsbury.com

BLOOMSBURY and the Diana logo are trademarks of Bloomsbury Publishing Plc

First published in Great Britain 2015

© Charles J. Greaves

Charles J. Greaves has asserted his right under the Copyright, Designs and Patents Act, 1988, to be identified as Author of this work.

British Library Cataloguing-in-Publication Data
A catalogue record for this book is available from the British Library.

ISBN: HB: 978-1-4088-6899-7
ISBN: TPB: 978-1-4088-6342-8
ISBN: ePub: 978-1-4088-6341-1

2 4 6 8 10 9 7 5 3

Typeset by RefineCatch Limited, Bungay, Suffolk
Printed and bound in Great Britain by CPI Group (UK) Ltd, Croydon CR0 4YY

MIX
Paper from
responsible sources
FSC® C013604
www.fsc.org

To find out more about our authors and books visit www.bloomsbury.com. Here you will find extracts, author interviews, details of forthcoming events and the option to sign up for our newsletters.

For the Tallow Lane Gang: Mike, Danny, Nancy, Roddy, and Tracey

Novels arise out of the shortcomings of history.
—Georg Philipp Friedrich von Hardenberg

THE YEAR WAS 1936.

Lucky Luciano was the most powerful gangster in America. Thomas E. Dewey was an ambitious young prosecutor determined to bring him down, and Cokey Flo Brown—grifter, heroin addict, and sometimes prostitute—was the witness who claimed she could do it. Only George Morton Levy, a courtly Long Island defense attorney, stood between Lucky and a life behind bars and between Dewey and the New York governor's mansion.

This is their story.

One

Lucky

"SIX IS THE POINT. Six."

Salvatore Lucania weighs the cool dice in his hand. Small in stature, lost in the shapeless tweed of a borrowed jacket, he watches through hooded eyes as bills flutter and settle like autumn leaves on the green expanse before him, there to be sorted and matched in concordance with the shouted wagers of the sporting men who elbow and jostle, their polyglot ruckus evolving under a hazy trinity of overhead lamps into order and then, finally, into silence.

He gives the dice a slow rattle.

"Come on, kid. You jackin off or shootin crap?"

Laughter.

Lucania's eyes, cold and reptilian, search out the voice. The laughter dies.

1

He blows into his fist.

"Comin out."

He tosses the dice backhanded. They short-hop and carom off the far rail and tumble to their final, immutable rest.

Double threes.

Whoops, and jeers, and a rough hand slapping his back.

Lucania glances at his pal Meyer, who stands quietly by the side pocket. Their eyes meet and hold. Meyer's eyebrows lift.

"Hose him down, Frankie. This kid is hot!"

"Twenty clams."

"Covered."

"Abe's Cabe."

"Covered!"

"Sawbuck."

"You're off."

"Fade 'im!"

"Snake eyes!"

"Boxcars!"

"Baby needs a new pair of shoes!"

The process repeats, as it has throughout the night and into the bleary morning, with only the shooters changing in their rotation until the men by acclamation, their number winnowed by the inertial forces of loss and fatigue, finally call it quits.

At nearly five A.M., Lucania watches as winnings are counted, and outcomes assessed, and maledictions quietly uttered. A cigar is lit with a flourish. The croupier is tipped and bows obsequiously as he moves through the shadows toward the stairs leading up from their basement redoubt.

The men sort hats and topcoats, don mufflers and gloves. They stamp or pace like stallions in a tight and skittish cluster.

"Excellent evening," Meyer says as the two boys stand with hands in pockets, waiting for the alley door to be opened.

"Not too shabby," Lucania agrees.

They make for a curious pair, the young Sicilian and the younger Russian Jew where they stand flanked by older and larger men whose body odors and rancid breaths mingle in the dead basement air with the acrid smells of bleach and oil, coal dust and smoke.

Yawns are stifled. Coats open and flap.

"You boys done real good tonight." A fat man—Pazzano, the Calabrian baker from Mott Street—has turned and is speaking to Lucania. "Whatta you plan to do with all that money?"

"You see my friend here? He's savin up for college."

The man laughs. "Hey, you hear that? We got a couple college boys over here."

One of the redheaded brothers from Brooklyn, the one with the pink facial scar, shoulders his way through the men until he is standing beside Lucania.

"Nice night, kid. In case you was worried about gettin home safe, my brother and me'll walk you right to your doorstep. Safer than a police escort we are. Only cost you a fiver."

"No thanks."

"You sure about that? It's a dangerous world out there. Anythin's liable to happen, you ain't got the proper protection."

"You heard me the first time."

"Okay, kid, have it your way. Just tryin to be helpful is all. Don't say you wasn't warned."

And still they wait for the alley door to open. Connor, the Tammany man, resumes his rambling yarn about a whorehouse fire in Five Points.

"—and not a one of 'em wearin more than the smile she was born with. And Timulty, the station chief, with his wife off visitin her sister in Philly, he steps forward like the gentleman that he is and says he's got an empty bedroom at his apartment, see—"

"Christ, the wife is gonna skin me."

"What's takin so goddamn long?"

"Frankie! What the fuck are you doin up there?"

3

A door opens above. All heads turn to the staccato clatter of shoes on wooden stairs.

"What the—"

Three men have descended, each with his hat pulled low and a muffler covering his face. They move silently into position with their guns leveled and steady—one by the furnace and one at either end of the billiard table, the three guns forming a deadly triangle.

The room is suddenly silent.

"Let's go, cash on the table," a gunman orders, gesturing with his weapon. He wears a topcoat of gray herringbone and gloves of black kid.

None of the gamblers moves.

"I said—"

"Do you have any idea who you're talkin to, boyo?"

The gunman turns and raises his pistol and thumbs back the hammer. Connor's hands lift in slow surrender.

"Cash on the table, Micky! Let's go, chop-chop!"

This time all do as instructed, each man either emptying his pockets onto the hard green felt or turning them inside out for the gunmen's inspections. Soon, over eight hundred dollars stands in a greasy, crumpled heap.

"You too, Junior."

The gun points at Lucania, who meets it with eyes as hard and black as the muzzle staring back at him.

"Go fuck yourself."

The gunman steps closer. His hand blurs as his pistol lashes, smashing Lucania's cheek.

All the men flinch. All, that is, except Lucania, who tastes the blood as it trickles toward his chin.

"Let's go, tough guy. Cash on the table."

Lucania tosses a fistful of folded bills onto the felt. Meyer's eyes, alert throughout, watch as the gunmen stuff cash into their pockets.

4

"Thanks, boys," their leader sing-songs as he backs toward the staircase, his gun sweeping left and right. "It was nice doin business."

One by one the gunmen make their way up the narrow steps, with the leader the last to ascend, crouching as he backs until, with a whirl of gray herringbone, the door slams shut behind him.

The room erupts.

Men are shouting and swearing, and some are fumbling for pistols. The alley door is rattled and tested by heavy shoulders. Amid the heat and frenzy, Meyer offers a handkerchief to his friend, who presses it to his cheek.

"Thanks."

One of the men, his gun at the ready, has sidled to the staircase. He ducks his head for a look, then raises a hand to the others.

"Quiet!"

Above him, the door creaks open.

"Don't shoot! It's me, Frankie!"

The men crowd the staircase as the croupier descends on wobbly legs, a bloodied bar rag pressed to his head. He is swept and spun as if by a surging tide and backed against the table, where he stammers his story of how the gunmen had lain in wait and coldcocked him and left him for dead. The man who holds him by the shirt collar pulls the rag-hand free and turns him by the chin, so all can witness the bloody, purplish lump above his ear.

He is released.

"Somebody's a dead man!" bellows Connor.

"Open the fuckin door," another orders, and Frankie, his keys jingling, hurries to oblige.

Snow has fallen during the night, and the men emerge from the basement single file like hibernates smoked from a den with their greatcoats steaming and their breaths billowing frosty white in the cold light of daybreak.

They confer but briefly. Theories are advanced, and names ventured, and vengeance crudely sworn until, one by one, the men drift away, trudging heavily down the alley and into the blanketed morning.

Meyer is alongside Lucania as both boys, hurrying now, raise their collars and duck into the icy headwinds buffeting a Third Avenue whose flocked expanse is yet untracked by car or horse or man.

The boys watch over their shoulders.

"Son of a bitch, that hurt."

"Here, let me see it."

They stop, and Lucania lowers the bloody handkerchief.

"It's all right, you won't need stitches. Put some snow on it."

"Son of a fucking bitch."

They are moving again, hastening against the risen dawn.

"By the way," Meyer says, "what did I tell you about betting the four and ten?"

"Hey, I won, didn't I? And besides, what's the difference now?"

"Dumb luck is nothing to be proud of."

Lucania pauses once more to crane his neck. "Keep an eye out for that scar-faced Mick bastard."

"What for? He knows you've just been robbed. That's the beauty of it. I'll bet you nobody goes to the cops. Statistics show that crimes perpetrated against other criminals are very rarely reported."

"Whatever you say, Meyer."

"Risk management," the younger boy proclaims with a finger raised. "First you figure the odds, then you figure out how to shave 'em."

"What are the odds my old man kicks my ass when I get home?"

"Just tell him you went to the library and fell asleep in the stacks. That's what I always say."

"Yeah, right," Lucania says, examining the bloody handkerchief. "At least you been in a fuckin library."

They arrive at the corner of 12th Street, where they stop and wait, shuffling their feet and blowing warmth into their hands. Soon a figure emerges from out of the sunrise, furtive in its approach, ducking from pushcart to car, from stoop to storefront.

The boys move into a sheltering alcove and wait for the new arrival. He too is a young man, flushed and winded when he finally appears.

"Like candy from a baby," the new man says, pulling an enormous roll of bills from his herringbone topcoat and handing it off to Meyer.

"Nice work. Is everybody square?"

"You bet."

"What about you?"

"I took my cut. Count it if you want."

Meyer pockets the cash without counting it.

"Your boys are in the dark?"

"Just like you said."

"You're absolutely sure about that?"

"Sure I'm sure. I done just like you told me."

The new man turns to Lucania, eying the bloody handkerchief. "Sorry about the knock, Sallie, but I hadda make it look good."

Meyer steps between them to survey the empty street. He exhumes the roll from his pocket and peels off a pair of bills.

"Here's a little bonus," he says to the new man, "for a job well done."

Before either can react to the *snik* of the knife blade, Lucania has jumped onto the new man's back and is pounding at his neck, jabbing and stabbing as though chipping ice from a block. The man's shrieks turn to gargles, viscous and strangled, and then to silence as Meyer ducks to avoid the spurting blood and Lucania, still stabbing, rides the falling body all the way to the sidewalk.

The alcove is an abattoir, its walls spattered and running. Meyer grabs Lucania's arm with both hands and wrestles him off the prostrate figure whose body is sprawled on the sidewalk with its legs on bare pavement and its head, or what remains of it, a crimson flower blossoming in the snow.

7

"What the hell'd you do that for?"

Lucania's breath comes in heaves as he wipes his face with a sleeve.

"Risk management."

"Christ, let's get out of here."

Meyer pulls him by the arm, but Lucania shrugs free and rummages the dead man's overcoat, counting out bills as he stands.

"Sorry, pal." Lucania leans forward and spits. "But I hadda make it look good."

Two

George

May 1915

HIS FIRST PROBLEM was the dictograph.

The device, purchased by Mrs. Florence Carman and installed by one Gaston Boissonnault, had allowed Mrs. Carman to eavesdrop from the safety of the marital bedroom on the conversations that her husband, Dr. Edwin Carman, had been having in the supposed privacy of his downstairs examining room. It was the discovery of this device that had changed the focus of the investigation from an assassination, dispassionately perpetrated by some unknown enemy of LuLu Bailey, into a crime of jealous passion.

His second problem was the maid, Celia Coleman. The current version of her story had Mrs. Carman tearing through the kitchen, gun in hand, on her way to the side of the house where she would thrust the weapon through the examining room window and shoot Mrs. Bailey dead, the bullet perhaps intended for the philandering doctor. In this latest, more dramatic telling, Mrs. Carman had then brandished the gun as she'd returned through the home's back door, announcing to the maid, "I've shot him!"

His third problem was the Burns Agency detective, Archer Owens, the man who'd originally been their savior. Employed by the Nassau County district attorney's office to keep watch over the maid, Owens had approached the defense team with a sensational tale in which Celia Coleman had been kidnapped by the D.A., held against her will, and browbeaten into fabricating her current testimony. This bombshell, although disputed by Coleman herself on the witness stand, was felt to have been largely responsible for the hung jury that had ended the first trial of Florence Carman. After that trial, however, Owens had visited Celia Coleman at her home in South Carolina and had, in the presence of at least two witnesses, been loudly accused by the maid of attempted bribery, effectively blunting the detective's further utility as a witness.

But all these problems paled in comparison to the one that had kept young George Morton Levy awake, tossing and turning, for the better part of a week. It wasn't so much the difficulty of the case, or the sudden resignation of John Graham as lead counsel for the defense—the first trial had, after all, taken a heavy toll on the aging barrister—but rather Mrs. Carman's adamancy that George and George alone was the one to take Graham's place.

"But I'm only twenty-six years old," George had reminded her, fidgeting in his chair.

"I realize that."

"And I've never tried a murder case. Or any major case, for that matter."

To this, the defendant had only shrugged. "You've tried other cases. Edwin told me as much."

George's imploring eyes shifted to Dr. Carman. "I really don't have the experience. And what if I make a mistake?"

"George, dear," Florence Carman told him then, her hand firm on his knee. "I'm not asking for another continuance. You know this case better than anyone. You helped with the investigation, you sat through the first trial, and you're the most capable young man I've ever met. I have complete confidence in your ability to win an acquittal."

The case, it must be said, was not without hope. The maid, Celia Coleman, had from the witness stand contradicted the very affidavit she'd signed on the day after LuLu Bailey's murder. In that document, which George himself had prepared, Celia had said nothing about a gun, or a side-yard excursion, or a dramatic back-door confession. But George had made the mistake—the rookie mistake—of obtaining her signature on only the last page of the document, which had given the maid, once in the custody of the district attorney, room in which to repudiate the first two pages of her testimony.

And then there was the gun itself. Or rather, the fact that no gun had ever been found in the Carman household, leaving a gaping hole in the prosecution's theory of the case. This was a hole that Lewis J. Smith, the dogged district attorney of Nassau County, had tried to fill with farfetched theories about gang connections and mystery accomplices. It was the missing gun, George had always believed, more so than Archer Owens's dramatic testimony, that had led ten members of the original Carman jury to cast their votes for acquittal.

The prospect of trying one's first murder case was enough to warrant any young lawyer's insomnia. Here, however, the trial's more salacious aspects—the beautiful defendant, her dashing doctor husband, and the heavy barrage of journalistic innuendo regarding the good doctor's other female patients—had turned the proceedings into a carnival sideshow the likes of which New York hadn't seen since the Harry Thaw trial of 1908. Indeed, when the first Carman trial had opened in October of 1914, more than three thousand spectators had crowded the Mineola courthouse, vying for three hundred available seats.

And now it would all fall to George. George, who'd been too busy with his semipro baseball and football careers to bother attending college. George, who'd worked his way through the night program at NYU Law School by taking odd legal jobs for three dollars a week, searching titles and serving process. George, who'd only recently taken the New York bar exam upon attaining the minimum age of twenty-one years.

But George Levy accepted the Carman case, and with it the butterflies and the lost appetite and the chronic insomnia. Really, what choice did he have?

The reporters scoffed, and the judge condescended, and the sneering D.A. ran roughshod over the earnest young lawyer in the stiff woolen suit, yet somehow George persevered. Better still, for two grueling weeks of thrust and parry, move and countermove, George Morton Levy rose to the occasion, his courtroom baptism culminating in a blistering cross-examination of Celia Coleman that had left the young maid in tears, breathing new life into the Owens version of events and, most important of all, exposing for the first time the maid's long-festering animosity toward her employer, the coldly imperious Florence Carman.

But all did not go smoothly for the defense, not by a long shot. A critical issue in the case was visibility, since all the other patients in Dr. Carman's waiting room testified that they'd seen nobody cross the front lawn after the fatal shot had been fired. This left the defense with two alternative scenarios with which to rebut Celia Coleman: Either the gunman had fled west, across the neighboring lawn, or else the falling twilight had obscured the patients' views from the waiting room's street-side window.

In the retrial, however, the district attorney slammed both doors shut with a trio of new witnesses.

The first was Dr. James Scarr of the New York Weather Bureau, who described from his record book the atmospheric conditions in Freeport, N.Y., on the night of the murder. The sun had set at 7:32 P.M., he testified, with astronomical twilight lasting until 9:31. Therefore, between 7:50 and 8:10, when the crime had unquestionably occurred, there had been more than adequate daylight by which to observe a running figure from several blocks away.

George cross-examined Dr. Scarr with a single question: "Are you the man who prepares the weather forecasts for the papers?"

"Some of them."

"That's enough," said George with a wave, and the courtroom erupted in laughter.

The other two witnesses were not so easily dismissed. May Black and her daughter Ruth had been summer renters of the house next door to the Carmans', and yet had never been questioned by police. With no ax to grind, and no reason to color their testimony in favor of either prosecution or defense, both described hearing the fatal gunshot from where they'd sat on their front porch, and both described hurrying to the fence that separated their house from that of the Carmans.

Neither saw any fleeing assailant.

This was devastating testimony on two levels. First, it corroborated Celia Coleman's version of events in which the killer—Mrs. Carman—had fled neither westward nor into the street, but rather back to the rear door of the house. Second, it sent a subliminal message to the jury that if the police had been so slipshod in their investigation as to have missed these two critical eyewitnesses, then might they also have overlooked the murder weapon hidden somewhere inside the Carman home?

Thrust and parry, punch and counterpunch, with both sides bloodied and exhausted after two weeks of mortal combat. Thus was set the stage onto which young George Levy rose with shaking knees to present his final argument. The apogee of his nascent career, his summation would be delivered to a packed courtroom, before a skeptical judge, and with the national press scrutinizing his every word and gesture. And also, as George was acutely aware, with his client's very life on the line.

George began by reviewing the evidence, both pro and con. Then he lambasted the district attorney for effectively kidnapping Celia

Coleman and forcing her to commit perjury. And then, sensing the need for a tenth-round knockout, he closed with a haymaker.

"Gentlemen of the jury," he said, "let me share with you my greatest fear. You may feel that you cannot decide between myself and my worthy opponent, the district attorney, and so might find that there has not been a major guilt, but only a minor one. Well, let me disabuse you of that notion. Mrs. Bailey has been murdered. Either Mrs. Carman killed her, or she did not. There can be no compromise on that point. You must either free Mrs. Carman," he said, his voice rising as his finger swung toward his client, "or you must send her to the electric chair!"

There occurs in all jury trials, be they criminal or civil in nature, a kind of subconscious transference in which the jurors assign to a party their like or dislike, their collective trust or mistrust of that party's counsel, who speaks on his client's behalf. And therein lay Florence Carman's salvation, because any animus those Long Island farmers and fishermen might have harbored for the icy, statuesque beauty on trial before them was more than overcome by her slight, bandy-legged counsel's inherent good nature. George Levy was not only genial; he was also sincere and trustworthy, and his voice fairly hummed with the righteousness of his cause.

"Scrappy," they would call him afterward. "A good egg. Just a regular guy."

The acquittal of Florence Carman was a national sensation, and it made George Morton Levy the talk of the New York trial bar.

Three

Tom

THE SCHOOL BELL, muted at first behind thick sandstone walls, trilled with clamorous rapture as the doors flew wide and the children spilled tumbling and laughing down the broad concrete steps and onto the emerald lawn.

First came the younger grades—a bright terrazzo of knee-skinned boys in summer knickers and pigtailed girls in sailor dresses and shiny Mary Janes. Among the older children who followed, the girls bunched and giggling and the boys in attitudes of boredom or roughhouse, one stood apart from the rest.

Tommy Dewey strode through the throng, whistling as he went, oblivious to the tumult around him. Inured, perhaps, to the girls' stolen glances and the boys' hopeful voices raised in greeting or farewell. Secure—some might even say smug—in his role as Central High's newest and brightest young light.

His route to the train depot covered six familiar blocks that Tommy pedaled languidly, his bike carving lazy serpentines on the sun-dappled macadam. The houses he passed—the Millers' and the Jameses' and old Mrs. Pulver's—were spruce and tidy, the lawns still midsummer-green even as the elms and maples, as if sensing their incipient nakedness, were blushing their first autumnal hues.

The 4:15 from Detroit was right on schedule, and Tommy leaned his brand-new Cadillac alongside the older, rustier bikes on the north wall of the platform, where Jenks and Lacy stood waiting by the ticket window. Tommy joined his old grade-school pals just as the hulking locomotive chuffed and screeched to a halt.

"Ducky," Lacy said without turning.

"Buck up. You could be at Cadet Corps doing push-ups."

"At least I'd be home by five."

"With nothing in your pockets but lint."

"Hey," Jenks said to Tommy. "Did you get a load of Mary Watkins today?"

"Steady, man. Don't be a cad."

The boys watched in silence as the doors opened and the passengers alighted, several nodding or waving to Annie Dewey's only son while the porters handed down luggage. Then, finally, the cargo door opened and Jackson waved the boys over.

"Don't tell me you gents got all slicked up for me," the old Negro grinned as he hefted the heavy bundles and carefully handed them down. Tommy liked Jackson best of all the porters because he never tossed the bundles, scuffing or shredding the bottommost newspaper.

"Junior high," Tommy explained. "It started today."

Jackson stood akimbo, his gaze drifting toward the horizon.

"Junior high." He sighed. "All them pretty young things in itty-bitty skirts and white ankle socks."

"Steady, man," Jenks told him. "Don't be a cad."

Their bundles secured and balanced, the boys retraced their route, wobbling over the Main Street bridge before turning up Water Street, standing on their pedals and straining against the weight of their cargo, as if the grim tidings they bore from France and Belgium carried with them a palpable mass.

The others were assembled at the neat Victorian bungalow on West Oliver Street. There a half-dozen bicycles leaned against trees or sprawled haphazard below the freshly painted steps that led to where the boys themselves were already goldbricking on the porch, drinking milk and choosing cookies from a passing silver tray.

"Mater!" Tommy cried as he lowered his kickstand. "If you keep feeding them, I'll never get them to work!"

"Nonsense, dear," his mother replied as she turned toward the kitchen. "An army travels on its stomach."

By the time Tommy had divvied the papers and dispatched his minions and finished his own delivery route, a purplish dusk had settled over central Michigan, and the lights along River Street reflected a familiar constellation on the mirrored face of the Shiawassee. Inside the glowing Victorian on West Oliver, where a fire now crackled in the parlor and where Vivaldi swooped and soared from the phonograph, Tommy's father sat clucking at the day's headlines.

"They're estimating half a million Christians have been killed in Asia Minor!" George Dewey thundered, glaring over the page to where his wife and son stood watching from the doorway to the kitchen. "And now I suppose the Democrats will blame *that* on Taft!"

"Careful, George M. You'll have a thrombosis."

"The world is going to Hades in a handbasket!"

"Not here, darling. Here in Owosso we're having pot roast for dinner."

The mealtime conversation strayed only briefly from its usual fare of national politics, state politics, and local politics to include a smattering of Annie Dewey's afternoon bridge and a generous helping of Tommy's first day of school, complete with a grilling on teachers, classes, and classmates.

No, debate was not offered this year. Yes, he'd signed up for choir. No, he didn't think the new civics teacher was a Bull Moose. Yes, he was certain there was no junior high newspaper.

Seizing on a lull in the inquisition, his mother passed Tommy the carrots. "I ran into Glenna Watkins this afternoon."

"Oh, dear. Was she injured badly?"

"Don't be impertinent. She told me that Mary had quite the time in Chicago this summer. The symphony and the ballet and *tout* the art museums. Glenna said that she'd positively *blossomed*. That was the word she used."

"I'll bet she did."

"You bet she did what, dear? Said, in the case of Glenna, or blossomed, in the case of Mary?"

"Let the boy eat his supper."

"I was only recounting a conversation, that's all. It's not as if I were *prying* or anything."

"Might we please change the subject? Father, did the Tigers win today?"

"Five-two. Cobb went three for four."

"Hot socks!"

"We'll have no more of *that*, young man. People will think you were raised in a saloon. I'll wager that Mary Watkins doesn't go around spouting vulgarities in front of *her* parents . . ."

Tommy perched on the piano bench with his mother seated behind him, the click and clash of her knitting lapsing into unconscious rhythm with the tick and tock of his metronome. He played Chopin's "Revolutionary" Étude and Beethoven's "Für Elise." After Debussy's "Clair de lune," he noticed that the sounds of her knitting had ceased.

"Sing for me, my angel."

He sang. Bizet's "Habanera" and Bach's "Bist du Bei Mir." He closed with her favorite, Schubert's "Ave Maria," and when he'd finished "*In hora mortis nostrae, Ave Maria!*" she'd dabbed at her eyes before again taking up her needles.

"Someday," she told him, "mark my words, Thomas Edwin Dewey will sing in the great opera houses of Europe."

He turned on the bench to face her.

"Correction, Mater. Father says that someday he'll be president of the United States."

Four

Flo

VIOLET'S BROTHER RALPH looked like Joe Brooks in his best Sunday getup—a double-breasted number with a white pocket hankie and spectator shoes. We watched as he strolled past the shop window like some Ridge Avenue high-hat out taking the air, just walking and smoking and eyeballing the merchandise. Then he glanced over his shoulder and crushed out his cigarette and disappeared through the door.

We could hear the little bell go *tinkle, tinkle* from clear across the street, where we sat with the top down and our feet up on the dash.

"Don't worry," Vi said, reading the look on my face. "Ralph knows his onions. Besides, you can't cheat an honest man."

She reached into her bag and pulled out her hope chest and shook loose a couple of ciggies. I made sure my hand was nice and steady when she lit me up.

20

"Okay, you know the script," she said after another few minutes of slouching and smoking and me tapping my foot on the windshield. "Don't ball it up."

I took the photograph from the envelope and stepped out onto the sidewalk. It was hot and muggy and my armpits were already sweating as I peeled the dress off the small of my back. What little breeze there was came from the west, off the Allegheny, like stink off a burning tire. I fanned myself with the photo as I hurried across the street.

The shop was called Larry's Loan & Pawn. According to Ralph, Larry was a cheap kike bastard who sucked the blood out of working stiffs like him, which made it okay to pull the old fakeloo so long as we didn't get caught. Me personally, I didn't care about blood or money—all's I wanted was to get in jake with Vi and her crowd at school. That, and maybe catch a pass from Ralph, who was a swell-looking hunk but was also around twenty-five, which made him ten years older than Violet and me, so who was I kidding anyway?

Tinkle, tinkle. The shop looked like your grandfather's attic might look if your grandfather played the accordion and the saxophone and collected old typewriters and dusty sets of china. The guy behind the counter was tall and stoop-shouldered and looked like a vulture, right down to his bony neck and his Adam's apple and his great big honker of a nose. He wore a vest and a necktie but no jacket, and he give me a quick once-over before pointing the beak back at Ralph, who was all matter-of-fact while feeding him the hooey about the museum he worked for in New York and how he liked to browse around in joints like this whenever he traveled because you never know what hidden treasures, blah blah blah.

I walked up to the counter and laid the photograph on the glass.

"What's this?" Larry asked, pinching cheaters from his vest.

I gave Ralph the fish-eye and walked Larry down to the far end of the counter. I'll admit that my heart was thumping so loud I thought maybe Ralph could hear it from where he'd moved to stand behind me, pretending to study some junk up on the wall above Larry's head.

I read Larry the script about my sick mother and my dead father who collected old photographs. All of which was a yarn, because my dad was alive and usually drunk and using my mom as a punching bag, and also because the photo on the counter—which showed some long-haired Indian on a spotted horse with a rifle across his lap—had actually come from Ralph, who'd bought it for a penny at the Carnegie Library and browned it under a flatiron.

I looked up at Larry, who was glancing over my shoulder at Ralph, who, I knew without looking, was making a slicing motion with a finger across his throat.

"Uh, look here, young lady," Larry said, taking the photo and holding it up to the milky light from the window. "I'm busy just now with this gentleman, but if you'll leave this with me, I'll look it over when I have a free moment."

I reached my hand for the photo. "I can't do that, sir. Mama would kill me if I let it out of my sight. Heck, she'd kill me if she knew I'd taken it from Papa's collection in the first place."

Larry made a face like he'd bit into a lemon.

"All right then." He glanced at Ralph again before walking over to the cash register and jabbing one key and banging his fist on another. The drawer slid open with a loud *cha-ching*, which was the exact sound Ralph had made out in the car when he'd described to us the dough we'd soon be splitting three ways—half to him, a quarter to Violet, and a lousy quarter to me, who was the one taking all the risk.

I jumped when Larry slapped a dime down on the glass.

"There's a drugstore just around the corner," he said. "Go have a soda and come back in fifteen minutes. I'll be finished with this gentleman then, and we can talk about this picture business."

I was supposed to make a fuss about leaving the photo, only I didn't see the point in it anymore, so I just turned for the door and scrammed. I gave Violet the high sign after I'd passed clear of the

22

window, and then I ducked around the corner and into the drugstore and ordered myself an egg cream, plus a second one for Ralph.

I twirled on the counter stool and waited.

"You were supposed to make a stink," Ralph said when he entered, tossing his hat onto the counter.

"Did he bite?"

He took the stool one down from mine. He picked up his drink and took a long sip and half turned to face me.

"Hook, line, and sinker," he said. "If you weren't such a little squirt, I'd kiss you smack on the mouth."

"Applesauce," I told him, turning my face to the door.

Violet appeared then, backlit in the doorway, posing like Theda Bara with a hand on her hip.

"Well?"

"Fish in a barrel," her brother said. "Corn in a can."

"How much?"

He looked down the counter to make sure the jerk was busy.

"I told him I'd pay twenty now, and another twenty if it proved to be the genuine article. I told him if it didn't, then he could keep the first twenty as a gesture of good faith."

Violet took a long drag on her cigarette and flicked it to the sidewalk. She sashayed in and sat between me and her brother and helped herself to my soda. She was always doing stuff like that—taking my magazines or my lipstick—just to show that she could.

"Okay, Flo, now it's your turn." She gestured toward the door with her chin. "Don't take any wooden nickels."

What I took was a long drink of Ralph before sliding off my stool and giving my dress a tug. The material was cotton—yellow flowers on a white background—and I imagined Ralph's eyes on my chassis as I stepped into the sunlight and paused there long enough to give him a gander.

Tinkle, tinkle. Larry was standing behind the counter with the cheaters up on his head. He was polishing some kind of a lantern, like he was hoping for a genie to appear and grant him three wishes. Or like he'd already gotten one wish, and now he was hoping to squeeze out a couple more.

"That was fast," he said, setting the lantern aside. "Did you bring any change from my dime?"

I'll admit, that threw me a little. I started to answer, but he waved it off.

"Never mind. Let's have a look at this picture."

He slapped the rag over his shoulder as he walked to where we'd been standing before. He lowered the cheaters onto his nose and lifted the photo up to the light again, tilting it this way and that. Only now, I noticed, he was holding it carefully by the edges.

"I'm no expert," he finally said. "Where'd you say your father got this?"

"I don't know for certain, sir. I only know that Grandpa was an Indian scout before the Civil War and that Papa got most of his pictures from him."

Larry made a low humming sound.

"Mama's got a whole box of old pictures like that," I improvised, then immediately regretted it as Larry frowned and set the photo down and removed his cheaters and slipped them into his vest.

"I don't get customers in here looking for photographs," he said, sliding the picture across the counter. "Not my stock in trade. But I'll tell you what I will do, just this once, because I'm softheaded and I'm sorry about your mother taking ill. I'll give you two bits. That's my best offer, take it or leave it."

I took the photo and studied it. "That won't help Mama very much," I said as I turned for the door.

I got as far as the saxophone.

The apartment, Ralph said, belonged to a friend. The crowd was young and noisy, and there was phonograph music and booze for sale and a few shuffling dancers, but mostly it was some kind of a petting party with college boys curled up on sofas whispering sweet nothings into their girlfriends' shell-like ears.

"Say, what kind of a joint is this, anyway?" Violet shouted over the din.

Ralph fanned himself with his hat. "Go grab a seat. Those people are getting up."

We slid into the chairs, and Vi lit up a smoke without offering one to me. Ralph returned after a minute with three skinny glasses that he held in both hands like he'd brought us a bouquet of flowers.

"What's this?"

"Bubbly," he said, passing off the drinks. "We're celebrating!"

We certainly were. The take from Larry's Loan & Pawn had been an even sawbuck, which Ralph said was double what he'd expected. He must've made change from the bartender, because he gave us each our two-fifty, meaning he'd sprung for the drinks himself. He picked up his glass and raised it in a toast.

"The kid did all right," he said to his sister. "I think she's got the goods."

Violet didn't answer, and she practically gulped down her drink before dropping her cigarette into the empty glass and setting it on the floor. She stood to leave, brushing some ash from her skirt.

"Come on, Flo, let's ankle. This place is all wet."

"What's the rush?" Ralph said, taking hold of my hand. "We only just got here."

"Yeah," I said. "We only just got here."

"Suit yourself." Violet hiked her purse and made for the door, threading her way through the dancers and disappearing without so much as a backward glance. I felt a twinge of something—regret maybe, or guilt—like somehow I'd just scotched my initiation, until Ralph moved his chair closer to mine.

"Hey, baby, don't cast a kitten," he said, resting a hand on my knee. "She's just a little sore is all, on account of you doing so good."

So we had us another drink, and we punched the bag for a while, and then we got up and danced. The next thing I knew, we were sitting in a corner—Ralph in an armchair and me in his lap—and his tongue was playing Uncle Wiggily inside my mouth.

"You're a swell kid, do you know that?"

"Shut up," I said, "and do that again."

I know this sounds silly, but I actually thought about Larry then—just a flash of him standing behind the counter, polishing his lantern and waiting for Ralph to return. Not realizing that it was me, not him, who'd got her wish granted. Or was about to, anyway.

"I need to go iron my shoelaces," I told Ralph, slapping his hand as I stood and tugged my dress into place. "You keep the motor running."

There was a line for the bathroom, but the girl at the front took one look at me and said, "You'd better go first, honey. You look blotto."

After finishing my business, I stood for a minute with my hands on the cold porcelain, studying the glassy-eyed girl in the mirror. She looked, I thought, an awful lot like my mother. Not the tired house-wife in the frayed dress and apron, but the hopeful young bride in the photo that hung by the door in my parents' bedroom—the pretty Jewish girl in the cloud of white lace with the smile that seemed equal parts joy and terror.

A fist pounded the door. I licked my lips and gave my bubs a lift.

"Okay, kiddo," I said to the mirror. "The bank is open."

Ralph was right where I'd left him, sitting and smoking, his smile all lopsided and dirty.

"Hey, beautiful," he said, standing and taking my hand. "Let me show you something."

He led me down the hallway to one of the bedrooms, where he locked the door behind us and then disappeared into the little bathroom and returned with a towel in his hands.

I didn't resist, not even a little.

It was Ralph, in fact, who ended up saying, "Slow down, willya," and "Take it easy," and "Save some for next time." Not that I really heard him. Because what he'd shown me was a little like double-dutch jump rope, in that once you got past the tricky part at the beginning, the rest was just nothing but fun.

When we'd caught our breath and cleaned up our mess, we shimmied back into our clothes. That's when I grabbed Ralph by the lapels and pulled him close and looked him square in the eye.

"I know this is gonna sound crazy," I said, "but how's about you and me blow this two-bit town and never look back?"

Ralph met me at dawn, and helped with my bag, and watched as I took a long backward glance at the only home I'd ever known. It looked small and crummy, especially compared to what I knew was out there waiting.

"It's your fairy tale, baby," Ralph said as he wrestled the car into gear. "Where do you wanna go?"

I pointed north.

Five

Lansky's Law

December 1921

As the train lurches and rattles southbound, two men make their way toward the dining car. Both are young, and both darkly handsome in new business suits with hats in their hands and topcoats over their arms. The shorter man—the one now known to his friends as Charlie—waits as the taller man hurries forward to open the door.

A Sal or Sallie—a grown man with a little girl's name—would never command that kind of respect.

The dining car resembles a hospital ward, with its crisp white tablecloths stretching in ordered pairs along a narrow center aisle. Heads turn as the two men enter, and more than one woman's gaze lingers on the taller man's face, with its high cheekbones and its deeply cleft chin.

"There they are."

Two other men, both younger still, sit with their backs to the bulkhead at the last table on the right-hand side of the car. Meyer Lansky, the shorter of the pair, wears a suit of gray flannel, while Benjamin Siegel, his baby-faced companion, sports a garish houndstooth jacket.

Both stand to greet the new arrivals. All break into grins.

"Meyer, Benny. You boys remember Joey A."

Pleasantries are exchanged as the men shake hands and settle in, arranging themselves and their hats and topcoats on the soft leather banquettes, their high spirits contrasting with the gray parade of bare trees scrolling past the train car's rain-streaked windows. After the Negro waiter has left with their breakfast orders, Charlie Lucania twists in his seat to survey the neighboring tables.

When he leans forward to speak, his voice is barely a whisper.

"So I talked to Cousin Alphonse. He says this Gordon is a Polack named Irving Wexler used to bust heads for Benny Fein. Says they call him Waxey on account of he was a pickpocket before he fell in somehow with Rothstein, who bankrolls the whole operation. Al says they got boats, trucks, money, and muscle, and all of it in spades."

"Yeah? Then what's he need us for?"

"He don't need us, Benny, but we need him. Tell 'em, Joe."

Like his companion before him, Joe Adonis turns to study the car before leaning forward to speak.

"I'm down in Philly the day after Christmas to watch Frankie Genaro fight Kid Wolfe, see, and the promoter, this guy named Boo-Boo, he introduces me to Waxey Gordon. Says the name like he's some big shot I should know who he is. Turns out he's from the old neighborhood and we know a few people, so he invites me out to dinner after the fight. Come to find out the guy owns two or three speaks plus a legit nightclub in Philly, and get this—he's buildin a barrel house over in Jersey. Meanwhile, he's bringin in train cars of rye from Canada, he's bringin in boatloads of Scotch and gin from

Europe, and he's got more bonded whiskey stored in a warehouse in Philly than he's got trucks he can move it in."

"Al says Gordon and Rothstein are like the fuckin funnel for half the booze comin into the country," Charlie adds. "Them and this Nucky Johnson in Atlantic City, they got the whole East Coast tied up with a bow."

"Anyway, Gordon gives me a ride to the train after dinner and says to me, you put together thirty-five grand and I'll sell you a thousand cases of hundred-proof bottled-in-bond rye whiskey I gotta get rid of on account I got no place left to store it. Says it would normally go for around fifty Gs, but seein as how I'm a Genaro fan from the old neighborhood, he'll sell it to me on the cheap."

The men all look to Meyer, who composes his hands on the table. Only nineteen, and boyish still despite his sharp suit and tie, Meyer Lansky remains one of Charlie Lucania's closest and most trusted friends. Charlie remembers their very first meeting, when fourteen-year-old Salvatore Lucania had tried to extort lunch money from ten-year-old Maier Suchowljansky, a skinny little Yid from Grand Street. Although only half his aggressor's size, the younger boy's answer had been immediate and emphatic. "Go fuck yourself," he'd told Lucania, and a friendship was born on the spot.

"Thank you, Joey, for that background," Meyer now says, unfolding his hands and picking some lint from the tablecloth. "The question before us, gentlemen, is whether we want to get any deeper into this bootlegging racket. There's a lot of competition out there, and we're making good money as things presently stand. Moving booze on the scale Joey's talking about would represent a major expansion of our operations. It would require more capital and more guns and more risk. We'd need to triple the buy-money bank and get Frank and maybe Joey if he's interested to use their influence to move us into midtown in a much bigger way. I don't have to tell you that that will make certain people very unhappy. People like Dwyer and D'Aquila and Masseria, to name a few."

"Fuck Masseria. I'll piss in his fat fuckin ear."

"Thank you, Benny, for that turgid insight. The point is, we'll be crossing a Rubicon if we do this deal. And that assumes the booze is genuine and that Gordon can deliver as promised. It also assumes . . . Ixnay, here comes the dinge."

The waiter returns with a second Negro in tow. They place four silver cloches on the table and remove them with a flourish.

"Hey, Charlie, what the fuck is that?"

"It's supposed to be corned beef hash."

"Look at Rockefeller, eatin corned beef hash. What's that on top?"

Charlie pokes at his food with a fork. "What, don't you know nothin? It's a fried egg for Christ sake."

"It *also* assumes"—Meyer watches the waiters depart—"that Gordon can keep on delivering into the future, because the capital outlay we're talking about won't be recouped with a thousand cases of whiskey, no matter how good it turns out to be."

Here he pauses, looking to each of his traveling companions.

"So, gentlemen. Do we stand pat and enjoy what we have now, or do we raise the stakes and become full-time bootleggers? I put the matter to a vote. Benny?"

The youngest boy shifts in his seat. "I say fuck yes. We're already takin the risk so's other guys can make the big dough. I say we get in the game while the gettin's still good. This Volstead Act ain't gonna last forever."

"What about you, Joey? If we do this deal, it means you're in for a one-fifth share, along with the three of us and Frankie Costello."

"Heck, you guys know my vote. That's why I called Charlie in the first place. It's why we're on this train, ain't it?"

All eyes shift to Lucania.

"Charlie?"

Once again Lucania turns, his eyes sweeping the half-empty dining car.

"Don't turn around or nothin, but you see them two guys over there? The ones who look like a couple of Wall Street big shots? I'm tellin ya, that's gonna be us a year from now. Only difference is, they're the ones gonna be comin to us on bended knee to get booze for their parties and their fancy restaurants and their best out-of-town customers. But here's what I wanna make clear. If we do this thing, I don't wanna be some nickel-and-dime bum sellin watered-down coffin varnish. So I say we make a pact right here and now. We buy only the best, and we sell only the best. If we do that, then pretty soon we'll make a name for ourselves in all the right places. Between our friends in the garment district and Frank and Joey's connections on Broadway, we'll have half the fuckin city by spring. And as far as guys like Dwyer and Masseria go, I agree with Benny. Fuck them old-timers. We work with 'em where we can, and we piss on 'em when we can't."

The men grunt and nod in agreement.

"Okay, so what about you, Meyer?"

The smaller man tugs the napkin from his shirt collar and dabs at the corners of his mouth.

"I've been reading a book. It's by a Harvard professor, an economist, and he talks about a concept called the law of supply and demand. It goes something like this. In summer, when peaches are ripe and plentiful, the price of peaches falls because the available supply exceeds the demand. In other words, there are more peach sellers than there are peach buyers. But come fall, when the local supply runs out, then the price of peaches rises. And why is that, Benny?"

"Because there's more people want peaches than there are peaches to buy, so people will pay more."

"Precisely. Demand exceeds supply, so prices rise. Before this Volstead Act, there was a rough equilibrium between supply and demand for beer and wine and liquor. Availability was constant, demand was constant, so prices held steady. Only now, everything's been thrown out of whack. The demand is still there, but supply has been artificially suppressed, so naturally prices have gone through the roof. Especially, as Charlie points out, for the real McCoy. And that unmet demand represents opportunity."

"Come on, Meyer, just say yes, for Christ sake."

"Patience, Charlie. I'm trying to make a larger point. This law of supply and demand operates beyond just peaches and booze. It applies to anything that the people want but that the law suppresses. Policy. Dope. Broads. If we play our cards right, this deal with Gordon could be just the beginning for us. I've been running some numbers."

Meyer removes a folded envelope from his pocket.

"If we can move a thousand cases of rye whiskey, we stand to clear over a hundred grand in just a few months' time. Think about that. That's more money than our parents will see in their lifetimes. And Benny's right about this Volstead Act—it ain't gonna last forever. So this is no time for half measures. With the connections we've already made, and with the dough we can earn from selling as much booze as we can as fast as we can, we could move ourselves into every racket in town. Diversify, in other words. Position ourselves for the long run, for after Prohibition is over."

"And get ourselves shot in the process."

"No, Joey, not if we play it smart. Look at us. Two Jews, a Sicilian, and a Neapolitan. Frank's a Calabrian. We're like the fucking League of Nations. We have our separate interests, sure, and those we'll continue to pursue. But on this Gordon deal, and on any other deals we decide to do with the money we make, we'll combine our varied resources and connections."

"Like a trade union," Joey suggests.

"I was thinking more like an all-star team in baseball. But let's not kid ourselves. This ain't gonna be easy. Our trucks are gonna get hit, and we'll have to hit back and hit back hard. But if we make the right friends and we watch each other's backs, then pretty soon we'll have chips on the table in every game in the city."

Charlie is laughing.

.

"What's so funny?"

"You, Meyer, you little bastard. You're startin to sound just like me."

Meyer signals the waiter for their check.

"Then God help me, Charlie, because in all the years I've known you, that's about the scariest thing I've ever heard you say."

Six

Alchemy

December 1921

HIS PUBLIC DENUNCIATION of District Attorney Lew Smith for witness tampering in the Carman case would return to haunt George Morton Levy in 1916, when Smith was appointed to the Nassau County bench and promptly dedicated himself to making George's courtroom life miserable.

Smith's revenge took many nefarious forms. During George's closing arguments, for example, the judge would descend from his bench, stroll to the windows, and ask in a bored voice, "How much longer is this going to take, counselor?" More often, however, the judge's sabotage was solely visual—rolled eyes or a shaking head during George's arguments, with smiles and nods of approval for the district attorney—all carefully calibrated to leave no record of judicial misconduct on appeal.

In response to these tactics, George developed a repertoire of tools and tricks with which to blunt the judge's influence. During the examination of jurors, for example, George would liken the jury's role as the exclusive judge of the facts to a "juror garden" in which the judge should not be allowed to trespass. Similarly, the jurors were to respect the judge's function as the exclusive arbiter of the law. "You stay on your side of the fence," George would tell them, and then, with a nod to the scowling figure on the bench, "make him stay on his."

George, you see, believed in the American jury system; he trusted in the collective wisdom and life experience of twelve ordinary citizens as a bulwark against the prejudices and peccadillos of any single jurist. He revered the concept of equal justice under law personified by the statuary image of a blindfolded lady with her scales held high in equipoise—scales on which no thumb should ever tilt the balance. And especially no thumb belonging to Lewis J. Smith.

For the most part, George's strategy worked. "We could tell the judge hated your client," jurors would tell him in confidence after a verdict, "but we didn't pay him any mind. We knew he was trespassing." But since Smith was the sort of judge who'd never met an accused he didn't long to incarcerate, George's growing string of acquittals merely served to roil the simmering animosity between the former district attorney and the affable young defense attorney.

It was thus the misfortune of Louis Enright to learn that his prosecution for grand larceny—that is, for the felonious receipt of money or property under false pretenses—had been assigned to Lewis J. Smith for trial.

The accused was a tall man, gray and solemn, some seventy-five years in age. An engineer by training and a tinkerer by profession, Enright had come to Long Island from the oil fields of West Texas with, George would later learn to his dismay, a wake of angry investors foaming at his stern.

No sooner had Enright landed in Nassau County than he'd formed a new company to exploit his latest invention, which he described as a secret process by which to extract gasoline from Long Island's abundant deposits of peat. After raising some quarter-million dollars in equity capital from a group of starry-eyed investors that included several of the county's leading citizens, Enright then proposed a second stock offering to augment the first. This latter proposal, combined with a dearth of demonstrable progress in the commercialization of Enright's invention, sent a group of suspicious shareholders to the office of then-D.A. Charles R. Weeks.

A grand jury indictment for grand larceny soon followed.

Despite the daunting prospect of yet another trial before Judge Smith, George remained hopeful. One reason for his optimism was that Professor Enright, as he insisted on being called, had been careful to make no express promises to his investors. Moreover, all the shareholders had been warned in writing both that the venture would be time-consuming and that it would be expensive. Lastly, Enright himself appeared sober, intelligent, and well-spoken—in short, credible—and could be expected to make an excellent witness on his own behalf.

But George took his greatest comfort from the professor's own resolute self-confidence. "I've said I can make gasoline from peat," he told his lawyer, "and I can prove it!"

With Judge Smith on relatively good behavior, the trial went about as smoothly as George could have hoped. The D.A.'s witnesses each conceded on cross-examination that Enright had merely opined that he could make gasoline from peat, and had candidly acknowledged never having done so in any commercial quantity. Since the crime of grand larceny required the knowingly false representation of a material fact—not merely an exaggerated opinion—the case appeared to have died a quiet death by the time the prosecution finally rested.

At the close of the state's evidence, George stood and moved for dismissal of the indictment. But no sooner had he done so than Professor Enright, greatly agitated, clamped a bony hand on George's arm.

37

"My professional honor has been impugned!" the old man remonstrated in a stage whisper. "That is the one thing I cannot abide!"

"What do you want me to do about it? The case is already in the bag."

"I want to perform a demonstration! I want to prove to the world that I can turn peat into gasoline!"

A frowning Judge Smith interrupted this huddled colloquy.

"Counsel? Is there something the matter?"

Against his better judgment, George rose again to his feet.

"Your Honor, Professor Enright has just informed me that he would like to demonstrate his secret process for the jury."

"You mean now? Show us the actual procedure?"

"Yes, Your Honor."

"Permission granted!"

Enright sprang from his chair and hurried to the rear of the courtroom where, from a large leather satchel, he removed a strange apparatus consisting of a glass beaker, an alcohol lamp with a hand crank, and several lengths of rubber tubing. The jurors stood with excitement as the old man carried his device past the gawking reporters and courtroom spectators—many of them skeptical investors—all the way to the witness box.

"This will only take a moment," Enright said as he lit the wick and removed from his pocket a chunk of ordinary peat, which he then crushed in his hands and sprinkled inside the lamp. Once the lamp was sufficiently heated, Enright began turning the crank. After a minute, a pale amber liquid began dripping from the rubber tubing into the beaker. After another full minute, Enright lifted the beaker and carried it to the foreman of the jury.

The foreman sniffed at the beaker and pronounced his verdict.

"Gasoline!"

Great commotion engulfed the courtroom as Judge Smith, banging his gavel, grumbled that he'd take George's dismissal motion under advisement. He then called the noon recess.

"What does that mean?" Enright asked George.

"It means we've won. Congratulations."

Satisfied, the professor returned his device to the satchel before wading out to the hallway through a pressing throng of admirers.

George was busy gathering his papers when an even greater commotion arose from the hallway door through which all had just departed.

"Judge! Judge!" came the foreman's voice as he ran back into the courtroom. "We need to see the judge!"

By now all the jurors had returned to the courtroom, and Judge Smith, hearing the disturbance, appeared at the door to his chambers.

"What is it? What's going on?"

"Judge! There's gasoline all over the hallway! The man's a fake!"

Lewis J. Smith's eye-daggers pinned George to the wall, where he stood openmouthed.

"Well, Mr. Levy? What have you got to say about this?"

"Uh, maybe it's the gasoline he'd already made?"

"Oh no," said the foreman. "He put the contraption back in his bag, but there's a trail of gasoline running clear down the hallway!"

A brief investigation proved the truth of the accusation, revealing as it did a thin scrim of yellow liquid leading down the marble corridor, down the stairs, and straight to the downstairs restroom where the professor had taken refuge. And so it was that after the noon recess, and despite the technical shortcomings of the prosecution's case, the jury returned an emphatic verdict of guilty on the charge of grand larceny.

Which wasn't, it turned out, the end of the story.

Prior to the sentencing hearing, which had been scheduled for some weeks later, George and a committee of Enright's creditors conducted a review of the old man's assets. The search confirmed exactly what the professor had long maintained—namely, that he'd actually spent all the money he'd raised on the invention, leaving only five thousand dollars of his own personal funds on deposit in a bank in Hicksville. This, plus a hodgepodge of old oil and mining stocks, was the sum total of Louis Enright's net worth.

The creditors, many now sympathetic to the chastened old man, agreed to recommend a suspended sentence in exchange for relinquishment of the professor's oil and mining stocks to the committee. Enright readily agreed, and to George's surprise, so did the judge. All was well that had ended well, until a few months later, when George received a telephone call at his office from an irate Judge Smith, who demanded George's immediate presence.

"Your man Enright is not only a crook," the judge fumed upon George's arrival, "he's also a double-eyed villain!"

"What do you mean?"

"Look here," the judge said, slapping before George a stack of bank statements for the Hicksville account. They showed over a hundred thousand dollars in post-trial deposits.

"There must be some mistake," George protested. "We went through his finances with a fine-tooth comb."

"There was a mistake all right, and it was mine for being soft-headed and suspending the old man's sentence. Now I'm sending him to Sing Sing."

"Wait a minute, Judge. Give me a few days to look into this. Something's obviously not kosher here."

On that they both agreed, but for entirely different reasons. Nevertheless, George was afforded the opportunity to visit the bank and inquire about the account. What he learned from a helpful young cashier surprised even him.

"Professor Enright said he was afraid of having his account attacked by creditors," the clerk explained. "So what he'd do is leave a hundred dollars in the account for living expenses, then withdraw the rest in a cashier's check. The first check was for four thousand nine hundred dollars. Then when he needed money again, he'd redeposit the cashier's check, leave a hundred in the account, and then withdraw the rest in another cashier's check. He did that over and over again—so many times that he'd soon deposited over a hundred grand. But it was really just the same five thousand dollars."

Relieved, George brought the cashier to Judge Smith, who listened to the young man's story with barely disguised incredulity.

"I don't believe it for a minute," the judge snapped. "But even if I did, it just goes to prove that the old fraud is up to something. I don't know what it is, but I damned well know how to stop it. I'm sending him to prison!" Which the judge did before the week was out.

George was still downcast from these events when he ran into District Attorney Charlie Weeks in court a few days later. The two men sat in a back bench, waiting for their cases to be called.

"You know, Charlie, I had a football coach once, a pretty gruff fellow, and he used to tell us that quitters never win, and winners never quit. He drummed it into our skulls." George shook his head wistfully. "Maybe that's what explains it."

"Explains what?"

"Why I never seem to know when to quit while I'm ahead."

Seven

Chicago

July 1923

ALERTED BY THE squeak of new brogans on pile carpet, Leonard Reid looked up in time to glimpse a blur of blue serge streaking past his office door.

"Tommy? Tom!"

The jug-eared law clerk appeared in the doorway, his body bent like a sapling in the wind.

"Sir?"

"For God's sake, son, where's the fire? Did you look into that title question I—"

"Yes, sir. I've dictated a memo that'll be on your desk in the morning."

"And what about—"

"I posted the court calendar in the conference room, and I pulled all the documents I think you'll want to use for the Spencer deposition."

42

Reid studied the earnest young whirlwind. He recalled when his cousin Annie had telephoned in May to ask him to hire her son for the summer, and that his first impulse had been to decline. After all, it was not the general practice of firms like Litzinger, Healy & Reid to employ first-year students, even top students from a top law school like the University of Michigan. More daunting still was the prospect of having to tell Annie Thomas Dewey that her only son's performance wasn't up to snuff. Now Reid could only smile at the memory of that conversation.

While it was true that some in the firm thought the young man from Owosso priggish and smug, none could deny that, less than three weeks into his summer clerkship, Thomas E. Dewey had made himself as indispensable as any of the firm's junior partners.

"Where are you off to now?"

"Voice class. The studio's holding a scholarship contest tonight, and the winner gets the whole summer program free."

"I suppose that's the infernal song I've heard you humming all week?"

"No, sir. That was just me horsing around."

And like that, the boy was gone again, his rich baritone trailing him down the hallway.

"I wish I'd had time to practice! I only just heard about the scholarship contest this morning!"

Tom closed the door carefully behind him. Up on the darkened stage, her blonde curls blazing under a single white spot, stood the young mezzo-soprano from Wisconsin, Marilyn something-or-other. Or was it Marian? He crept down the aisle and took an empty seat among his classmates. They were an odd assortment of seasoned performers and starry-eyed amateurs, as varied as vaudeville, united by the singular honor of having been accepted into the Stephens Studio's traveling master class.

Once his eyes had adjusted to the darkness, Tom could make out the heads of what he assumed was the panel of contest judges seated in the front of the theater and, centermost among them, the leonine mane of Percy Rector Stephens. The piece being performed was "O Don Fatale" from Verdi's *Don Carlos*, and when the girl had finished, Tom lifted his hands to applaud.

Only nobody else was clapping.

"Thank you, Mary Ann." Stephens cleared his throat as he consulted a clipboard. "Next up is Miss Rose Winters."

Tom's performance came late in the program, and by the time he'd mounted the creaking stage, the audience had shrunk to under a dozen dark and indecipherable shapes—including the front-row quintet whose haggard faces he could barely discern beyond the spotlight's harsh radiance. He'd chosen for his recital Handel's "Hear Me, Ye Winds and Waves," which he performed in English, in G minor. And when he'd sung the final "I pray for death alone," he was startled to hear a pattering of applause waft toward him from out of the darkness.

His scholarship was awarded the following week.

"You've got it, you know."

Tom recognized the voice, and the recognition slowed his steps even as it quickened his pulse.

"Oh, hello, Frances," he said, trying for casual. "Are you walking my way?"

Frances Hutt fell into stride beside him. The petite brunette with the porcelain skin hailed from Oklahoma, Tom believed, by way of New York. As Percy Stephens's personal secretary and studio manager, not to mention a dazzling mezzo-soprano in her own right, Frances had excited the imaginations of every bachelor in class.

"This thing I have, I do hope it isn't contagious."

"Save the false modesty for amateur night. I'm from the big city, and I know about these things."

44

Scuttlebutt had Frances Hutt as an athlete of some sort, and a Methodist. Tom knew for a fact she was single, because that was an issue he'd already researched.

"I can assure you that any modesty I might possess, I come by honestly. Take this evening, for example. I plan a modest dinner in the city, followed by an elevated train ride to a modest little park in Lake Forest, where I'm meeting some brothers of the Phi Mu Alpha for an evening of Brahms concertos. Modestly performed, I have no doubt."

"Gosh, that sounds idyllic."

"What about you? I thought you and Stephens were yoked to the plow this week."

"Oh, Stevie's having dinner with friends from New York, and I've managed to slip the yoke for one night at least. I thought I'd celebrate by walking the Loop and doing a little shopping."

Tom stopped and turned to face her on the crowded sidewalk.

"See here. Not on an empty stomach, I hope?"

"Why, Mr. Dewey. Is that how they ask girls out to dinner in Owosso?"

"Oh, no. In Owosso we do it like this."

He dropped to a knee, taking both of her hands in his.

"Miss Frances Hutt, would you do me the great honor of joining me for an evening repast?"

The restaurant was called Raklios. It was a Greek place—a greasy spoon, really—wedged into a crowded block of storefronts whose plate-glass views of Washington Boulevard were framed by the El tracks across the street. The front door was open and the radio behind the counter bleated "Toot, Toot, Tootsie" into the rattle and rumble, the hiss and clang of a sultry Chicago rush hour.

Tom ordered a Hamburg steak. Frances ordered a salad. Both ordered lemonade. Frances insisted on separate checks. Tom objected, was overruled, and heard his appeal summarily denied.

"How are you enjoying Chicago?" he asked her—feebly, he knew—ending the silence that had hung awkwardly in the wake of the waiter's departure.

"Oh, it's all right, I guess. I love the lake, and the art museum, and watching all the sailboats. What about you?"

"Me? I think Chicago's a wonderful town for speakeasies and floozies and gangsters with tommy guns. Crooked cops and fixed baseball games, for goodness sake. For the life of me, I can't understand how the people of a city this large and sophisticated continue putting up with it."

He couldn't read her smile, or the sparkling eyes that danced behind it.

"Listen to me," he said, arranging his silverware. "I must sound like Pollyanna from Podunk."

"Is that why you're studying law, Tom? To come and clean up Chicago?"

"Not me, thank you. I wouldn't even *be* in Chicago if it wasn't for Stephens. And as for the law, well, you might say I'm conflicted on the subject."

"You mean you're impaled on the horns of a dilemma."

"Well, yes, something like—"

"For what it's worth, I think you have a wonderful voice, and a real future in opera or musical theater. And I'm not just saying that. I know plenty of singers who delude themselves into thinking they've got the goods—that they're the next Caruso or the next Jolson. In your case, Tom, it's no delusion, and you need to hear that from somebody who knows."

"You're very kind, Frances. But even if I believed you, that still doesn't solve my dilemma. A man doesn't have the luxury of thinking only about today, or next week, or the next couple of years. He's got to plan for the long haul. I enjoy performing, don't get me wrong, but the human voice is a fragile instrument. What if I were to give up the law and then lose my voice? Where would I be then?"

"Pursuing your dream. Doing what you were born to do."

Now it was Tom's turn to smile.

"Did I say something funny?"

"No, of course not. It's just that who's to say what one is born to do? Maybe I was born to clean up Chicago."

"No, that sounds awfully messy. Leave that to the police and the politicians."

"Now you *are* being funny. The police need all the help they can get, and as for the politicians, well, they're the ones most in need of a good scrubbing."

Her smile, he realized then, had vanished.

"Would you listen to me? Out to dinner with a swell girl and here I am blathering like an idiot. I'm sure you weren't expecting a hayseed civics lesson."

"Don't be silly. It's refreshing to discuss something besides music, music, music. Sometimes I think Stevie and his friends all live in a big glass bubble. All they ever talk about is this performer or that concert. After a while, it gets to be like ice cream. I enjoy ice cream, but not every day. Not every meal."

"It's just that where I come from, a man in public office would be tarred and feathered if he so much as looked the other way at corruption. Here it's not only tolerated; it's practically part of the Democratic Party platform."

"You make Chicago sound like Gomorrah."

"In some ways it's worse than Gomorrah. If there were ten righteous men—"

"Wait, I have an idea! Why don't you come to New York and clean up Tammany Hall? Then while you're at it, you can audition for the Met, or maybe a role in the Follies. There are so many opportunities for a singer in New York, Tom, you have no idea. I'm sure for a lawyer as well, what with Wall Street and everything."

"You make it sound easy. The problem is, I've got two more years left at Michigan."

"They have law schools in New York, don't they?"

"You mean transfer? I'm afraid it's not that simple. Besides, my mother would pitch a fit."

"Uh-oh. We mustn't upset Mother."

"You haven't met my mother. And besides, my father owns the local newspaper. His goal in life is to make me the governor of Michigan."

"Far be it from me to deprive the good people of Michigan. But come September, I'm heading back to New York. So if you had any ideas in that thick skull of yours about the two of us going steady, well, then you'll have no choice but to come along."

"Now hold on a minute. I didn't—"

"Careful, Tom Dewey, your Podunk is showing. Women have the vote now, haven't you heard? And I'll let you in on another little secret."

She leaned across the table.

"We have to think of the long haul as well."

Eight

The Speak

August 1923

WE NEVER EVEN gave it a name.

When we talked about it at all, we just called it the place, or the joint, or sometimes even the office. We didn't want the hoi polloi showing up at our door. Or the revenue agents, for that matter. You had to know somebody to get in, or else know somebody who knew somebody, and that somebody had to be someone we trusted.

Sure, there were classier joints in town. The Blaue Club, for instance, or the Sachsenheim. And the booze we served wasn't always bonded, but we poured an honest drink and offered beer on tap and peanuts in a barrel, plus live piano on Friday and Saturday nights. It wasn't a blind pig, I can tell you that much. Or one of those crummy shine boxes.

My partner's name was Pearl, Pearl Callahan, and she was a real tomato. I'd met her in Youngstown, just before Ralph had split back to Pittsburgh, and we got along good. We ran a picture gag

49

together—she was the roper and I was the spieler—and after a year or so we'd banked enough kale to wash the coal dust out of our hair and make for the bright lights of the city.

Pearl was twenty-four then, and I was what she called "fifteen going on thirty." She had a bunch of funny expressions like that. She said I was slicker than snot on a doorknob, and that I could talk a hungry dog off a meat wagon. She was like the crazy big sister I never had—the one with the horse laugh who drank like a catfish and cussed like a stevedore—and ours was a partnership made in grifter heaven.

Pearl was the one who'd said there was dough to be made in bootleg liquor. So we raided our piggy banks and rented a three-story building on the east side of Cleveland for a hundred and twenty a month plus utilities. We ran the joint downstairs, and used the second floor for storage, and then me and Pearl lived on top, in what we called the penthouse. We scrubbed and painted the place ourselves, and then we hung old boxing posters on the walls. We rented our furniture and glassware from a restaurant supply store on Euclid Avenue where we paid cash and nobody asked any questions.

I kept the books and managed the inventory, while Pearl was in charge of customer relations. We paid five clams a week to the precinct captain, plus twenty a month to the Murray Hill Mob, who also sold us our hooch. The precinct captain was named Tierney, and his bag man was a great big mulligan named Quinn, who called us colleens and usually let Pearl suck his cock for the fiver.

We took turns, Pearl and me, tending bar and waiting tables and working the door, plus we had a shine in on Mondays to mop out the joint. The piano man worked for tips. Once we were up and running, we were clearing almost eighty dollars a week, and in summer we did even better. Me and Pearl split the net fifty-fifty, with a small weekly adjustment for what she called the tonsil tax.

We sent Ralph a postcard once. It said, "Who's crying now, you lousy crumb? Drop dead soon. Love, Flo." And below that, Pearl had scribbled, "Piker!" That was good for a giggle.

With Ralph out of the picture, there were always a few drunks at last call wanting to walk me home—meaning up to the third floor—only most were so splifficated they couldn't of climbed the stairs if I'd let 'em, which I almost never did. But Pearl had a regular fella, a postman named Wally Stein, who she called Wally the Whale even though on account of his job he was actually pretty skinny, if you get my meaning.

Cleveland was a boomtown then, and the fifth-largest city in America. It had auto factories and a railroad line and a baseball team called the Indians, who'd apparently won the World Series in 1920, which people there were still talking about. Sometimes it was all they talked about, that and the union riots. But all things considered, it was actually a pretty swell town.

Like I said earlier, I hardly ever dated the customers. But there was this one Saturday night in early August when the joint was jumping and we had to call in the shine, whose name was Marcus, to work the door on account of us being so busy. Well, Marcus, who was probably close to sixty and had the brains of an Irish setter, he let four bohunks into the joint who we'd never seen before and who took a table by the door and ordered beers and then sat there like bumps on a log all night and weren't dancing or playing cards or even talking, not even to each other.

Anyway, these guys just sat there nursing their beers until around midnight, when the crowd started to thin a little. Then all of a sudden they stood up, and one of them sapped down Marcus, and two of them pulled guns and came around the bar and shoved Pearl aside to open the register.

We raised bloody hell, and Pearl even jumped on the one guy's back as he turned to leave with our money, which, on account of it being a good night, was probably thirty or forty bucks. Well, two of the guys—I'm thinking they must've been Polacks—they pulled Pearl off their buddy's back and tossed her onto a table, splashing the suds and breaking a few of our glasses in the process. Wally happened to be in that night, and while he ran over to help Pearl to her feet, he didn't try to stop the robbers. I can't say as I blame him for it, but Pearl was awfully sore at him afterwards.

And that's when this funny thing happened. Just as the piano man quit playing and the rumpus settled and the bohunks were on their way out, this big guy, who I hadn't really noticed until then, stepped in front of the door and blocked their getaway.

"Scram," said the guy with the money, and to emphasize his point he poked his gat right in the stranger's belly. Only the stranger, who was maybe six foot four with a face like a side of beef, he didn't bat an eyelash.

"Turn around and put the money back," the stranger said, nice and calm, like he was ordering a cup of tea.

The gunman cocked his pistol. "Says who?"

"Says Joe Porrello," the stranger said, and then he opened a cigarette case and tapped out a smoke like a guy who was waiting for a bus.

Well, that was the end of the robbery. The gunman walked back to Pearl and handed her the whole wad of dough. "I'm real sorry, Miss," he told her, loud enough for everyone to hear, and then he gestured to his buddies, who all huddled up and shuffled out the front door like choirboys leaving the midnight Mass.

And that's how I first come to meet Big Joe Porrello.

It was also the last time our joint ever got robbed.

Nine

Wild Bull

September 1923

CHARLIE HAS NEVER seen a crowd quite like the one that greets his hired limousine as it rolls to the curb on West 155th Street. It appears to him like a rally, or a riot, or like the ninety thousand spectators expected at the evening's main event have somehow managed to swarm the Polo Grounds en masse. And indeed, the elevated ramp connecting the grandstand to the Ninth Avenue train is packed with men in coats and straw boaters, pushing and shoving, moving like prodded cattle past truncheon-wielding policemen on foot and on horseback, funneling into the vast holding pen that awaits them beyond the stadium turnstiles.

"Christ, would you get a load of this," Charlie says, parting the velvet curtains, his attention shifting from the older man beside him. "This could be a million-dollar gate."

Johnny Torrio leans to take in the sight. "You handlin any action on this thing?"

Charlie shares a smile with his honored guest from Chicago. "I'll take your action, Pops. Who do you like?"

"At three-to-one, I like the spic. Al went to that training camp up in Saratoga. He said if Dempsey's six feet tall, then so is he."

"You know what they say. The bigger they are, the harder they fall."

"You better hope that ain't true, Charlie, or else you and your pal Lansky are gonna make one helluva noise. How's about three fifty to your grand?"

"Sure, why not. What's another grand among friends?"

The car has stopped, and the driver is opening the curbside door. Charlie alights in a double-breasted suit of oxford gray paired with a crisp white shirt and a tie of navy silk. His topcoat and fedora are in matching pearl. The clothes, purchased specially for the occasion, are the brainchild of Arnold Rothstein, Charlie's friend and mentor. If you want to change your image, Rothstein told his young protégé, then start with what people can see.

Charlie Lucania badly wants to change his image.

Foolishly, Charlie was arrested three months earlier for selling heroin to a police informant while agents of the Secret Service looked on. A search of his apartment yielded a small cache of morphine, heroin, and opium. Once in the custody of federal authorities immune to the blandishments of Frank Costello's buy-money bank, Charlie Lucania—with a 1916 narcotics rap already on his record—had no choice but to bargain for his freedom. After two hours of interrogation and three hours of negotiation, a deal was finally struck: Charlie would direct the agents to a trunk full of heroin, its street value in excess of a hundred and fifty thousand dollars, in exchange for dismissal of the charges against him.

For Charlie the deal meant freedom, but at a heavy price. News accounts of his arrest labeled him a major purveyor of narcotics—an albatross that has threatened the carefully cultivated image of gentleman bootlegger that has been Charlie's entre to the private clubs and glittering soirees of New York society. Worse, despite a promise they wouldn't do so, the police had branded Charlie a stool pigeon, and even though the dope he was forced to sacrifice had been his own, its ownership could never, for obvious reasons, be publicly acknowledged.

The net result of the whole debacle was wary looks from both sides of the street. Nothing short of a biblical resurrection is required, and tonight, Charlie hopes, will be his personal Easter.

Dempsey-Firpo is the hottest ticket of 1923, which meant that Charlie had to shell out twenty-five thousand dollars to assemble his two hundred seats in the first five rows at ringside. Working with Costello and Joe Adonis, Charlie drew up a list of the hundred most influential figures in New York and beyond—a veritable who's who in politics, sports, entertainment, and the rackets—with each receiving a pair of complimentary ducats from Charlie Lucania.

"This is worse than a fucking wedding," Costello had groused as the roster of invitees was winnowed from the original list of five hundred.

"Tell me about it," Charlie replied. "At a wedding, at least you get cake before the fightin starts."

Torrio takes the lead as the men wend their way through the crowd. Heads do not turn and fingers do not point as they approach the clubhouse turnstiles, because they, unlike some of their less reticent contemporaries, are men who understand the value of anonymity. Understand that the tallest trees in the forest are the first to get cut. Which is why Charlie's arrest and its attendant publicity had been all the more vexing.

The ticket taker hesitates as he tears the stub and returns the rain check to the man in the new pearl fedora.

"Row A, Seat One," he says. "Mister, you must really be somebody."

The empty ring stands like an altar near what would normally be second base; and like an altar, it exerts an invisible magnetism to which all heads in the vast, open-air stadium orient. The crush of bodies only intensifies as the men are escorted to their ringside seats by a stoop-shouldered usher, who parts the surging multitude with a practiced repertoire of prods and pleas, shrugs and sidling shuffles.

A dozen patrons stand to greet the pair's arrival as the usher whisks their seats and then bows, newly fawning, at the younger man's proffered twenty.

"Charlie!"

"Hey, Charlie!"

"Hiya, Charlie. How ya doin, Johnny? How's Chicago?"

The men are surrounded. Hands are shaken, and shoulders grabbed and squeezed. Benny Siegel and Frank Costello are already there, as are Joe Adonis and Vito Genovese. There's Charlie Murphy and Jimmy Hines from Tammany Hall, along with Flo Ziegfeld and Earl Carroll from Broadway. Ben Gimbel is there, and John Ringling, and the dapper Kenny Sutherland. The men form a bright constellation of disparate stars whose gravitational pull captures the awestruck and the merely curious along with a healthy smattering of showgirls and flappers who crowd in closer, vamping and giggling, to bask in the reflected glow.

A bell rings, and an announcer appears. Charlie takes his seat and is handed a flask as the crowd settles down for the preliminary bouts. Cigars are proffered, and another flask, and soon a purple twilight has settled over Coogan's Hollow.

Others, meanwhile, continue to arrive. King Solomon from Boston, and Waxey Gordon from Philly. Al Capone and his entourage from Chicago. Police Commissioner Enright, along with Chief Inspector Lahey. All stop to pump the hand of their front-row benefactor.

"I gotta hand it to you, Charlie. I never seen nothin like this," Torrio says after Babe Ruth has paid his respects. "You got this whole fuckin town in your pocket."

"Supply and demand," Charlie says, turning to eyeball the seats behind him. "Life is sure funny, ain't it Johnny? When I was in grade school, I had this teacher, Mrs. Goldfarb. I didn't speak English so good, and I missed a lot of classes, and I got sent to this truant school over in Brooklyn. Mrs. Goldfarb, she's the one who done it. Told my parents I was a bad influence. Said I'd never amount to nothin and that someday I'd wind up in jail. Made my mother cry."

"What a cunt."

"Then maybe a year ago I'm comin out of the Copa with Rothstein and Joey A. We got these girls from the Follies with us, and we're on our way to this party on Long Island. Anyway, I stop to get my coat, and guess who's workin the hatcheck counter in back? It's Mrs. Goldfarb. She's an old lady by then, but I recognize her plain as day."

"So what did you do?"

"I called her over. I said, 'Mrs. Goldfarb, do you remember me? I'm Sal Lucania from First Avenue.' I said I wanted her to know she was absolutely right about me. I said I been in trouble my whole fuckin life, and I been in jail, and I've caused my parents nothin but grief. And then I gave her a C-note and kissed her on top of the head and said she'd have to excuse me, because Mr. Rothstein and I didn't want to keep Mr. Whitney waiting."

Darkness thickens, blanketing the main event. In the glare of the overhead lights, amid the oompah brass of a marching band, the gladiators finally arrive. First comes Firpo, the massive Argentine, looking every inch the Wild Bull of the Pampas—a circus animal snared and tamed and gaudily costumed in silks of yellow and purple. He is followed by the champion, Gentleman Jack, the Manassa Mauler, whose muscled neck and shoulders are wrapped in a simple white sweatshirt.

"Care to double that bet?" Torrio shouts over the bellicose roars of the crowd.

"You're on, Pops. Don't ever underestimate the little guy."

57

As the crowd quiets and the fighters and seconds gather for their final instructions, a rotund figure rises from his seat and moves through the shadows on the far side of the ring. Giuseppe Masseria is trailed by two bodyguards as he circles the apron, and most of the sportswriters and all the policemen at ringside turn to watch as the fat man waddles in Charlie's direction.

"Christ," Costello leans forward to whisper. "Get a load of what's comin."

Masseria stops before Row A, Seat 1. He nods to Johnny Torrio, then offers a meaty hand to the dapper young Sicilian seated beside him.

"Salvatore Lucania," the fat man says, his grip an iron vise. "I think it's high time you and me had us a little talk."

Ten

The Devil They Knew

October 1924

LIKE ALL MEN, George Morton Levy had his fair share of vices. Cuban cigars, for instance, were a habit to which he'd taken as a kitten takes to string. Also, try though he might, the sight of a well-turned ankle never failed to slow his step. And since George, unlike many of his colleagues at the trial bar, was never much of a drinker, he often sought refuge from the toils and stresses of the courtroom at the poker table.

Stud was his game, and George soon fell into a weekly contest with a group of his old Freeport cronies. These included George Loft, the candy man, and Victor Moore, the actor. Steve Pettit, a real estate broker and the former sheriff of Nassau County, and George Bennett Smith, the local Cadillac dealer. The men would meet on Saturday nights at the Elks Lodge, and their games would last into the wee hours of Sunday morning, whereupon sums as large as two thousand or three thousand dollars would ultimately change hands.

Beatrice, George's second wife, viewed these weekly conclaves with an increasingly jaundiced eye—to the point that, when her hints gave way to objections and her objections to ultimatums, she became downright creative in demonstrating her displeasure. She would, for instance, show up at the Elks Lodge after midnight with her knitting—and later, with her infant son, George Jr.—nestled in her lap. After a while, these antics forced George to accept a difficult but necessary truth.

He needed a new place to gamble.

Jack McDermott was a lawyer from Manhattan who'd long been urging George to try his hand at craps. George had resisted at first— as Exalted Ruler, he'd even barred dice games from the Freeport Elks Lodge—but McDermott persisted, telling George he had a line on a big floating game in the city. So one day George relented, and the two men, joined by a younger partner of McDermott's, planned a clandestine reconnaissance outing for the following weekend.

The location, it turned out, was a furnished loft over a garage on East 48th Street. McDermott somehow knew the password. George had arrived for the evening with two hundred dollars in his pocket, while McDermott and his partner brought less. A lively crowd surrounded the brightly lit table, and it was through a bluish haze of cigarette smoke that the wide-eyed lawyers recognized such notable high rollers as Subway Sam Rosoff and Nick the Greek Dandolos shouting and laughing and clutching fistfuls of bills like bridal bouquets.

The rules of the game were deceptively simple. The point to be made by the shooter determined the odds. If another customer took your action, then you had a bet, either for or against the shooter. If nobody wanted your action, then you could play against the house for a nominal fee of 5 percent of your winnings.

The lawyers wormed their way to the table, where they were welcomed, and introduced, and given free drinks. Then, before the ice in their glasses had even melted, they were relieved of all their cash. As they thanked their hosts and began shuffling for the door, they were stopped by a shouted voice from the other side of the table.

"Counselor! Hold on a minute! Are you short of money? Here."

A thick roll of bills hit the felt with a thud. George returned to the table and retrieved it, counting out five thousand dollars as he circled the table to address his would-be financier.

"I don't believe we've met. I'm George Morton Levy."

"Sure we have, Counselor. Earlier this year, at Max Hirsch's house."

Now George remembered. Max Hirsch trained thoroughbreds at Belmont Park, and George recognized Arnold Rothstein as the man whose horse Sporting Blood had won the 1921 Travers Stakes. Rothstein had requested that George represent two of his nephews who'd been charged with stock fraud. George had taken the case, had won a quick dismissal of the indictments, and had promptly forgotten the whole affair.

George, of course, knew Rothstein's reputation as a high-dollar gambler, and that his nickname, the Big Bankroll, derived from his alleged investments in bootlegging and bookmaking and any number of dubious ventures.

And then there was the small matter of the 1919 World Series.

"Listen. Don't let a run of bad luck send you boys home early," Rothstein told the men in a low, silken voice. "You fellows are smart. Think of gambling not as random chance, but as a rough kind of science. Like a sine wave that oscillates within a limited range of probabilities. You'll win a few and you'll lose a few, but in the end it'll all even out. And if you're adequately capitalized, then you'll be the ones—not Lady Luck—who decide when to call it a night."

The lawyers elected to stay, each borrowing five hundred dollars from Rothstein. Eventually, their collective fortunes—waxing and waning in accordance with their benefactor's mathematical hypothesis—reached a post-midnight apex that found them up over five thousand dollars.

In deference to both the lateness of the hour and the amplitude of their positions, they huddled to discuss an exit strategy.

"This looks like a pretty rough place to take your money out," McDermott said, eyeing the other players, several of whom were shadowed by bodyguards.

George nodded. "Let me talk to Rothstein."

The Big Bankroll laughed, clapping a hand on George's shoulder. "Tell you what, Counselor. Leave your winnings with me, and when you're ready to pick them up, they'll be waiting for you at Lindy's."

George knew the restaurant-deli, which was just around the corner on Broadway. He also knew that it served as a kind of unofficial headquarters for Rothstein, who was known to stand out front on the sidewalk most evenings, paying and collecting his manifold wagers.

The lawyers conferred again. Concluding that the devil they knew was preferable to whatever might be lurking outside, they voted to leave their money with Rothstein.

Two weeks later, George found himself back in Manhattan, at a sheriff's department smoker with his Long Island friends Steve Pettit and Grover Walsh. It was Walsh, short on cash, who hit George up for a loan.

"I haven't ten dollars on me," George said, patting his pockets. And then he remembered. "But let me make a call."

The cashier at Lindy's confirmed that he was, indeed, holding an envelope bearing George's name, so George arranged for its delivery by messenger. This transaction completed George's introduction to a stratum of New York society whose conduct, George thought, well illustrated the distinction he'd learned in law school between that which is *malum in se*, or inherently wrong, and that which is *malum prohibitum*, or "wrong" merely because it's forbidden by law.

And so, George Levy became a regular at Saturday night craps. What right had the state, he reasoned, to govern a man's private vices? Besides which, the men he was meeting and the friendships he was forming might well open new and lucrative vistas for a man in his line of work.

Beatrice took a somewhat different view. "It's unbecoming for a man of your stature to go around consorting with hoodlums and gangsters."

"But criminals are my stock in trade," George reminded her. "They pay the bills around here."

"We should be mixing with a better class of people. Long Island society people."

"I'll mention that to Willie Vanderbilt the next time I see him. He generally plays on alternate Saturdays."

One night George was leaving a game near First Avenue and 49th Street with over four thousand dollars in his pocket when he heard footsteps on the sidewalk behind him. The street ahead was dark and empty, and George felt his heart beating faster.

Spying no taxis on First Avenue, he proceeded to Second Avenue at a somewhat brisker pace, but the footsteps did not slacken. And so it went—past Third Avenue and Fourth Avenue, and then finally to Fifth Avenue, where, to his enormous relief, a taxi had pulled to the curb to disgorge a laughing young couple.

George dove into the backseat of the cab, and as it merged into traffic, he turned to see through the rear window the receding figure of a man, tall and powerfully built, with a flattened potato for a nose.

George's pulse had returned to normal by the time he reached Pennsylvania Station, where he proceeded down the stairs to his platform. The platform was wide and mostly empty, with only scattered newspapers and a few snoring drunks to keep him company. He chose an empty bench by the staircase, where he lit a cigar to calm his nerves.

Soon the Long Island train rumbled into view. George snuffed his cigar and had just started toward the track when a pair of ragged men appeared from behind a tiled pillar.

"Hey, pal, what's the hurry?"

"Yeah, where's the fire?"

George halted. He sidestepped, but the men did likewise. Ahead of him, he noticed, the train doors had opened and swallowed the eastbound passengers. The platform, George realized with growing alarm, was now otherwise deserted.

George backed as the two men advanced. He knew he couldn't fight them, and he doubted he could outrun them in his suit and wing-tipped brogues.

For the second time that evening, he felt a shadow pass over his heart.

"Now hold on, fellows," George said, still backing up, but the men had stopped in their tracks. Their gaze, George realized then, had shifted over his shoulder.

He spun around to look.

The large man with the flattened-potato nose was hurrying down the stairs with a hand thrust into his overcoat. As George turned again to confront his assailants, the platform before him was empty.

The big man, his breathing labored, skidded to a halt beside him.

"Who are you?" George demanded. "Why are you following me?"

"I'm sorry if I frightened you, Mr. Levy," the big man said, removing his hat, "but you usually leave your money with the house, so I was sent to protect you."

"Sent? Sent by whom?"

"Why, by Mr. Rothstein, of course."

The man trotted ahead to the waiting train and held the door for George.

"You can never be too careful, Mr. Levy," he said as George stepped on board. "This town is full of crooks."

Eleven

Tammany Hall

November 1926

EVEN THE MAYOR was a songwriter.

James J. Walker, a grinning, glad-handing son of Greenwich Village, had already penned such popular ditties as "There's Music in the Rustle of a Skirt" and "Will You Love Me in December as You Do in May?" before dipping a cap-toed brogan into the murky waters of elective politics. He was soon a Democratic assemblyman and then a popular state senator, and he took the oath of mayoral office in January of 1926 amid a national economic boom of historic proportions.

With Al Smith in the governor's mansion and Democratic strangleholds on the city's legislature and judiciary, its public works and public safety departments, the New York into which Tom Dewey graduated from the Columbia University School of Law was a testament to the strength of the Tammany Hall political machine at the height of its storied powers.

Uptown, they'd dubbed it the Harlem Renaissance. Downtown, in the windswept canyons of Wall Street, they were calling it the Roaring Twenties. And in a midtown bathed in the golden footlights of Broadway—in its nightclubs and speakeasies, its theaters and dance halls—it was known as the Jazz Age. But whatever you called it, and from whatever vantage you witnessed its glittering abundance, the second decade of the twentieth century had found in New York a host city of unique incandescence.

Ever dapper in his silk hat and spats, Mayor Jimmy Walker played the strutting drum major to this trombone parade of enterprise and decadence that roused New York from its postwar doldrums and led it, high-stepping, to its manifest destiny as a world capital of art and culture, industry and finance—a city of six restless million whose skyscrapers tickled the heavens, whose stages hung the stars, and whose hustling, bustling streets carried more automobile traffic than all of Europe combined.

But the roar of the steam shovel and the syncopated din of Tin Pan Alley masked another, darker sound in a city where the raking claws of graft were audible to all but the willfully deaf. It was a city in which a police captain's bars might be bought for a few thousand dollars, or a magistrate's robes for ten. A city in which the population grew by 15 percent as the municipal budget swelled fourfold. Where the mayor, dubbed Beau James by an adoring press, held court at the Central Park Casino—refurbished at a taxpayer cost of over $350,000—with bootleggers at his table and a showgirl on either arm.

Meanwhile, in the ground-floor apartment of a modest brown-stone on West 22nd Street, the mustachioed young lawyer newly associated with the Wall Street firm of Larkin, Rathbone & Perry rubbed a circle on his bathroom mirror. Tom Dewey paused a moment to listen, razor in hand, to the bright, tinkling melody emanating from the piano in the parlor. But when Frances Hutt's delicate etude was joined by a reedy vocal tenor, Tom's smile morphed into a frown. Grabbing a towel, he threw the door wide and stalked, fully lathered, into the carpeted hallway.

"For God's sake, man, put some guts into it!"

The music stopped as Frances shielded her eyes. "Goodness, Tom, put some clothes on."

"I told you that'd smoke him out of his hole." Marland Gale dropped to a knee and splayed both hands over his heart. "*If you knew Dewey, like I know Dewey, oh, oh, oh, what a guy!*"

Frances's hands clapped to her ears as she pivoted on the bench. "Now see what you've gone and started?"

"What do you say, Tom? How's about a little Eddie Cantor for old time sake? *Yes, we have no bananaaas*—"

"C'mon, knock it off." Sewell Tyng, the third man in the room, squared a thick stack of handbills as he rose from the couch. "Let's get going. We've got a governorship to win."

The three lawyers were soon striding eastbound toward Fifth Avenue with their overcoats buttoned, the gauzy lights of the Flatiron Building guiding them like a beacon. The night was damp and unseasonably cold for the first Tuesday of November, and the sidewalk would have stretched dark and empty before them save for a lone pedestrian, stooped and shuffling, on whom the three men rapidly gained.

Sewell Tyng held a gloved fist to his throat. "You're a damn lucky man, Dewey. When are you going to make an honest woman out of that songbird back there?"

"Not so fast," Marland Gale protested. "What are you trying to do, get me evicted?"

"I can't evict you, Marty—Frances needs the piano. Besides, she's been offered a part in the *Scandals*, only this time for the road show."

"What?" Gale grabbed his roommate's coat sleeve, spinning him to a halt. "Any guy who'd let a classy dame like that ride the rails with a bunch of clowns and chorus girls ought to have his head examined!"

"You're preaching to the choir, Marty. Only women have the vote now, haven't you heard?" Tom shrugged free, and the men were moving again. "I've told her I don't like it—either the work or the company. But she's no shrinking violet, in case you haven't noticed. She says she has her *future* to think of. If he didn't know any better, a fella'd think she was trying to send him a message . . . Excuse me, sir? Have you voted yet?"

The shuffling pedestrian started, backing a step at the younger man's proffered handbill.

"I most certainly have. For Ogden Mills."

"That's a good fellow. Here." Tom stuffed a handbill into the old man's jacket. "If you've got any Republican neighbors, remind them the polls close at eight!"

The lawyers were hurrying now, cutting across the empty street.

"A million more like him and we'll send the Happy Warrior back to the Second."

"Don't kid yourself," Tyng said. "If we could find a million like him, Tammany would find two million more."

"That's a damn cynical thing to say."

"I'll forgive your naïveté, Tom, but only because you're new at this. Let me tell you a little story. I was working the polls two years ago, right here in the Tenth, when all of a sudden a bunch of hoodlums showed up—great big apes with hairy knuckles and guns sticking out of their jackets. They hung around for a while, making everybody nervous, and then a bus rolled to the curb and maybe two dozen floaters came strolling in. None of them registered, of course. Probably all from out of state."

"What did you do?"

"What could we do? We called the police, but they never came. Heck, it was probably a cop who was driving the bus. All we could do was protest the votes, which earned us a horselaugh from the hoodlums. Then once the bus pulled out, they all moved on to the next precinct. Those guys on the bus must have voted a dozen times that day, and do you want to hear the corker? Someone filed a complaint with the Board of Elections saying *we* were the ones intimidating voters. Can you beat that?"

"You make it sound worse than Chicago."

"Chicago? Chicago's for amateurs, brother. There's a saying in these parts you'll do well to remember, and that's that nobody's ever lost a nickel betting on Tammany Hall."

"If you believed that for a minute, Sewell, you wouldn't be out here tonight. You wouldn't have spent the last six weeks knocking on doors and passing out handbills. And for that matter, neither would I."

"Maybe we're just a pair of cockeyed optimists."

"We're Republicans, damn it. We think the people of this city deserve decent, honest government. We think it's a crime the way public projects come in at twice over budget, and the way government payrolls are padded with hacks and cronies, and the way every loaf of bread sold in this city carries a ten-percent kickback to union gangsters and the crooked politicians they pay to look the other way."

"Start printing the campaign signs." Marland Gale made a frame with his hands as he walked. " 'Dewey for Attorney General.' "

"Not me, friend. I've got a living to make. Maybe Sewell here should run for assembly. 'A war hero who's too rich to be corrupted.' Now there's a slogan for you."

"I heard when they probated Boss Murphy's estate it was worth over two million simoleans," Gale said as the men turned north into the headlights on Fifth Avenue. "Not bad for a guy who hadn't held a job for twenty years."

"You mean the man who elected three mayors and three governors? I'd call that a job well done."

The men divvied their handbills and took up positions on the corner, waiting for prospective voters.

"The fellow I don't understand is this Buckner," Tom said. "He's the United States attorney for God's sake, with all the power of the federal courts on his side. He's got the FBI, the Intelligence Service of the Treasury, the Secret Service, the Postal Inspection Service, and the Narcotics Squad all at his beck and call. He should be busting these rackets and blanketing this town with grand jury subpoenas. Come to think of it, he should be posting federal marshals at every polling place in the city."

"Easy, Dewey. You've got a chorus girl to support."

"Tell you what, Tom. Why don't you tell that to Buckner in person? He's invited some of us to lunch at the Lawyer's Club on Thursday. Sam Koenig will be there, and so will Tom Desmond and some younger fellows from Buckner's staff. We're getting the Young Republicans back together, and we all think you should be part of it."

"Thank you, Sewell, but the last time I checked, there were only twenty-four hours in a day."

"Suit yourself," the older man said as a clutch of shoppers approached. "But Desmond will be very disappointed. He and Koenig both made a point of asking for you by name."

Twelve

Broad Shoulders

May 1927

THE WAY I figured it, three was my lucky number. I left Cleveland in
March of '26—that's the third month, see?—and headed for Chicago
with the three grand I'd cleared after selling my share of the speak to
Pearl. Big Joe Porrello had set me up in a suite on the third floor of
the Hotel Metropole, and he'd promised to visit me whenever he was
in town, which he said was usually around three times a month.

Lucky three, get it? But it wasn't too long before three didn't seem
so lucky after all.

I liked Big Joe, don't get me wrong, and I know he was sweet on
me. More than his other girlfriends, that's for sure, and maybe more
than his own wife even. But after a while, a girl comes to realize that
sweet only gets you so far, and that she needs to have certain things in
a city like Chicago that she don't necessarily need in a place like
Pittsburgh or Youngstown or even Cleveland.

Take food, for instance. Do you have any idea what a room service meal costs in a joint like the Metropole? A girl could go broke without leaving her room! And then there's dinner out, and let me tell you something, you don't go out to dinner in Chicago wearing any old thing you pull out of your closet. You need gowns, not to mention hats and gloves and a half-decent fur, or else you look like some kind of a crumb.

I tried to explain all this to Big Joe, and at first he bought me a few nice things like lingerie and stockings and frilly girl stuff he wanted to see me wearing. Or not wearing. Or putting on and then taking off again. Or leaving on, in the case of the stockings. But when it came to going out, what did he care if I wore the same lousy dress I wore the last time we went out together? *Ish kabibble*, that's what he cared.

Plus I was getting bored. I know, you'd think lying around in bed all day listening to the radio and farting through silk underpants would be the elephant's eyebrows after running that joint in Cleveland for three years, working ten, twelve hours a day waiting on tables and washing glasses and scrubbing up other folks' puke. But you'd be wrong. The truth of it was, I was going off my nuts. I felt like that bird you hear about, the one that lives in the gold-plated cage.

I needed to stretch my wings.

I met Jack Zuta on one of Big Joe's visits around Christmastime. Big Joe and me went to this club on the south side where Al Capone was supposed to be, and Frankie Rio, but instead it turned out to be a bunch of third-rate palookas sitting around smoking cigars and getting drunk on their own bootleg hooch. I was bored out of my skull, and pretty soon Big Joe and me had us a humdinger of a row.

It started over Big Joe taking lip from this guy half his size about some deal involving a boat and who it was that was supposed to have registered it. I asked Big Joe how come if he was such a big shot now he didn't just tell the pipsqueak to chase himself. Big Joe got all sore and told me to dry up. I said he should dry up, 'cause I was only asking a question, and then he told me I didn't know from nothing and I should go downstairs and powder my nose.

So that's what I done. And when I came back to the dining room, instead of going to the table where Big Joe was waiting, I walked over to this guy at the bar who'd been giving me the big eye all night, and I asked if he wanted to dance.

Now, normally I wouldn't of done something like that, on account of it making Big Joe look like a heel in front of his gangster friends. Also on account of Big Joe being the jealous type as far as his nature goes, and a baby grand as far as his size goes. But I was madder than a wet hen by then, and I'd had a couple of drinks too many, and I suppose, looking back on the situation, I was only trying to get some kind of a rise out of the big galoot.

At first I thought this guy at the bar was a Jew, but then he told me that his name was Jack Zuta, which sounded Italian, and that he worked for Capone. Now if I had a nickel for every guy in Chicago who claimed to work for Capone, I could of bought myself a Duesenberg. Only this guy seemed on the level, and if he was even the slightest bit afraid of Big Joe, who was staring pitchforks at us the whole time we were dancing, he sure as hell didn't show it.

He wasn't the best-looking guy in the joint, this Jack Zuta, but he had real nice manners, and he wore a flower on his lapel, and he cut a rug like Oliver Twist. I guess you could say he had class, and it'd been years since I'd been around any of that. Plus he had these long, dark lashes like Valentino that made my knees a little wobbly when we danced up close and he looked me straight in the eye.

I could see Big Joe at the table getting madder and madder, swelling up like an overpumped tire, and so I told Jack Zuta I'd better get back to my date. He asked me where I was staying, and I before I could stop myself, I told him the Metropole. Then he asked me what room, and I told him to slow down a little, and that made him laugh. He said, "Okay, the Metropole then," and he went back to the bar, and I went back to Big Joe.

Big Joe, of course, burned like a fuse for the rest of the evening, until we got out to the car, and then he really exploded. Called me a bitch, and a slut, and an ungrateful little whore. Said he should slap me silly and make me walk back to the hotel. Said that the guy I was dancing with used to run a string of five-dollar houses and that my even talking with him in public made me look like a quiff and made him, meaning Big Joe, look like some kind of a sucker who had to pay cash for his nookie.

To which I was about to make a smart-ass remark, but then thought the better of it under the circumstances. The circumstances being that I was in a speeding car with two hundred and forty pounds of angry Dago with a gun under his arm and a straight razor strapped to his ankle.

Big Joe always carried that goddamn razor. I'd asked him once what it was for, and he said it was for when he ran out of bullets.

Big Joe had cooled down by the time we got to the hotel, and by the time he finally went to sleep, we'd already kissed and made up. But in the meantime, I'd found out a few things about this Jack Zuta fellow. Like that he wasn't really Italian but a Polak. And that he really *did* work for Capone, as some kind of a fixer. And that the Guzik brothers had run him out of the whorehouse business a few years earlier, before he'd somehow managed to catch on with the Capone outfit.

So anyway, Big Joe went back to Cleveland the next morning, and I went back to my radio. Then in the afternoon, at around three o'clock, a bellboy knocked on my door and handed me a bunch of flowers with a note that said, "Pick you up at six. We'll dance. Jack Z."

I gotta tell you, it made me a little sore, that note, but it also made me smile. Jack Zuta had moxie, and I liked a man with moxie. Besides, I figured, if he worked for Capone, then I'd be doing Big Joe a favor by making connections he could use someday in his rackets. At least that's what I told myself. But the main reason I was smiling was on account of this whorehouse business, because there was this idea I'd been chewing on even before I'd met Jack Zuta, and here was my chance to finally do something about it.

We went to dinner at the Blackhawk. Carlton Coon was there with his Kansas City Nighthawks, and me and Jack danced a few waltzes with both of us laughing and me all the time keeping an eye out over his shoulder for any of Big Joe's bootlegger friends.

When we finally sat down to eat, I told Jack what Big Joe had said about the Guzik brothers and Jack laughed it off, saying it was the best thing that'd ever happened to him, what with him connecting first with Johnny Torrio and then later with Capone. He said he was a bookkeeper now and was strictly legit, which I thought was sweet of him, thinking he had to appear legit in order for me to be interested.

"Let me ask you something," I said once the food had arrived. "How hard would it be to set up a whorehouse in this town? And not some two-dollar crib, but a swanky joint with real booze and clean sheets and girls who know how to behave?"

"What?" he said, acting all surprised.

"Look honey," I told him, "I think you're a swell guy, so let's not kid each other and get off on the wrong foot. I'm no debutante, and you know it. I ran a drum in Cleveland, and I worked the short con in Youngstown before that. That's how I met Big Joe, during a robbery at my speak. Only now he's got me squirreled away in that hotel all day with nothing to do but stare at the wallpaper, and I'm starting to go buggy."

Jack shook his head as he lit us a couple of smokes.

"You're buggy all right," he said, handing me my cigarette. "To run a house in Chicago you'd need the okay from the cops and the outfit both, and you'd never get either one, so forget about it. Believe me, I know. And if you tried to go independent, you'd still need a booker and a bondsman, and you'd never get either of those."

"What's a booker?"

He rolled his eyes. "A booker is sort of like an employment agent. Every week he sends fresh girls to the houses—like shuffling a deck of cards. It mixes things up for the customers."

"So what if I didn't use a booker? What if I found my own girls and I was smart about it and never got pinched?"

"Then I'd still say no dice. If the outfit ever found out, you'd get your joint robbed or wrecked or both. Maybe that pretty face of yours, too. This isn't beanbag, kiddo. There was one guy I heard about who tried to muscle in on the Guziks, and they found his body in the bathtub. They found his head in the sink. I hope you're getting the picture here. And I've yet to meet the pro skirt whose mouth wasn't bigger than her handbag. So, like I said, don't even think about it."

If there was one thing that got me sore, it was some mug telling me what I could and couldn't do. It was my mother who used to say that if she wanted me to do something, all's she had to do was tell me not to.

"But you'd know how, right? Even if we're just beating our gums, you'd know how to set one up?"

His head was still shaking, but at least this time he was smiling.

"Yeah, Flo, I'd know how to set one up. And I'll tell you all about it, but first you gotta promise me two things."

"Anything."

"First you gotta promise you ain't serious, 'cause even loose talk like this could get us both killed."

I nodded. He reached a hand under the table and rested it on my thigh.

"Second, you gotta promise me you'll ditch that goon Porrello, because I ain't in the habit of sharing my girlfriends with nobody, understand?"

So that's how I came to be dating two guys at the same time. It was also about then that lucky number three walked into the picture.

I explained to Jack Zuta that if I was gonna break it off with Big Joe, then it had to be real gentle-like, on account of Big Joe being a hothead. Jack said that if Joe Porrello ever gave me any trouble, he'd personally cut Joe's balls off with a butter knife and feed 'em to his goldfish. Which, sweet though it was, I knew to be strictly patter, on account of while Big Joe carried a gun and a razor, the only weapon I'd ever known Jack Zuta to carry was a gold fountain pen.

As far as Big Joe was concerned, I never saw Jack Zuta again. And as far as Jack was concerned, I'd broken it off with Big Joe for good. So when me and Big Joe spent New Year's together, Jack thought I was in Pittsburgh visiting family. And when Big Joe called the hotel after midnight and found out I was gone, I'd say I'd been sitting up with some girlfriend's elderly mother. Best of all, whenever the rent was due on my suite at the Metropole, I got two checks every month, and both for the full amount.

Things, as the man said on the radio, were copacetic. And then all of a sudden they weren't.

Joe Sussman was a friend of Jack Zuta's who used to run a whorehouse on Madison Street. Jack introduced me to Suss with the idea, I think, of getting me to quit talking all the time about going into the business, on account of Suss getting roughed up pretty good by Mike Heitler and having to lam it up to Duluth. Only there were two things Jack didn't see coming, and come to think of it, neither did I. The first was that Suss wanted back into the business and was actively looking for a partner. The second was that Suss fell for me like a sack of rolled oats, and the truth of the matter was, I fell for him just as hard.

Pretty soon I had what you might call a romantic triangle on my hands. Or maybe it was a rectangle. Whatever it was, I was the one who had to work out the angles.

The nice thing about Suss was that he wasn't so full of himself. Most of the guys I'd met in Chicago, they were either hard-boiled or else they wanted you to think they were. Guys who all they ever talked about was this big shot they knew, or this racket they were part of, or this boss they were gonna bump off. But never Joe Sussman.

For one thing, he didn't weigh more than a buck sixty, so who was he gonna kid? Plus he liked to poke fun at himself for being yellow, or being slow on the uptake, or having a tiny dick, when in fact he turned out to be braver, smarter, and better in the feathers than Jack Zuta and Big Joe Porrello put together.

The first time me and Suss made it, even the guests in the adjoining rooms lit up cigarettes.

But the best thing of all, Suss wasn't the jealous type. He knew all about me and Big Joe and, of course, all about me and his pal Jack Zuta. Yet he never asked stupid questions, even when he knew I'd spent the night with Joe or I'd just come back from a weekend out of town with Jack. All's he'd say was that he was glad I'd had a swell time, and that he was happy I'd made it home safe. Also that for a big ape from Cleveland, he thought Big Joe had excellent taste in women's underwear.

At first we debated whether to open our house in Chicago or Duluth. Suss's argument was that Duluth was a wide open city that was full of good-looking blondes and had easy access to Canadian booze. My argument was that Duluth might as well be the North fucking Pole, and what good would it do us to run a first-class joint only to freeze to death or get eaten by wolves?

In the end, we settled on Duluth. Not on account of Suss winning me over, but because we had no other choice in the matter, given what happened next.

It started in April, when Big Joe had the bright idea to surprise me for my twentieth birthday, which I'd forgot he even knew about. And because I forgot, I'd made a date to meet Jack at the Hotel Sherman for dinner. And because I'd also made plans to meet Suss later that night, I left word at the Metropole as to where I was gonna be.

Geometry, I'm sorry to say, was never my strong suit.

The evening got off to a good-enough start when Jack and me got back to our table from the dance floor and the waiter came over with one of those fancy plates with a silver dome on top. And when he lifted up the dome, there was a pair of sapphire earrings with little diamond sparkles staring me smack in the kisser. I squealed and ran around the table and gave Jack a big hug. Even the eggs at the other tables were smiling, and some even clapped like we'd just gotten engaged or something.

After that we had our dinner. Then the band started up with a slow number, and we were back on the dance floor cheek to cheek when over Jack's shoulder I seen Big Joe come charging into the dining room, looking around like he wanted to rip somebody's head off.

That somebody being me.

"Uh-oh," I said.

"What?"

"Don't look now, but Big Joe Porrello's standing over there by the doorway."

Jack spun me around to get a gander at Joe. I felt his body go limp in my arms.

"Jesus Christ," he said. "What're we gonna do?"

"I don't know about you," I told him, "but I think I'll go powder my nose. If he does happen to see you, watch for that razor he wears on his ankle."

I made for the powder room posthaste, while Jack went the other way, toward the big swinging doors to the kitchen. Big Joe saw me first and headed to cut me off. Then Jack must've reached the doors just as a waiter was coming out, because there was this loud crashing sound, and everybody in the joint—Big Joe included—turned their heads to look.

"Son of a bitch," I heard Joe say as he started across the dance floor.

Jack, who by then had soup all over his shirtfront, saw Big Joe coming and hightailed it into the kitchen. I changed directions and made for the hotel lobby. I figured if I could catch a taxi, I could get to the Metropole and maybe pack a bag before Big Joe'd finished dicing Jack Zuta into chicken à la king.

79

Then I heard, "Flo! *Pssst*. Over here!"

Joe Sussman was standing by a door off the lobby with that crooked grin on his face. He had one hand on the crash bar and was waving me over with the other.

"Suss!" I said. "What're you doing here?"

"Never mind that," he said. "Let's go, baby."

He grabbed my wrist and yanked me onto the sidewalk. We stumbled around the corner onto 23rd Street, where Suss had parked his old Buick near the rear entrance to the hotel. Then, just as he'd opened the passenger door, we both heard a familiar voice calling from back near the loading dock.

"Flo!" Jack was hollering and waving his arms like a castaway who'd just spotted a passing freighter. And then . . . "Joe?"

Suss circled the car, tipping his hat to his old pal Jack Zuta just as the rear doors to the hotel flew open and Big Joe Porrello came charging out like a train that had jumped the tracks.

Suss fell in behind the wheel. He turned the ignition, and the engine sputtered and caught, and then he paused long enough to give me the once-over.

"Nice earrings, baby," he said, throwing the car into gear. "They'll be the bee's knees in Duluth."

Thirteen

The Ride

October 1929

THE TROUBLE BEGINS, as it always does, with his father. Antonino Lucania had not been forewarned that his middle son, Salvatore— or Charlie, as the boy now calls himself—would be joining the family for dinner. When Charlie arrives, late as usual, with a bagful of gifts and is promptly swarmed by his mother and siblings, Antonino does not rise from the table to join them. Instead the old man opens his newspaper and finishes his meal in silence, then stands without speaking to grab his coat and hat and head for the door to the stairwell.

"What's the matter, Papa? First no hello, and now no goodbye?"

Antonino pauses without turning. Then the door slams shut behind him.

What else does Charlie expect? His father, who'd been a sulfur miner in their Sicilian hometown of Lercara Friddi, believes in three things above all others: the infallible mercy of Our Lord Jesus Christ, the virtues of honest labor, and the honor of his family's name. This was a man who'd paid for their passage to America by saving his centesimi for years in a glass jar under his bed. A man who'd come to America with neither a dollar in his pocket nor a word of English to his name, but who'd managed to feed and clothe and house his wife and their five children by the sweat of his brow and the sheer determination of his fifteen-hour workdays.

To Antonino Lucania, his son Salvatore's life is a mockery of all he holds dear. Godless, the boy had quit attending Mass when, at age fourteen, he'd quit attending school to hang around with the neighborhood Jews. Lazy, the boy had chosen the gaudy flash of hoodlum life over the value of an honest day's wages. But worst of all to Antonino Lucania is the way in which his son has tainted the family name with his drug dealing, and his arrests, and his criminal reputation in the neighborhood. And thus it was no insult to Antonino when he learned through a friend that his son Salvatore was calling himself "Luciano" now.

Good, the father thought. Maybe now their neighbors would forget that the thug named Charlie Luciano is the flesh and the blood of Antonino and Rosalia Lucania.

Charlie, for his part, laughs off the old man's performance. If not for Charlie's money, and his gifts, and the respect he's accorded in the neighborhood, the Lucania family would still be living in that squalid cold-water flat on First Avenue. His mother would still be working in rags, and his siblings mocked and taunted for their hand-me-down clothes. Instead of ignoring him, the old man should be thanking Charlie—or better yet, kissing his feet—for all he's done for this family. For their comfort, and for the deference they're rightfully paid. Because he, Charlie Luciano, is the one risking life, limb, and prison to provide for the family as his father never could— for the family who's so-called reputation the old man so worries about.

82

Someday his father would own up to the truth. Someday he'd have no choice, because someday Charlie Luciano would be too damn big for even his father to ignore.

An hour after the old man's departure, Charlie stands at the kitchen window, a damp dishcloth cooling in his hands. Tenth Street yawns dark and cavernous below him with its sidewalks empty and its curbside automobiles quietly slumbering. To the east he can see the cars on Avenue A, their headlights revealing the tall gothic arches of the corner church and, on the sidewalk beyond, the figures passing in dark silhouette—the nightly promenade of junkies and whores, toughs and downtown hustlers.

This is Charlie's old neighborhood, and his lips curl into a smile.

Charlie excuses himself when the telephone rings. He touches his mother's arm as he exits the kitchen, plucking a grape from the fruit bowl and lifting the heavy receiver to the sound of a familiar voice.

"Salvatore, *a cussi tardu!*" his mother cries as he emerges moments later from his parents' bedroom, shrugging into his overcoat.

"*Nun ma aspittari,*" he tells her, kissing her forehead while palming a wad of folded bills into the pocket of her housecoat. "*Ci sta nu problema a putia ca u devu risolviri.*"

Outside his parents' apartment the night is crisp, the air redolent of wood smoke and coal smoke and a hint of rotting garbage. Charlie pauses for one deep breath before continuing westbound along 10th Street. He turns into the colder air on Second Avenue, where the comforting thrum and bustle of flaring headlights and laughing pedestrians bathed in storefront neon restore a spring to his step. Instinctively he scans for patrol cars up and down the avenue, his right hand hefting the .38 revolver in his overcoat pocket, easing the weight that would otherwise break the perfect line of his lapel.

He turns west again at 15th Street, his pace quickening, and by midblock he is eyeing the curb line, searching for the car that will carry him uptown. Farther ahead, at the corner of 15th and Third

Avenue, he spies a familiar form, hunched and smoking, loitering under a streetlamp.

"Let's go!" Charlie calls, still walking, still checking the sidewalks front and rear.

The man stamps out his cigarette. He steps to the curb and opens the rear door to an idling Packard with darkened headlights.

Charlie knows in an instant that everything is wrong. The car is unfamiliar, and the Irishman in the backseat is a stranger, hatless and hulking. But before Charlie can react, the hard muzzle of a pistol jabs into his spine, forcing him inside the car as another, smaller man appears from the shadows and shoves into the backseat beside him.

"What the fuck is this?"

As Charlie's hand closes on the revolver in his pocket, the pistol presses at his skull, forcing his head sideways and down to where the Irishman grabs him, pinning his arms. From the front seat, the twin barrels of a sawed-off shotgun swing into view.

The rear door slams, and the car is already moving.

"Okay, wise guy, show me both hands." The shotgun barrels dip. "Nice and easy."

The speaker is hidden in shadow. Charlie releases his grip on the revolver and frees his hands from his pockets. Fingers claw into his overcoat, his suit jacket, his pants, removing his gun and his cigarette case and lighter.

The shotgun withdraws.

"Relax, Charlie. Everything's gonna be fine." The front-seat voice is calm, reassuring. "*Nun ti preoccupari*. If we wanted you dead, you'd be dead already. Just sit back and be quiet and we'll have you home before midnight."

The car reeks of men long at close quarters—of body odor and garlic and gun oil. It stinks of stale cigarettes and, from the slab-faced Irishman seated beside him, of cheap rotgut whiskey.

Charlie settles into the seatback. He recovers his hat and rests it on a knee.

Although he is outwardly calm, Charlie's mind is racing wildly. Is this a hit, or merely a summons? Are these the men in charge, or are they flunkies? Do they want information, or something more tangible?

There are only two things that Charlie knows for certain. The first is that the men who surround him are cops. The second is that wherever it is they're taking him, it's not to any station house.

"Joe the Boss ain't gonna like this," Charlie says. He is addressing the Italian in the shotgun seat, but it's the Irishman beside him who responds.

"Is that a fact? Well, that's too fucking bad for—"

"Shut up, both of you."

The big man glares at the front-seat voice but, Charlie notices, does as he is told. And so they ride in brittle silence, west at first and then south along the river, their progress slowed by traffic snarls and construction barriers and the tweet and shriek of police whistles.

It takes them twenty minutes to reach the Battery.

"You guys are makin a big mistake," Charlie tries again, probing. "If I knew where he was, I'd give him up in a heartbeat. I got no reason to protect that crazy son of a bitch."

The man in the front seat turns. Although his face is backlit by the oncoming headlights, Charlie can detect the outlines of a smile.

"Listen to you, already squealin like a baby. I guess it shouldn't surprise me, a stool pigeon like you. And here I heard you were a big shot now, you and your pals down in Atlantic City. Well, guess what, big shot? Ain't no pals around to help you tonight. And none of your payroll coppers neither. So do like I said and shut your yap. You'll do plenty of squealin before the night is over."

Charlie is focusing now, marking time in his head. It takes them fifteen minutes to load the Packard into the belly of the ferryboat. The men remain inside the car, cramped and hot in their woolen overcoats, shrouded behind windows raised and fogging. All around them, doors are slamming and voices are trailing away toward the iron stairs to the deck.

"I can't fuckin breathe," Charlie finally says, and the leader rubs a circle on the shotgun window with his fist. The ferry engines are rumbling as the window cranks open and a cooling combination of salt air and diesel fumes floods into the car.

Charlie can hear seagulls somewhere above them as the boat shudders and lurches into motion.

"Hey, wise guy. Is it true you know Al Capone?" asks the little guy on Charlie's right.

"Yeah, sure. Gimme your address and I'll have him pay you a visit."

"I said shut up, all of you."

The passage takes twenty minutes. Then on the Richmond County side the process is reversed as voices return and the window cranks closed and the surrounding car engines stutter and catch. Soon they are part of a long procession of headlights that climbs and levels and wends its way through the ferry terminal and thence onto Bay Street, where the Packard pulls to the side to allow the other cars to pass.

The shotgun reappears.

"Now," says the leader, and Charlie is shoved forward with his face pressed into the seatback as his arms are twisted behind him. He feels rope scratching, burning, biting into his wrists.

"You fucking bastards," he says. "I'll tear your fuckin heads off. I'll cut your fuck—"

Zip, zip, zip. A roll of adhesive tape is passed from man to man beside him. Three, four times it circles his head, trapping the words in his mouth.

"All right, let's go."

The car is moving again, merging onto a Hylan Boulevard that's deserted at this hour, the roadside houses dark and abandoned. Charlie struggles against his bonds, testing at first, then thrashing and flailing in earnest. What he feels in that instant is neither fear nor panic, but a hot, blinding rage that overwhelms his reason and sends his legs kicking and his body crashing over the seatback like an errant torpedo.

Rough hands yank him backward, and Charlie catches the glint of the brass knuckles only in the final instant before the big man's fist slams the side of Charlie's face, shattering his cheekbone in an explosion of swirling embers.

Charlie's last memory inside the car is of blood—his own blood—running in thin rivulets down the seatback, the image playing to a score of shrieking seagulls that circle and descend, hundreds of gulls, their cries growing louder and louder until he hears nothing but the gulls and then he hears nothing at all.

"Wake up!"

Charlie wakes to find that there are five men now, with a porcine newcomer in a vested suit standing slightly apart from the others. The new man keeps his hands in his pockets and is rocking on the heels of his polished brogans. The others stand in a square around Charlie where he lies in the mud with a cold wind at his back and the putrid stink of dead fish and rotting garbage filling his nostrils.

Charlie tries to stand, but his wrists remain bound and he only manages to extend one leg and roll awkwardly to a seated position. His breath comes in short, clotted snorts. His face, he knows, is badly swollen and he notes with his one sighted eye the piles of windswept trash and the angled cars behind the men that block his view of the street and the wooded hillside rising above it.

"Help him up," says the fat man.

Charlie is hoisted to his feet and stands weak-kneed and wobbling before his captors.

"Ask him nice, just the one time."

The Irishman from the backseat grabs Charlie by the lapels and lifts him onto his toes.

"Jack Diamond! You tell us where to find him, and you go home tonight on the boat. Clam up, and your body washes up tomorrow in

Jersey. You hear me, wise guy?" He shakes Charlie as if he were weightless. "You hear me? Nod once for yes."

Charlie knows now they are homicide dicks—a special squad of some sort, tasked with finding Legs Diamond. In July, the night that two men were killed in his Hotsy Totsy Club on Broadway, Legs had mysteriously vanished. Now eyewitnesses to the murders have been disappearing, and the cops are growing desperate. They are tearing the city apart, searching for the loudmouthed bootlegger who'd once been Arnold Rothstein's bodyguard and therefore, in the minds of the police, Charlie Luciano's ally.

Since he can neither curse nor spit at the man who holds him, Charlie arches his back and thrusts his head forward, targeting the Irishman's nose. The blow connects with a satisfying *crunch* that leaves Charlie once again heaped on the muddy ground.

He waits for it. He is kicked once, twice in the ribs before a shoe presses down on his shattered cheekbone, grinding his head into the mud. The embers return, orange and dancing, and he is screaming beneath his gag.

Voices burble, then a sharp command. Charlie can see on Hylan Boulevard the lights of a passing car. He struggles at his bonds, his hands balled into fists.

He is lifted again by his overcoat, and a fist is driven into his belly. But he remains standing because, he realizes now, another man is behind him, holding him upright.

The Irishman is back, only this time with a knife.

The blade is short and sharp and jagged along its cutting edge. It sways hypnotically in the reflected lights off the bay. The face behind the blade is flushed and bloody and the blood has soaked the Irishman's shirtfront.

Whiskey breath comes at Charlie in gusts.

"You dirty wop bastard," the Irishman wheezes. "You'd better talk to us. Nod once and I cut the tape." The blade is cold on Charlie's cheek, where it lingers for but a second before inching higher. "If not, I swear to Christ, I'll carve your fuckin eye out."

"For God's sake," says the fat man. "It's not like we wanna be out here freezing our asses any more than you do. Speaking for myself, I'd rather be home in front of a fire. And what do you owe Jack Diamond, anyway? I hope he ain't your bodyguard, 'cause he didn't do too great a job for your pals Rothstein and Little Augie, did he?"

The fat man stops talking and rocking long enough to light a cigarette.

"Besides, it seems like every hoodlum in New York is trying to kill the guy, so stop and think for a minute. Is it really worth losing an eyeball to protect some trigger-happy asshole who's already as good as dead? Come on, Charlie, don't be a sap. It's only a matter of time. Be a smart boy, and go ahead and nod."

The men wait, all looking at Charlie.

The Irishman turns. The fat man shrugs.

"Okay, tough guy. Have it your way."

The blade digs into his face. Charlie screams under his gag while his blood spurts as from a burst balloon onto the Irishman's sleeve, his pants, the ground under his feet.

"Jesus," says the smaller man behind him.

Charlie slumps again, his knees turned to jelly, but still he is held upright. He cannot tell whether his eye is gone, on the ground along with the trash, but he knows that in order to live, he must do something and do it quickly.

His fists ball and twist, the rope cutting deeper into his wrists.

Charlie nods, with grunts meant to approximate speech.

The fat man flicks his cigarette to the ground.

"About time. Here, give me that."

The fat man takes the knife from the Irishman. He wipes it clean with a handkerchief, then runs his fingers along Charlie's face, probing for the edge of the tape.

The man behind Charlie loosens his grip. Charlie balls his numbing hands and twists again and feels for the first time that the rope is beginning to slacken.

The tape is ripping free. Then it stops, and Charlie sees the heads of the men turning one by one toward a sound that he recognizes as the whine of a distant siren.

"Shite," the fat man says.

The other men are anxious, pacing now as the fat man switches the knife to his right hand. He feints toward Charlie's abdomen, then slashes upward so that, although Charlie has jerked his head backward, the blade catches the underside of his jaw.

Charlie is gagging now, sprawled on his side, choking on mud and blood. He sees the fat man's polished brogans, then feels the heavy thud of a body blow, the blade plunging deep into his back.

"So long, tough guy. You shoulda talked when you had the chance."

The brogans are gone. Charlie hears two automobiles starting. His hands, although still tangled in the rope, have come unbound.

The sirens are several, and they are growing louder.

Somehow Charlie is on his knees, then on his feet, and he is making his way toward the roadway like a man wading in heavy surf. He himself feels heavy, and his clothes are stiff as oilcloth. First he sheds the rope, and then the tape, which, as he rips it from his head, is sticky in his hands.

Headlights rake his body, and he raises a shielding hand. The cherry strobes and the garbage stink and the banshee scream of the sirens blend together, disorienting him, turning him in a circle.

He is seated on cold, hard blacktop.

Running feet and flashlights.

"Hey, are you all right? Jesus, look at this guy."

Charlie lies back, freezing now, longing for sleep. His head lifts from the pavement and a light shines in his eye.

"Call an ambulance!" one voice shouts, while another says, "See if he's got a wallet."

More fumbling hands. Squinting into the headlights, Charlie can see the shapes of running men. He hears the crackle of a two-way radio.

He tries to speak.

"What's that? What'd he say?"

Charlie licks his lips and starts again.

"Fifty bucks."

"What?"

He shields his eye with a hand. "I said call me a cab, and I'll pay you fifty bucks."

The patrolman turns away. "Can you believe this guy? He wants us to get him a taxi."

"Lucania," reads a patrolman with a flashlight. "Salvatore Lucania."

"Hey, Sal. What happened here? Who did this to you?"

Charlie waves them off. "Go on, scram. Take a day off. I'll handle this myself."

Another car arrives and then, finally, the ambulance. Charlie is numb by now, light-headed and empty, the warmth drained from his body. A stretcher lies on the cold pavement beside him.

"You're lucky to be alive, mister," the ambulance driver tells him.

"Yeah, sure," Charlie says, the scene blurring again, fading to white. "That's me. I've always been lucky."

Fourteen

Word of Honor

As the thundering roar of the 1920s echoed across the American landscape, George Levy found to his surprise that his courtroom exploits had made him a modestly wealthy man. And like other wealthy men living on a still-rural Long Island suddenly booming both in population and prosperity, George decided to dabble in real estate.

With his growing circle of well-heeled friends and a reputation for honesty and sound judgment, George had little trouble finding other speculators eager to reap the rewards of turning the day's bucolic duck and potato farms into the morrow's bustling residential suburbs.

In May of 1928, George purchased a 557-acre tract of farmland in Massapequa for $306,000—or roughly $550 per acre—with the notion of subdividing the land for homes. He paid $32,000 down and signed a promissory note for the balance. He then put the word out to his wealthier friends in Manhattan.

William Fox, the studio mogul, jumped at the opportunity to invest. Fox, in fact, agreed to repay the $32,000 George had advanced, and further agreed to put up, along with two other investor-partners, whatever funds were required to develop the property. Under the terms of this handshake proposal, a corporation was to be formed in which George would own 25 percent of the capital stock while risking none of his own money. Saul Rogers, an attorney for the Fox Film Company, was tasked with drafting the papers that would memorialize the parties' agreement.

Enter Edward West Browning, husband of the notorious Frances "Peaches" Browning—a man whose personal life had left him a national laughingstock but whose real estate acumen had made him one of Manhattan's largest and wealthiest landlords. Browning caught wind of the deal with Fox and approached George personally, offering $2,000 per acre for the Massapequa property, 50 percent of which would be payable in cash.

At a time when a Steinway grand piano cost $400 and a new Cadillac $2,000, the Browning offer represented a profit to George Levy in the life-altering sum of one million dollars. And since New York law required that any agreement concerning real property must first be reduced to writing before it could be enforced, George had every legal right to accept the Browning offer for his own personal benefit. All it would have taken was George's signature on the confirmatory letter from Browning.

Despite having no legal obligation to Fox or his colleagues, and despite the urging of friends who questioned his sanity, George nonetheless presented the Browning proposal to his prospective partners. Even under the terms of their oral agreement, George still stood to net a cool quarter-million dollars if they accepted the offer from Browning—not bad for a $32,000 investment.

William Fox, however, had other ideas.

"We'd be crazy to accept this offer," Fox harrumphed, tossing the Browning letter aside. "If he wants the property this badly, it means it's worth a hell of a lot more than he's offering. I say no deal!"

George, nonplussed, pointed out that none of them was really a real estate developer in the first place and that a profit, after all, was a profit. He refrained from explaining that he could, as a matter of law, not only accept Browning's offer without their approval but also cut them out of the deal entirely.

The men put the matter to a vote. George lost 3-to-1.

Enter the stock market crash of 1929. With a suddenness that was all but unimaginable only a few months earlier, many of the nation's largest fortunes were lost in October of that year, leaving rich men nearly poor and poor men newly destitute. Soon half the nation's banks failed, and fifteen million Americans lost their jobs. Unemployment swelled to 25 percent, while crop prices fell by half. Foreclosures skyrocketed, and displaced families flooded the homeless shelters and soup kitchens of every American city.

The Browning offer evaporated, of course, along with the personal fortune of William Fox, who soon declared bankruptcy. By the time the tangled tendrils of the Massapequa real estate deal were finally unraveled, George was out over one hundred thousand dollars, a sum that represented almost the entirety of his life savings.

According to Saul Rogers, Fox's lawyer, "It was the most honorable thing I've ever seen in my life. I told George so at the time, and I also told Fox he was taking advantage of George. It almost cost me my job with the Fox Film Company, but it was true. Instead of making a million dollars or a quarter of a million dollars, George Levy ended up owing a hundred thousand. How nuts can you get?"

George, for his part, was more sanguine. "Saul was wrong," he later said. "I'd promised Fox and his partners seventy-five percent of the deal, and that was that. A man is only as good as his word."

If adversity reveals the true character of a man, then the Great Depression served as a kind of national litmus test—a test that George Morton Levy passed with highest honors.

Prior to October 1929, George had been hired by the Paraiso Realty Corporation to handle the mortgage transactions from another real estate development, this time in the Long Island hamlet of Wantagh. While George had no ownership interest in Paraiso and no control over its operations, he did deal directly with the buyers of the subdivided lots, each of whom came to George's Freeport office to sign their mortgage documents. So when the Great Depression hit and the buyers were unable to obtain deeds to the lots for which they'd been faithfully paying on installment, George became angry. And since most of the mortgage transactions had been handled by his office, George felt an obligation to do something about it.

"A lot of those contracts went through my firm," he explained to an incredulous colleague. "Those people didn't know Paraiso from pineapples. They depended on me."

George called the Long Island Title Company to inform them that, beginning immediately, he would assume personal responsibility for all the unpaid mortgages. Ultimately, George paid out more than thirty thousand dollars—effectively the rest of his dwindling nest egg—to assure that his clients received their titles.

Nor was that the end of the affair. George had also recommended a friend—a contractor named Arthur Hendrickson—to perform grading work on the Wantagh project, and by the time Paraiso went under, Hendrickson had been paid only half of his fourteen-thousand-dollar contract. George pledged to pay him the balance.

"But you don't owe it, George," Hendrickson told him, flabbergasted. "Paraiso owes it."

"Can you handle the loss if you don't get paid?"

"No," said Hendrickson. "If we don't get it, then we'll have to close up. We're through."

"Well then, stop talking about it. You wouldn't be in this mess if I hadn't put you there. Let's go to the bank and work something out."

To the bank they went, where George signed eleven promissory notes of seven hundred dollars each, all payable to Hendrickson. Why eleven? The extra note, George explained, represented interest for the delay in full payment. Thereafter, as Hendrickson would present a note to the bank, George would scramble to deposit funds from his law practice to cover it. Eventually, all the notes were paid in full.

"The Hendrickson Company is now one of the largest heavy equipment contracting firms in the country," Hendrickson would later tell an interviewer, "and we wouldn't be here at all if it hadn't been for George Levy. We were absolutely down and out when he took on that obligation that didn't belong to him. I don't know of any other case like it, and we've been in business a long time."

For George, the explanation was simple. To a man who'd never ventured far from his boyhood home, friendships were more important than the material trappings of success. This was a man, after all, who still drove the same Abbott-Detroit roadster he'd bought on his thirtieth birthday. A man who used scissors to cut the sleeves off his dress shirts because he felt they restricted his arm movements in court.

But George had another, perhaps more philosophical rationale for behaving as he did. Unlike ordinary tradesmen such as the butcher, the baker, and the candlestick maker, a successful lawyer depended almost exclusively on his reputation for integrity and trust. Pro bono work—cases undertaken with no expectation of payment—was an honored tradition as old as the law itself. George Levy believed in the lawyer's unique and privileged place in American society. He felt that the awesome powers conferred by admission to the bar—the powers to subpoena, to sue, and to prosecute—came with commensurate responsibilities.

And so every evening after dinner, old pals in distress—George's so-called parishioners—began appearing at the Levy home, and few if any ever left empty-handed. George could still work, he told his fretting wife, Beatrice, and he could still borrow money, and what was the point of it all if their neighbors were homeless and hungry?

"How he did it, I don't know," George's third wife, Margaret, later recalled. "At one point during the Depression it seemed as though George was keeping just about everybody in Freeport afloat. If you ask me, George invented Social Security before Congress ever heard of it."

Fifteen

Uncle Sam

January 1931

THE YOUNGER OF the men could barely hide his disappointment.

"If only he'd taken the time to read the papers," Tom Dewey groused to George Medalie as the two lawyers trudged the four frigid blocks from Foley Square—the downtown plaza crowded with apple hawkers and chestnut vendors and a young girl playing the accordion—to the office building their law firms shared at 120 Broadway.

"Juries are complex organisms, Tom. Never forget that. At best, they're the conscience of the community. At worst, they're an angry mob with torches and sharpened pitchforks. In this economic climate, defending a firm like Empire Trust against a widow claiming she'd been swindled was no easier task than slaying the Nemean lion."

"Yet Heracles somehow managed it."

The older man smiled. "That he did. And the Appellate Division, unless I'm greatly mistaken, will be our avenging Zeus."

The widow in question, one Nanny Glover Kaufman, had sued the Empire Trust Company alleging that, without her knowledge or consent, it had exchanged certain preferred stock she'd owned for common, with disastrous consequences come the crash of October 1929. Empire Trust was a client of McNamara & Seymour, the litigation boutique to which Tom had migrated in 1927 after a volatile exit from the Augean stables of Larkin, Rathbone & Perry. George Z. Medalie, age forty-seven, was a respected courtroom veteran whom Stuart McNamara had retained to guide his firm's newest associate through his first jury trial.

"What was that phone call this morning?" Tom asked as they turned the corner onto Broadway. "It must have been important for the clerk to interrupt like that."

"It was Bill Mitchell."

"As in William D. Mitchell, the attorney general?"

"The same."

"My God, what did he want?"

Medalie sighed. "It seems that President Hoover, in an appalling lapse in judgment, has just appointed me to be the next United States attorney for the Southern District of New York."

Tom stopped and clapped a hand on the older man's shoulder.

"Why, that's fantastic! Congratulations!"

Medalie turned away as he sneezed, pulling a handkerchief from his pocket. "I won't lie to you, Tom. It's an honor to be following in the footsteps of men like Elihu Root and Henry Stimson." He blew his nose. "But it's also a damnable business."

Medalie was moving again, with Tom hurrying to catch up.

"Why? What do you mean?"

"I mean that with Tom Crain as the district attorney, it'll be up to the Justice Department to tackle Tammany Hall single-handed, and that's just what I plan to do. This Seabury investigation is going to open a whole new front in the war on public corruption, and I'm going to need fresh troops to mount an offensive. At least a dozen or more talented, dedicated young men willing to perform public service for their Uncle Sam at great personal sacrifice. Men like your friends in the Young Republican Club. Lawyers from the best schools and the biggest firms on Wall Street."

"But I thought the federal prosecutors were already top-notch."

"One would hope so, but then let's face the facts. The U.S. attorney's office hasn't been as proactive or as effective as the times require. Graft is eating at this city like a cancer, and bootleggers like Waxey Gordon and Dutch Schultz are operating in broad daylight without the slightest fear of arrest or prosecution. It's nothing less than a civic disgrace. When times were good, the public was willing to laugh and look the other way. But the public mood is changing, Tom, I can sense it. Meaning now is the time to act."

"I'll be happy to put the word out. I know a few fellows who'd be perfect candidates for the job."

"I was hoping you'd say that. Perhaps you could ask around and work up a list for my consideration. Then we could meet for lunch next week sometime, assuming I'm not at death's door with this infernal cold."

"I'd be honored."

"Oh, and there's one other thing." Medalie turned to Tom as they reached the building entrance. "I'll be very disappointed if the name Thomas Dewey isn't at the top of that list."

"*Leave* McNamara and Seymour?"

Frances Dewey twisted on the piano bench.

"Why, Tom, you've only just started there! And after all Mr. McNamara's done for us. He's promised to make you a partner!"

"I didn't say I'd apply. I only said I'd think it over."

"And?"

"And that's what I'm doing. What *we're* doing. It's not my decision, you know. We're in this together now."

"And what does your mother say?"

"Who says I consulted with Mother?"

Frances, her arms folded, tapped the toe of her slipper.

"All right, so I cabled her on the ship. If you want to know, she's against it. She said if I stay with McNamara, then at least I won't be sending men to Sing Sing."

"And what about Mr. McNamara? Have you even talked to him?"

"Not yet, but I know he thinks the world of George Medalie. You should have seen him in that courtroom, honey. Seen the respect he commands. And not just from the judge, but from every one of those jurors. Did you know that his father's a rabbi? And that he speaks fluent Greek?"

"But it's a political appointment, isn't it? What will happen if Hoover is defeated next year? They'll bring in a Democrat to replace Medalie, that's what. And you'll be out of a job."

"You're right, and that's one for the minus column. Along with the pay cut, and the longer hours, and the not-so-incidental fact that I've never tried a criminal case in my life."

To Tom's relief, Frances hadn't flinched at the words "pay cut." After turning down offers from the "Scandals" and the San Francisco Light Opera, both at Tom's insistence, she'd have been well within her rights to veto the whole idea of his leaving McNamara & Seymour. Over two thousand banks had failed in the United States that year. Times were harder than ever, the future never less certain, and Tom had promised his new bride that he alone would be the family's breadwinner.

"So what's in the plus column?"

"Lots of things. Foremost is the opportunity to get some real trial experience, and plenty of it. That'll give me a leg up in the long run, no matter how the job market tightens. Plus, the men George will be hiring are some of the very best in town. Columbia, Yale, and Harvard men. I've already talked to Barry Ten Eyck, and he's going to apply. Even if the job lasts only a couple of years, connections like those will last a lifetime."

"You mean political connections."

"But most important of all is the work, honey. Medalie's got his sights set on the big game—the top crooks like Dutch Schultz and Waxey Gordon. Not just to grab a few headlines, but to smash the criminal rackets once and for all."

Tom knelt beside Frances where she sat.

"Don't you see? This is more than just a political opportunity. It's a chance to clean up this city before the Democrats are back in office and things return to business as usual."

Frances ran a hand through her husband's hair.

"What?"

"Nothing. I was thinking about our first dinner together, do you remember? About how you didn't want to clean up Chicago, and how I was the one who said you should come and clean up New York instead. I guess I have no one to blame but myself."

Tom edged closer, wrapping her in his arms.

"I know this would be a huge sacrifice, honey. I wouldn't even consider it unless you were behind me all the way."

"I'm not worried about me, you silly man. I'm only concerned that it's the right move for my husband and his career. A very wise boy once told me that a man's got to think of the long haul."

Tom kissed the crown of her head. "I'm supposed to meet Lowell for dinner this evening. I have a hunch Medalie's recruited him to twist my arm. Why don't you come along? We'll listen to what he has to say, and then we can make an informed decision. Together, the two of us, and Mother can mind her own business."

The car was on its third pass through a Central Park growing steadily whiter in the still-falling snow. Lowell Wadmond, one of Tom's Young Republican colleagues and the chief assistant to outgoing U.S. attorney Charles H. Tuttle, was hunched behind the wheel, his head bobbing in time with the wipers.

"If this is such a great opportunity, Lowell, then why aren't you staying on?"

Wadmond glanced at Frances Dewey in the front seat beside him.

"For one thing, Mary would brain me with a poker. Four years of public service were three too many, as far as she's concerned. Plus there's that office at White and Case with my name on the door. But for a fellow like Tom, this could be the chance of a lifetime. I know George Medalie, and I think he's capable of great things. Tom would be crazy to miss out on it."

"What do you mean, 'a fellow like Tom'?"

"I mean a bright-eyed bulldog with his sights set on elective office. Do you know what we call him down at the Young Republicans? Among other names best unspoken in mixed company, he's known as Governor Dewey."

"I'll tell you my greatest fear, Lowell." Tom leaned his chin on the seatback. "I'm worried I'll get lost in the shuffle down there."

"Hold on a minute. Tom Dewey afraid? Not the same Tom Dewey who told Albert Stickney to go sit on his thumb."

"Tom!"

"And got himself fired for it. I'm serious, Lowell. What have you got there now, fifty assistants?"

"Closer to sixty. And when Medalie's finished his hiring and firing, they'll be sixty of the best young lawyers in this city. And when he's finished training them, they'll be the top prosecutorial agency in the country. With no disrespect to McNamara and Seymour, Tom, this is like being called up from the sandlot and offered a starting spot with the Yankees."

"So how's a bright-eyed bulldog to distinguish himself in a crowd like that? I could wind up trying bankruptcy frauds or mailbox burglaries."

Wadmond's eyes found Tom's in the mirror.

"Not if you're head of the Criminal Division you won't."

"What are you talking about?"

"You lunkhead. I'm saying Medalie's prepared to make you head of Criminal. He'd of made you the offer himself but he's flat on his back with the flu. I don't know what you did in that courtroom, but you'll be pleased to know you impressed the hell out of him. He called you a force of nature. Said he'd never seen a harder-working or a better-prepared young lawyer in all his years of practice."

"For all the good it did us."

"Heck, Tom, losing is part of the game. Nobody bats a thousand, not even a federal prosecutor. Not even Governor Dewey."

"Who's never tried a criminal case in his life."

"Never mind that. After a year in that office you could try a case in your sleep. Besides, when you're head of Criminal, your responsibilities are mostly administrative. You've always talked about opening your own firm someday. What better preparation than running a sixty-lawyer division of the U.S. Department of Justice?"

"Last I checked, they don't accept experience at the grocery store. The fact is, I'm earning eighty-five hundred this year at McNamara, with a promise of partnership next year. And being the bluebeard that I am, I made Frances give up her singing career with the promise that I'd provide for the both of us. I'd be nuts to even consider the kind of pay cut you're talking about, and besides—"

"All right, you drive a hard bargain. Medalie told me if you didn't go for head of Criminal, I was authorized to offer you my job."

"*What?*"

"You heard me. And if you turn this down, I'm making you walk the rest of the way home."

Again his eyes found Tom's in the mirror.

"Congratulations, my friend. You're the new chief assistant United States attorney for the Southern District of New York."

Sixteen

Kicking the Gong

March 1931

THE GUY AT the end of the bar had heavy sugar written all over his cashmere suit and his onyx cuff links and the gold chain he wore on his vest. An older gent with a ferret face and a pencil mustache, he looked kind of like that movie actor—what was his name?—Warner Baxter. He wore no wedding ring, but from clear across the room I could see the band of lighter skin on the third finger of his left hand.

If he were a book, he'd be one I'd already read a hundred times before.

He'd been eyeing me like cotton candy ever since I'd walked through the door. I gave him a few minutes to make his move, but when the time was up and he still hadn't budged, I took up my coat and my Scotch and I walked them over to where he was sitting.

"You'd better be careful, mister," I told him, setting my drink next to his. "You look any harder, they might burn right off me."

He leaned back to take in my dress. It was mostly silk, and mostly thin, and it showed a lot of leg.

"That would make for an awfully small fire," he said. "Barely enough to warm a man's hands."

"You got cold hands, I know a nice warm place you could put 'em."

"Say, there's nothing bashful about you, is there?"

"Oh, I can be shy all right, if that's what you like." I peeked down the top of my dress. "Heck, I can blush all the way to my garters."

"I suppose you realize you're young enough to be my daughter."

I leaned in close to whisper. "I'll bet when your daughter was naughty, you used to give her a spanking. Nothing too hard. Just enough to turn her bottom all pink and hot."

Like I said, I'd already read the book. I figured him for a banker, or maybe a judge. Straight as a ruler on the outside, but inside wound tighter than that gold watch in his pocket.

He took a sip of his drink, and his hand was practically trembling.

"Have you been a naughty girl?"

"Not yet I haven't, but the night is young. Let me make a phone call first and see if the coast is clear."

We left in my car, with weasel-face holding his hat in his lap, twisting the brim in his hands. It was dinner hour, and uptown traffic was light. We made small talk until around 79th Street, when he surprised me and asked me my name. I said it was Brown, Flo Brown, but he could call me Smith if he wanted, or maybe Jones. Whatever was easy to remember.

My apartment was on the ground floor, left off the lobby. I knocked shave-and-a-haircut, and when the door swung inward and weasel-face got both barrels of Dolly in her black negligee, he took a step backward.

Men tended to do that. It was like seeing Grand Central Terminal for the first time. Big, and breathtaking, and full of possibilities.

"Relax, Professor. This is my friend from Chicago," I told him, prying his hat loose and tossing it onto the divan. "She's a nice girl, and I think the two of you are gonna get along swell."

106

Fifteen minutes later and I was back in midtown, this time at the Three Hundred Club, one of my regular haunts. The joint was so busy I had to elbow my way to the bar. Right away this old Jew in a shabby raincoat appeared out of nowhere and offered to buy me a drink. He was an odd-looking bird with heavy spectacles and eyes that kind of crossed. I had to pick which one to look at when I thanked him for the Scotch.

"Pleasure's all mine," he said, having to shout over the music. He raised his glass. "That's what I like about this place, it attracts all the best-looking dames."

The guy was strange all right, and he dressed like a brush salesman, but I could see he was no Rube. I cut the baloney and got straight down to cases.

"It's too loud here," I told him. "You seem like a sport. How's about you and me go find someplace a little more quiet?"

"You read me like a meter, sister." He knocked back his drink. "I'm right behind you."

I offered to drive, but he wanted to take his own car, so I waited around the corner on Seventh Avenue until he pulled up behind me and tooted his horn. He was driving a Cadillac that looked like it had just rolled off the assembly line. So maybe he wasn't a salesman. Maybe he was some kind of eccentric millionaire, out mingling with the common folk. That was one thing about this racket—you never knew who you were gonna meet next.

The uptown traffic had grown heavier, and it took us another thirty minutes to get to Yorkville. That gave Dolly plenty of time to finish with the professor, because nobody lasted more than forty-five minutes with Dolly. It was a matter of professional pride with her. She was real dependable that way.

I stood outside the apartment building while four-eyes parked his car someplace that it wouldn't get scratched. When he finally appeared on the sidewalk, I took his arm and we walked together up the steps and into the lobby, where again I knocked shave-and-a-haircut.

Only when the door opened this time, it was Dolly who took a step backward. And she kept on backing all the way to the sofa, where she plopped on her ass with folded arms and a crooked slant to her mouth.

"Cockeyed Louis," she said.

The old Jew was turning a circle, eyeballing the joint like he might make an offer to buy it.

"Nice," he said, nodding his approval. "Real classy."

"What's going on?" I asked Dolly. "Who's Cockeyed Louis?"

"Louis Weiner," she said, "meet Flo Brown."

"Is Dolly your only girl?" the guy asked me, already knowing her name.

"Who wants to know?"

"What's the matter, you got wax in your ears? I'm Louis Weiner. I book all the best girls in this town. I used to book this *nafka* here, only I ain't heard from her for four whole months, and now I see why. What're you charging these days, Dolly? Two dollars? Three?"

"Five!"

"Listen, cockamamie, you're wearin out my carpet. I'd hand you your hat, but it looks like you already got it, so why don't you scram before I call somebody."

He laughed at that, tossing his hat onto the coffee table and making himself comfortable on the divan.

"Ain't you the live wire," he said, feeling the fabric with his fingers. "The thing is, we need to have a little talk, you and me. But first, how's about that drink you promised?"

"Sure thing," I told him. "Arsenic or strychnine?"

"Don't get sore about it. You seem like a smart girl. How long did you think you could operate like this with nobody being the wiser?"

"What're you gonna do, call the cops on me?"

"The cops? Sister, the cops are the least of your problems. Sit down, relax, and let Uncle Louis tell you what's what. But first, how's about that drink?"

I went to the kitchen and made us three highballs, all the time muttering under my breath. The old Jew was right—I did know this day was coming. I just didn't think it was coming today.

When I returned with the drinks, me and Dolly sat like schoolgirls with our knees to our chins while Cockeyed Louis Weiner explained the ways of the world, starting with how we should be grateful it was him who'd found us first and ending with how, from that day forward, I had to book all my girls through him.

"So today's actually your lucky day," he concluded, finally tasting his drink.

"I'm pinching myself."

He had blondes and brunettes, he told me. Black girls and white girls, two-way girls and three-way girls, with over a hundred to choose from. He made it sound like he ran the doll department at FAO Schwarz.

When he finished his pitch I said, "Thanks all the same, but I don't need help from you or anyone else."

Cockeyed Louis thought that was funny.

"Listen, *bubbala*, I'd soft-pedal that if I was you. Or else maybe you'd like a visit from Jimmy Fredericks?"

I looked at Dolly, whose face told me that was one visit I definitely didn't want.

"All right, so what's it gonna cost me, this service of yours?"

"Ten percent of the action. Not your half, but the whole shebang. And from now on, you gotta keep track. I'll send over some punch cards in the morning. And don't give me that look, because it'll be easy to make up my cut. You go on a weekly schedule, see? You charge each girl two bucks for the maid, plus eighteen for board and five for the doctor. The doctor comes on Mondays. Also, you pay an up-front deposit of two hundred and fifty for fall money."

"Don't make me laugh."

"Please, this isn't a negotiation. You want my five-dollar girls, you gotta bond. I use Jesse Jacobs, who's the best in the business. Ask

Dolly, she knows. If your place gets hit, you pay half and the bonding pays half."

"Let me guess. And if I don't pay bond, then my place gets hit."

He shrugged. "Cost of doing business. Everybody bonds."

"That's a lie. I know for a fact that Polly Adler don't bond."

"That's because she's been around, sister, and we know she's good for it. You we don't know from bupkes. We won't place a girl in a house that can't bail her out within twenty-four hours."

"You mean so she won't rat you out."

"I mean so she ain't out of commission all week on account of some greenhorn madam tried to save herself a few bucks."

"And who's this 'we' I keep hearing about? All's I see is a cross-eyed creep in a cheap raincoat."

"That's right, sister. And if you mind your potatoes, that's all you'll have to see."

"Tough guy, is that it?"

"Not me. I'm just a small businessman trying to weather the hard times like everyone else. But I'll tell you what I am willing to do, because I'm a mensch. We'll start you off with a clean slate and forgive what you already owe."

He reached into a pocket and pulled out a pad and a pencil.

"Here's my phone number. Memorize it, then throw it away. I'll bring the punch cards tomorrow, and you can pay your deposit then. From now on you'll call that number on Fridays and I'll send you the pick of the litter. And just to be clear, this bitch over here is back in my kennel. Ain't that right, Dolly?"

Dolly nodded.

"Good," he said. "I was afraid we'd have to send out the dogcatcher, but now I can see that we all understand each other."

He stood and collected his hat. To me, he said, "Cheer up, sister. You've got protection now, plus you won't have to schlep all over the city trolling for suckers. My five-dollar girls, they bring their own trade. You can stay home and put your feet up. Listen to the radio, or read a good book. And eat more, you're too skinny."

What I was too much of was tired—too tired to drive downtown again. Besides, I had a lot to think about. Me and Dolly both. We needed a jag. After Cockeyed Louis left, I went into the bedroom and got down my hat box and broke out the opium pipe.

"Well, kiddo," Dolly said, "it was fun while it lasted."

"The nerve of that guy, sayin he'd send out the dogcatcher. So what are you gonna do now?"

She shrugged, lighting the lamp and blowing out the match. "Go back to booking with Louis, I guess. It beats working a sewing machine."

I opened the can and prized out a thick wad of gum. I made the pills extra big on account of my nerves being jangled like they were.

"Who is this Fredericks character anyway? Some kind of a leg-breaker?"

"Jimmy Frederico. He's Italian, and a real gorilla. He wrecks the houses that hold out their girls. You ever see him outside your door, honey, don't let him in."

"Who does he work for? And don't tell me it's Cockeyed Louis, 'cause that guy couldn't lead a dog on a leash."

"I don't know exactly. Some wiseguys downtown. You want my advice, you don't want to go asking too many questions."

I closed up the can and took up the lamp and made a small adjustment to the flame. My hand, I noticed then, was shaking.

"There was a time I could've snapped my fingers and had a mutt like Cockeyed Louis put in his place," I told Dolly. "You ever heard of Jack Zuta? He was my sugar daddy in Chicago until that rat bastard Capone had him killed. The same with Big Joe Porrello in Cleveland, only it was the Mayfield Road Mob that rubbed him out. It's always the goddamn Italians. They're like the cockroaches that show up whenever you turn off a light."

Dolly got up and closed the street-side curtains. Then she got a towel from the bathroom and laid it at the base of the door. She was real careful like that. It was one of the reasons we got along.

"Whatever happened to that nice Jewish boy from Duluth?"

"You mean Joe Sussman? After Zuta got killed, Joe went back to Chicago. Said New York had him all balled up. Last I heard he was doin okay, but things are pretty rough in Chicago these days. Ain't nobody's safe, not even little kids on the street. I told that to Suss, but he just laughed. Said if I found a place that was safe, to be sure and let him know. Now I hear they're gonna put Capone on trial, and do you know what for? Not paying taxes. Ain't that a scream."

I gave Dolly the first go with the pipe. She worked the pan over the lamp and took the smoke in short, jerky puffs. She coughed and passed it to me, then laid down on the divan.

"You could always close up and move," she said. "Just tell Louis you're quitting the game. I know madams who do it all the time. Sometimes they just move across the hall. But if Jimmy finds out, there'll be hell to pay."

I took my turn with the pipe and then set it back on the table. I stretched out on the divan next to Dolly, who scooted over and pulled me into her bosom.

"You know that last creep with the mustache?" she said, already sounding sleepy. "He told me he was the principal, and I was a naughty schoolgirl for talking in class. Asked if we had a ruler anywhere."

"What'd you tell him?"

"I said sure, King George was in the other bedroom."

We both giggled.

"I ain't gonna run like a rabbit," I told her after a while, snuggling my head on her arm. "I'm finished running from guys like Cockeyed Louis."

"What'll you do?" she asked, her voice barely a whisper.

"I'm gonna find this Jimmy Fredericks, that's what. And then I'm gonna become his special girl."

Seventeen

Ace of Diamonds

April 1931

DESPITE THE HOUR, Lucky cannot sleep. He lies on his back and studies the high ceiling, listening to the traffic sounds and the human sounds and the torpid castanet-clatter of horses' hooves on cobblestone. There are no crying babies here on 59th Street, no shouting wives or drunken husbands, breaking glass or screaming sirens. And yet the night sounds of the city still find a way, like rats in a tenement wall, to claw into his head.

The telephone on the nightstand rings, jolting Lucky upright. It is the front desk calling to announce a visitor.

The clock reads three A.M., and he is not expecting visitors.

"Who the hell is it?"

"I'm terribly sorry, Mr. Lane. It's a Mr. Adonis. He says he knows you. Shall I have him call tomorrow, or—"

"No, no, it's okay. Wait. Ask him what cigarette he smokes."

Lucky holds the line.

"He says Chesterfields."

"Okay, send him up."

Lucky dons slippers and a silk robe from the closet. From the bar in the sitting room he retrieves a bottle of King's Ransom and two crystal glasses and arranges them on the breakfast table. Then he sits, listening for the chime of the elevator.

Abruptly he stands, returning to his bedroom and removing a .38 revolver from the drawer of his nightstand. He goes back to the kitchen and places the gun on the table.

The knock, when it comes, is loud and urgent. Lucky takes up the gun and crosses to the door and peers through the peephole. He slips the gun under a sofa cushion before returning to the door.

"Joey, come on in."

"Thanks, Charlie. I'm sorry to call so late."

The men repair to the table, where Lucky pours them each two fingers of Scotch.

"I got news," Adonis says, swirling his drink, "and I'm afraid it ain't the good kind. Joe the Boss called me tonight around midnight. Said we hadda talk right away over at his place. As soon as I get there, the fat bastard sits me down and says he's got proof it was you behind the Morello hit. Says you're a dead man, and on account of us goin way back and everything, he says I'm the guy's gotta take you out. To demonstrate my loyalty, he says. Says I gotta 'remove that stone from my shoe.' "

"Shit!"

"I'm tellin ya, Charlie, the guy's off his nut. First he starts this thing with Maranzano, and now that we're all in the trenches, he wants to whack his best soldier? What kind of a fucking strategy is that?"

Lucky stands and crosses to the window. The dark oblong of Central Park stretches before him like a tombstone.

"That ain't why I said 'shit,' Joey. Listen. I'm gonna tell you somethin, and I'm sorry you're only hearin it now, but believe me, it was for your own protection. Me and a few of the guys, Albert and Vito and some others, we been studyin this thing for a while now. The truth is, we backed the wrong horse. This Maranzano is tougher and smarter and better organized than Masseria, and now it's to the point where he's got more muscle to boot."

Lucky turns to face his would-be assassin.

"We're on the wrong side of history, Joey. And if we don't do somethin soon, we stand to lose everything we been workin for."

"Christ, I been waitin to hear you to say that, Charlie, and I ain't the only one. What can I do to help?"

Lucky returns to stand by the table. He pats his friend on the face.

"You helped already, Joey, comin straight here. I won't forget that."

"Hell, Charlie. Everything I got, I owe to you."

Lucky collects his drink and returns to the window. His voice, when he speaks again, is distant, contemplative.

"Everybody wants this thing to be over. Business is lousy, the cops are crawlin up our asses, and nobody can take a crap without lookin over his shoulder. At first it was just two Mustache Petes fightin over who's got the biggest dick. Only it's been eighteen months now and everybody's been pulled into it, not just the Sicilians. We all know it's gotta stop, but nobody can figure out how to stop it, right? Well, I know how to stop it. Maranzano's gotta know that with the Clutch and Mineo dead, there's only one guy that can get close enough to Masseria, and that's me."

"What are you sayin, Charlie?"

Lucky turns again to his friend.

"We've already made the arrangements, Joey. Me and Benny and Tommy Lucchese are gonna meet Maranzano on Monday. The deal's gonna be real simple. I kill Joe the Boss, and Maranzano becomes top dog. In exchange, Maranzano guarantees our safety. I get Masseria's rackets, and we get a free hand again in runnin our business."

"Geez, Charlie. What about the others? What about Capone?"

"Al's on board, and so are Meyer and Frank. So are Ciro Terranova and Frank Scalise."

"Holy crap."

"For a minute there I thought maybe you'd dropped a turd in the punchbowl, on account of if Joe don't trust me no more, then maybe I missed my chance to take him out, and that puts the kibosh on the whole deal. But the more I think about it, this is exactly the break I been lookin for. So if you really wanna help, Joey, here's what you can do."

"Name it, Charlie."

"I want you to go back to Masseria. Tell him you got a meet set up for Wednesday. Let's make it on Coney Island, at Jerry Scarpato's place. That fat bastard loves the food there. You tell him he's invited to come and witness my execution."

"What time?"

"Make it one o'clock for lunch."

"And what about his bodyguards?"

"Don't worry, I'll handle them. And if he asks who you're usin for the hit, you tell him Vito and Albert. But whatever you do, don't say nothin about Benny. You mention Benny, he'll smell a rat."

"What if he don't wanna come?"

"Then we'll find another way. But if he thinks I killed his pal Morello, then this is one show he won't wanna miss."

Adonis nods without speaking. Lucky lays a hand on his shoulder.

"Joey A. You sure you're okay with this? 'Cause if it works out like I think, word's gonna get around."

"What, you think I'm scared? You think I've gone soft or somethin?"

Lucky tousles his old friend's hair.

"You might get them manicured fingernails dirty."

"Fuck you, Charlie. Go look at your face in the mirror. That's what happened the last time I wasn't there to cover your back."

★ ★ ★

The children have returned to their buses, and the Monday afternoon crowd, generally small to begin with, has thinned to a handful of stragglers, leaving few to witness firsthand the four men in gray fedoras as they pass through the Bronx Zoo's squeaking wooden turnstile.

"It's over this way," Benny Siegel says, tilting the map he'd received at the ticket booth.

"This way's faster," says Tommy Lucchese. "Trust me, I practically grew up in this place."

They follow a winding blacktopped path in which benches are set at regular intervals. In their hats and overcoats, the four men draw looks from the mothers still shepherding their children, fussing and dragging, toward the exit.

"Hey look," says Joe Adonis as they pass the elephant exhibit. "It says right here, Giuseppe Masseria."

"Smells just like him."

"Hey, Charlie. This guy's got bigger balls than you do."

"Knock it off you guys. Come here and listen up."

The men cluster around Lucky as he removes a map from his pocket.

"The lion cage is right around this corner, so remember what we talked about. Everyone know what they're supposed to be doin?"

Hands pat overcoats or dip into pockets. One by one, the men nod.

"Benny? Do me a favor and don't shoot nobody who don't shoot you first, okay?"

"Sure thing," Siegel says, rolling his shoulders. "I'll be on my best behavior."

"That's what I'm worried about. Okay, any questions? No? All right then, let's do this thing."

The men are moving again, strolling now, affecting a careless ease as they round the next corner. Ahead of them the pathway stands empty save for a seated man on a bench.

"I count three," Lucchese says.

Behind the seated figure and flanking him on either side stand two men with their hands in their pockets. They are stationed out of earshot, their backs to an iron railing.

Salvatore Maranzano turns his attention from the sleeping lion. He does not stand to greet the new arrivals. Siegel, Adonis, and Lucchese fan out with their backs to the lion cage, each man facing his counterparts who guard the Castellammarese leader.

Maranzano pats the bench beside him. "*Buon giorno*, Salvatore. Come and sit. You must be tired, carrying such a heavy burden."

Lucky sits. The lion lies on open concrete, its body striped by the canted shadows of the tall iron bars. It is a male, old and dirty, and its mane is flecked with flies.

"Behold the king of beasts," Maranzano says, following Lucky's gaze. "Reduced to a life of captivity and humiliation. If he had known this to be his fate, I venture to guess he would have chosen instead an honorable death. At least, I prefer to imagine so."

Benny Siegel tenses as Maranzano removes a silver case from his pocket. He selects a thin cigar and lights it as Lucky watches.

"That is one important difference between man and beast," Maranzano continues, shaking out the match. "The beast is difficult to capture, but he is very easy to kill. With man, the opposite is true. *Nun si d'accordu?*"

Lucky shrugs. "I wouldn't know. I ain't never tried to capture nobody."

Maranzano chuckles. "No, of course you haven't. Today we associate the lion with gladiatorial contests held in the Coliseum, but it was actually the elephant that symbolized Roman power and privilege. Do you know your Roman history, Salvatore?"

"Can't say that I do."

"Indulge me, then, in a little story. When Caesar returned triumphant from Egypt in 46 B.C., he arrived at nightfall in the company of forty trained elephants bearing torches in their trunks. They marched alongside him, right up the steps of the Roman capitol. Caesar, you see, understood the power of spectacle. The power of symbols."

Maranzano turns to face the younger man. He takes hold of Lucky's chin. Siegel's hand moves into a pocket, but Lucky stops him with a look.

Maranzano is examining Lucky's scars, his drooping eyelid.

"Charlie Lucky," he says, withdrawing his hand. "The man who went for a ride and lived. That is powerful symbolism right there. Maybe the stuff of which legends are made. One should never underestimate the power of symbols, Salvatore. They are invaluable to men like us—men who were born to command."

"If you say so."

"But of course, you already know this. Bringing the Jew, for example. That is making a statement. Do not for one minute imagine it is lost on me."

Lucky gives the man a second look. Maranzano is smart—maybe even as smart as they say. Although his accent is heavy, his command of the English language is impressive for so recent an immigrant. Charlie has heard that Maranzano once studied for the priesthood in Sicily.

"When this war is over, Salvatore, I intend impose a new order among our Sicilian brethren, all patterned after Caesar's Roman legion. *Decini* led by a *capo*. Each *capodecina* reporting to a *sottocapo*. Five *capo famiglia* in total, myself included, and no more of this nonsense where dozens of independent outfits are fighting each other for turf. Discipline and organization will be the new order of things. What do you think of such an idea?"

"I'm all for organization. Like the man said, the business of America is business."

"Precisely. And that would make you, Lucky Luciano, one of the five most powerful mafiosi in New York. Truly a man to be reckoned with. A man to be respected, and a man to be feared. What are you now, thirty-five years of age?"

"Thirty-three."

"Thirty-three. So young. Do you believe you are prepared for that kind of responsibility?"

"Does that mean we got a deal?"

Maranzano smiles. He takes a final draw on his cigar before stamping it underfoot.

"What it means is that I've considered your proposal." Maranzano's eyes return to the lion. "I accept all of your conditions, but I also impose one of my own."

"What's that?"

"You, Salvatore, must be the one. As much as Giuseppe Masseria and I have disagreed, it simply would not do to have a Jew or an Irishman pull the trigger that ends his miserable life."

"What's that, another symbol?"

"No, my young friend, it is much more than that. Call it a question of honor. Me honoring him, and you honoring me. His death will come as a mercy. Don Giuseppe may be my enemy, but he is also Sicilian, and in his own way, he is a lion."

Maranzano nods to the cage.

"Even he deserves a better fate than this."

Nuova Villa Tammaro is crowded when Lucky arrives on Wednesday afternoon, but still Anna Tammaro hurries forward to greet him. She grabs a menu from the rack and leads her honored guest to a table in the rear of the restaurant, where Joe Adonis and Giuseppe Masseria have already tucked into heaping plates of antipasti.

Adonis stands, wiping his mouth with a napkin.

"Sorry I'm late," Lucky says as he sits, his eyes searching the surrounding tables for Masseria's bodyguards. "Geez, boss, I didn't know you was gonna be here too."

Masseria chews as he speaks. "When Joey told me where he was goin, I sez to myself Joe, you can kill two boids with one stone. You can eat at your favorite restaurant, and you can spend a little time with your most trusted soldier. Joey, pour Charlie Lucky some wine."

"No thanks, I got a long day ahead."

"Come on, Charlie. Piddu Morello and me, we used to sit for hours, just eatin and drinkin and talkin things out. Plannin for the future. I miss them conversations, so humor a lonely man and have a glass of wine."

The meal lasts over two hours, the antipasti followed by clams casino, and linguini with red clam sauce, and lobster Fra Diavolo. The dishes are served family-style, with the largest portion—the lion's share—taken by Masseria, who washes it down with a second bottle of nero d'Avola. The conversation ranges from Benito Mussolini to Gaspare Messina to the murder of Joe the Baker. By the time the cannoli arrive, the restaurant is almost empty.

"I gotta get goin soon," Lucky says, reading his watch.

Adonis grabs hold of his arm. "C'mon, Charlie, what's the rush? How's about a little cards?"

"Yeah," Masseria tells him. "You're always in a hurry. Relax a little. It's good for the digestion. And besides, we still got business to discuss."

Masseria unbuttons his vest as he leans back in his chair. He belches. One of the bodyguards is sent to procure playing cards from the kitchen.

"Hey, I just realized somethin," Masseria says as he shuffles. "You and me, Charlie, we ain't never played poker before. What kind of stakes you like?"

"Whatever you say, boss."

"I say nickels and dimes. You, Charlie, you're a big-shot gambler, but me, not so much. I don't trust things to chance. I think chance is for suckers. Ain't that right, Joey?"

Masseria deals. Lucky gathers his cards and fans them. He holds a pair of queens.

"Arnold Rothstein taught me one thing about poker," Lucky says, opening with a dime. "He said the mistake most guys make is that they only play the cards, but the cards even out in the end. The thing to do, if you want an edge over the long run, is to play the man."

"Call," Joey says.

Masseria slides two nickels into the pot. "What does that mean, 'play the man?' "

Lucky discards three.

"You know how some guys are. Set in their ways. Scared to take a chance. Easy to bluff. Or else too pigheaded to know when to fold."

Masseria nods. "Sure, I get it. Or maybe too cocky for their own good."

Lucky gathers his cards again. He frowns as he squeezes a peek at queens and sixes.

"Cocky's the worst of all," Charlie agrees. "Guys that get cocky, they're the ones who never know what hit 'em. I'll check."

"Check," Joey says.

"Dime. So what kind of gambler are you, Charlie? I think you play it close to the vest. Never give too much away."

"You read me like a book, Don Giuseppe. Dime and dime again."

"Hey, you can't check and raise!"

"Sure I can. I just did."

"Fold," Joey says.

"Okay then, fuck you. I call," Masseria says, slapping down three aces. "Read 'em and weep."

Charlie mucks his cards. Masseria cackles, his belly quivering under his vest.

"I'll always remember this day, Joey. Beatin Charlie Lucky in the first poker hand we ever played together."

Lucky checks his watch. It is three fifteen.

"I gotta take a leak. Go ahead and deal me in."

Lucky stands, and suddenly time seems to slow, as it will in a dream. He is crossing the empty dining room, his footfalls echoing on the polished hardwood as his gaze slides to the picture windows in front. There he sees Masseria's armored limousine, huge and black in the afternoon sun, while at the curb opposite he sees car doors opening and three men stepping into the street. Behind him, chairs are scraping. In the kitchen, the muffled clatter of pots and pans has ceased.

The bathroom is new, the tiles white and gleaming. Lucky steps to the toilet and unzips. Over the stream of his own water he hears the front door jingle, and then hurried footsteps, and then a shout.

Lucky pulls the chain. Four shots puncture the sound of swirling water as he steps to the sink and carefully washes his hands, shaking them once and running them through his hair, patting it into place. He tilts his head this way and that, studying his face in the mirror.

"Too big to ignore, Papa," he says aloud.

Lucky exits the bathroom. In the street beyond the windows, Masseria's limousine is gone. Benny Siegel, Vito Genovese, and Albert Anastasia are waiting for him at the table.

All have guns in their hands.

Masseria is slumped forward, moaning, his head resting on the table. Blood trickles down his chair, wetting the floor at his feet.

Using a napkin, Joe Adonis hands Lucky a revolver. It is a .38, snub-nosed and nickel-plated, heavy in Lucky's hands.

Lucky takes the gun and the napkin and stands directly behind Masseria. He places the muzzle at the back of the groaning man's head.

"So long, pal."

He fires a single shot.

Lucky steps back to examine his handiwork. Blood and brains spatter the tabletop while the rest of Masseria's body, toppled by the final bullet, lays faceup on the hardwood with the dark blood pooling around him in a kind of saintly aura. Lucky pictures the image in black-and-white, as it will appear on the front page of every evening newspaper.

Lucky wipes his prints from the gun. He flaps the napkin once, draping it over the dead man's face.

"Okay, let's go," he says, stealing a final backward glance at Joe the Boss. The dead man's hand, Lucky notices then, still clutches a playing card.

It is the ace of diamonds.

Eighteen

Saratoga

August 1932

PERHAPS IT WAS inevitable that George Levy, a gambler by nature, would discover the twin diversions of golf and thoroughbred horse-racing, and that he'd find the ideal setting in which to pursue both these pastimes in the verdant, neo-Victorian ambience of Saratoga Springs, New York.

The historic Saratoga Race Course, America's oldest, officially opened for business on August 2, 1863, less than a month after the Civil War battle of Gettysburg. Known as the Graveyard of Champions, Saratoga was where Samuel D. Riddle watched his great steed Man o'War suffer its only lifetime defeat at the thundering hooves of the appropriately named Upset in 1919. And it was in the Travers Stakes of 1930 that America's second-ever Triple Crown champion, Gallant Fox, lost by eight lengths to the upstart Jim Dandy, an incredible 100-to-1 longshot.

After years of cajoling by his friend and client Mortimer Lynch, a professional bookmaker, George was finally persuaded to visit Saratoga in 1932 for what was promised to be a weekend of golf and relaxation in the mineral springs that had made the resort town famous. His guide for the occasion was to be Oscar Rhodes, a fellow Elk's Lodge member and the son of Walter Rhodes, who was a successful Freeport hotelier and the rear commodore of the South Shore Yacht Club.

Flamboyantly eccentric, with his signature monocle and walking stick, dandy young Oscar was only too happy to show Uncle Georgie the ropes, and George—having just emerged, exhausted but victorious, from the second of the notorious Dubert Armstrong vote-rigging trials in Queens—was only too happy to be shown. And so the unlikely pair made plans to meet that Friday evening at Throggs Neck to catch the last car ferry to Albany.

It was during the overnight boat passage that George had his first inkling of what he'd gotten himself into when, close to midnight, he was awakened by an urgent rapping on his stateroom door. Opening it, he faced an ashen Oscar Rhodes, who informed George that he'd been involved in a game called Spin the Top with "a couple of rough characters," and could he possibly borrow ninety-seven dollars until they made it to Saratoga?

At the racetrack the following day, Oscar led George past the queues and the touts and the ticket takers—all the way to the special clubhouse entrance, where, removing and fogging his monocle, he breezily inquired whether the guards there had received the fish he had sent them. One responded that he'd received no fish and, more to the point, where were Oscar's clubhouse passes? To which Oscar responded by flapping his gloves in the direction of the admissions supervisor.

"Harry, this is George," Oscar announced. "Don't worry, he's with me."

The day proceeded without incident, and George found himself captivated by the pageantry and excitement of the program. It was only after the seventh race that Mortimer Lynch, George's old client, pulled George aside to ask in a low voice how far Lynch should go in extending credit to this Rhodes fellow. Startled, George replied that as far as he knew, Oscar hadn't two nickels to rub together. In fact, George explained, he'd been lending Oscar five or ten dollars per race throughout the day, just to keep him occupied.

Lynch's face went as white as Wonder Bread.

"What's the matter?" George demanded.

"Hell, George. We figured if he was a friend of yours, he must be good for it."

"Good for what?"

"Why, the guy's been betting big all day. He's into us for around forty thousand dollars!"

As George looked on in horror, Lynch convened a hasty conference with his fellow bookmakers. In the midst of the shouting and finger-pointing, Oscar Rhodes blithely strolled in from the clubhouse bar, pulling up short in the doorway.

"Georgie," he said, eying the melee, "I think you've been talking . . ."

Sunday morning found George lighting the week's first cigar alongside three of his newer golfing buddies up to Saratoga from the Lakeville Club in Great Neck. Dave was a lawyer, Lou was a vaudeville actor, and Frank was a former bootlegger. The men had planned an early start to their round in order to make it to the track for the first post. They kicked off the day's wagers with a $250 Nassau as George regaled them with the tragic saga of Oscar Rhodes.

"Jesus Christ," Lou said, once the laughter had died. "What'd they do to the guy?"

"Nothing, I hope. He checked out of the hotel last night, and I haven't seen or heard from him since."

"That's the problem with on-track bookmaking," Frank said in his graveled voice, lighting his own first cigar. "Between the long shots and the welshers, those guys take a terrible risk. It's why we need pari-mutuel wagering in New York. I hear they're installing a tote board at Arlington Park in Chicago."

"Pari-mutuel wagering will never be legal in New York," Dave declared. "Hell, even Jimmy Walker couldn't fix that."

"Maybe," George replied, bending to tee up his ball. "Then again, maybe it's already legal."

"What do you mean, already legal? It's right there in the state constitution, plain as the nose on your face."

"I have a client who's running a dog track at the Mineola Fairgrounds," George informed the men as he took his practice swings. "He wants to install a totalisator for pari-mutuel wagering. He's got a scheme to make it work, and there's a Florida appellate court decision that says he might just succeed."

"Come on, Levy. What's the angle?"

"It's ingenious, really. You see, you don't *bet* on the dog, but rather you purchase an option to *buy* the dog. The option certificate costs two dollars, but if the dog wins, of course, then its value increases. In that event, the house will buy back your option certificate at a premium that's determined by the odds on the tote board."

Frank roared, a meaty hand on his belly. "You fucking lawyers. I gotta hand it to you."

"Why, that's a blatant subterfuge!" Dave sputtered. "It's not only illegal, it's . . . it's borderline unethical!"

"Is it? I contend it's no different than the commodities markets, where people buy options on things like soybeans and pork bellies all the time. They have no intention of ever taking possession. They're just betting the price will rise."

"Maybe so, but I still say it's illegal."

"You'll be pleased to know you're in good company, Dave, because that's what the district attorney thinks. I've invited him to settle the question in court."

George had caddied in his youth, and he'd been a star shortstop and quarterback in high school. Although relatively new to golf, his native athleticism had translated seamlessly from the diamond and the gridiron to the rolling links of his new country club.

George and Lou were two-handicaps, while Dave was a solid five. Frank, on the other hand, although known as a heavy gambler and a hail-fellow-well-met, was actually a terrible golfer—a fact that never diminished his enthusiasm for the game.

As the men teed off and the round progressed, their bets became ever larger and more exotic. By the time the foursome had reached the seventeenth tee, Frank stood to win over three thousand dollars if he only could break 99—a feat he'd never before accomplished but that, thanks to a front-nine score of 42, was well within his sights.

The seventeenth was a par three, with the tee box fronting a lake. The distance to the flag was only 170 yards, but the carry to a dry landing was over 130. George, Lou, and Dave had all reached the green safely. Frank was laying 89 for the round, with just the par-three seventeenth and the four-par eighteenth standing between him and a healthy payday.

Bogey-bogey was all it would take. For his tee shot, Frank had chosen a four iron.

"Press?" Lou inquired as Frank took a practice swing and then turned to the grinning men on the bench.

"Hell, yes. And I'll press you right back."

Higher mathematics ensued. All eventually agreed that the total bet was now $7,500.

Frank plucked some grass to test the wind. Licking his lips, he gave his club a final waggle as he stood over the ball, his hands fumbling for the perfect grip.

"Hundred bucks says it's in the drink."

"Geez, Frank. Sure you don't wanna use a practice ball?"

"Don't forget to breathe."

Frank stepped away. He took another practice swing as the lake before him grew to the size of the Great South Bay. Again he addressed his ball as the bench behind him fell mortally silent.

Thwack!

Frank had swung with everything he had. Swung so hard, in fact, that his clubhead had barely grazed the ball, which squibbed a few feet to the side. His four iron, however, rose in a majestic arc, rotating as it soared, eventually finding the center of the lake with a towering splash.

The laughter carried all the way to the clubhouse.

It was on the eighteenth fairway, after Frank had carded his triple-bogey six and then sliced his final drive into the rough, that Dave sidled up to George as the two men trailed after their caddies.

"I don't know if I've mentioned this," the lawyer said, his voice discreetly lowered, "but I have an application currently pending for a seat on the Supreme Court bench."

"Why, that's splendid, Dave! You'd make a wonderful judge."

"Thanks, George. It's something I've wanted my entire life. And not to be a burden, but I was wondering if you might put in a good word with Frank. I don't know him that well, but I know he respects you an awful lot."

"Frank? What's Frank got to do with it?"

"Come on, George. Quit kidding."

George stopped, turning to face his colleague.

"I'm not kidding. You have a fine reputation, and I'm sure the bar association will support you a hundred percent. What's Frank got to do with anything?"

"My God," the younger lawyer said, placing a hand on George's arm. "You really don't know, do you?"

"Know what?"

"Frank Costello is the power behind the throne at Tammany Hall. Rumor is he controls every patronage job and every public official in the state of New York."

Nineteen

Waxey Gordon

November 1933

THE OTHER MEN sprang to their feet as George Medalie entered the long conference room. Without speaking, the United States attorney for the Southern District of New York strode to the end of the twenty-foot table and sat. Two easels had been set up at the far end of the room, one on either side of a rolling blackboard covered with names and numbers, all written in a tight, precise hand.

Medalie checked his wristwatch. "Go," he said.

The other men sat as Tom Dewey stepped to the head of the table. He cleared his throat and pointed a pencil toward the blackboard.

"The defendant, Irving Wexler, was born in New York City in January of eighteen eighty-eight. His first arrest, for picking pockets, came at the age of nineteen when—"

"Stop," Medalie said. "That's backstory. Save the backstory for later, if you need it at all. Right now I'm a juror. Tell me why it's so important that I'm here at the courthouse today instead of working to feed my family."

Tom swallowed. He turned to study the blackboard for a moment, and then he began again.

"The evidence in this case will show that the defendant, known among his underworld associates as Waxey Gordon, earned over four-and-a-half-million dollars during the years nineteen thirty and nineteen thirty-one from his various criminal enterprises, and yet he paid less than one hundred dollars in federal income taxes."

"Much better," Medalie said, shifting in his chair. "But let me ask you a question, Tom. Forget your opening for a second. You've been preparing this case for how long now?"

"I don't know. The better part of thirty months."

"You started with a single deposit slip, and since then you've had an army of lawyers, accountants, and T-men working two shifts per day for almost three years. How many bank records would you say you've examined during that time?"

Dewey looked to the seated men. "Over two hundred thousand, I'd guess."

"All for accounts under phony names. You've painstakingly matched deposits and withdrawals, following a paper trail from here to New Jersey to Pennsylvania and back again. You've interviewed a thousand witnesses, and traced over a hundred thousand telephone calls. You've reviewed letters, bills, receipts, loan records, truck registrations, insurance policies, and God knows what else until your eyes were practically bleeding. In short, you've been hacking your way through a forest of paperwork for so long that it's all you can see at night when you lay your head on the pillow."

"All right, so what's your point?"

"My point is, you've got to put a ruby-red nose on it. You've got to give the jurors something meaty, something juicy they can sink their teeth into. Something that sits in their gut and stays there for the rest of the trial. For example, how many cars does Wexler own?"

"Personally? He's got three Pierce-Arrows and a Cadillac limousine."

"There you go. I drive a Ford. Where does his kid go to school?"

"Staunton Military Academy."

"Mine goes to P.S. Nineteen. You see what I'm driving at? You're a bona fide savant, Tom, not to mention the most meticulous human being I've ever met. But in front of a jury, you need to forget all the hours you've logged and all the facts and figures you've gathered and collated and committed to memory. You need to step back for just a moment and ignore those trees and take a good, hard look at the forest. If you start out with numbers and dates and documents, you'll have the jury asleep before the first recess. What's the girl's name? That waitress who worked across from the brewery?"

"Helen Denbeck."

"Helen Denbeck. I even like the name. Okay, how about this? Gentlemen of the jury, we will prove that the accused, Irving Wexler, is the biggest bootlegger in America, and that he heads up a criminal enterprise that includes a dozen speakeasies, two hotels, five nightclubs, three warehouses, four garages, sixty delivery trucks, and at least three breweries in New Jersey alone. And do you know what else we'll prove? We'll prove that in the year nineteen thirty, when his income was nearly two million dollars, Mr. Wexler paid only ten dollars and seventy-five cents in federal income taxes. Why, that's barely enough money to fill the tanks of his three Pierce-Arrow automobiles, let alone his chauffeur-driven Cadillac.

"Now, in order to prove all this, we're going to show you a whole bunch of documents, and you'll be hearing from experts in the fields of accounting and banking, voice recognition and handwriting analysis. But you don't need a mountain of documents and a team of expert witnesses to know that a man who has two hundred bank accounts, a man who can afford to send his son to the Staunton Military Academy, a man who lives in a ten-room apartment on the Upper West Side and who maintains a luxury penthouse at the

Piccadilly Hotel, is cheating Uncle Sam when he declares eight thousand dollars in annual income. Oh, and by the way, we'll also prove that Mr. Wexler owns the Piccadilly Hotel.

"Now, Mr. Wexler, he's going to deny that he owns all this, because you know that a man who's crooked enough to be a big-time bootlegger is too crooked to put things in his own name, let alone to be bothered with paying taxes like the rest of us working stiffs. And that's where the documents and the experts will come in. But you'll also be hearing from ordinary folks like Helen Denbeck, who used to wait tables across the street from one of Mr. Wexler's breweries. She'll tell you how Mr. Wexler's employees used to come into her restaurant for lunch soaked in beer. She'll tell you about the truckers and armed bodyguards and keg rollers who came and went from Mr. Wexler's plant at all hours of the day and night, and about the lookouts who waved handkerchiefs in the street whenever the coast was clear for the beer trucks to roll.

"Once you've heard all this evidence, you gentlemen will be afforded a great privilege. You'll get to do what no crooked cop or feckless politician has been able or willing to do for the past dozen years. You'll get to act as the conscience of this community and throw the book at Mr. Wexler and send him to jail, where he belongs. So I'm going to sit down now and let Mr. Wexler's lawyer do his little dance, and then we can all get to the business we came here to do. I'm looking forward to it, and I know you are too, so thank you in advance for your service, and let's roll up our sleeves and get busy."

The room was silent. Then, one by one, the men began to clap.

"Gentlemen," Medalie said, showing his hands for quiet, "if you'll excuse us for a moment, I'd like to have a word with my chief assistant."

Chairs scraped and papers rustled as the other men stood and filtered out, closing the door behind them.

"Am I in some kind of trouble?"

"No, Tom, not at all. In fact, just the opposite. I wanted you to know how proud I am of the work you've done on this case. I don't think you realize how extraordinary it is for one man to have the tenacity it's taken to accomplish what you've been able to accomplish here. Never before, not even in the Capone trial, has a prosecutor faced the kinds of obstacles you've had to overcome. I'm talking about forged and altered bank records, and murdered witnesses, and local cops arresting federal agents. Do you remember what Wexler said to us that day we first questioned him?"

Tom smiled. " 'When you get your figures together so they prove something, come back and we'll talk again.' "

"He could afford to be cocky then. He had the D.A., the New York Police Department, the banks, and even the magistrate's court in his pocket. Everything he owned he'd hidden behind false names and dummy accounts. He was virtually untouchable—a crown prince living safely within the fortress of Tammany Hall, waving at the poor folks down below. But the thing he didn't count on was that there was one man standing among them with the patience and the fortitude to penetrate his castle keep."

"And the resources, thanks to you."

Medalie stood. He removed a silver dollar from his pocket and, as was his habit, worked it through his fingers as he paced.

"I have news, Tom, and I wanted my chief assistant to hear it first. I'm stepping down as United States attorney, effective at the end of next week."

"*What?*"

"I know it's sudden, but it can't be helped. In any event, I've done what I came here to do. I've hired new personnel, instituted new policies, and inculcated what I hope has been a renewed sense of purpose and determination. Our conviction rate is up to eighty-two percent, with nineteen of twenty-one verdicts affirmed on appeal. But this kind of trial work—this exhaustive, round-the-clock racket busting—is a young man's game. That's why next week a special panel of judges from the Southern District will appoint Thomas E. Dewey as the acting U.S. attorney until the A.G. chooses my replacement."

"Me? But . . . but what about—"

"The trial? Don't worry about that. I've timed it so that nobody can derail this case, even if they wanted to. You'll convict Waxey Gordon, Tom. And if we ever get our hands on Dutch Schultz, you'll convict him as well. A few months from now, you'll not only be the youngest man ever to hold the office of United States attorney for the Southern District of New York; you'll also be the most feared crime-buster this town has ever known. And if you play your cards right, you'll ride that reputation all the way to the governor's mansion."

Tom felt a little dizzy. He groped for the table, sinking into a chair.

"I don't know what to say."

Medalie laughed. "I'd suggest you say, 'I accept.' That way I can make a formal announcement tomorrow."

"You know I do. And George, I also want—"

"Stop. You don't need to say another word. This isn't a gift, you know. It's a promotion that you've earned, and you've earned it in spades. There's just one thing I'd ask you to keep in mind after I'm gone."

"What's that?"

"Seneca taught us that those who hold great power must wield it lightly. I've watched you these past few years, Tom—the sixteen-hour workdays, the obsessive perfectionism, the demands you've placed on the others. That's all fine for a chief assistant, but as the acting U.S. attorney, you'll need to be a leader as well as a commander, and those are very different roles. I don't think it would surprise you to hear that there are some in this office who think you're a pompous son of a bitch. 'The only man who can strut sitting down.' You've already won their admiration, Tom, grudging or otherwise. But starting next week, you'll also need to earn their respect."

"Yes, of course. I won't let you down, chief."

"I know you won't. I wouldn't be doing this if I had any doubts. But I also want you to remember something else. The only thing standing between order and anarchy in our society is the law, and the law is only as effective as the men who are charged with enforcing it. I'm not talking about the law that's found in statutes and casebooks. I'm talking about the verdicts that are rendered by juries every day in America's courtrooms."

He placed a hand on his young protégé's shoulder.

"In law school they teach us metallurgy, but in practice we learn how to weld. It's time to take up the blowtorch, Tom. Silver medals are great in track and field, but inside the courtroom, all that counts is the gold. You remember that, my boy, and the world will be your oyster."

Twenty

The Combination

February 1934

"What do you mean you're on salary now?"

I was standing in the open doorway to the bathroom watching Jimmy shave his neck with my safety razor. You know how a guy will get sore when his girlfriend uses his razor on her legs? On account of the way it dulls the blade? With me and Jimmy, it was just the opposite, and I had the nicks on my shins to prove it.

"You heard me," he said. "Nick Montana's out. Charlie Spinach and Cockeyed Louis are on the way out. There's a new combination taking over their books."

"Says who?"

"Says Little Davie and Tommy the Bull."

"Tommy Pennochio? I thought that guy peddled dope."

"They both pedal dope. Only now they're moving into prosti-tution."

Jimmy told me this all matter-of-fact, like he's reading a weather report in the newspaper. Like there's a cold front moving into the area and I better drip my faucets so the pipes don't freeze.

"What the fuck are you even talking about?"

He rinsed off the razor and set it down on the sink. He took up his brush and painted more soap on his face.

"I told ya, Tommy and Davie are taking over. The bookers are going on salary, and everything's getting organized."

This was great. First Chicago, I thought, and now New York. And it figured it was the Italians who were the ones behind it. It was always the fucking Italians.

"So what's it mean for us, this new combination?"

"For one thing, it means you gotta start bonding again. Only now it's a regular thing. Ten dollars a week for each girl, and no exceptions for nobody."

"That's bullshit and you know it. Peggy Wild and Jenny the Factory ain't gonna pay no ten dollars a week."

"That's where you're wrong, Flo. Anybody tries to hold out, me and Little Abie, we pay 'em a visit. That's why we're on salary now."

I nudged him over and got my works out from under the sink. I kept them in an old Kotex box. I sat on the toilet and got out the spoon and lit the candle stub with a match. I broke off a quarter cube, on account of that cold front was moving in fast.

"How am I supposed to find girls if I gotta start charging 'em ten dollars a week and I got no booker?"

"That's the thing. Davie says that if everybody bonds, then after a while it becomes normal and nobody squawks. But if some madams hold out, then it ruins it for everybody. That's where me and Abie come in. And there's still gonna be bookers, just some new guys is all."

"What new guys?"

"Dave Miller and Pete Harris. And a guy named Jack Eller."

I fixed myself a shot while Jimmy watched in the mirror. It gave him the heebie-jeebies, he said, when the needle went in, but I noticed he always watched. I usually shot myself in the leg, up over the knee. That way it didn't show, and I could move it around. Taking three shots a day, my thighs looked like I had the chicken pox.

"What kind of a salary?"

"What's it to you?"

"What's it to me? First you were gonna be my butter-and-egg man, and now you tell me you're on salary to a couple of Mott Street hoodlums? Oh, and by the way, I gotta start bonding again? I ought to start charging you rent. I'll bet you wouldn't like that, would you?"

"How would you like I take that junk and flush it down the goddamn toilet?"

"I'd like to see you try it."

Most people who dealt with Jimmy Fredericks thought he was just a big ape. And while it was true that Jimmy could be a loud-mouth, and that ruffling feathers was part of his job description, the Jimmy I knew was more like a coconut—all hard and hairy on the outside, but actually soft and sweet once you cracked him open and got inside.

We had a lot in common, me and Jimmy. He'd had it pretty rough as a kid, and then he'd quit school when he was fourteen and started living on his own, just like I did. Only Jimmy wasn't real bright, so he'd done a few stretches in places like Elmira and Sing Sing and Dannemora. Most of his life, in fact, he'd been in and out of the slammer. In Dannemora, he told me, on account of him being so big, the bulls made him fight with the niggers. They'd bet money on him, like he was some kind of a dog. Then when he finally got paroled a few years ago, they just dumped him off at Grand Central where he wound up sleeping for weeks on a dirty mattress in a subway tunnel.

What did they expect a guy like Jimmy to do, get himself a job on Wall Street?

They're hypocrites, every last one of 'em. I've had clients who were lawyers and doctors and even a politician once I recognized from the newspapers. The same teetotaling bluenoses who talk all day about the evils of vice and corruption, then grab their high hats and stop by the local cathouse on the way home to the wife and kiddies.

It's enough to make you puke. Give me a choice between a hypocrite and an honest crook and I'll take the honest crook every day of the week.

And it ain't like jobs was growing on trees, even for the Ivy League college boys. So Jimmy done what he had to do, lifting himself up by his own bootstraps, and I respected him for that. He had moxie. It ain't like he enjoyed being a leg-breaker, but he had a wife to support, and that Lillian of his was a real piece of work. That's why he spent most of the week at my place. That's why I had nicks all over my shins.

"I need a lift uptown," Jimmy said, drying his face with a towel. "I'm meeting Tommy and Davie."

"At three in the morning?"

"You want I should take a cab, go ahead and say so."

Jimmy never did learn to drive, on account of him being either broke or behind bars for most of his life. But before you get the wrong idea about Jimmy, and think maybe I was soft in the head for putting him up and driving him around and everything, there's a few things you need to understand. For instance, when word gets around that you're Jimmy Fredericks's girl, ain't nobody gives you any trouble. Like that time Cockeyed Louis refunded my two hundred and fifty bucks bond money, and included an extra sawbuck for interest. You think anyone else ever got a refund, let alone interest? Or like whenever Cockeyed Louis or Charlie Spinach tried to send me some girl who was hopped up or on the rag, all's it took was one phone call to straighten things out.

Little things like that, believe me, they made a difference in this business.

Oh, and there's one other thing you should know about Jimmy Fredericks. You remember Wally the Whale, Pearl's old boyfriend from Cleveland? Well, I'm sure you get the picture.

My latest joint was a two-story brownstone on West End Avenue where I had a colored maid named Addie who changed the sheets and didn't steal the silver and kept her big mouth shut. I lived upstairs and usually used both the downstairs bedrooms for business, but they were empty right at that particular moment on account of business having ended an hour ago. So my choices were to drive Jimmy uptown to his meeting or else to lay in bed and listen to Jack Armstrong on the radio.

I grabbed my keys off the dresser.

"Thirty-five bucks," Jimmy said after we'd rounded the block and turned uptown onto Broadway.

"What?"

"My salary. You wanted to know. It's thirty-five a week."

I started to say something but decided to hold my tongue. Back when he was working with Jerry Bruno, Jimmy was making fifty, sometimes even a hundred bucks a week.

"Go ahead and say it."

"Say what?"

"You think I'm a sap for sticking my neck out for a lousy thirty-five bucks."

I looked over at Jimmy. His face was turned to the sidewalk, and his fists were balled in his lap. Maybe it was the morphine, or the hour, or the wounded expression I pictured on his face, but I didn't have the heart to tell him that was exactly what it was I'd been thinking.

"Listen, honey. At least you're still in the racket. That beats selling apples in the park."

One of his fists opened up, and he reached over and patted my knee.

The drive was seventy blocks, and when we pulled to the curb outside a Chinese joint near 130th Street, Jimmy leaned over and gave me a peck on the cheek.

"Don't wait up, Flo. Sleep tight, and don't let the bedbugs bite."

The joint was dark inside, and a Closed sign hung in the door. I watched Jimmy walk into the restaurant and take a seat by the window. It looked like there were three other guys in the booth.

None of them stood. None of them offered to shake his hand.

Twenty-One

Boss of Bosses

May 1934

CHARLIE LUCKY AND Frank Costello watch from the shade of the open-air terminal as the Sikorsky S-40 flying boat trims its engines and glides like an overfed goose toward the crowded passenger dock. Men scramble and shout as fenders are readied and lines tossed and the hulking seaplane is captured and turned and lashed to its moorings.

"Right on time," Costello says, reading his watch.

A floating platform is lowered into the water just fore of the dock-side wing. Only then does the passenger door open and a uniformed hostess alight. She is young and blonde and wearing the smart blue uniform of Pan American Airways. She steps to the auxiliary plat-form and helps the other passengers as they duck their heads and descend from the still-rocking aircraft into the blinding Florida sunshine.

"There he is."

Costello nods to the tanned little man in the white guayabera shirt who is stepping down from the plane. Once on the dock, the man sways his hips and with his free hand twirls the laughing hostess in an impromptu cha-cha step.

"Christ. Guy's been gone for a week and he thinks he's Xavier Cugat."

From his dockside rhumba and from the smile still lighting Meyer Lansky's burnished face, the men know that their friend's mission to Cuba has been a success. It's only the details that concern them now as they stroll toward the baggage claim area.

"Somethin tells me that's an empty briefcase you got in your hand," Lucky says as Lansky stops amid the throng of arriving passengers and draws a cigar from his shirt pocket and runs it under his nose.

"Not exactly. I got my dirty laundry inside."

"We'll take your word on that one."

The old friends embrace. Meanwhile, two men from the Santo Trafficante's outfit in Tampa are pacing, watching them from the curb. Charlie raises a finger, indicating they'll be ready in a moment, and then guides Lansky to a quieter corner of the terminal.

"We want any privacy, now's the time to talk."

Lansky lights the cigar, turning it slowly over the flame.

"Gentlemen," he says, shaking and tossing the match, "if there was a mirror on that wall over there, you'd be looking at the new casino managers of the Hotel Nacional. We also have the gaming license, the rights to develop our own luxury hotel and casino, and an island-wide exclusive on slot machines and pari-mutuel wagering. I tried for the parking meters, but you know what the colonel told me? He said if he gave those away, even the president would notice."

"You beautiful bastard. So what's Batista's end?"

"Three million down, with a credit for our little gift. After that it's a percentage of our gross against a sliding-scale guarantee. I'll lay it out for you later. But the important thing is, we need to have the three mil on deposit in Zurich by the first of July. Once that happens, we can start moving our people into the casino. And Frankie's slots, of course. That is if La Guardia hasn't impounded them all by then. Excuse me, Tracey?"

The hostess in the blue uniform turns at the sound of her name.

"Tracey, these are my friends Frank and Charlie from New York. We're having a little celebration tonight at the Biltmore. We'd be delighted to have you join us as our special guest."

"Why, thank you Mr. Meyers, but I lay over tonight in Havana."

"Such a shame. Next time, perhaps."

Costello holds his tongue until the girl is out of earshot.

"Okay, so Batista gets our money. But what do we get besides a greasy handshake?"

"Don't worry, Frankie, it'll all be nice and legal. Better than legal. It'll be backed by the full faith and credit of the Cuban army."

Once the luggage is ready, Lucky signals to Trafficante's men, one of whom turns and whistles. Within moments, three black Cadillac Fleetwoods pull forward to the curb. While one man opens the trunk of the middle car, another hurries for Lansky's suitcase. A third man holds the rear door open for the three honored guests from New York.

The drive from Dinner Key to the Biltmore Hotel is fifteen minutes, and after some terse and coded conversation, the three friends lapse into a shared silence, each lulled by the rush of ocean air and the steady drone of the Cadillac's powerful V-16 engine.

Lucky finds himself, as he often does lately, dwelling on the past. In this case, on how the imperial reign of Salvatore Maranzano had proved to be so short-lived, its downfall hastened by an ill-considered ceremony in which the newly crowned Caesar, addressing a blue-ribbon assembly of the nation's top mafiosi, declared himself *capo di tutti capi* to which all in attendance must pay homage. He then unveiled his new organizational plan, further alienating the hard-eyed men who'd been led to believe that their two bloody years of street combat had been a war of independence.

It wasn't long before these same men were turning to Lucky Luciano for counsel. Not just Masseria loyalists like Vito Genovese, Tom Gagliano, and Carlo Gambino, but also those who'd fought on the Maranzano side. Men like Joe Bonnano, and the estimable Joe Profaci.

What had been touted by Maranzano as the dawn of a new era of peace and prosperity had proved to be a summer of disillusionment and anger, in which men already bent by the twin hardships of Depression and gang warfare were soon bowed by the heavy thumb of yet another imperious Mustache Pete. Adding to that burden was Maranzano's ill-conceived battle with Louis "Lepke" Buchalter over control of the Amalgamated Clothing Workers, a fight in which civilian casualties were again garnering unwanted newspaper headlines.

For Lucky, the penultimate straw came in May of 1931, at a meeting called to prepare for a planned national crime summit in Chicago. When Lucky mentioned that Meyer Lansky would be part of his delegation, Maranzano replied, "The Jew can come, but he can't be in the room when we meet." The final straw came soon after, when rumors of a Maranzano hit list that included Luciano and his so-called Broadway Mob of Vito Genovese, Frank Costello, and Joe Adonis began making the rounds.

It was, Lucky concluded, either kill or be killed.

While the impetus came from Lucky, the final plan was vintage Meyer Lansky. Maranzano, Lansky had learned, was the subject of an ongoing Internal Revenue audit, thus presenting a perfect ruse by which to separate the new boss from his omnipresent bodyguards. Lansky hired Red Levine to assemble a team of Jewish hit men to pose as revenue agents. On the appointed day—Thursday, September 10, 1931—four briefcase-wielding torpedoes arrived at Maranzano's headquarters in the New York Central Building, where they retired to an inner office and then butchered the Boss of Bosses with carving knives.

A fittingly symbolic end, Lucky thought, for a man who aspired to be Caesar.

Only later did Lucky learn that while Red Levine's men were making their getaway, they'd passed Vincent "Mad Dog" Coll in the stairwell. Coll, a notorious killer for hire, had apparently been given the Maranzano contract on Luciano. Upon learning that his employer had been killed, Coll coolly turned around and followed Levine's men down the stairs, pocketing his twenty-five-thousand-dollar advance.

"What're you smiling at?" Lansky asks.

"Elephants with torches."

"What?"

"Nothing. I was only daydreamin."

With Maranzano out of the way, Lucky moved quickly to consolidate power. He embarked on a national goodwill tour in which he personally assured both friend and wary foe alike that Charlie Luciano harbored no sovereign ambitions, but instead sought to foster real cooperation, and regional autonomy, and the establishment of a national crime commission to demark territories and settle disputes.

Styling himself as the anti-Maranzano—as a modern American businessman working to create an environment in which all might prosper—Lucky managed to achieve in a few short months of suitcase diplomacy that which had eluded three generations of Sicilian strongmen with their stilettos and their garrotes and their interminable bloodshed.

And so the son of Antonino and Rosalia Lucania from First Avenue was now the de facto head of organized crime in America.

While Charlie is lost in his memories, Frank Costello, his gaze out the driver's-side window, is also deep in thought. Frank has the utmost respect for Meyer Lansky, but he worries about his old friend's naïveté when it comes to Fulgencio Batista. It was Frank, after all, who'd slapped the backs and greased the palms of every city alderman and state assemblyman in New York. It was Frank who rubbed elbows with the judges and congressmen, who broke bread with the governors and senators, and whose name appeared in the little black books of every political operative working this side of the Mississippi.

Meyer is smart all right, Frank thinks, and maybe he's even a genius, but what does he know about politics?

Take the FDR debacle as an example. With Hoover on the ropes and the Oval Office just waiting for whoever could win the Democratic nomination for president, it was Meyer and Charlie who'd wanted to back Al Smith. Frank could still recall their first discussion at the Hotel Claridge, when he'd explained to his friends that with two New Yorkers as the Democratic front-runners, the road to the White House ran straight through Tammany Hall. At the Democratic National Convention in Chicago, the New York delegation would hold unprecedented sway and could, he'd told them, if they played their cards right, actually decide the outcome.

Smith, it was true, had been a longtime friend and ally. A machine pol of the old school, the Happy Warrior had carried their water in Albany for years, and had a mattress full of their money to show for it. But Smith was a Catholic, Frank had argued, which all but disqualified him in a national contest. Even if Roosevelt was a gimp and a high-hat, Frank was certain that the Harvard man and fifth cousin of Teddy Roosevelt would be the preferred candidate of the other states' delegations.

As the convention approached, both camps pleaded for Frank's endorsement. They would, as he told Meyer and Charlie, suck his cock in Macy's front window if that's what it took to win the support of Tammany Hall. Now was the time, Frank argued, to dump Smith and strike a deal with Roosevelt. They could bargain for an end to the Seabury investigation, or for replacing George Medalie as U.S. attorney, or for keeping Jimmy Walker as mayor.

But Charlie and Meyer were loyal—Frank has to give them that—and so when they all arrived in Chicago, it was at the Drake Hotel, Smith's campaign headquarters, that they took their six-bedroom suite. And while the hookers ebbed and the booze flowed, Frank watched with quiet resignation as the national delegates moved inexorably toward Roosevelt. It was a once-in-a-lifetime opportunity to expand their reach all the way into the White House, and now it was lost forever.

They were still weathering the fallout. The Seabury Commission's crusade against public corruption had ushered in a new wave of reform politicians, from Herb Lehman in Albany to Butch La Guardia in New York. "Good government" was all the rage, and organized crime the national bogeyman. Worst of all, in a direct rebuke to Tammany Hall, a Democratic president had allowed Tom Dewey, an unabashed Republican, to remain in office as acting U.S. attorney for the Southern District of New York.

So what does Meyer really know about the political situation in Havana? Nothing, that's what. Betting the house on Batista is like betting on Masseria in the Castellammarese war, another Lansky blunder. Thank God Charlie had bailed them out of that one. But even Charlie Lucky couldn't shoot his way out of a malarial rat-hole like Cuba.

"Everything okay?" Meyer asks, patting Frank's knee.

"Sure. Just tired is all."

Meyer Lansky nods. He, too, is tired—exhausted, in fact, after a solid week of breakfast meetings, working lunches, cocktail summits, and ceremonial dinners. If only his friends could be made to fully appreciate the importance of what they've just accomplished—what *he's* just accomplished—in being the first foreign investors to wet their beaks in the heady nectar of Cuban tourism.

"Diversification" is the watchword now, and with Prohibition ended, gambling is the locomotive that will pull their gravy train. Frank, of all people, should understand that. He'll soon have his slots—thousands of them—in every hotel in Havana, just as he recently moved into Louisiana, thanks again to Meyer's efforts.

Come to think of it, Batista isn't very different from Huey Long. Both are personally ruthless, and politically adroit, and as greedy as Old King Midas. Not only will they make millions in Havana, Meyer is certain, but they'll also launder millions more from their various stateside interests. Instead of sitting there fretting like an *alter cocker*, Frank should be thanking him on bended knee.

Diversification. They have carpet joints in New Orleans, Palm Beach, Hot Springs, and Saratoga. In New York they have the unions and the industrial rackets, as well as loan sharking and protection. They have hotels and, of course, they have nightclubs. Plus they have stakes in dozens of legitimate businesses, from dairies and bakeries to real estate and trucking. And they have drugs and the Italian lottery. Each of the men sitting beside him is clearing over five million a year and, once Dutch Schultz is dead or behind bars, they'll move into the uptown policy, which represents another fifty million gross.

On a cash-flow basis, they'll soon be bigger than U.S. Steel.

As far as booze goes, Meyer and his friends part company. Charlie seems to think that once they liquidate their inventories, they'll be out of the game entirely. To Meyer, this is shortsighted. Although legally barred from the liquor business, they could still parlay their old alliances and distribution channels into profits, since bootleg booze is cheaper than liquor that's taxed. Frank understands this, and so does Joey. Charlie will soon come around. But Meyer has another idea—one that will take it even further.

It's like the California gold rush, Meyer has told his father-in-law. Some prospectors got rich and some went bust, but none did better than the men who sold the shovels.

In November Meyer formed Molaska Corporation, and thanks to the side deal he's just negotiated with Colonel Batista, Molaska will soon be importing Cuban molasses by the boatload. They'll open a factory in Cleveland, in Moe Dalitz's territory, and while the front room is making table sugar, the loading dock will be delivering raw material to every distillery in the country.

This is diversification of another kind—the first salvo in Meyer's own little war of independence. He has repeatedly warned Frank and Charlie to keep their names out of the newspapers. Look what happened to Legs Diamond, he's told them, and to Waxey Gordon, and will soon be happening to the Dutchman. Think of Icarus, he said, and then, of course, had to explain the allusion.

It's obvious to Meyer that the national mood is changing. Gangsters, once viewed as modern-day Robin Hoods, are lately considered crumbs—and worse, as leaches sucking the lifeblood from a newly anemic nation. Nowadays the public wants scalps, and the politicians want headlines. And when they come for Lucky's scalp, Meyer is planning to be ready.

The cars are passing under a double row of palm trees, approaching the hotel entrance. When they pull to a stop at the curb, Trafficante's men alight.

"If you'll wait here, gentlemen," their captain says, and the three friends sit and watch as the bodyguards enter the lobby of the same hotel where, just five years earlier, their old friend Fatty Walsh famously met his maker.

A signal is given, and the rear doors open wide.

"Meyer! Don Luciano!"

Santo Trafficante stands in the cavernous lobby, his arms thrown open in greeting. Forty-three years old, Trafficante is short and powerfully built, with the rugged face of a prizefighter. He embraces his old friend Meyer, then bends to kiss the hand of Charlie Lucky.

"All right, Santo, I ain't the fuckin pope. I don't think you've met my consigliere, Frank Costello."

The men shake hands. "It's good to finally meet you, Frank. I've heard so many good things. And this is my son, Santo Junior. Santo, may you always remember the day that you met the Boss of Bosses, Charlie Luciano."

Trafficante's kid doesn't look like much to Lucky. He's around twenty, taller than his old man, but softer too—like a college boy, with thick eyeglasses and a limp handshake. Charlie wonders why Santo has brought him all the way to Miami.

"My men will check you in and bring your keys to my suite. Come, it's this way, right next to the swimming pool."

Two of the bodyguards fall in beside them as they make their way through the lobby and out a glass door and down an open-air loggia echoing with laughter and the sounds of water splashing. Soon Charlie is gazing over the largest swimming pool he's ever seen, the turquoise oblong studded with emerald and sapphire and ruby swimsuits.

"I have a cabana reserved for the weekend," Trafficante says, waving toward the pool, "and I made starting times for tomorrow morning if you'd like to play golf. The room is just ahead."

Once inside the luxury suite, Trafficante dismisses his bodyguards. He latches the door and lowers the window blinds. The four men are alone now, with Junior in the kitchen wrestling the cork from a bottle of French champagne. They take seats in the spacious living room, the sofas plush and white. Stacked on the coffee table is a pyramid of bundled C-notes totaling fifty thousand or so by Lucky's estimation.

"It sure was a shame about Waxey," Trafficante says, waiting for Junior to finish topping the men's glasses before raising his own in a toast. "I know you had your differences, Meyer, but he sure made a lot of guys rich. *Salute!*"

They all touch glasses, the euphonic chime of crystal filling the suite.

"Waxey was already history," Meyer says, draining his glass and setting it on the table. "If Dewey hadn't nailed him, then the Dutchman certainly would have. The feds could've saved themselves the trouble."

"The fucking Dutchman." Trafficante shakes his head. "I was just telling Santo he is . . . what's the word again?"

"Anachronism," Junior says.

"Exactly. A man out of place with his time. Like your man Maranzano, all bang-bang and rat-a-tat-tat. Good for headlines, but not so good for business."

Lucky sets down his glass and takes up a packet of bills. He riffles it with his thumb.

"Some guys when they was kids, Santo, they never learned to play nice. Take Charlie Wall for instance."

Trafficante's glass pauses halfway to his mouth. He sets it back on the table.

"So, you've heard of my little problem."

"Your problem ain't so little, Santo. Wall has friends on the commission. I can't come down here and wave a magic wand."

"But my father thought—"

"*Zittite*! Never question Don Luciano!"

The kid goes white at his father's outburst. He sets the bottle on the table and crosses to the windows, where he pinches the blinds and looks out toward the swimming pool, his toe tapping impatiently on the carpet.

"You know I'll do what I can, Santo, but there's interests on both sides of this. If I go around sayin Wall's out and Trafficante's in, then I'm no different than Masseria or Maranzano. And to be perfectly honest, I don't have that kind of juice."

Lucky tosses the packet of bills to Trafficante, who catches it and sets it back atop the others. The older man sighs.

"I understand, of course. When Iggy Antinori and I disagreed, we sat down like gentlemen and worked out our differences. But this Wall, he is like your Dutchman, who knows only the gun. I'm not afraid for myself, Charlie, you know that. But if we start losing shipments, I'm worried that our friends in Corsica might begin to have second thoughts."

"That would be a problem," Meyer agrees, lighting a cigarette.

"You want my advice, Santo? I say let Antinori and Wall shoot it out. If you're lucky, maybe they'll knock each other off. Meanwhile, you keep your head down and your powder dry, and just be ready when the time comes to step in and pick up the pieces."

"The same strategy you used in the Castellammarese war?"

"Somethin like that. Only do me a favor, willya? Don't get your ass caught in the cross-fire. We're gonna need a friend we can trust when things heat up in Havana."

At the sound of the knock, Trafficante stands and crosses the room. He squints through the peephole, then slides the latch and throws the door open.

"*Surprise!*"

The girls wear skimpy swimwear and very high heels. They are tanned and long-legged, and each has a room key tied with a ribbon around her neck.

"Ladies," Trafficante says, taking one on either arm. "I'll trust you to escort my special guests to their rooms. And when you get there, be sure to show them everything there is that Miami has to offer."

Twenty-Two

Madman

June 1934

"YOU HEARD ME. I demand that you try my client for murder."

Elvin Edwards, the district attorney of Nassau County, already knew he had one madman on his hands. Now, it appeared, he was dealing with two.

"What the hell are you talking about?" he demanded of his old friend and nemesis, George Morton Levy. "Your man's an escaped lunatic who's lucky he isn't on death row. Now you want me to put him there?"

"I want to exonerate him, and to clear his name, and that means you putting him on trial for murder."

George's client, the notorious Joseph Ustica, was indeed an escapee from the King's Park State Hospital for the Criminally Insane, to which he'd been committed in 1928, thereby avoiding trial for the bludgeoning murder of William Gilbride, a wealthy Long Island sport fisherman. That sensational killing, the legal wrangling that followed, and his dramatic escape from the asylum in 1930 had made Ustica both a household name and a kind of regional bogeyman to whom several subsequent murders had been attributed. For years, Long Island parents had coerced their recalcitrant children with the threat that "Ustica will get you if you don't behave!"

The peculiar saga of Joseph Ustica had begun in July of 1928, when Gilbride's burlap-wrapped body was discovered near a wooded lane in Bellmore, four miles from the Freeport restaurant in which he'd last been seen alive. That waterfront dive was jointly owned by Ustica, a shell-shocked veteran of the Great War, and Anthony D'Apolito, a petty criminal and suspected rum runner. Ustica's car had been found abandoned two miles from the body, with Gilbride's bloodstains on the backseat. When an eyewitness—Lucille McDermott, the owner of a Freeport employment agency—placed all three men together at lunch on the day Gilbride went missing, police arrested Ustica and D'Apolito and charged them both with Gilbride's murder.

After days of coercive questioning, Ustica became unstable. His attorney, Peter Beck, promptly moved for a trial continuance and a mental evaluation of his client. This led to Ustica's involuntary commitment at King's Park until such time as he might be deemed competent to stand trial.

D'Apolito, meanwhile, had hired Fiorello La Guardia as his attorney, and La Guardia had retained Charlie Weeks—the same Long Island lawyer who'd been district attorney back in the Louis Enright peat-to-gasoline case—as D'Apolito's local counsel. To Weeks, D'Apolito admitted having struck Gilbride with a rolling pin, but insisted that it was Ustica who'd then delivered the fatal blow with a tire iron. Together the men had wrapped Gilbride's body in burlap, dragged it to Ustica's car, and deposited it in the woods.

With Ustica institutionalized and unable to testify, Weeks and Edwards struck a deal by which D'Apolito would plead guilty to a lesser charge of manslaughter, thereby avoiding the death penalty, and would be sentenced instead to a maximum of twenty years in state prison.

And so with D'Apolito in Sing Sing and Ustica safely at King's Park, the case of the William Gilbride bludgeoning murder was finally and officially closed.

That is, until Ustica escaped.

During his years as a fugitive, Ustica's name would crop up in connection with every unsolved homicide on the eastern seaboard, or so it seemed, garnering headlines from Plattsburgh, New York, to Pittsburgh, Pennsylvania. As his notoriety grew, so, too, did the tales of his savagery and cunning. So imagine George Levy's surprise when, on a blustery afternoon in February, Joseph Ustica's elderly parents appeared in George's office, begging him to take their son's case.

"How can I," asked George, "when nobody even knows where he is?"

"We know where he is."

"Well, then, either bring him in or stop talking about it. Otherwise we'll all be arrested for harboring a known criminal."

And so Ustica surrendered. To George's surprise, his new client appeared to be a gentle soul—a little fragile, perhaps, but as sane as any man. Even more surprising was that when Ustica professed his innocence in connection with the murder of William Gilbride, George actually believed him.

And therein lay a dilemma.

"You can avoid trial and return to King's Park," George explained, "or you can stand trial for murder and risk the death penalty."

"Then let's go to trial, Mr. Levy, because I'd rather die than go back to that loony bin."

George's first order of business was to have Ustica examined by experts and declared by a court to be mentally competent. His next hurdle—the one that found him in Elvin Edwards's office—was to convince the district attorney to prosecute Ustica for the Gilbride murder.

"George, you're as crazy as he is," Edwards said. "This case is closed. Why not leave well enough alone?"

"Because the man's reputation is at stake, not to mention his freedom. What's the matter, Elvin? Are you afraid that if Ustica's found innocent, your deal with D'Apolito won't look so good with the voters?"

"But Ustica's not innocent. Hell, everybody knows that. D'Apolito will say so, and an independent eyewitness will corroborate him. And besides, Gilbride's blood was all over Ustica's car!"

"There you go," George said, lighting a cigar. "Now all you have to do is prove it."

The trial of Joseph Ustica for the 1928 murder of William Gilbride finally began on June 6, 1934, before the Honorable Cortland A. Johnson and a packed courtroom on Franklin Avenue in Garden City. And no sooner had the trial begun than matters took a strange and unexpected turn.

Transported from Sing Sing to appear as the star witness for the prosecution, Anthony D'Apolito, Ustica's erstwhile partner and co-defendant, flatly refused to testify.

"But you can't plead the Fifth!" an angry Judge Johnson thundered at the witness in chambers. "Double jeopardy precludes your retrial for murder!"

"I don't care," said D'Apolito. "I ain't talking."

"Then you'll leave me no choice but to hold you in contempt. That means prison!"

"I'm already in prison."

"I'll add time to your sentence!"

"What, an extra six months? C'mon, Judge, don't make me laugh."

So while the prosecution lost a key witness, George Levy gained a valuable insight. If D'Apolito had nothing to lose, yet remained

159

unwilling to testify, then who, George wondered, was he still trying to protect?

Undaunted, the district attorney called as his next witness the estimable Lucille McDermott. A proud woman of regal bearing, Mrs. McDermott described to the jury her visit to the Freeport restaurant on the day of the murder, where she'd seen both Ustica and D'Apolito eating lunch with William Gilbride. Ustica's car, she testified, had been parked just outside the restaurant. Gilbride had been drinking heavily, and with each drink order would produce from his pocket a thick wad of cash.

George began his cross-examination of Lucile McDermott gingerly, working purely from an instinct honed by nearly twenty-five years at the bar.

Why had a woman like her been at such a seedy restaurant in the first place? She'd come, McDermott testified, to upbraid the owners for constantly firing waitresses she'd sent from her employment agency.

Wasn't it unusual for a customer to pay cash for each drink as it was ordered? That was the policy D'Apolito had instituted at the restaurant.

How did she know the restaurant's drink policy? It was one of the issues about which the waitresses had complained to her.

How did she recognize Ustica's car? She assumed it was his car because Ustica had been sitting in it when she'd first arrived at the restaurant by taxi.

The woman seemed to have a ready answer for each of his questions, and the longer she testified in her stiff and imperious manner, the louder the alarm bells sounded inside George Levy's skull. Something wasn't right, but George couldn't put his finger on exactly what it was. Finally, he asked an innocuous question that provoked an unusual response.

"Where do you currently reside, Mrs. McDermott?"

"That's none of your business. I don't have to answer that."

After the judge informed her otherwise, she grudgingly replied, "Franklin Avenue."

George raised an eyebrow.

"Where on Franklin Avenue?"

She shifted uneasily in her chair. "Fifteen hundred."

"I'm sorry?"

"I said fifteen hundred!"

Now both eyebrows were up.

"Why, that's the Nassau County Jail, isn't it?"

Lucille McDermott didn't respond.

"And you're an inmate at the jail, isn't that correct?"

Again no reply.

"For what crime are you presently incarcerated in the Nassau County Jail?"

This time the judge required an answer.

"Check forgery," the witness sobbed, collapsing forward in her chair.

The dam was broken then, and the truth poured out with the tears. Yes, she'd gone to the restaurant that day. No, it wasn't on business. Yes, she and D'Apolito had been lovers. No, Ustica wasn't present when she'd arrived. Yes, she'd witnessed Anthony D'Apolito murder William Gilbride. No, Ustica had not been involved. Yes, D'Apolito had taken Ustica's car to dispose of the body.

George's acquittal of the notorious madman was a tabloid sensation. Doubly satisfying, in light of the Louis Enright debacle, was that George had won the case without having to put his vulnerable client on the witness stand.

Twenty-Three

Runaway Jury

June 1935

WHILE FEDERAL PROSECUTORS working first under George Medalie and then under Thomas E. Dewey grabbed national headlines with their high-profile racketeering and public corruption convictions, their state counterparts under Manhattan district attorney Thomas C. T. Crain seemed almost moribund by comparison.

While Crain had convened grand juries to investigate both the 1928 murder of Arnold Rothstein and George F. Ewald's 1930 purchase of his own magistrate's robes, neither grand jury returned an indictment. Meanwhile, the extent of Crain's efforts against the policy and industrial racketeers who were terrorizing the city and draining an estimated half-billion dollars each year from the local economy was to post a "Complaints" box in the hallway outside his office door.

The janitors emptied the box every evening at six.

But this institutional indifference to organized crime ended with a bang once the March 1935 New York County Grand Jury was impaneled.

The grand jury, a British gift to American jurisprudence, is an assembly of twenty-three ordinary citizens tasked with hearing evidence and, if they believe the evidence so warrants, voting indictments against criminal wrongdoers. Because grand jury proceedings are conducted in secret, both to protect the innocent and to confound the guilty, no judge is allowed in the grand jury room, nor are counsel for the witnesses or the targeted malefactors. The purpose of a grand jury proceeding is not to adjudicate guilt or innocence, but simply to determine whether probable cause exists to bring a person to trial.

At the state level, evidence is presented to the grand jury by an assistant district attorney, who serves as the jury's gatekeeper and adviser. A grand jury also has the power to conduct independent investigations, write reports, and issue subpoenas to compel the testimony of witnesses.

Lee Thompson Smith, the pugnacious president of the New York County Grand Jurors Association, was elected foreman of the March 1935 grand jury. William Copeland Dodge, another Tammany Hall stalwart who'd succeeded Thomas Crain as district attorney in 1934, assigned his youngest and least-experienced deputy, Lyon Boston, to serve as the grand jury's adviser. When Boston suggested that prostitution and Communism—rather than, say, racketeering or public corruption—might be worthy subjects for the grand jury's attention, the enraged Smith took the unprecedented step of barring Boston from the grand jury room and instead hired Samuel Marcus, the former counsel for the Society for the Prevention of Crime, to act as the grand jury's attorney.

Unmoored from both the constraints and cooperation of the district attorney's office, the Smith grand jury sought to undertake an independent investigation into the twin scourges of policy—

the so-called numbers racket—and corrupt bail bonding. Dodge, incensed by Smith's impudence, actively obstructed the grand jury's efforts, at one point even refusing to authorize the payment of twenty dollars in travel expenses requested by a witness whom the grand jury had subpoenaed.

The situation quickly devolved into an acrimonious stalemate, with attorney Marcus resigning his unofficial post in frustration.

As this very public standoff between district attorney and grand jury foreman dragged into its third month, newspapers and civic groups, churches and bar associations joined in the chorus decrying Dodge as the stooge of Tammany assemblyman Jimmy Hines. Dodge, for his part, railed against the "runaway grand jury," proclaiming, "I don't intend to surrender!"

Having exhausted all other remedies, foreman Smith finally pleaded his case directly to Governor Herbert H. Lehman, requesting the appointment of a special prosecutor "of unusual vigor and ability" to act independently of Dodge in investigating and prosecuting New York public corruption.

Bending to this shift in the political winds, Lehman announced in early June his intention to call an extraordinary term of the state supreme court and to appoint an independent prosecutor whose task it would be to root out organized crime and civic corruption in New York County. And to blunt any suggestion of whitewash, Democrat Lehman appointed a staunchly Republican jurist to preside over this extraordinary term, in the person of sixty-three-year-old New York Supreme Court Justice Philip J. McCook.

McCook, a flinty New Englander, was a veteran of the Great War and a scion of the famous "fighting McCooks of Ohio" who'd burnished his crime-busting credentials as the presiding judge in the Westchester County land fraud scandals. McCook had also, just eighteen months earlier, administered the oath of mayoral office to his close friend and political ally, Republican Fiorello La Guardia.

More problematic for Lehman was the question of whom to select for the role of special prosecutor—the man whose task it would be to work hand-in-glove with McCook and a newly empaneled special grand jury. Lehman's decision was freighted with considerations more political than practical. The chosen candidate could, for example, demand enormous resources, and any parsimony on Lehman's part would be criticized as protectionism on the part of the Democratic governor. So while it went without saying that the man selected to act as special prosecutor would have to be independent of Dodge, Hines, and the Tammany Hall political machine, there was a corollary risk in naming an ambitious young Republican who might one day aspire to occupy the governor's own office.

In consultation with his political advisers—as well as with bar leaders, La Guardia, and Police Commissioner Lewis Valentine—Lehman compiled a list of four candidates who he felt met his exacting criteria. The men Lehman selected were George Z. Medalie, Charles H. Tuttle, Charles Evans Hughes, and Thomas D. Thacher. All were prominent lawyers. Each was over fifty. And while all were Republicans, none was viewed by Lehman as a likely political threat.

In Washington, meanwhile, even larger forces were at work. William O. Douglas, a Yale Law School professor newly appointed to the Securities and Exchange Commission, was urging the candidacy of one of his Columbia Law School classmates. Tom Dewey's painstaking prosecution of Waxey Gordon, Douglas argued to President Roosevelt, was the very example to which the office of special prosecutor should aspire.

But whither Thomas E. Dewey?

Eighteen months earlier, following FDR's appointment of Democrat Martin Conboy as U.S. attorney for the Southern District of New York, Tom had at last returned to private practice. Spurning offers from the big Wall Street firms, he'd instead taken over his mentor George Medalie's old lease at 120 Broadway, hung out his shingle, and immersed himself in a succession of lucrative civil cases.

On the domestic front, Tom and Frances had moved to an eight-room apartment at 1148 Fifth Avenue—a home large enough to accommodate Tom Jr., then age two, and the second child the happy couple was expecting in October. On weekends, the Dewey clan decamped to a modest country home in Tuxedo Park, where Tom kept a sailboat. Alongside his manifold professional and personal obligations, Tom continued his work with the Young Republican Club, even leading a successful campaign to depose the hidebound Samuel Koenig as New York's Republican county chairman.

Only thirty-two years of age, Tom Dewey was already a man of reputation and substance. A real comer, it was said within Republican Party circles. "He has the sizzle, and he's got the steak." What he lacked, however, with the Republicans out of power both in Washington and Albany, was a high-profile platform from which to launch his quiescent political ambitions.

"The world is full of lawyers, Tom," George Medalie told his young friend in one of their many back-channel telephone discussions, "but it's critically short of leaders."

"But I'm not even on the short-list of candidates."

"Never mind that. I need to know whether you'd accept if the opportunity presented itself."

"I don't know, George . . ."

"This won't be a political appointment. And by that I mean no change in administration will affect you once you've been named. The governor's over a barrel, Tom, with the president sitting on his chest. You can set your own budget, hire your own team, and run your own show. Best of all, you can see it all the way through to the end, and politics be damned. My God, son, an opportunity like this comes along once in a lifetime."

"So why aren't you taking it?"

"We've already had that conversation. The fact of the matter is, there's nobody better qualified than you. Hell, you know it and I know it. And besides, I feel like I owe you one."

"Don't be ridiculous. Owe me how?"

"I once promised you that the U.S. attorney's office would be your ticket to the governor's mansion. Well, Roosevelt had other ideas. So think of this as a do-over. A second bite at the apple, for both of us."

By late June of 1935, all four men on Governor Lehman's list of preferred candidates had declined the appointment, each citing personal or professional obligations. Then, in a show of unity that even the governor couldn't ignore, all joined in a public announcement urging Thomas E. Dewey for the role of special prosecutor. Lee Thompson Smith, the grand jury foreman whose obstinacy had ignited the controversy, soon joined in the motion to draft Dewey. The press followed suit, demanding, "Make it Dewey!"

June 29, 1935, was a Saturday. In Boston, Tom was taking the place of his late uncle Edmund in giving his cousin Elizabeth away in holy matrimony. In Manhattan, meanwhile, Governor Lehman had convened a special meeting at his Park Avenue apartment in a last-ditch effort to change the mind of at least one of his handpicked candidates for the post of special prosecutor.

The meeting lasted two hours. The wedding ceremony was shorter. Both ended at approximately one o'clock in the afternoon.

For his part, Tom danced at the reception that followed the nuptials, and offered a toast, and even joined the band in a ballad he dedicated to the young bride and groom. Meanwhile, on the broiling sidewalk outside his apartment, a weary Governor Lehman addressed a small group of reporters to announce his final choice for the post of special prosecutor.

Later that evening, still in his tuxedo, Tom stepped off the train at Grand Central. As he walked through the bustling terminal, the headlines of a dozen evening newspapers screamed for his attention, all featuring the same blockbuster announcement.

He couldn't suppress a smile.

Twenty-Four

The Cure

January 1936

AIN'T THAT A hot sketch? The one time I ran upstairs and left Addie in charge of the show, she let a couple of dicks in the joint.

The next thing I knew, there were men shouting and girls scream-ing and a fist pounding on the bathroom door. I turned around to lift up the toilet seat just as the door frame splintered and one of the dicks grabbed my arm and dragged me into the hallway. Pretty soon we were all lined up in the parlor downstairs, all of us facing the wall and waiting for the paddy wagon, and they had my works and all my junk laid out like tchotchkes on the coffee table behind us.

Rhatz!

And you want to hear the screwiest part? With all the things I should've been worried about at that moment—getting booked, and making bail, and maybe doing time—what I was actually thinking was, wait till Pete finds out. That's because Pete Harris had already

168

been calling me Cokey Flo behind my back, and here I went and got myself pinched with a needle in my leg and a pair of his three-dollar girls downstairs in the sheets.

Shit!

And then, of course, there was Jimmy. I knew he'd start right away on the dope angle, on account of me having only a grand or so left in the bank. Like it was my fault I was the one who paid for every little thing around the house while he bought his wife a mink coat for Christmas and didn't even send me so much as a penny postcard, the big cheapskate, let alone money for rent or food or gasoline.

"Think we should call an ambulance for this one?" one of the dicks said to the other.

"How about it, sweetheart? You gonna be okay to ride down-town?"

I told him, "If it's all the same with you, I vote for Coney Island."

He didn't even smile. "Couple hours from now," he said to his partner, "she won't need to go to Coney Island. The walls of her cell will be spinning all by themselves. Ain't that right, dopey?"

"Go chase yourself."

They both had a laugh, but from where I was standing there was nothing funny about it. Even if everything went exactly like it should, it'd still be hours before Pete and Jimmy could bail me out. And then I'd need to score right away, which Jimmy wouldn't like one little bit, especially if I had to borrow his money to do it.

"Okay, let's go."

They led the four of us—me, Addie, and the two girls, Kitty and Joan—out to the wagon in handcuffs. The johns, of course, they'd already cut loose. A lady I recognized from across the hall was standing on the sidewalk with her mouth hanging open, and I was tempted to kick it shut but instead just lowered my head and looked the other way.

At least Addie and me were dressed for the weather. The girls they didn't let change or put on an overcoat on account of the nightgowns were some kind of evidence, I suppose. They weren't even wearing underwear, the two girls, and both of 'em were hugging themselves in the back of the wagon, their teeth already chattering.

Pretty soon I'd be the one whose teeth would be chattering.

They took us down to the Jefferson Market Women's Court, where they booked us and split us up and dumped me in a cell in the basement. It was only my second pinch in New York, and I gave 'em the name Frances Martin, which was the name I'd used on the lease. They said the night session began at eight, which was more than two hours away, and that I should relax and make myself comfortable. And when I asked about making a telephone call, the matron with the key ring laughed as she walked down the corridor.

It seemed more like two days before they finally came to get me, and by then I was already feeling the hunger. Somehow Jesse Jacobs was waiting in the courtroom, and so were Jimmy and Pete Harris, and I'd never been happier to see either of them in my life. Together they posted a $2,800 bond for the three misdemeanor counts, which were maintaining a house of prostitution, possession of a hypodermic syringe, and possession of a cube and a half of morphine. So while I was out on bail, I was also in hock to the combination for their half of the bail money, and Jimmy or no Jimmy, I knew I'd have to pay that back at the rate of six for five.

Jimmy, bless his heart, had brought along a morphine tablet that I chopped up and snorted right there on Pete's dashboard. After that, everything got kind of fuzzy, and I told Pete to pull over to where I stepped out on Sixth Avenue and puked my guts in the gutter in front of maybe a dozen bystanders. Then the sidewalk started spinning, like I'd gone to Coney Island after all, and that was the last thing I remembered.

My first thought when I awoke in the morning was that the whole episode had been a bad dream. But then I smelled bacon frying downstairs, and coffee, and when I tried to sit up in bed, my stomach did a back somersault.

I made it to the toilet just in time, and after I'd finished puking and I'd sat down on the floor, I opened the cabinet under the sink and saw that my Kotex box wasn't just empty—it was gone altogether.

And then I knew it wasn't a dream.

Meanwhile, silverware was rattling in the kitchen, and pretty soon Jimmy's voice was calling up the stairs.

"Flo? C'mon, Flo! Time to rise and shine!"

I started bawling then, sitting on the cold tile floor and wiping my face with my arm.

"In a minute!"

First I brushed my teeth, then I grabbed a robe and held on to the bannister all the way down to where I saw Jimmy in the kitchen wearing Addie's ruffled apron. He hadn't shaved yet, and his suspenders were hanging down to his knees, and he had a chewed-up cigar stub sticking out of his craw.

I had to smile, despite how lousy I felt.

"There's my princess. Sit down, I'm makin pancakes."

"Thanks all the same, honey, but I ain't hungry."

Truth was, the smell of the frying batter was making me sick all over again. But I sat and watched his back, as broad as an icebox. He was humming like my mom used to do, after my dad had left home for the day.

"I need a shot, baby," I told him. "I need it awful bad."

He didn't answer. After a while he turned around with two steaming plates and set one down in front of me. Pancakes and bacon were usually my favorites, but I shoved it away.

"You gotta eat, Flo. You're already thin as a dime."

"I will. I just need to settle my stomach first."

Jimmy ate, and it didn't take long. I used to tell him to count his fingers when he got up from the table.

"Look, honey, we need to work this out," he finally said, wiping his mouth and carrying his plate to the sink, where he turned on the water tap.

"Don't I know it."

"You owe a grand to Jesse now, and they ain't gonna send you no more girls until you pay it back with the interest and then start bonding again."

"How am I supposed to pay it back if I can't open a new joint?"

Jimmy looked at me over his shoulder. I was in a jam. At least he understood.

"Can't you talk to somebody?" I asked him.

"I can try, but it ain't gonna do no good until you get yourself off the junk. People are sayin you can't be trusted, Flo. Plus you'll probably do time on the pinch, and you don't wanna take the cure in jail, do you?"

I shook my head, still staring down at the pancakes.

"I been askin around. There's this place on Central Park West. They say the doctor's okay, and he don't ask too many questions."

"Oh yeah? And who's gonna pay for that, do you suppose?"

He turned all the way around to face me.

"I will, that's who. You can pay me back after you've paid off Jesse Jacobs."

I started crying again. Jimmy walked over to the table and stood beside me.

"I know it ain't gonna be easy, baby, but you really got no other choice. So what do you say, will you give it a try? For me?"

I nodded. Jimmy fished something from his trouser pocket and set it on the table next to my plate.

It was another morphine tablet.

"Last one, Flo. After this, you're getting straight."

Twenty-Five

The Dutchman

January 1936

"THAT COCKSUCKER IS comin after me? After *me*? Don't he know I'm the one saved his fuckin life?"

"He knows," Frank Costello tells Charlie Lucky. "And you know what he said? He said, 'Tell Luciano that someday I'll show my gratitude in court.' "

"Yeah? You think maybe that's good?"

"No, Charlie. I think that's a threat."

Lucky throws up his hands. He retreats to the bar and returns with an open bottle of wine. He fills the trio of glasses that flank the still-steaming bowl of pasta in tomato sauce.

"Okay you mugs. *Salute.* To Mama Castiglia."

Meyer Lansky and Frank Costello raise their glasses just as a knock sounds from the hallway.

Lucky peers through the peephole, then swings the door wide for a nervous little man in a flawless blue suit, who leans over the threshold without setting a toe in the suite.

"*Buona sera*, Mr. Ross. I just wanted to make sure everything turned out to your satisfaction."

"Everything's jake, Henry. I hope I ain't hurt nobody's feelins. It's just that a guy's gotta get some home cookin every once in a while."

"Of course, Mr. Ross."

"You tell the boys in the kitchen not to take it personal, okay?"

"Of course, Mr. Ross. Have a wonderful evening, and call downstairs whenever you're ready."

Frank is dishing up the pasta. "Charlie, you're the only guy I know who lives in the fucking Waldorf and still sends out to Brooklyn for tagliatelle Bolognese."

"I'd eat your mother's tagliatelle if I lived in the fuckin White House."

"You could of been eating in the White House if you'd listened to me about Roosevelt."

"Please, Frankie," Meyer says, "do we have to hear this again?"

"Instead you've got Dewey back on the scene, and now he's crawlin up your ass like a bedbug."

Dewey. It's all Lucky's been hearing of late, ever since the Dutchman's string of banner headlines has finally reached its end.

Arthur "Dutch Schultz" Flegenheimer has been the white whale to Tom Dewey's Ahab ever since the special prosecutor's days as an assistant U.S. attorney under George Medalie. It was Schultz, in fact—the Bronx beer baron turned industrial and numbers racketeer—who was Medalie's first target back in 1931. But no sooner had the Medalie team indicted Schultz for income tax fraud than the Dutchman went into hiding, and he remained in hiding until both Medalie and Dewey returned to private practice.

Far from sitting idle during his self-imposed exile, Schultz instead used the opportunity to consolidate his bloody grip on both the numbers racket in Harlem and the city's restaurant service unions. He fought shooting wars with Legs Diamond and Mad Dog Coll, and he embarked on a protracted territorial struggle with Waxey Gordon that ended, ironically enough, with Gordon's own federal income tax conviction by Dewey. By 1934, the ephemeral Dutchman was declared the nation's "Public Enemy No. 1" by J. Edgar Hoover, and reform mayor Fiorello La Guardia staked his personal reputation on finding Schultz and finally bringing him to justice.

Then, with the noose tightening, Schultz did a curious thing. After sending out feelers through lawyer Dixie Davis, the Dutchman offered to settle the tax charges against him for the princely sum of one hundred thousand dollars in cash. When U.S. Treasury Secretary Henry Morgenthau Jr. flatly rejected the Davis offer, Schultz finally surrendered himself to the authorities. Not in Manhattan—where the felony indictment had been handed down, and where a thousand Wanted posters bearing Schultz's doe-eyed image were blanketing the city—but rather in Albany, where the delinquent taxes should theoretically have been paid.

Free on bail while awaiting his trial upstate, Schultz was forced to manage his Harlem interests from a distance. So when Jules "Julie Martin" Modgilewsky, a fearsome enforcer for Schultz's restaurants racket, was alleged to have shorted the Dutchman some seventy thousand dollars in protection money, Schultz summoned Martin to the Harmony Hotel in Cohoes, New York. During the course of their heated meeting on March 2, 1935, Martin denied having skimmed the seventy grand, but eventually admitted to taking twenty thousand, a sum to which he'd claimed a moral entitlement.

With a horrified Dixie Davis looking on, Schultz yanked a gun from his waistband, forced the muzzle into Julie Martin's mouth, and pulled the trigger. Afterward, Schultz apologized to his lawyer for having murdered a man in his presence. Later still, when Martin's body was found in the snowy upstate woods with deep and grisly chest wounds, Schultz explained the tableau to Davis over breakfast.

"Oh, that," the Dutchman said, digging into his oatmeal. "I cut his fucking heart out."

The trial of Arthur Flegenheimer for the willful evasion of U.S. income taxes began on April 16, 1935, in the United States Courthouse in Syracuse, New York. Using the very documents amassed by Dewey and Medalie back in 1933, attorney John H. McEvers—a veteran of the Capone prosecution team who'd been brought to New York as a special assistant to Attorney General Homer Cummings—presented indisputable evidence of the Dutchman's undeclared income totaling $2.8 million over the three-year period from 1928 to 1931.

Employing an ingenious defense strategy, Schultz acknowledged the nonpayment, but blamed the oversight on erroneous legal advice he'd received, to the effect that no taxes were owed on income derived from an illegal activity—namely, bootlegging. He further claimed that once he'd been properly advised, he'd made a good-faith effort to resolve the matter, only to be rebuffed by Henry Morgenthau. As defense attorney James Noonan told the jurors, "It shows he was on the level, and that there was no willfulness in his heart. The government wouldn't take his money!"

The jury hung, 7-to-5.

A retrial was scheduled for July, but with venue now moved to the small Canadian border town of Malone, New York, where the prosecutorial baton was passed to Martin Conboy, the man who'd succeeded Thomas Dewey as U.S. attorney for New York's Southern District.

In a cynical bid to ingratiate himself with the local citizenry, Schultz and his entourage arrived in Malone several weeks in advance of the trial date and proceeded to spend lavishly, replenishing local coffers badly depleted by the Depression. This continued until the pastor of Malone's First Congregational Church cried foul from the pulpit after Schultz was seen at a semipro baseball game in the company of the town's mayor. The resulting public outcry forced District Judge Frederick H. Bryant to revoke the Dutchman's bail.

By then, however, the proper tone had already been set.

The Malone trial was, in essence, a reprise of the earlier trial in Syracuse, but with a very different outcome. This time, the jurors voted unanimously to acquit Arthur Flegenheimer on all counts. Judge Bryant spoke for many stunned observers when he said that the verdict "shakes the confidence of law-abiding people in integrity and truth," telling the erstwhile jurors, "You will have to go home with the satisfaction, if it is a satisfaction, that you have rendered a blow against law enforcement and given aid and encouragement to the people who would flout the law. In all probability, they will commend you. I cannot."

Downstate in Manhattan, a furious Mayor La Guardia was even more succinct. "Dutch Schultz won't be a resident of New York City," he vowed. "We have no place for him here." To which the Dutchman responded, "So there ain't room for me in New York? Well, I'm goin there anyway." And go there he did, to reassemble the pieces of his shattered criminal empire that rival mobsters had already begun to collect.

Months before the Dutchman's acquittal, and with a view toward preserving his own lucrative sinecure, Bo Weinberg, Schultz's chief enforcer, had met with New Jersey crime boss Longie Zwillman to prepare for life after Arthur Flegenheimer. Zwillman called in Charlie Lucky, and a summit was held at the Waldorf Towers. They drafted a blueprint for the division of Schultz's rackets should the Dutchman—as was universally expected—join Al Capone and Waxey Gordon as guests of the federal government. Weinberg, in exchange for retaining his usual 15-percent override, agreed to disclose to Zwillman and Charlie Lucky all aspects of the Dutchman's operations.

And so it was that, upon his Lazarus-like return from upstate, Schultz made a beeline to Charlie Lucky. The two men discussed not only the business at hand but also, surprisingly, the Catholic religion. Schultz, a lifelong Jew, confided to his astonished host a promise he'd made to himself while in the Malone city jail, to the effect that if he were to be acquitted on the income tax charges, he would convert to Catholicism. Jesus Christ, the Dutchman told Lucky, had been the one who'd answered his prayers.

There was nothing Christian, however, about the Dutchman's appraisal of Bo Weinberg. Correctly suspecting his chief lieutenant's disloyalty, Schultz ordered his men to stake out Longie Zwillman's house in New Jersey. In September, the stakeout finally paid a deadly dividend. Informed that Weinberg's car had just pulled into Zwillman's driveway, Schultz personally rushed to the scene, and when Weinberg emerged from his meeting a few hours later, the Dutchman was outside waiting.

Bo Weinberg was neither seen nor heard from again.

As the newly appointed special prosecutor of organized crime in New York, Thomas E. Dewey was all but salivating at the prospect of finally getting his crack at the Dutchman. Because double jeopardy precluded a prosecution for felony income tax evasion, Dewey instead focused his army of twenty all-star lawyers, twenty stenographers, ten accountants, four process servers, four clerks, four messengers, two grand jury reporters, and seventy-five specially recruited police detectives on Schultz's policy racket—the so-called numbers game or Harlem lottery—which by Dewey's estimation was grossing some twenty million to fifty million dollars annually.

But before Dewey could secure a state grand jury indictment, a federal grand jury in October of 1935 accused Schultz of eleven misdemeanor counts of failing to file income tax returns for the very same years—1929 through 1931—for which the Dutchman had already been acquitted in Malone on the more serious felony counts of willful income tax evasion.

Schultz, who'd moved his headquarters to Newark while fighting extradition across the Hudson, was enraged at the prospect of having to re-wage a legal battle he'd thought was already won. Blaming Dewey for his ongoing woes, the Dutchman devised a crude but effective solution to his problems.

He would simply murder the special prosecutor.

Dewey had already been receiving death threats, including one call to his Park Avenue apartment in which Frances, then eight months pregnant with the couple's second child, was asked to come to the morgue to identify her husband's body. Those threats—together with an ominous warning letter from J. Edgar Hoover—had convinced the special prosecutor to accept two full-time bodyguards, whose job it was to shadow him everywhere in public.

Could a gunman bypass the bodyguards and get to Thomas Dewey?

Schultz hired contract killer Albert Anastasia, of Murder Inc. fame, to undertake surveillance of Dewey's daily routine. A week later, Anastasia reported that Dewey had a habit of stopping at the same drugstore every morning on the way to his office in the Woolworth Building. Convinced that an assassination could succeed, Schultz requested approval for his plan from the new national crime commission. At a meeting held in mid-October, the commission, chaired by Charlie Lucky, rejected Schultz's plan, fearing the backlash that such a high-profile execution would almost certainly engender.

To an increasingly isolated and embattled Dutch Schultz, the commission's vote was further proof of Lucky's personal designs on the Dutchman's rackets. Furious, Schultz decided to defy the commission and proceed with his plan. When word of that decision got back to Charlie Lucky, a second, emergency commission meeting was held, this time to approve the assassination of Dutch Schultz.

And so the race was on.

Responsibility for the Dutchman's murder was delegated to Lepke Buchalter, who assigned the actual hit to his lieutenants Bug Workman and Mendy Weiss. On October 24, 1935, the two assassins entered the Palace Chop House in Newark, where Schultz was eating dinner alongside henchmen Otto Berman, Abe Landau, and Lulu Rosenkrantz.

The ensuing bloodbath left Schultz and his three lieutenants mortally wounded. All succumbed within hours, with Schultz receiving last rites from a Catholic priest at Newark City Hospital.

And that's how Lucky Luciano saved the life of Thomas E. Dewey.

In Lucky's suite at the Waldorf Towers, the three friends tuck napkins into shirt collars as they sit down to their steaming plates of tagliatelle.

"Anyway, I ain't losin sleep over Dewey," Lucky is saying. "What's Dewey got on me? I pay my taxes like a good American."

"Come on, Charlie. You paid six years of back taxes in July."

"Ain't that what you told me to do?"

"Yes," Meyer says, "but don't you think that looks a little fishy? I mean, six years is the statute of limitations. And what did you claim by way of income, twenty grand a year?"

"Somethin like that. Maybe a little less."

"That's your first problem. And what about state taxes?"

"Come on, Meyer. You didn't say nothin about that."

"All right, Charlie, relax. All I'm saying is that Waxey paid some taxes too, but that didn't stop Dewey from nailing him."

"Jesus Christ. Maybe I shoulda let the Dutchman kill the little cocksucker after all."

"Or maybe you should take a page from the Dutchman's playbook and lam it for a while. Take Gay and go to Miami until things settle down. The way it is now, you've got a big red target on your back. Some actress gets killed in California, and they blame it on Charlie Lucky. It's got to the point where every stink-bombing or drugstore holdup, the papers say you're the one's behind it."

"Maybe you're right, Meyer. Or maybe I'll go to Cleveland and inspect your little molasses operation."

Meyer sets down his fork.

"What, you thought I wouldn't find out? Christ, I knew about it before the first boat ever left Cuba."

"My molasses deal has nothing to do with you, Charlie. Molaska was a legit partnership between me and Anna's father."

"And your pal Moe Dalitz. Relax, I ain't mad or nothin. But the thing is, you made that deal while you was in Havana on our business, and that makes it part of our business. I don't care about the sugar end, because that part's legit, but on the liquor side, everything goes into the kitty. You know the rules, Meyer. Hell, you're the one helped me to make 'em."

"All right, Charlie, if that's how you feel about it."

"How I feel's got nothin to do with it. It was up to me, I'd let you do whatever the fuck you wanted, you know that. But then word would get around that Lansky's gettin special treatment, and pretty soon every wise guy would think it was okay to cut their own side-deals."

"You're right, Charlie. I'm not arguing with you."

"You're goddamn right I'm right. Look at us, Meyer. We're a couple of shits from First Avenue livin like Morgan and Rockefeller. We're in the fuckin Waldorf, for Christ sake. But you know what? So was Cousin Alphonse, and so were Rothstein and Waxey and the Dutchman. All of 'em up to their eyebrows in booze and broads and cash. But you know what the difference is between them guys and us?"

"What's that?"

"Enemies. Them guys made enemies like that lady from Canada makes babies. Us, we just make other guys rich, and we treat 'em fair, and we play by the same set of rules. That's why we're on top, Meyer, and that's why Molaska goes into the kitty. And you wanna know somethin else? It's why we're gonna stay on top for as long as we fucking feel like it."

"*Salute,*" Frank says.

"And as for Dewey," Lucky says, touching his glass to the others, "he can suck my cock, because at the end of the day, he ain't got nothin on Charlie Lucky."

Twenty-Six

Loss and Memory

January 1936

IN THE FALL of 1931, at the intersection of Southside and Roosevelt Avenues in Freeport, nine-year-old George Levy Jr., the only child of the noted Long Island defense attorney and his second wife, Beatrice, lost the brakes on his soapbox derby racer and veered into the path of an oncoming car.

The accident occurred late on a Thursday afternoon, and by the time George and Bea arrived at the hospital, their beloved son's body, horribly crushed and mangled, was undergoing a complex surgical repair that even the county's top orthopedic specialists were hesitant to undertake.

It was nothing short of a miracle that George Jr. survived his crippling injuries. It was less of a surprise, at least to those who knew them, that his parents' already rocky marriage did not.

Further surgeries and hospitalizations would leave George Jr. wheelchair-bound for life, his symptoms mirroring those of cerebral palsy. His mother would throw herself into the role of full-time caregiver, even trading her smart frocks and butterfly blouses for a nurse's starched white uniform. Even feeding and bathing her son, and changing his bandages, and tending to his most intimate physical needs. Even taking the boy with her to Reno when she filed for the divorce.

Although George Levy continued to provide financially for his son and namesake, the divorce and custody orders marked the end of their daily interactions, leaving a gap in George's life that would only grow larger as the boy over whom he'd once so fiercely doted—the boy he'd taken to Lourdes in his frantic search for a cure—matured into adolescence.

That void was very much on George's mind when, less than a year after his son's near-fatal accident, he stood at the foot of yet another hospital bed, this one in Hempstead, where young Ormond LeMaire lay battling for his life.

"Are you a family member?" asked the duty nurse, startled to find a pre-dawn visitor in the young man's private room.

"No. Just a concerned well-wisher."

"I'm afraid visiting hours don't begin until nine," the nurse said, reading her watch as she consulted the boy's chart. "If you'd like, you can wait . . ."

But the man was already gone.

On Saturday night of the previous weekend, Ormond LeMaire had attended a party near his home in Rockville Center that was hosted by the parents of his old high school friends Emily and Irma Groesbeck. There were twenty or more of his former classmates in attendance, the bright young collegians laughing and chatting and dancing to the phonograph even as a furious thunderstorm lashed the Groesbeck home on Capitolian Boulevard, the wind-driven rain and the loud, syncopated music combining to muffle an urgent pounding on the front door that only LeMaire, as he passed through the foyer from the kitchen, happened to hear.

LeMaire opened the door. He then backed into the crowded living room with his hands held high in surrender.

First the laughter died, then all conversation as the guests, one by one, took notice of the dripping figure holding a gun.

"Frank? Frank, is that you?"

Jack Wulforst stepped forward to stand beside LeMaire as the other guests crowded behind them. All now recognized Frank Murphy, their old high school classmate, beneath his hat and shimmering slicker.

Murphy's eyes were dark and hollow as they scanned the faces in the room. And then without warning, his gun burst to life.

Three shots punctuated the ragtime piano still playing on the phonograph. The first and second caught Jack Wulforst in the arm and thigh, while the third hit Ormond LeMaire squarely in the back when the young man turned away from his assailant.

As girls screamed and boys dove for cover, the gunman then turned and strode through the still-open doorway, disappearing into the storm.

It was after midnight by the time the police arrived. William Groesbeck, a sobbing daughter under each arm, urged the investigating officers to perform their duties quickly. Since the witnesses were many and their conditions ranged from fatigue to shock to outright hysteria, all were allowed to leave without giving formal statements. No crime-scene photographs were taken, no spent bullets were recovered, and no effort was made to identify or trace the assailant's weapon.

Murphy was arrested the following morning, the Rockville Centre police finding him asleep in his bedroom at his parents' house on Princeton Road, one block north of the Groesbeck residence. Belligerent, Murphy denied ever owning or possessing a firearm, and further denied having visited the Groesbeck party, claiming instead to have spent the night drinking bootleg whiskey at the Turf Inn in the nearby village of Hempstead.

Despite his protestations, Murphy was arrested and booked on a charge of felonious assault with a deadly weapon. The clothing he'd worn on the previous night, however, was never collected as evidence or tested for powder burns.

It wasn't until Monday afternoon, some forty hours after the shooting had occurred, that Elvin Edwards, the district attorney of Nassau County, first learned of the events on Capitolian Boulevard. Incensed both by the delay and the slipshod investigation, Edwards nonetheless sprang into action, dispatching Assistant District Attorney Martin Littleton Jr. to track down and interview all the young men and women who'd been present at the Groesbeck party.

Sixteen of the eyewitnesses said they'd gotten a clear look at the assailant. All identified Frank Murphy, whom they'd known since childhood, as the silent gunman.

It was three days after the shooting that the telephone rang in the law office of George Morton Levy. Later that afternoon, during an emotional face-to-face meeting with the distraught parents of the accused, George learned how young Frank Murphy had fractured his skull as a child and had thereafter suffered from epilepsy and various mental illnesses requiring a series of hospitalizations at Bellevue and other psychiatric facilities. Worse, George learned that the boy had been aware of the Groesbeck party and had, just before leaving the Murphy home on Saturday evening, vowed revenge at not having been invited.

"It's all our fault," his mother concluded, burying her face in a hand.

"Don't be ridiculous!" snapped her husband, a prominent Wall Street broker. "You can't blame yourself for something like this. Nobody could have anticipated—"

"I wasn't blaming myself."

"Oh, I see. I suppose it's *my* fault that—"

"Perhaps if you'd been more involved. Perhaps if you weren't holed up in your office at all hours of the day and night."

"And how do you propose that we pay for all these doctors and headshrinkers? Do you think money grows on trees? Do you think that—"

"All I'm saying is that if you'd been around more often, if you'd spent more *time* with the boy, then perhaps . . ."

George listened to the familiar argument in silence. Then, once the combatants had arrived at a weary détente, he agreed to represent Frank Murphy to the best of his abilities.

His first order of business was to visit Mercy Hospital to witness firsthand the crippling injuries that the shooter had inflicted. His second was to visit his new client at the Nassau County Jail, where, to George's dismay, Frank Murphy continued to deny any role in the Groesbeck shootings. George's third and final destination was the office of Martin Littleton, the assistant district attorney assigned to handle the prosecution.

As this would be his first actual exposure to the storied George Morton Levy, Littleton asked Elvin Edwards, the veteran D.A., what kinds of tricks and sharp practices he might expect to encounter.

"None whatsoever," Edwards told him. "You can trust George with your life."

"I beg your pardon?"

"You heard me. Just don't let him light one of his damned cigars in the conference room."

Despite the young prosecutor's wariness, the meeting proved surprisingly cordial. Levy, Littleton quickly discovered, was more interested in learning the facts of the matter than in probing for any sort of advantage. At the end of the day, Littleton agreed to turn over copies of all the sworn statements he'd amassed, and also to arrange for the sixteen eyewitnesses to return to his office the following day to be personally questioned by George.

"The police investigation was fairly well bungled," George later informed the Murphys, "and we might make some hay out of that. Make the police look like monkeys, and embarrass the district attorney with a few scathing headlines. And make no mistake, there are plenty of lawyers out there who'd be only too happy to take your money and put on that kind of a show. But the unavoidable fact is that sixteen of your son's closest friends will all testify without reservation that it was Frank who shot Ormond LeMaire."

"Then what are our options?"

"There's only one option. Hire an alienist and plead temporary insanity. Try to keep your son out of prison and get him into a hospital setting where he'll receive some proper treatment."

The trial, which lasted a week, quickly devolved to a battle of experts. Littleton recalled, "The very fact that [Levy's] record of wins was so large predisposed me against him. He might be a pretty clever customer, I thought to myself, but he wasn't going to take me in. Gradually it occurred to me that he had no tricks at all. It was an extraordinary trial, and the judge might as well have stayed at home around his fire. There was no dispute about the facts and not a single objection was raised during the trial; it was strictly a dispute between medical experts."

In his closing, Littleton echoed the state's medical expert in arguing that the planning involved before and after the shooting—specifically, Murphy's acquisition and disposal of the weapon—evidenced premeditation and a clear state of mind. To this George countered, also consistent with his medical experts, that young Murphy's medical history, coupled with his amnesia on the night of the shooting, were themselves the best evidence of his mental incapacity.

On July 7, 1932, after five hours of deliberation, the jury returned a guilty verdict, with an express recommendation for mercy.

Two lives ruined; two families left fractured and grieving. But the case had become personal to George, whom Littleton would describe as having "the tenacity of a toy bulldog when he got hold of a pertinent fact." George continued to pursue the Murphy case through a maze of post-trial motions and appeals until, almost four contentious years after the verdict, George finally won an order of executive clemency that saw his client transferred from state prison to the bucolic Matteawan State Hospital in Fishkill, where Frank Murphy could finally begin receiving the medical attention he desperately needed. It was, in practical effect, the same outcome that would have resulted had the jury's verdict been one of acquittal.

It was only a small victory, to be sure, in a career of greater triumphs. But to a parent who was himself no stranger to the lingering effects of personal tragedy—to the loss, and the estrangement, and the gnawing recriminations—it was an outcome well worth the effort.

Twenty-Seven

The Roundup

February 1936

IT ALL BEGAN with Eunice Carter.

The only woman, and the only African American, on Tom Dewey's handpicked team of courtroom sluggers, Carter had been an assistant district attorney under the feckless William Copeland Dodge but had distinguished herself as a tireless and incorruptible Women's Court advocate. Tom had originally recruited her in the hope that, as a black woman, Carter might prove useful in his planned extirpation of the Dutch Schultz numbers racket in Harlem. But when the Dutchman's brutal murder left Lucky Luciano as the special prosecutor's primary target of interest, it was Carter who'd first suggested a means by which to breach the walls within walls of stony silence that seemed to surround the Sicilian mob boss.

It was a tried-and-true formula for prosecutorial success: start at the bottom by arresting and flipping the small-fry in order to land the bigger fish. At the U.S. attorney's office, both Medalie and Dewey had employed it to perfection in building their painstaking cases against Legs Diamond and Waxey Gordon. But the Italian gangsters, in contrast with their more colorful Irish and Jewish forebears, had proved an opaque confederation whose insularity, discipline, and strict code of silence frustrated even a cursory understanding of its structures and methods, let alone its leadership and inner workings.

Employing tips and phone taps, the special prosecutor's team of crack assistants soon focused its attention on the familiar territory of the Women's Court and its revolving-door cast of madams and prostitutes, bookers and bondsmen. Word on the street, which had reached the attuned ear of Eunice Carter, was that a new downtown combination was using violence and intimidation to organize and centralize the formerly freelance world of New York prostitution. Here, then, was the toehold—the first rung on a rickety ladder that might, with luck and perseverance, lead all the way to Luciano's Waldorf-Astoria penthouse.

Tom, at first, was skeptical. "I didn't take this job to go after prostitutes!" he'd snapped when Carter and fellow assistant Murray Gurfein first broached the vice-racket angle. But then Frank Hogan signed on to the investigative team, as did Charlie Grimes and Harry Cole. Before long, a succession of aggrieved madams was giving grand jury testimony about a shadowy combination involving up to two thousand prostitutes, three hundred disorderly houses, and a menacing cadre of bookers and bondsmen, enforcers and loan sharks—a veritable "NRA of prostitution," as Tom came to describe the rapidly unfolding landscape.

"But it still doesn't get us there," he told his assembled team of assistants. "Who's going to believe that the head of the Unione Siciliana, the so-called Boss of Bosses, is taking pocket change from two-dollar prostitutes?"

"A jury will believe it," Cole replied, "when we prove that Tommy the Bull Pennochio and Little Davie Betillo, two known Luciano associates, are in charge of the whole operation."

It may have taken a while to convince the special prosecutor as to the merits of the Carter approach, but once he was on board, Tom translated his conviction into immediate action.

From the outset, secrecy had been a central tenet of the special prosecutor's office. Adopting the guidelines first laid down by his mentor, George Medalie, Tom had forbidden private practice by any assistant, or discussion of any pending investigation with the press or public, or fraternization of any kind with the criminal element. His assistants were to live as Caesar's wives, he'd told them, avoiding even the appearance of impropriety. Cases were to be tried in court, not in the newspapers. He'd even forbidden assistants working on one case from discussing their efforts with their colleagues within the office, except on a need-to-know basis.

It was not surprising, then, that the great vice raid of 1936 bore all the hallmarks of a covert military operation.

In the waning hours of Friday, January 31, undercover detectives arrested Betillo and Pennochio, along with combination enforcer Abie Wahrman and loan shark Benny Spiller, as the four men left a party on 16th Street in Manhattan. Elsewhere in the city, detectives were descending on restaurants and nightclubs, sidewalks and apartment houses, hauling in enforcer Jimmy Fredericks, bondsmen Jesse Jacobs and Meyer Berkman, and bookers Al Weiner, Jack Eller, and Dave Miller. In Philadelphia, they arrested booker Pete Harris. In total, sixteen key members of the vice combination were held incommunicado at various precinct houses throughout the city in what proved to be but a preliminary bout to the next night's main event.

Saturday, the first of February, was cold and overcast in Manhattan. At precisely 8:55 P.M., at eighty different locations throughout the city, plainclothes officers opened sealed envelopes bearing only the addresses to which they'd been dispatched. Following the instructions inside, the 160 officers descended on the suspected disorderly houses at nine o'clock sharp, arresting any prostitutes or madams they found working within.

Preferring unmarked cars and taxicabs to conspicuous paddy wagons, the arresting officers delivered their haul of 87 prisoners to the Greenwich Street police station, where the protesting women were booked and then transported, again by taxicab, to the Barclay Street side entrance to the Woolworth Building. There the entire Dewey team of twenty lawyers, twenty stenographers, and dozens of aides and clerical assistants were waiting on the fourteenth floor, ready to take their statements.

It was an extraordinary tableau. Brightly rouged women in silk evening gowns and little else slouched and smoked, paced and slept while awaiting their turns to be interviewed. The special prosecutor's offices reeked of cigarettes and cheap perfume. The women, inured to the revolving door of the Women's Court, were defiant—even dismissive. They were from out of town, they told their interrogators, just visiting a friend. They were only playing bridge. They were models or manicurists, shopgirls or dressmakers. Virtually all, it seemed, claimed to be virgins.

The worldlier of the madams—Polack Frances and Sadie the Chink among them—counseled the younger, more skittish girls. "Keep your yap shut and everything will be fine," they instructed. "Remember, you don't know from nothin."

Tom patrolled the crowded hallways alongside John Lyons, his chief of detectives, assuring the agitated women that it was the higher-ups he was after, not the prostitutes or madams. "Cooperate," he told them, "and the charges against you will be dropped. Moreover, you'll receive complete immunity for your grand jury testimony."

But his assurances fell on calloused ears. "So, you're Dewey," one of the prostitutes sneered, towering over the special prosecutor in her patent leather heels. "Run along, Boy Scout, and peddle your papers."

As gray dawn broke over Manhattan, frustratingly little progress had been made. At noon, Philip J. McCook, his Sunday brunch interrupted by a call from Tom Dewey, appeared on the fourteenth floor of the Woolworth Building, where the jurist and the special prosecutor, joined by his chief assistants Bill Herlands, Murray Gurfein, Jake Rosenblum, and Barent Ten Eyck, huddled to strategize in Tom's private office.

"So that's where matters stand," Tom concluded, lighting a cigarette. "We've got close to a hundred suspects in custody, but none of the girls is talking. They assume this is business as usual, and that they'll be back on the street by Monday. I've told them we've got their bookers and their bondsmen in custody, but either they don't believe it or they think someone else will be coming to their rescue. We need to send them a message that will really get their attention."

"What did you have in mind, Tom?"

"I want all the girls held as material witnesses, each on a ten-thousand-dollar bond."

McCook was skeptical. "The usual bond on a prostitution charge is something like three hundred dollars."

"Usual is exactly our problem. If these girls make bail, which is what *usually* happens, then we'll lose them forever. They'll either disappear or else their lives will be threatened and all of our effort will have been wasted. We need time to work on them, Judge, and they need to understand that this is no laughing matter."

"With bail that high, you're practically inviting a constitutional challenge."

"Which is all the more reason why the girls should be held incommunicado, without access to lawyers."

"What?"

"Hear me out a moment. If these girls have access to counsel, we'll be up to our necks in habeas petitions before the week is out. And once they're back in the hands of the gangsters, our case will go right down the drain. I'm telling you, this is the only way we're going to get to Luciano."

Still frowning, McCook found a chair and sat.

"Let's not lose sight of the bigger picture, Judge. We've got a lot riding on this extraordinary term, and as you well know, our initial focus was on Schultz. We can't afford another false start. The public expects results, and so does the governor. So does the mayor. We need to give them something tangible, and we need to give it to them soon."

McCook grunted, filling a pipe.

"If word gets around that we hauled in a bunch of prostitutes and nothing comes of it, I'll be a laughingstock, which is exactly what Hines and Dodge have been hoping for. I can already see the head-lines, Judge. Not to mention our pictures, yours and mine, side by side on page one."

McCook lit his pipe. He watched the bluish smoke waft and curl toward the ceiling.

"All right, Tom. I know you're in a tight spot. If you're quite certain this is our only avenue . . ."

"Thanks, Judge. I promise you won't regret it."

The arraignments, conducted there in Tom's office, took most of the afternoon. Seventy prostitutes pleaded not guilty, and each was remanded to the custody of the Women's House of Detention on a material witness bond of ten thousand dollars. For the combination men, each charged with the crime of compulsory prostitution, justice was even harsher. Little Davie Betillo's bail was set at twenty-five thousand. For Jimmy Fredericks it was forty, and for Tommy the Bull Pennochio, a whopping seventy-five grand. All were returned to the Raymond Street Jail in Brooklyn to await trial.

In the elevator lobby of the Woolworth Building, as prostitute Nancy Presser waited to descend to the idling paddy wagons now lining the curb downstairs, she caught the eye of Ralph Liguori, her former boyfriend and now a stickup man for the combination. Liguori ambled over, hands in pockets, with an easy smile on his face. Looking left and right, he leaned in close to whisper.

"If you squeal," he told her softly, "I'll kill you myself."

Twenty-Eight

Rock Bottom

May 1936

To THIS DAY, I swear to God, I blame the fucking dogs.

Mrs. Calvit—that's Dorothy Russell to you—had a pair of furry monsters that were too big for her old apartment, let alone for the crummy two-bedroom she was leasing at the Hotel Alamac on West 71st Street. So when I moved in to live with her, well, let's just say things got a little too close for comfort.

I got the job through Dr. Gardiner from the sanitarium. Dorothy Russell, he told me, the daughter of actress Lillian Russell, was an old patient of his who was looking for a caretaker that could also act as a stenographer, and could I type worth a damn? I told him, "If I could practice a little," and so he let me bang away on a brand-new Underwood that he kept at one of his nurse's desks. The quick brown fox jumped over that same lazy dog three hours a day for two solid weeks, and the faster I typed and the more accurate I got, the more I started to think that maybe I was that quick little fox and that Dewey was the lazy old dog who, while he may have gotten Jimmy, would never lay a paw on me because from now on, brother, I was strictly legit.

That was a laugh, I realize now, but don't forget this was right after I'd heard about Jimmy getting pinched along with everybody else, and what with all the bookers and most of the girls in town cooling their heels in jail, it was a cinch I wasn't opening up a new joint even if I had the money to do it, which I didn't. Besides which, I'd jumped my bail on the misdemeanor charges back in January, so I couldn't very well risk another fall or else I'd be looking at some serious time in prison.

I needed to keep my head down and my nose clean. I needed to go legit. That was the plan, anyway. And what looks more legit than a girl with her very own dog?

I named her Pearlie, after my old pal from Ohio. I'd found her in the park one day, all skinny and dirty and shivering, and I knew right away that she'd been abandoned. She had no collar, and at first she wouldn't even come to me when I called her. Finally I bought some caramel nuts off a guy on the street and used those to gain her trust. I'd leave one and walk away, and then another, and pretty soon Pearlie was following me through the park with her little tail wagging, and I had myself a pet.

Mrs. Calvit didn't mind, at least not at first. She was a real dog lover, she said, and Pearlie was such a cute little thing. The other beasts would chase her around the apartment, drooling and slobbering, and I had to close her up in my bedroom until they all got used to each other, but after a while they let Pearlie play with them, and sleep with them, and even eat her little meals in a bowl right next to theirs.

More than once I thought to myself that Pearlie was kind of like me, small and scrappy, while the big dogs were more like Jimmy, all gruff on the outside but really more bark than bite.

Poor Jimmy. I missed him something awful, locked up in that crummy old jail. He'd hired a lawyer named Siegel, who I went to visit a few times, just to see what I could do to help with Jimmy's case. But every time I went down there, Siegel would give me the brush-off. Too busy, he was, to even sit with me. Like I had some kind of disease or something, and he didn't want it going around his fancy office.

Word on the street was that five of the girls who'd been arrested had already cut deals with Dewey and were ready to rat out the others. Word also was that if you spun a good enough yarn to Dewey, you got out of jail free and they put you up in a hotel and paid for your room and board with cigarettes and candy and trips to the movies included. They even took you out drinking and dancing, with everything on the house.

That's some system of so-called justice, ain't it? With times being hard like they were, I knew girls who'd rat out their own mothers if it meant getting three hot squares and a roof over their head, never mind movies and cigarettes.

I walked the big dogs twice a day, once in the morning and once before dinnertime. Every now and again I'd pop into one of the fancy hotels along 59th Street and pinch a few pieces of stationery from the lobby. Then I'd type these long letters to Jimmy when Mrs. Calvit was taking one of her naps. Here's one that I sent to him back in April:

My Dear Cousin:

Well, it's the day after Easter and everything is still the same. There is nothing new. I feel very melancholy to-night. Very blue. I'm disgusted with the whole world. There is no justice at all. I wish Uncle Dee would die of cancer, the louse! He should of died from leprosy when he was a baby.

I think it's terrible to make a person do time before they are even convicted. Its not fair. They let lousy murderers go free. But a person that never did anyone any harm in their life, has to rot in

197

jail. Look at that Vera Stretz case. A confessed murderess! She even admitted doing it, on the witness chair, yet she is freed. But a person that hasn't even been convicted yet has to stay in jail, until some louse gets good and ready to bring them to trial! Look at all the money that was spent on Hauptman! The Governor himself intervening for a filthy foreigner of a baby-killer. The worst kind of killer there is. That's why I say there is no justice in this world.

Gee, I'm so blue, and lonesome for you. I don't know what to do. Believe me, if I had about five minutes, with a few certain people, alone, I'd know what to say and do. There would be just five rats less, to bother people.

Well, it's no use wishing. I'm going down to see Siegel Wednesday, I guess. I want to know what he intends to do. What defense has he worked out? I want him to get busy, and try to get his head to working. Not to think he is going to get money for nothing. He should never mind bull shi--ing so much, but get something done. I can't stand this suspense and inactivity much longer.

Well, don't worry, old pal, everything will be O.K. Just have faith and courage. That's the main thing. Maybe you'll thumb your nose at all these louses that are lying like hell, just to save their own skin.

Take care of yourself, and ask them if they will allow you to buy some linement, so you could rub your legs. Maybe if you massaged them with something, you'd get a little releif, so you could get some sleep. I worry about your legs an awful lot. I wish I could rub them for you.

Regards from all, and all my love,
    your Faithful,
    Cousin

So yeah, I missed my Jimmy something awful. The one silver lining to my situation was that Jesse Jacobs was in jail too, and so were Pete Harris and Benny Spiller, so I didn't have to go around looking over my shoulder, worrying about getting my nose broke on account of my so-called loan, which, with the vig still running, was now somewhere north of three grand and counting.

I'd become Mildred Nelson—the name Jimmy and me'd used when I checked into Dr. Gardiner's sanitarium. I was Mrs. Calvit's personal assistant, earning twenty-five dollars a week and living on the Upper West Side and typing her book and story manuscripts. I even gave her a few story ideas of my own, about a "friend" who was tied up in the rackets, with the understanding that if she sold one to *Liberty* magazine, we'd split the take fifty-fifty. I had a dog and, after a few weeks on salary, I had a little money put aside. Which was good, because the so-called cure I'd taken at Dr. Gardiner's sanitarium hadn't worked worth a damn, and I'd taken to using heroin on account of morphine being so expensive and all.

Still, things could've been worse, believe me, and things might have actually worked out in the end except, like I said, for the fucking dogs.

Pearlie had energy, see, and she was getting on Mrs. Calvit's nerves. She needed a yard, only we didn't have one. But there was this basement apartment on West 75th that came on the market real cheap that had a little fenced yard out back, and I told Mrs. Calvit that if we went in as partners we could rent it and park all our dogs over there during the day and get more work done without tripping over ourselves all the time. She thought that was a "grand idea." But then she must've forgotten, because after I'd signed the lease, she said she couldn't possibly afford "such an extravagance" and was "quite contented" to have her dogs with her at the hotel like she'd always had.

Joe Sussman used to say that if life gives you lemons, the first thing you need to do is make a little lemonade, then go out and find someone who life gave vodka and have yourselves a party. So I decided that the new apartment wasn't a problem, really, but an opportunity. As in, what if I took the money I'd been saving and bought a bed and a dresser and moved into the new place myself? And better yet, what if I used the new apartment to make a little lemonade on the side?

The way I figured it, with most of the working girls still in jail and the rest of 'em running scared, there was a whole bunch of johns out there with nothing to do and nobody to do it with. So I started calling some old numbers I had. Nice guys mostly, none of the creeps. "Want to meet for a drink?" I'd ask them, and most of them did. I figured they might have an extra five dollars to spend, even if times were tough. And I was right about that too.

Only now if I brought a guy back to the apartment, I was the one who had to do Dolly's old job. Chief cook and bottle washer, that was me. Which is why I'd started buying an extra cube a week, just to settle my nerves. What the heck, I had the money. Meanwhile, as far as Mrs. Calvit was concerned, the reason I was busy most nights was because I was working in a dance studio.

So all in all, things were going okay. Until all of a sudden when they weren't.

He had dark hair, thick and wavy, and dreamy blue eyes and no wedding band. I'd seen him once before, hanging out on the sidewalk near the new apartment. He'd made a joke about the dogs, about who was walking who. I made him for a drugstore cowboy— just a single guy who was bored and restless and liked to take the air.

On the night in question, which was May 8, three days before Jimmy's trial was scheduled to start, I was walking to the new apartment with Pearlie on her little leash. When I saw my drugstore cowboy, he was standing on the corner under a streetlamp, smoking a cigarette. I didn't know if he remembered me or not, but I stopped and bummed a smoke.

"Pretty night, ain't it?" I said, just to chew the rag.

"I'll say."

"What's the matter, your girlfriend stand you up?"

He smiled. "Nah. I just like to be outside is all. Can't stand being cooped up. It makes me squirrely."

"You live around here?"

"Close by."

We stood there smoking, watching the cars.

"Well," I told him, "thanks for the ciggy."

"You bet."

I started on my way, and then I stopped and turned around.

"Hey," I said. "You like lemonade?"

"What?"

"What I mean is, if you're lookin for a little company, I might be available."

"Available how?"

"Come on, honey," I told him, offering my arm. "We'll discuss that part later."

His smile turned into a grin as he took my arm and spun me around and shoved my face against the building. Then he slapped the handcuffs onto my wrists while Pearlie circled around us, back and forth, barking her little head off.

Twenty-Nine

Hot Springs

April 1936

OUTSIDE THE SOUTHERN CLUB, the sidewalk on Central Avenue is crowded with lunch-hour strollers, the men in white ducks and boaters and more than a few of the women shouldering brightly colored parasols. Lucky waits while Dutch Akers, his local body-guard, stands and stretches and sucks a final drag from his cigarette before grinding it out underfoot.

"How'd it go?"

Lucky dips a hand into the pocket of his trousers. Discreetly, he fans five C-notes for the bodyguard's inspection.

"I'd be impressed if I didn't know you'd started with two grand."

Lucky laughs. "Tell you what. If it wasn't for suckers like me, smart guys like you'd be forced to retire on your pensions."

The men walk slowly, taking the air and eyeing the women. They soon make their way over to Bathhouse Row where, behind them, the towers of the Arlington Hotel rise from the Valley of the Vapors like the twin spires of some mythic Moorish citadel.

"Hey, Charlie. Is it true what they say about Mr. Madden? Did they really used to call him the Killer?"

Akers, Lucky knows, loves to hear the old Prohibition stories of the rum runs and rubouts that put Hot Springs, Arkansas on the national map and made men like Owen Madden and Charlie Luciano rich.

"It's no secret that Owney done time for murder," Lucky tells him, "but that ain't what made him a legend. It took more than balls and bullets to make it in them days. Lots of guys had both in spades, but the ones who come out on top were the guys who had the smarts to go with it. I'll tell you a little story, only you didn't hear it from me, understand?"

"Sure, Charlie."

"During Prohibition, Owney had this gin joint up in Harlem."

"The Cotton Club."

"That's right. And one day his partner, Frenchy DeMange, got himself kidnapped by Vincent Coll. You ever heard of him?"

"Sure. Mad Dog Coll, the baby killer."

Lucky nods. "Coll was a torpedo for hire, with over fifty notches on his gun. One was almost mine, but that's another story. Anyway, Owney pays fifty grand to ransom Big Frenchy, who's like a brother to him. Meanwhile, Coll and Dutch Schultz are fightin it out like it's the Marne, and pretty soon the bodies are pilin up like cordwood all over Harlem and the Bronx."

"What year are we talking about?"

"I don't know. Thirty, thirty-one. Anyway, Coll needs money, see, to pay for his war with the Dutchman, and he figures Owney for a soft touch on account of him payin so quick on his pal Frenchy. So Coll kidnaps Owney's brother-in-law and then calls Owney up on the phone. Sure, Owney tells him, not a problem, just don't hurt the poor guy. But while Owney's talkin to Coll with his left hand, he dials Dutch Schultz with his right and holds the two phones together so's the Dutchman can hear what they're sayin. The Dutchman, who's got a fifty-grand bounty on Coll's head, he gets the picture, see, and he has an inside man at the phone company put a trace on Owney's line. Ten minutes later, just as they're makin the final arrangements for the drop, Owney hears a Chicago typewriter on the other end of the phone, rat-a-tat-tat, glass flyin and tires squealin, and that was the end of Mad Dog Coll, shot to ribbons in a phone booth. Fuckin Owney freed his brother-in-law, got revenge on Mad Dog, and got his fifty grand back, all without leavin the chair he was sittin in. And that's what I mean about smarts."

Farther down the promenade, amid the crush of ambling couples and baby strollers and tourists hurrying to catch the daily double at Oaklawn Park, Lucky spies a pair of men. The big one is Irish, he figures, and the other Italian. They're wearing wool suits and fedoras, and might as well have "New York City Police" tattooed on their foreheads.

"Uh-oh," Lucky says. "Get ready for trouble."

"Pardon me," the Irishman says, wading through the crowd and blocking Lucky's advance, "but aren't you Charles Luciano?"

Akers steps forward. "There some kind of problem here?"

"Detective Brennan," the big man says, opening his coat to display a badge he wears on his belt. "This is Detective Di Rosa. We're with the New York Police Department. I'm afraid we'll have to ask you to come with us, Mr. Luciano."

"Come with you where? What for?"

"There's a magistrate's warrant outstanding for your arrest."

"Magistrate's warrant? What is this, some kind of a joke?"

"No, sir. I'm sure a judge will explain everything in due course."

Brennan reaches for Lucky's elbow, but Akers clamps a hand on the policeman's wrist.

"Hey, pal." Di Rosa rushes forward like a bulldog. "You don't wanna be doin that. Just mind your own business and nobody'll get hurt."

Lucky is chuckling, shaking his head.

"This is Arkansas, gentlemen," Akers reminds them. "You're out of your jurisdiction, and you're not taking anyone anywhere."

Di Rosa leads with his chin, getting up in the bodyguard's grill. "What are you, some kind of wise guy?"

"No, sir," Akers says, pulling a thin leather case from his pocket and dropping it open. "I'm Herbert Akers, and I'm the chief of detectives here in Hot Springs."

"Can you believe this fuckin bullshit?" Lucky calls from his hotel bathroom over the sound of running water. "Them guys is in town lookin for Al Karpis, and who do they find? That Dewey, he oughta come down and shoot craps, the luck he's got."

Galina Orlova is like a yearling filly, Akers thinks as he watches the New York showgirl pace in her short flapper dress. Gay All Over, he knows they call her, and here she is in the flesh, striding and turning, all legs and arms, pausing only when Lucky emerges from the bathroom freshly shaved and shrugging into a linen suit jacket.

"Okay, let's get this over with. What's the judge's name?"

"Garratt, Sam Garratt. My boys went to fetch him from the track. Sonny Davies is already at the courthouse. This shouldn't take but half an hour."

"Zat's good," the girlfriend says, straightening Lucky's tie, "because he promised to take me shopping."

"Don't worry, baby, I'll be back before three. Ain't that right, Dutch?"

"Yes, sir," Akers says. "But first we need to swing by the club and pick up the bail money."

"If Owney gives you any shit, you remind him I dropped fifteen hundred at roulette this morning."

"But Lucky, you told me zat you alvays vin," Orlova purrs, rubbing up against Lucky like a housecat.

"In the end, baby," he tells her, patting her bottom. "I said in the end I always win."

The courtroom is empty, save for the five silent men seated three on the left and two on the right in the hard wooden benches up front. When the door finally opens, four of the men stand as Samuel W. Garratt, chancellor of the Circuit Court of Garland County, enters while buttoning his robe.

The judge is tall and stoop-shouldered and sports a toupee that is slightly askew. He carries a folded newspaper under his arm that Lucky, smiling where he sits, recognizes as a copy of the *Daily Racing Form.*

"Pleasant afternoon, gentlemen," the judge says as he takes his place on the bench and spreads the paper open before him. "Mr. Davies, what trouble have we gotten ourselves into today?"

Allen T. Davies, the city attorney of Hot Springs, is a fleshy man with thinning blond hair and a suit of rumpled seersucker. He steps forward and hands a document up to the judge.

"Good afternoon, Your Honor. It seems these gentlemen here were part of that cock-up down in Malvern yesterday, and as if they haven't done enough damage in our community for one visit, today they've accosted Mr. Luciano on the promenade. They have in their possession what they claim is a warrant from a magistrate judge in New York charging Mr. Luciano with trying to extort—and I'm paraphrasing here, Your Honor—trying to extort a hundred bucks from a pimp. Do I have that right, gentlemen? A hundred dollars? In any event, Mr. Luciano wishes to put this matter behind him and get back to enjoying the fine weather we're having. As such, he's agreed to appear voluntarily and do whatever is necessary to allow these gentlemen to get home to their jobs and their families as soon as possible."

The judge frowns, first at the warrant and then at the fidgeting duo in the pew.

"Officers? Is there anything you'd care to add to Mr. Davies's remarks?"

The men share a look. Brennan, the Irishman, stands and clears his throat.

"Your Honor, the warrant you're holding compels the arrest of Charles Luciano for extortion accompanied by threats of violence and flight from prosecution. Specifically, it charges a violation of the Federal Kidnapping Act, which makes it a federal crime to avoid giving testimony in a proceeding—"

"I can read, Officer. But let's cut the bullshit, shall we? Y'all didn't travel a thousand miles just to serve paper on a chicken-shit charge like this. So how's about one of you tells the court what the hell is really going on here?"

Brennan looks to his partner for help. Di Rosa shrugs.

"Uh, we're not real clear on the underlying facts, Your Honor. Only that Mr. Dewey, the special prosecutor in New York County, heard we were coming to Arkansas and asked us to look for Mr. Luciano while we were here."

"I see." The judge is nodding now. "Mr. Dewey's reputation precedes him. A regular Dick Tracy, or so it's been said. Mr. Davies, what do the people have in mind, exactly?"

"Well, Your Honor, it seems to me that bail"—and here he glances at Akers, who splays five fingers next to his hat—"in the sum of five thousand dollars ought to suffice under the circumstances. That should buy us some time to clear up this whole misunderstanding."

The judge bangs his gavel. "So ordered. Mr. Davies, I'm sure you can handle the paperwork. Mr. Luciano? The court thanks you for your cooperation and hopes this hasn't been too great of an inconvenience. But since we're all here, and if you'll forgive my impertinence in asking, who do you like in the seventh today at Oaklawn?"

Lucky stands and tugs at his jacket. "Tomahawk, across the board."

"Tomahawk." The judge licks a finger and turns the page of his paper. "By God, maybe this wasn't such a waste after all. Very well, gentlemen. Y'all skedaddle back to New York. Our docket gets a bit crowded this time of year, but I'm sure Mr. Davies here will let you know as soon as your matter comes up for hearing."

On Friday afternoon, two days after his court appearance, Lucky sits in his usual box at Oaklawn Park with Gay Orlova beside him, her blonde waves tucked into a fetching new sunhat. Both are watching through heavy binoculars as the horses in the third race round the clubhouse turn and thunder into the stretch. Both rise to their feet as the co-favorites, dueling neck and neck, gallop for home.

"Come on, Eastport! Come on, baby! Eastport! Eastport! Yeah!"

They whoop and hug, the showgirl bouncing like a cocktail shaker inside of Lucky's embrace. Over her shoulder, Lucky frowns at the sight of the three suited men picking their way down the steps of the grandstand.

"Here, baby. Run up and cash these like a good girl."

As the showgirl shoulders her way past the new arrivals, Lucky stands and braces himself for the blow that the sullen face of Allen T. Davies is already telegraphing.

"Hello, Charlie. You remember Rich Ryan and Jimmy Campbell."

"I don't suppose you boys are here for the fourth race?"

"No, Charlie," Davies says, scanning the seats around them. "I'm afraid we've got ourselves what you might call a situation."

A rap on the heavy oak door quiets the conference room chatter. James Campbell, the Arkansas state assemblyman, opens it to a breathless Dutch Akers.

"Is she okay?" Lucky asks Akers, turning from where he stands at the window.

Akers nods as he takes a seat at the table. Lucky returns his gaze to the street as Richard Ryan, the criminal defense attorney, resumes his interrupted narrative.

"The point is, Carl Bailey is no friend of ours. He ran for attorney general on a law-and-order platform whose first plank was cleaning up Hot Springs. Hot Mess, he likes to call us in the press. Says we're a pustular pimple on the face of the great state of Arkansas. Which means this is exactly the kind of fight he's been itching to have."

"What fight?" Akers surveys the faces at the table. "What's going on?"

"Dewey," Davies tells him. "He's flown one of his Harvard boys down with a grand jury indictment and an extradition warrant signed by the governor of New York. It seems they plan to try Charlie on some sort of a prostitution rap. The A.G.'s gotten wind of it, and he's driving from Little Rock with the capitol press corps in tow. That kind of attention will limit our options, gentlemen, and means we'll have to fight this thing out in public. But at least we've got Sam Garratt in our corner."

Again Lucky turns from the window.

"C'mon you guys, what am I payin ya for? Dewey must be out of his fuckin gourd. I expected income taxes, but prostitution? The bastard's just grabbin at straws."

"Sounds like a rap you can beat, Charlie."

"Normally, I'd say sure, but here's the thing about Dewey. From what I hear about this judge he's got in his pocket, he could convict the pope of bein Jewish. Which means we gotta fight this extradition with everything we got. At least buy ourselves some time so we can figure out what the hell's goin on."

Campbell turns to Ryan, the defense attorney. "What are you thinking, Rich?"

"I don't know. This Dewey's been making a hell of a racket. Sam's gotten telegrams from the governor in Little Rock and the police commissioner in New York. He'll have to increase the bail; that much is certain. Which means you might have to spend a couple of nights in jail, Charlie, but that might be the safest place for you with those two detectives running around. Meanwhile, maybe we can make some hay out of these competing warrants. One's a federal rap and one's state, right? So Al, how's about if you issue a fugitive warrant for Charlie's arrest on the federal charge, and on that basis we oppose extradition on the state warrant? Take the position we plan to put Charlie on trial for the federal rap right here in Hot Springs. That should buy us some time to plan our next move."

"Sorry, Charlie, but you're under arrest."

The men laugh.

"Once the hubbub quiets down and Bailey gets his headlines, then we'll arrange bail for Charlie and see if we can't get him acquitted on this extortion charge. How does that sound?"

The men fall silent as Lucky moves from the window. Ryan steps aside, ceding his place at the head of the table.

"All right you guys." Lucky's palms are flat on the tabletop. "If that's the plan, then here's what I wanna see. Al, you call Moe Polakoff in New York and tell him to get his ass down here on the next available plane. Dutch, go tell Gay we're havin dinner tonight at the jail, and have her bring some decent chow and some clean sheets from the hotel. And my shaving kit. And my pajamas—the blue ones with the piping. As for you, Richie, you and Al get in there and kick the shit out of Dewey's Harvard boy—what's his name again?"

"McLean."

"You kick the shit out of McLean and send a message back to New York that Dewey's bullshit don't wash down here in Arkansas. And last of all, Jimmy"—here Lucky turns his attention to the Arkansas assemblyman—"I still don't know what the fuck I'm payin you for."

Again the men laugh.

"Okay, that's it. And don't screw this up, 'cause there's a horse I really like in the feature race on Sunday."

★ ★ ★

Lucky is still in his pajamas on Saturday morning when he hears the distant commotion. Sheriff Roy Ermey of Garland County lays down his cards and hurries through the open door of the cell. Dutch Akers and Jimmy Campbell share a puzzled look.

"What the hell is that?"

Ermey returns at a run, his key ring jangling as he bypasses the cell and heads straight for his office without so much as a sideward glance.

Now all the men lay down their cards.

"Dutch, go see what the fuck is going on."

But before any can move, a squadron of men—at least a dozen by Lucky's count—darkens the narrow hallway. All have shotguns or rifles, and all are wearing the belted blue uniform of the Arkansas State Police. With them are the two New York detectives, Brennan and Di Rosa, along with Dewey's redheaded assistant, Edward McLean.

"Charles Luciano?" the police captain reads from a blue-backed document. "By order of Governor Junius Marion Futrell and the Circuit Court of Pulaski County, you are hereby under arrest as a fugitive from justice in the state of New York."

"Get dressed, Lucky." Brennan removes a cigarette and taps it on the pack. "We're takin a ride to Little Rock."

"Habeas corpus. It means to deliver the body—your body—back to Hot Springs so they can try you on the federal charge."

Moses Polakoff sits opposite his client at a wide wooden table, his pin-striped suit and bow tie in sharp contrast to Lucky's work shirt and jeans of matching blue denim with the words "Pulaski County" stenciled over the breast pocket. A guard stands at attention behind him, cradling a short-barreled shotgun.

"I've heard that song before, Moe. Richie Ryan sang it to me in Hot Springs. Then the National Guard came along and broke up the show."

"That was just a stunt by Futrell, the Arkansas governor, repaying some favor to Lehman. Dave Panich is the best appellate lawyer in Arkansas, Charlie. He says we've got a good judge here who's not in anyone's pocket. We have a ten-day stay to pursue an appeal, and Panich is on his way up to Kansas City as we speak. What's not helping matters is that Bailey, the attorney general, is running around claiming Owney Madden tried to bribe him with fifty grand."

"Fuck the attorney general. Our problem ain't the politicians or the judges down here, Moe. Our problem is Dewey. What are you hearin about this pandering bullshit?"

Polakoff lowers his voice. "Dewey's got something like a hundred prostitutes already in custody, and some of them are pointing the finger at Little Davie. I guess the theory is that Davie answers to you, so it must be your racket."

Lucky swears in Italian. The guard frowns.

"That's bullshit and Dewey knows it. He couldn't lay a glove on me, so he tries to pull a freshman stunt like this."

"I know, Charlie, I know."

"I've never taken a dime off a skirt in my life! And anyway, who's gonna believe a bunch of junked-up whores in the first place? Somethin ain't right here, Moe. Dewey wants to be governor so bad he can taste it. He wouldn't be stickin his neck out like this unless the fix was already in."

"Here's something else you're not going to like. As we speak, Dewey and Lehman are ramming a bill through the New York legislature that will allow the trial of multiple defendants for a series of related offenses under a single indictment."

"Try that again in English."

"It's called a joinder law. It means he's planning to put you, Davie, Tommy Pennochio, the bookers, the bondsmen—this whole so-called vice combination—on trial together. He wants to sit you all at the same table, then let the girls throw mud at the bookers, and get the bookers to point the finger at Tommy and Davie. Then he'll ask the jury to return a verdict against everyone, including you."

"Jesus Christ."

"Dewey held a press conference the other day and said you were the biggest gangster in America, in charge of the worst vice racket in New York history. He basically made his opening statement to every potential juror in the city, with nobody around to contradict him."

"That little cocksucker."

"And that's not all. According to Chappie, Tommy and Davie were dropping your name all over town, trying to get the madams and bookers in line."

"Why the fuck didn't Chappie say anything to me?"

"I don't know. Maybe he figured you'd given Davie the okay."

"Jesus Christ, it's like a bad fuckin dream. What are we gonna do about it?"

"For right now, we sit tight and hope that Panich can find a sympathetic judge to hear our appeal."

"And what if he can't?"

Moses Polakoff shrugs. "Then we'll find you the best criminal defense lawyer in the state of New York."

Lucky wakes at midnight to the *clang* of an iron door. He lifts his head on an elbow. Footsteps echo in the corridor of the Pulaski County Jail. Three, maybe four men are heading his way.

"Now what?" he grumbles, reading his watch.

He is seated and scratching at his head by the time they arrive. There are four men in total, three of whom he recognizes by their backlit silhouettes.

"Here you go, Lucky." A pile of folded clothes hits the floor at his feet. "Time to go home."

They are hurrying in darkness. Down the polished corridor, past the cells of the slumbering inmates. Through the guard's room, and then down a carpeted hallway past the sheriff's office.

"Where are you guys takin me? My ten days ain't up till tomorrow."

"Wrong, Charlie. Your ten days expired at midnight."

One detective is on each of Lucky's arms. They guide him through the intake area and to the front desk, where a jailer is already waiting.

"Cuff him," Brennan tells Di Rosa, and Lucky feels the cold embrace of metal on his wrists.

A clipboard is signed, and the jailer opens the outside door. The cold air meets Lucky's face like a slap.

"Where's my lawyer? You guys can't just yank me outta here. This is America, for Christ sake."

Nobody responds. Down at the curb, a patrol car is idling. McLean claims the shotgun seat, while Lucky is wedged between the detectives into the middle seat in back.

He feels a sickening sense of déjà vu.

The patrol car travels without lights or siren. It is a short drive to the train yard. The car stops well short of the platform, where the men haul Lucky onto a graveled sidetrack. A train is waiting, hulking in the darkness, and Lucky can see lights filtering through the steam. Ahead, a cluster of men has gathered on the platform.

"Jesus," McLean says. "Fucking Bailey."

As the four men march past the caboose, a cry echoes from the platform. The waiting reporters surge to the railing.

"Lucky! Hey, Lucky! Any last words for the people of Arkansas?"

A camera flashes. Lucky is lifted and placed on the first iron step of the train car. He twists in the grip of his captors and manages a single shouted plea as the door slams closed behind him.

"Help! I'm bein kidnapped!"

Thirty

Mouthpiece

GEORGE LEVY HAILED a taxi outside the courthouse and took it straight to his hotel. He'd arrived in Albany on Thursday evening, just fourteen hours earlier, and he had every intention of returning to Freeport in time for Friday night dinner. He'd packed but a single change of clothes—the very suit he was wearing as he paid the cabbie and bounded up the steps and entered the hotel lobby.

If George had been a drinker, he'd perhaps have detoured into the bar for a celebratory cocktail. As it was, his plan was to check out immediately, grab a quick bite at the little sit-down deli across the street, then catch the two fifty train for Grand Central. That left him an hour for lunch and, with any luck, enough time for a victory cigar on the platform at the railway station.

Celebration was certainly in order. Earlier that year, George had obtained a declaratory judgment from the New York Supreme

215

Court that the dog racing purchase-option scheme employed by his clients at the Mineola Fairgrounds, while clearly an avoidance of the state's gambling laws, was not a violation of them. In a judicial opinion that was still being chuckled over in New York legal circles, Judge Paul Bonynge had waxed philosophical about the small hypocrisies that the law endures in order to attain the ends of justice:

> Does not the Supreme Court grind out thousands of divorces annually upon the stereotyped sin of the same big blonde attired in the same black silk pajamas? Is not access to the chamber of love quite uniformly obtained by announcing that it is a maid bringing towels or a messenger boy with an urgent telegram? Do we not daily pretend to hush up the fact that an offending defendant is insured when every juror with an ounce of wit recognizes the defendant's lawyer and his entourage as old friends?
>
> More than half a century ago P. T. Barnum recorded the fact that the American people delight in being humbugged, and such is still the national mood. Nowhere is this trait more clearly shown than in the field of gambling. A church fair or bazaar would scarcely be complete without a bevy of winsome damsels selling chances on bed quilts, radios, electric irons, and a host of other things. If the proceeds are to be devoted to the ladies' sewing circle or the domine's vacation, no sin is perceived and the local prosecutor, whoever or wherever he may be, stays his hand. But if a couple of dusky youths are apprehended rolling bones to a state of moderate warmth, blind justice perceives the infamy of the performance and the law takes its course.

Following the morning's oral arguments, the Appellate Division in Albany would at last lay the matter to rest and would, George was confident, uphold the legality of pari-mutuel wagering in the Empire State—a small victory for his clients, but one whose benefit to New York's horse racing industry would be measured in millions of dollars.

"Mr. Levy!" the receptionist called to George as he strode through the carpeted lobby.

"Yes?"

She waved a slip of paper. "There's an urgent message for you. A Mr. Polakoff has telephoned several times."

George carried the message slip to the phone booth in the hotel bar.

"Mr. Levy?" Even with the poor connection, George could hear relief in the stranger's voice. "Thank God I caught you. Your office gave me this number. I hope you can spare me a moment."

"What's this about?"

"My name is Moses Polakoff. I'm the attorney for Charles Lucania, better known as Lucky Luciano. As you're probably aware, my client has recently been indicted on multiple counts of compulsory prostitution. That's the crime of having placed women in houses of prostitution with the intention—"

"Yes, I know what it is. But what can I do for you?"

"My client needs a trial lawyer, Mr. Levy. A lawyer of impeccable reputation, but one with the guts to stand up to the special prosecutor and his army of Ivy League whiz kids. You've come highly recommended by Frank Costello and Lou Clayton, among others, and of course your reputation precedes you. But I'm not going to sugarcoat it. You've seen what Dewey's been doing to us in the newspapers. We're in a jam, George, and we need help. And just so you know, money is no object to Mr. Lucania."

"Now hold on a second. If I were to take the case—and I'm not saying I will—my rate is five hundred a day during trial. That's what I charge everyone."

"That's fine, obviously."

"And you'll have to forgive me, but I haven't been following the case all that closely. How much time would I have to prepare?"

Static filled the silence on the line.

"That's the other thing," the voice finally said. "The trial opens Monday, and there's no chance in the world of putting it off."

Saturday noon found George in a well-appointed office at 475 Fifth Avenue sitting opposite a small conference table from Moses Polakoff, age forty, and another, younger lawyer named Mezansky. Both men watched as George finished reading the sixty-one-page indictment. Both noted the furrows deepening on their visitor's forehead as he reached the final page.

"Ninety counts," George said, squaring the onionskin pages and sliding them across the table. "My God, all Dewey has to do is wave this thing in front of the jury. They'll figure Luciano must be guilty of something."

Polakoff nodded. "That's exactly what I've been saying."

"Do you have a list of the prosecution witnesses?"

"No. Dewey won't give us one, and the indictment, as you can see, fails to identify who testified before the grand jury."

"That's the new procedure, I suppose, with the repeal of section two seventy-one."

Polakoff shared a look with his colleague. "I can see you're up to speed. We've filed a motion arguing that the old procedure should apply, since the charged offenses predate the repeal. We've also demurred to the indictment on a similar ground—that the joinder law's application to the charged offenses would be ex post facto."

"That will turn on whether the joinder law is considered one of procedure or substance."

"Exactly. We think the trial of multiple counts and multiple defendants under a single indictment is both procedural and substantive in nature. That's our argument, anyway."

"Tell me about this judge."

Polakoff sighed. "Philip McCook is a clergyman's son from Connecticut—a law-and-order, God-and-country Republican. He and Dewey were appointed together and given the same marching orders: to convict the top racketeers, come hell or high water. Anything less will be seen as a black eye for both the mayor and the governor. McCook, who's close friends with La Guardia, knows that better than anyone. So far, he's let Dewey get away with murder. Have you heard about Luciano's bail?"

"No."

"Three hundred and fifty thousand, the highest in New York history."

"I see."

"Thanks to the pretrial conference, we've had some insight into Dewey's trial strategy. Basically, the prostitutes are innocent lambs, and the defendants are wolves and vultures growing fat on their degradation."

"And you take issue with that?"

"At least allow me to play devil's advocate. Assume for a moment that these girls are prostitutes by choice, for the simple reason that they can earn three to four hundred dollars a week compared to the eight or ten they'd be making as waitresses or cigarette girls. But one of the problems with prostitution is that if a girl gets arrested, no legitimate bonding company will post her bail. The default rates are simply too high. So the girls need cash, which they often don't have because many of them are also drug addicts. By those lights, Jacobs and Berkman, the two unlicensed bondsmen, were simply filling a need, to the benefit of all concerned. And at ten dollars a week, or roughly three percent of the girls' gross earnings, their rates were actually quite reasonable."

"But if a girl is never arrested, that's all profit to this so-called bonding combination."

"Just like any insurance premium. As for the rest of them, well, they're all part of the machinery that makes the system work.

Madams, bookers, lenders, upper management. If it wasn't illegal, and to some people immoral, you might say it's a fair and efficient system designed to protect the girls by keeping them off the streets and out of jail."

"And Luciano is part of it?"

"No, of course not. But we've been hearing rumors ever since that raid back in February that Dewey's putting tremendous pressure on the girls. They've been held for months now under constant threat of prosecution. Many were addicts who've gone through withdrawal, and God only knows what they've said or signed. Dewey's message seems to be, 'Tell us what we want to hear and the charges against you will be dropped and you'll be given immunity for your testimony.' And what he wants to hear, of course, is the name Charlie Lucky. Those who refuse are left in jail. Those who agree to finger Luciano are released from custody and moved to swanky hotels, where they're wined and dined by the handsome young lawyers from Dewey's office."

"That sounds a bit far-fetched."

"Except that it's true. We've had private operatives tailing the few we've been able to locate. Several of Dewey's assistants—Gelb, Cole, and Ten Eyck—have been taking the girls out for food and drinks on a regular basis. Dempsey's, the Villanova, Keane's Tavern. And not just one or two drinks, from what we can determine."

"If all that's true, then there's a defense right there: undue influence of witnesses. Witnesses, I have to assume, who weren't very credible to begin with. Have you tried talking with any of them?"

"Tried, yes, but Dewey won't allow it."

"What do you mean he won't allow it?"

Polakoff laughed. "Welcome to our world, George, where Dewey's word is law. We don't know how many will actually testify, but the indictment lists thirty prostitutes as potential witnesses. Dewey's got at least forty more stashed away, plus a handful of madams and low-level functionaries—the bookers and bondsmen and strong-arm types. If he can get even a few to say that Charlie Lucky's the boss, then we've got ourselves a hell of a problem. And the maddening thing is that other than David Betillo, who's an acquaintance from his old bootlegging days, Lucky doesn't know any of his co-defendants. He couldn't pick them out of a lineup."

George settled into his chair and pushed up his coat sleeves to reveal his bare forearms beneath. He'd heard of D.A.s woodshedding witnesses, of course—Lew Smith in the Carman case came to mind—but nothing on the scale of what Polakoff was describing.

"With thirteen defendants and a ninety-count indictment, it'll be a three-ring circus in that courtroom. Who are the other lawyers?"

"Ten defendants," Polakoff corrected. "We have it on good authority that three of the bookers will be pleading guilty. And there'll be no public spectators allowed—just the defendants, the lawyers, and a large pool of reporters. We'll ask that witnesses be excluded, of course, and McCook has hinted that he'll sequester the jury. As far as the lawyers go, they're all pretty solid. You know Jim Murray, I'm sure, and Maurice Cantor, who was Arnold Rothstein's lawyer. But I've made it clear to them that if you come on board, then you'll be the captain of the ship. As far as trial strategy is concerned, whatever you say goes, as long as their clients aren't prejudiced. And, of course, that you'll take the lead in jury selection."

Polakoff's look was imploring. To avoid it, George directed his gaze to the windows overlooking Bryant Park.

The time had come to decide. Undertaking to represent America's most notorious gangster in one of the most ballyhooed trials in history was no trifling matter. It was, in fact, a life-altering proposition. Until now, George had been known, where known at all, as a competent, affable barrister from Long Island. Should he take the Luciano case, he'd henceforth be called a mob lawyer—a mouthpiece. The label would follow him into every courtroom, every client meeting, and every social function he'd ever attend. It would shadow George Jr., his son and namesake, into an already difficult adulthood. It would appear in George's obituary.

And then there were the practical hurdles. This extraordinary session of the New York State Supreme Court involved two dedic- ated grand juries, a special prosecutor, a judge, and a so-called blue-ribbon panel of "experienced" petit jurors—meaning, George suspected, white businessmen who'd previously voted to convict—all of whom had been convened and constituted for the singular purpose of taking down Luciano.

Dewey, the special prosecutor, had spent untold taxpayer dollars, had tapped telephones and offered indulgences, and had run hundreds of witnesses through the two grand juries. He had, as Polakoff sug- gested, a small army of lawyers, accountants, and police detectives at his beck and call. He had a judge in his corner who seemed more of a co-prosecutor than a neutral referee, and he'd even enlisted the state legislature to tip the scales in his favor.

Never before in New York history had multiple crimes against multiple defendants been combined into a single trial. And to make matters worse, it would be a trial by surprise, with no foreknowledge as to who the witnesses would be, let alone what they might have been coached or coerced into saying.

Those were the downsides. George, on the other hand, was a lawyer and an officer of the court. He believed that every defendant, no matter how unsavory his reputation or heinous the crime alleged, was entitled to his day in court. All were innocent until proven guilty. To George, who'd aspired to the trial bar ever since his early teens, these were neither bromides nor hackneyed clichés, but rather the twin pillars upon which stood the greatest system of criminal justice the world had ever known.

George turned to Polakoff, who still was watching him, hanging as if on tenterhooks.

"Tell me the truth, Moe. Is Luciano really innocent?"

"Innocent?" Polakoff shook his head. "No, George, he's not innocent. He's a convicted drug dealer, a former bootlegger, and a notorious bookmaker and gambler. He's got his fingers in any number of murky deals with some very dicey characters. I don't ask, because I don't want to know. But he's no whoremonger, I can tell you that much. And he'd like the opportunity to tell you so himself."

"All right then, let's go see him."

Polakoff straightened. "Does that mean you're taking the case?"

"I may be crazy," George said, standing and gathering up the files, "but I wouldn't miss this thing for the world."

Thirty-One

The Wire

May 1936

"ALL RIGHT, PEOPLE. Listen up."

Tom leaned with his back to the desk, his fingers tracing the carved mahogany inlay. Of the twenty men and one woman crowded onto the chairs and couches hastily arrayed in a semicircle before him, it was Sol Gelb, Barry Ten Eyck, Jack Rosenblum, Stanley Fuld, and Harry Cole who appeared the most anxious. Which was only natural, since it was they, more so than the others—Charlie Grimes, Frank Hogan, Bill Herlands, Murray Gurfein, Thurston Greene, Paul Lockwood, Ed McLean, Vic Herwitz, Milt Schilback, Jack Grumet, Ed Joseph, Harry Steinberg, Livy Goddard, Manny Robbins, Charlie Breitel, and Eunice Carter—who'd be the ones standing shoulder to shoulder with the special prosecutor in the courtroom battle set to begin in less than an hour's time.

All the lawyers present, however, thanks to six solid weeks of fifteen-hour workdays, had an intensely personal stake in what was to come.

Outside the office where the prosecutorial team had gathered, the fourteenth floor of the Woolworth Building was a beehive of last-minute activity. Telephones rang and typewriters clattered. Stenographers and clerks, detectives and accountants bustled along a carpeted hallway glimpsed only in slatted fragments through the lowered window blinds.

"Is it just me," Tom began, affecting the tone of breezy confidence he'd learned from George Medalie, "or does this feel a little bit like Christmas morning? Some of you know what I mean. The shopping is done, the packages are wrapped, and now it's only a matter of tearing them open. We're down to the fun part, people! Especially when we know that somewhere in that pile of boxes is the one special gift we've been waiting the whole year to receive. The one we pestered our parents for. The one we wrote to Santa about."

"A Lucky doll!" someone warbled in falsetto, and the room erupted in laughter.

Tom waited for the merriment to subside.

"Allow me to be serious for a moment. I don't have to tell you how important the next three weeks are going to be. Not just for this office and the careers of those working here, but also for the people of New York and the cause of justice and decency in these United States. Because nothing less is what's at stake in this trial."

He paused there for effect, scanning the room, meeting the eyes of his audience.

"It's been a long road we've traveled, and God knows, it's been a rocky one. We've had to overcome frightened witnesses and drug addictions and threats from thugs and gangsters. We've had one of our own, Ray Ariola, prosecuted by a district attorney who's made it perfectly clear he'll do anything in his power to thwart us in our mission. And we've had to fight an epic extradition battle just to get our star defendant back in the jurisdiction. At times it's seemed as though we were twenty lawyers against the world. But all of that is behind us now, and our eyes must be focused from this moment forward on the task that lies ahead."

He circled the desk and perched on the edge of his swivel chair.

"An hour from now, jury selection will begin. We have a preliminary list of seventy witnesses, and as to those witnesses, each of you knows your assignment. Frank will be in charge of matters at this end. We have a dedicated wire running from the courtroom to the investigators' office, which will allow us to coordinate the transfer of witnesses from custody. Judge McCook is counting on us to monitor the proceedings and avoid any delays or interruptions due to the unavailability of witnesses."

Tom risked a glance in Gelb's direction. Little Sol, his chief trial strategist, was studying his shoelaces.

"With a venire of two hundred talesmen, I'm expecting voir dire to last at least two days, possibly three. The only witnesses we'll need for today are Weiner, Balitzer, and Marcus, each of whom will enter his guilty plea before jury selection begins. In front of the whole panel, I might add, which ought to give our esteemed colleagues for the defense a little something to think about."

Chuckles and murmurs rippled through the room.

"Speaking of defense counsel, I understand we have a new face in the crowd. Murray?"

Murray Gurfein flipped a page on his legal pad. "Sam Mezansky called on Saturday afternoon to say that George Morton Levy will be appearing as trial counsel for Luciano. Levy's a Long Island defense attorney with a sterling reputation and a hell of a track record. He's currently in partnership with Elvin Edwards, the former Nassau County D.A. You may recall that Levy represented Joseph Ustica in that Gilbride murder case a couple of years ago."

"Against Edwards, if memory serves."

"That's right, which tells you something right there. I spent most of Sunday asking around about Levy. Word is he's a quick study, good

226

on his feet, and that juries love him to death. He tried his first capital murder when he was all of twenty-six years old. George Medalie even used him once in a union-busting case in Rockville Centre. It's no stretch to say that Levy's the best defense lawyer on Long Island. He's also a member at the Lakeville Club, where he's golfing buddies with Frank Costello and Frank Erickson, which probably explains his connection to Luciano."

"Thank you, Murray. We've wondered whether Polakoff was going to try the case, and now we have our answer. If they hired Levy this late in the game, then I'm guessing he wasn't their first choice. Or maybe they've had him up their sleeve the whole time. In any event, it doesn't change anything we're planning to do."

Herwitz raised a hand. "What about peremptories?"

"What about them?"

"With ten defendants, is the judge going to limit them to twenty per side or twenty per defendant?"

"That's outside your bailiwick, Vic, and it's also beyond our control. In any event, we've already briefed it. Now if there are no other stupid questions, I'll conclude by thanking you all for your hard work to date, and for the even harder work I'll be expecting from each of you in the days and weeks ahead. It won't be easy, people, but nothing worth accomplishing ever is. Break a leg, gentlemen. You too, Mrs. Carter. And Sol, will you and Frank stick around for just a second?"

Chairs scraped as the lawyers stood and gathered their papers. When the hallway door opened, the tumult of the outer office gusted across Tom's desk until the door closed again, leaving the three men alone in the muted quiet.

Tom checked his watch. He stood and crossed to the hallway windows, where he adjusted the half-open blinds, further dimming the room.

"Don't go weak in the knees, Sol," he said without turning. "This is the part where we all need to stand our tallest."

"My knees are fine, chief."

"Even if McCook orders the witnesses excluded, we'll be in full compliance with that order."

Gelb didn't respond.

"Right?"

"I said I was fine with it, okay? Let's leave it at that."

Tom turned to face the two seated men.

"Look. McCook knows we have the wire. He knows we'll be monitoring the proceedings, and he knows we have witnesses here to prep. He can add two and two."

"But you're not going to tell the defense."

Tom removed a silver dollar from his pocket and worked it through his fingers as he returned to his desk.

"Come on, Sol. That bunch would object if I asked permission to use the men's room. You want to talk about cheating? Cheating is sending hoods to stand outside the House of Detention and shout threats up at the women. Cheating is offering money and drugs to those who don't cooperate. These aren't choirboys we're dealing with, and let's not forget it. These are vicious thugs who terrorize young women and live off the sweat of their disgusting, degrading labor. Young women who, but for the grace of God, could be our own sisters or daughters. These are the lowest of the low, Sol, and I, for one, am not going to apologize for the fact that hearing the others testify might stiffen their spines a little. Not to mention give us a few insights that will help us put Luciano behind bars where he belongs."

The telephone rang, the sound slightly muffled, and Tom yanked open a drawer.

"Yes? All right, Mrs. Rosse, just give us five more minutes."

He replaced the receiver and removed a cigarette holder from his pocket.

"Frank? Where do we stand with Presser and Balitzer? Other than a boat load of hearsay, they're our entire case against Luciano."

"Don't forget Bendix and Good-Time Charlie."

Tom tapped out a cigarette. "Neither of whom I'd trust to take out my garbage. Neither would you, and neither will the jury."

"Well," Hogan said, tipping back in his chair, "I think Nancy is pretty solid. As for Mildred, she'll do anything to help Pete, so as long as we have the one, we have the other. What we could really use is a witness who isn't a convict or a prostitute."

"You can't expect to see clergy testifying in a prostitution case. You like that? It's a line I'll be using in my opening."

Tom lit a match and leaned forward into the flame.

"Hell, I'll settle for another prostitute. I just hate going into that courtroom with only four eyewitnesses. For all the evidence we've got against the others, that's really all we have against Luciano—two prostitutes, one pimp, and a serial stool pigeon who's heading up the river for life. I feel like I'm walking into that courtroom half-naked."

"We'll keep working the others," Hogan said, "but at this point I wouldn't count on anything new. Not that you'll need it, chief. We've got Luciano in the bag."

"We'd better, or I'll be the national poster boy for prosecutorial incompetence."

Tom stood. He tugged at his lapels, then took his new hat down from the rack.

"How do I look?" he asked, tapping the bowler into place.

Frank Hogan smiled. "From where I'm sitting, you look an awful lot like the next governor of the great state of New York."

Thirty-Two

The Kite

May 1936

I FELT LIKE DEATH warmed over.

My head was throbbing, and my side was aching, and I hadn't kept down so much as a mouthful of food for nearly three days. I was burning a fever, sweating like a pig while shivering with the chills. I was too weak to stand, and I couldn't sleep, and my stomach felt like I'd swallowed a quart of battery acid.

And the next day, I knew, was going to be worse. That evening, at least, the nurse had come and given me a shot. But that was the last one—the end of my five-day cure—and from then on it would be strictly cold turkey.

After my pinch on 75th Street, I'd telegrammed Mrs. Calvit and asked her to call Sam Siegel to come and bail me out. But Siegel, the dirty bastard, never raised so much as a finger to help me out. So then I asked Mrs. Calvit if she'd at least come to the courthouse and testify,

230

but a fat lot of good that did. Siegel eventually sent some snot-nosed kid to handle my trial, and by the end of the day I'd been convicted of solicitation.

The only thing I had going for me was that I'd given my name as Fay Marston, and even though Mrs. Calvit testified that she'd known me as Mildred Nelson, the court never connected me with my first arrest as Florence Newman or the outstanding fugitive warrant for Frances Martin. That, and the fact that Mrs. Calvit agreed to take care of poor little Pearlie until I got out of jail.

So there I was, Fay Marston, convicted prostitute, awaiting sentence in the medical unit of the Women's House of Detention. The torture unit was more like it—a dungeon full of drunks and junkies screaming and crying and begging for one thing or another they knew perfectly well they were never gonna get.

And I was playing my part, curled up in my bunk, shivering and moaning, too weak even to use the toilet. I still hadn't heard from Jimmy, even though Siegel's kid must've told him where I was, and as bad as I felt physically, it was the silence from Jimmy that maybe hurt me most of all.

A bunch of the girls from the Dewey vice trial, which had started on Monday, were on the same floor as me, and I figured it was only a matter of time before word got around. That afternoon, sure enough, I got a kite from Gracie Hall, a girl who'd worked at my joint on West End Avenue.

Dear Flo: Some of the girls have seen you and reported you to the D.A.s. They will probably want to question you. Why don't you take the bull by the horns and send a note down to the D.A.s and tell them who you are? Mr. Ten Eyck and Mr. Hogan come to the building every evening. They are very nice and it won't hurt you to talk to them. Maybe it will be better that way. Grace

Gracie and her friend Judy came to see me that night. That was on Wednesday, the third day of the trial. From the expression on Gracie's face, I could guess what I must of looked like. I'd weighed around a hundred and ten pounds when I was arrested, and now, with nothing but a few mouthfuls of cereal over the past five days, I felt like a scarecrow. Like a stiff breeze could have lifted me up and blown me right through the bars.

They found me groaning under a pile of blankets.

"My God, Flo, look at you," Gracie said, laying a hand on my forehead. "You need to be in the hospital. Or at least over with us in the witness block. We get all kinds of special treatment."

"I'll bet you do. You and the other rats."

"Don't be like that. Just be quiet and listen."

She sat on the edge of the bunk, stroking my hair.

"Everything's changed, honey. All them guys, Jimmy and the rest of them, they're all going to prison. You need to talk to Mr. Ten Eyck. We all talk to him. He'll explain everything. If you help them, they'll take care of you. We get special food, and we wear our own clothes, and they take us out to the movies twice a month. Out to dinner too. We even get to go shopping once in a while."

"Tell it to Sweeney."

"It's true, I swear! Some of the girls have even been sprung. Helen Kelly, Irene Smith, Thelma Jordan—they're all living in hotels. Peggy Wild too, and Jenny Fischer. As a reward for being cooperative. Some of the other girls like Mildred Harris and Nancy Presser, the ones who were girlfriends with the combination guys, they're getting the deluxe treatment. I heard Thelma and Nancy are getting a cruise when the trial is over. As close as you were to Jimmy, I'll bet you could get all kinds of stuff. So don't be bullheaded. Here. Take this."

She pressed a pencil stub and some paper into my hand.

"Write a note to Mr. Ten Eyck. T-E-N E-Y-C-K. He'll want to see you, I know he will. And do me a favor, willya? Tell him I'm the one who said so. That'll help me out a little bit too."

Thursday came and went, again with no word from Jimmy. That's when I started to get angry. Angry about the sappy letters I'd written him. Angry about Siegel. Angry about the two of them leaving me here to rot in jail. Angry about little Pearlie, roaming around Mrs. Calvit's apartment, wondering where Mommy had gone. Feeling abandoned again, the poor little thing, and me with nothing I could do about it.

I knew exactly how she felt.

I thought about Christmas then—about when I'd given Jimmy that card with the C-note inside, only to find out he'd given his wife a fur coat. So what did I owe Jimmy Fredericks, anyway? I practically supported the big ape when times were tough for him. I cooked for him, and cleaned up after him, and drove him around like a coolie. And now that the shoe was on the other foot, what do I hear from him? Nothing, that's what. The big kiss-off. He didn't know if I was dead or alive, and I guess he didn't care.

If what Gracie said was true, and if all the combination guys were going down anyway, then I was a first-class sap for lying there with my mouth shut. I had leverage now, but once the trial was over, I'd have nothing but a sentence to serve and a record to live with for the rest of my life. And what was I gonna do then? There were no jobs out there, and even if there was, I'd never get a reference from Mrs. Calvit. I'd be back on the street, that's where I'd be, just another two-dollar whore with no Jimmy Fredericks to protect me. And every time some smelly creep was breathing hot in my ear, I'd be thinking about that one chance I'd had, and how I'd let it slip right through my fingers.

But what if Gracie was wrong? What if I ratted, and then Dewey rolled snake eyes? My life wouldn't be worth a ten-cent slug. I'd wind up in the river, or worse, and who'd take care of Pearlie then? There was no place you could hide from a guy like Charlie Lucky, and even if you could, you'd spend the rest of your life looking over your shoulder.

Goddamn fucking Jimmy. If only I could talk to him, or to Siegel, and get the inside dope. If I met with this Ten Eyck, he'd try to sell me a bill of goods about how great the trial is going and how the train is leaving the station without me. But for all I knew, that was a bunch of hooey. I needed to get my hands on a newspaper and see what the press was saying. Maybe that way I could make up my mind.

I used her pencil and paper to send a kite back to Gracie. I asked for a newspaper, and for another chance to talk.

The paper came with my dinner, which I still couldn't touch, and Mildred Curtis, one of the other girls I knew, came by and read it to me. She told me that June Gary, who was using the name Joan Martin in the trial, had gone on the stand and ratted out Jimmy, saying how he'd wrecked her joint and sapped her down and threatened to shoot her dog.

Shoot her little dog! I knew that was a lie because Jimmy would never do something like that. And then I was hopping mad all over again. Mad at June, who was a big troublemaker and was always moving her joint around, trying not to bond. Mad at Dewey for letting her spin a yarn like that on the witness stand. Mad at myself for lying there in my cell like a pile of dirty rags, unable to make up my mind.

That night, when the matron called the girls to the commissary wagon, I managed to get on my feet and walk, all weak and doubled-over though I was. Then when I saw June Gary standing there buying cigarettes, I couldn't help myself. I called her a dirty, lousy rat for what she'd said about Jimmy.

"I warned him I'd get even," she said, not backing down. "He didn't have to get rough like that. He didn't have to threaten my dog."

"You're a goddamn liar."

"Look at my head!" she said, bending forward and parting her hair. "Look what he done to me with his lead pipe. Go on, look!"

I had a different idea, and grabbed a fistful of hair.

"Owwww! Help! Guard!"

I yanked and twisted as hard as I could, and then Gracie jumped in and tried to pry my fingers loose, but June kept right on screaming. Pretty soon I heard running feet, and then I felt someone grabbing me and lifting me clear off the ground.

"All right, break it up!"

I ended up on the floor with the matron pinning me down with her knee.

"I guess you ain't so sick as you look," she said. "Not so sick you can't spend a little time in the hole."

They carried me there on a stretcher, with guards in front and back and the matron walking alongside. The other women laughing, or clapping, or hooting as I went by.

The cells in solitary were small, and they had only a narrow slot high up in the door for food. It was cold inside, and it smelled like piss, and when the door slammed shut behind me, everything went dark.

Only then did I start crying again.

I cried for a long time, and when I finally stopped crying, I fumbled in my pocket for the pencil and paper. I started to scribble, unable to see what I was writing through the darkness and the tears.

Mr. Ten Eyck

Dear Sir, I would like to see you on a matter of great importance in the Dewey Vice Case . . .

Thirty-Three

The Dock

May 1936

LUCKY IS KEEPING his head down.

He imagines that he is invisible and that the judge and all the lawyers and witnesses who are talking and arguing, swearing oaths and shouting objections, cannot see him. That he could simply stand up and walk, ghostlike, past the guards and reporters—down the stairs and out of the courthouse, where he could hail a cab and return to the Waldorf and slip into a silk robe with a drink in his hand and open up a newspaper and read all about the vice trial of Lucky Luciano, all with nobody being the wiser.

Except, of course, for the jury. Because while Lucky pretends he is a block of ice in a cold and flowing river, invisible and unmoved by the currents surging around him, the fourteen men in the jury box keep careful watch on the trial's star attraction with stares and side-long glances, as if checking to make sure he doesn't disappear from the courtroom like an ace that vanishes up the gambler's sleeve while the other players are distracted.

It is Saturday, the sixth day of the trial, and except for Dewey's opening statement, in which the special prosecutor branded Lucky "the czar of organized crime in this city" and called defendant Davie Betillo "the active general in the army under Luciano," not a single lawyer or witness has so much as mentioned Lucky's name. The whores and madams have instead been content—no, make that eager—to use their moment in the spotlight for settling old scores with the bookers and bondsmen and the strong-arm enforcers who'd fleeced them and intimidated them and in some cases beat them bloody in an effort to turn their loose amalgamation of independent houses into a kind of citywide chain.

Jimmy Fredericks, as far as Lucky can tell, is already sunk. Wahrman and Liguori too, if the jurors buy what the girls are selling. The girls, who are salesmen by nature, have been rehearsed to a fare-thee-well and are staging a bravura performance in their roles as fallen angels in calico dresses peddling sob stories of broken homes and broken lives and a final, miraculous shot at redemption thanks to their savior, Thomas E. Dewey, the great and incorruptible crime buster. The same girls who, as soon as the trial is over, will be back in their two-dollar houses posing as virgins, or as nymphos, or as whatever avatars of sweaty male lust will earn them their next cube of heroin.

Some of the lawyers—Siegel, for example, and Carlino—are rough on the girls, demanding the lurid details of their drug addictions, their sex lives. Scorning them for their aliases and their vagrancy and their lengthy records of arrest, implying that the girls will say or do just about anything to further their own interests. Lucky believes that this, while undeniably true, is also a mistake. A gentler approach, a more respectful tone, would stand them in better stead with the bluenosed jurors, who fidget and frown at the lawyers' bullying tactics.

It's a tricky business, Lucky admits, and the strategy that Polakoff and Levy have settled on is to let the others scuffle and brawl in the gutter while they remain above the fray. To portray Lucky as a gentleman gambler unfairly tarred by an overzealous prosecutor. And while it was Polakoff's idea to subpoena various witnesses who could attest to Lucky's gambling, it was Lucky himself who'd urged upon Levy that, with the exception of Davie Betillo from the old curbside liquor exchange, Lucky had never laid eyes on a single one of his co-defendants.

Dewey has placed a poster before the jury, a cast of characters, with the original thirteen defendants appearing above the line and other names—presumably witnesses or people whose names will otherwise be mentioned—appearing below. The poster reads:

Charlie Lucky	**Charles Luciano**
Tommy Bull	**Thomas Pennochio**
Little Davie	**David Betillo**
Abie	**Abraham Wahrman**
Bennie Spiller	
Jimmy Fredericks	**James Frederico**
Ralph Liguori	
Jesse Jacobs	
Meyer Berkman	
Pete Harris	**Peter Balitzer**
Jack Eller	**Jack Ellenstein**
Dave Miller	**David Marcus**
Al Weiner	

Cockeyed Louis	**Louis Weiner**
Nick Montana	
Binge	**Anthony Curcio**
Chappie	**Santos Scalfani**
Teddy	

Yoke	
Jo-Jo	Joseph Weintaub
Andy Coco	Andrew LeCoco
Charlie Spinach	Charles Pisano
Spike	Spike Green
Danny Brooks	Daniel Caputo
Billy Peluso	William Peluso
Joe Levine	
Abe Karp	Abraham Karp
Max Rachlin	
Vito	

Levy has objected to leaving the poster in sight of the jury, but this objection, like all the defense motions before it, has been promptly overruled.

Still, Lucky thinks, Levy was the perfect choice for the job. The little Jew is courtly but commanding, radiating an invisible magnetism that others in the courtroom can feel. Lucky is reminded of Meyer Lansky in the way that Levy fills the room when he enters, the way that others fall silent when he talks. Even McCook, who lets Dewey run roughshod over the other lawyers, is deferential to Levy, listening when he speaks and even sustaining one or two of his infrequent objections.

This is not to say that Lucky has grown overconfident. He knows from Dewey's opening statement that the special prosecutor plans to call witnesses who will claim that Lucky attended meetings with his various co-defendants, actively managing the day-to-day affairs of the so-called vice combination. But Dewey was vague, or probably just cagy, in never disclosing who would actually testify to what. Worried, perhaps, that Lucky might try to influence the witnesses. Or worse, make them disappear. The way he'd made Dutch Schultz disappear, saving Dewey's miserable life.

From where he sits at the defense table, Lucky can read Polakoff's hastily scribbled notes. Dewey had told the jury that in late summer of 1933, all the old bookers were summoned to a meeting downtown at which Lucky had walked into the room and announced, "You guys are through. I'm giving the business to Little Davie." This had turned the jurors' heads and, for that moment at least, Lucky was visible again. The story, however, is a complete fabrication, and Lucky wonders who Dewey has coerced into telling it on his behalf.

As for Tommy Pennochio and Davie Betillo, while not yet sunk, both are taking on water. Before jury selection even began, three of the four bookers named in the indictment—Dave Miller, Pete Harris and Al Weiner—stood before the judge and the roomful of prospective jurors and pleaded guilty to all ninety counts. These are the men who dealt with the whores on a week-to-week basis; the men who, having turned state's evidence, would soon be pointing their fingers up the so-called ladder that Dewey described, right at Little Davie's skinny behind.

But all in all, the trial is going well. Indeed, Dewey has overplayed his hand in at least one respect that he'll soon come to regret. Lucky knows, from reports of the private detectives Polakoff has hired, that Dewey's assistant prosecutors are taking the girls out to bars and restaurants on a regular basis. Yet when Siegel broaches the subject with a witness named Muriel Ryan, Dewey can't jump onto his high-horse fast enough. Again Lucky leans to read the handwriting of Moses Polakoff:

Q: *Were you out in the evenings from the House of Detention?*
A: *Twice.*
Q: *Twice in the evenings? With whom? Any of Mr. Dewey's assistants?*
A: *With a police officer and a matron.*
DEWEY: *I think that is a most offensive question. I object.*
COURT: *What do you object to?*
DEWEY: *The implication that my assistants were going out with these women held as prisoners.*

COURT: *Maybe the noise prevented me from hearing the exact words. If there was such implication, it should not be.*

So while certainly not cocky, Lucky is growing ever more comfortable where he sits. None of the bookers can claim to have met him, and neither Tommy Pennochio nor Davie Betillo will ever dare mention his name. Meanwhile, Dewey has marched into the first trap Polakoff has set for him, and there will be other traps waiting down the road.

The water will rise, Lucky thinks, drowning the Abie Wahrmans and the James Fredericos, submerging the Ralph Liguoris and the Benny Spillers. But it will stop just short of his own battle-scarred chin. And if by some combination of bad luck and perjury the water should engulf even Charlie Lucky, then George Morton Levy, the charismatic little Jew, will be there to rescue him.

In the meantime, Lucky sits and watches, content with being invisible.

Thirty-Four

Stacked Deck

May 1936

GEORGE LEVY WAS no stranger to crowded courtrooms or high-profile cases. He was inured to reporters and photographers, to police escorts and gawking spectators. But even he had never seen anything quite like the Luciano vice trial.

From the mobs thronging the barricades outside the Supreme Court building to the police snipers perched on the adjacent rooftops in Foley Square, the air outside the courthouse fairly crackled with electricity. Inside the second-floor courtroom, where a squadron of uniformed guards accompanied the defendants as they arrived from the jailhouse each morning in handcuffs and shackles, the daily ritual of chains and locks, truncheons and shotguns reminded George of a Dixie chain gang, or maybe a political show-trial held in the concrete bowels of some grim Baltic gulag.

However one might choose to describe it, it was definitely not an atmosphere conducive to the principle of presumed innocence. And if any fading ember of that glowing ideal had somehow managed to rekindle itself after the previous day's proceedings, it was extinguished each morning at ten o'clock sharp by the arrival of Philip J. McCook.

The old judge had set an early tone for the trial when, on the first day of jury selection, he'd summarily denied each and every one of the defense's pretrial motions. The grand jury was improperly constituted? Denied. The defendants are entitled to separate trials? Denied. The joinder law shouldn't apply retroactively? Denied. The defense was entitled to know the names of the witnesses who'd appeared before the grand jury? Denied. The so-called blue-ribbon venire panel had been improperly chosen? Denied. Each defendant is entitled to the same number of peremptory jury challenges as were accorded to the prosecution? Denied. Each defendant is entitled to know with which of the ninety alleged offenses he is specifically charged? Denied, denied, denied.

Next came the voir dire, at the outset of which Harry Kopp, veteran co-counsel for defendant Thomas Pennochio, had requested that the special prosecutor reveal the names of the witnesses he intended to call. This, Kopp argued, would allow the prospective jurors to identify in advance any potential conflicts that might arise if, for example, a witness personally known to a juror might later appear to give testimony, and would obviate the danger of jurors having to disqualify themselves in mid-trial. That motion was also denied.

McCook then allowed the special prosecutor to give a précis of his case—in effect, a preliminary opening statement—to the entire venire panel, on the theory that doing so would help "expedite the selection of jurors." Dewey used this unprecedented opportunity to tell the packed courtroom that which he'd already told the rest of the nation in newspaper and radio interviews: namely, that Charles "Lucky" Luciano was a vicious thug and gangster who "sat way up at the top in his apartment at the Waldorf as the czar of organized crime in this city."

So much for the presumption of innocence, George thought as he sat, dumbfounded, watching the scene unfold. And so much for limiting the people's proof to only those matters charged in the indictment.

While defense counsel were still pissing blood from these early kidney punches, another, graver problem became apparent to George on the trial's third day. It happened during the course of Dewey's formal opening statement, the one given after the twelve trial jurors and two alternates had finally been seated and sworn.

As George understood it, the whole rationale of the joinder law was one of convenience, in that it allowed a prosecutor to charge and try multiple felonies against multiple defendants under a single indictment. In making his case to the legislature, Dewey had argued that the crime of conspiracy—which allows a similar outcome, but constitutes only a misdemeanor—was inadequate to deal with the growing scourge of organized crime in New York. The legislature agreed, and New York's Code of Criminal Procedure was amended accordingly, just in time for the Luciano trial.

An attribute unique to the law of conspiracy, however, is that the hearsay statements of one co-conspirator are admissible as evidence against the others, even if the original speaker is unavailable to testify as a witness. Thus, what would otherwise be inadmissible hearsay— for example, when Wilma Witness testifies that Mike Missing told her that Danny Defendant said such-and-such—is admissible in a conspiracy case against the speaker's co-conspirators as long as the hearsay statement was made during the course of and in furtherance of the conspiracy.

Acting as a counterweight to this liberal rule of evidence is the requirement that, before a conviction can be had, the testimony of a co-conspirator must be corroborated "by such other evidence as tends to connect the defendant with the commission of the crime." In other words, the mere hearsay statements of co-conspirators are insufficient, by and of themselves, to uphold a conspiracy conviction.

But during his second opening statement, Dewey had described to the jurors threats allegedly made by unindicted individuals like former bookers Nick Montana and Cockeyed Louis Weiner—speakers who, Dewey acknowledged, he had no intention of ever calling to testify. When objection was made that such hearsay testimony would therefore be improper if offered at trial, since no conspiracy was alleged in the indictment, it was again overruled by McCook.

Thus, George realized, Dewey had chosen not to plead conspiracy in order to avoid the sentencing limitations of a misdemeanor prosecution, but now wanted the benefit of the liberal rules of evidence as they pertain to a conspiracy case. Moreover, Dewey wanted those rules to apply without the risk of the jury acquitting the defendants on the conspiracy charge—for example, due to lack of corroboration—which would ordinarily render all the co-conspirator testimony retroactively inadmissible. And McCook, it appeared, was perfectly willing to oblige him.

The ramifications of this development were profound. Dewey could, for example, claim that all the dozens of madams, bookers, bondsmen, and managers of the so-called vice combination were co-conspirators, even though no conspiracy had been alleged in the indictment. This meant that any of the madams, for example, could take the stand and say something like, "Cockeyed Louis told me I had to bond because Charlie Lucky said so," and that McCook was prepared to allow such rank hearsay into the record as evidence against Luciano.

George had played against stacked decks before. He'd survived a dozen trials before Lew Smith, for example, and he'd often come out on top. But this was a horse of a different color. George had had no role in the pretrial skirmishing and no chance to anticipate the prosecution's strategy. Indeed, he'd had no opportunity to even meet with the judge until the first day of trial, and it seemed to him now that whatever impressions his co-counsel had already made, they had served only to stoke McCook's innate hostility toward the defense side of the courtroom.

Polakoff, at least, was proving to be a competent, dignified trial attorney. The same could be said of Sam Siegel, Frederico's lawyer, and Maurice Cantor, who represented the fourth and final booker-defendant, Jack Eller. James Murray, appearing on behalf of the un-licensed bondsmen Jesse Jacobs and Meyer Berkman, and David Paley, counsel for the shylock Bennie Spiller, both seemed to be taking a page from the Levy-Polakoff playbook and keeping as low a profile as possible. As for Caesar Barra, who represented both Pennochio and Betillo, and David Siegel, who represented Abie Wahrman, George had yet to form an opinion.

The main burrs under McCook's saddle appeared to be Kopp, who also represented Pennochio, and attorney Lorenzo Carlino, counsel for defendant Ralph Liguori. Both lawyers were brash and outspoken and openly antagonistic toward Dewey, and both were irritating the judge with a steady stream of interruptions and talking objections. McCook, for his part, was tempering his anger and maintaining a clean appellate record. This, George knew from experience, was a sign that the old judge expected the case to end in conviction. George wondered if Kopp and Carlino could see this as well.

As for the man they called Charlie Lucky, George had to admit to actually liking his notorious client. Most men in Luciano's position would have been frightened, or angry, or some combination of both. They'd have blustered and bellowed, fulminated and fumed. But Luciano proved to be gracious and soft-spoken and showed a keen interest in his lawyers' discussions of trial strategy and tactics. It was Luciano, in fact, who'd first commented on Liguori's lawyer, saying, "McCook is like God to them guys on the jury, and that puts horns on that loudmouth Carlino."

"He's only protecting the record," George told him. "We all may burn in hell before this is over."

"Not you, counselor. Them jurors might worship McCook, but it's you they'd bring home to dinner."

"You think so?"

"Listen. If there's one thing I know, it's people. While you're watchin the judge and the witnesses, I'm studyin them guys in the jury box. As far as they're concerned there's only three people in that courtroom, and that's McCook, Dewey, and you. McCook they respect like a father. Dewey gets on their nerves a little, like a know-it-all kid brother, but at least they admire his moxie. You, Levy, you're like their favorite Jewish uncle."

"I wouldn't put too much stock in the lawyers, Charlie. Remember, what we say isn't evidence. If the jury likes Dewey's witnesses, then they'll believe Dewey's case. It's our job to see that they don't."

"I can't see 'em likin that bunch of sleazy pimps and whores."

"I hope you're right, and that the cumulative effect will work in our favor. I only wish we knew who Dewey plans to call about that supposed meeting downtown."

"It has to be one of the old bookers," Polakoff said. "Charlie Spinach, or maybe Spike Green. They're both up on the poster board."

"Don't lose any sleep over them guys," Lucky assured them. "They know better than to rat. Prison's a tough stretch to begin with, but it's hell for a guy who's a rat."

"It's clear that our friend Mr. Dewey has somebody up his sleeve. If he didn't, he wouldn't have said what he did in his opening."

"Yeah, well, you know what, counselor?" Lucky stretched his legs, lacing his hands behind his neck. "What Dewey's got and what Dewey thinks he's got might turn out to be two different things."

Thirty-Five

Cold Feet

May 1936

TOM STOOD, FISTS on hips, towering over the fidgeting man.

"What the hell are you trying to say?"

Charles Burke, the former whorehouse booker known in the trade as Good-Time Charlie, was hunched forward in his chair. Again he ran a hand over his face.

"I can't do it, Mr. Dewey. I won't do it."

"You haven't any choice, you ninny. You're under subpoena. We have your witness statement right here. You signed it under penalty of perjury!"

Tom snapped his fingers. Sol Gelb dug the document from his briefcase and handed it to the special prosecutor.

"You said right here . . . you were called to a meeting downtown . . . all the bookers were there. Then Little Davie came in . . . and when Charlie Lucky walked into the room, all the Italians stood up.

248

Lucky said, 'You guys are through. I'm giving the business to Little Davie.' Then Lucky walked out again, and all the Italians were still standing. Do you deny saying this?"

"I don't deny saying it. It's just that it ain't true, that's all."

"You testified before the grand jury!"

"Okay, so sue me. You asked me for a story and I gave you one. You put me on the stand now and that's exactly what I'm gonna say."

Barent Ten Eyck had entered from the courtroom. When he saw the look on his boss's face, he halted in the doorway.

"Listen, you. I'll put you on that stand, and if you so much as change a word of your sworn testimony, I'll prosecute you for perjury. I'll handle your trial myself, do you hear me?"

Good-Time Charlie shrugged. "Do what you gotta to do, Mr. Dewey, but I ain't gonna say what you want me to say."

Tom's face had turned crimson. He looked to Gelb, who gestured toward the doorway with his head.

"We'll be right back. Officer, keep a close eye on this man."

Tom stalked into the vacant courtroom, trailed by Gelb and Ten Eyck. The main doors to the hallway were closed and locked for the lunch recess, but the clerk and the court stenographer were still inside, still busy shuffling papers. Tom strode toward the door to the empty jury room.

"What?" Ten Eyck asked when the door had closed behind them.

"It's a run-out," Gelb told him. "He says he won't testify."

"Nuts."

"He's obviously been threatened." Tom was pacing now, slapping the witness statement against his thigh. "Luciano's boys got to him somehow. But how, Sol? How did you let this happen?"

"That's one possibility."

"What do you mean by that?"

Gelb shrugged. "I mean, maybe he's telling the truth. Maybe he made up the whole downtown meeting story. No one else has ever corroborated it."

"Damn it, Sol! I used that testimony in my opening! We've promised it to the jury!"

Gelb hiked his hip onto the conference table. He flipped a page on his legal pad, studying the list of witnesses.

"The whole point of calling Peluso was to set up Good-Time Charlie. Now what should we do?"

"Recover, that's what. We'll need another witness and pronto. Who's available?"

"We can move up a few of the girls. Betty Baker, Helen Hayes, Gussie Silver, and Helen Walsh. Run the clock out today and then start strong tomorrow with Pete Harris."

"Damn it all!"

Ten Eyck cleared his throat.

"What?"

"I was going to save this until later, but . . . I've got news. Good news, I think."

"Well?"

"I got a note the other night from a girl in the drug ward at the House of Detention. Fay Marston is her name, but she's known as Cokey Flo Brown."

"That's your good news? Another junkie inmate?"

"This junkie I think you're going to like. She wasn't part of the original sweep. She was picked up for solicitation on May the eighth. Turns out she's Frederico's girlfriend. That part's on the level. She ran a house that got busted in January, and she skipped bail on three misdemeanor counts. You remember those 'Dear Cousin' letters to Frederico?"

"Yes?"

"Well, she's the one who wrote 'em. Only now she's sore at the big guy and says she wants to cooperate."

"She's a plant," Gelb said. "A ringer."

"Could be, but I don't think so."

Tom had stopped pacing and stood with his fists on his hips.

"Can she give us Luciano?"

"I don't know. She's playing it cute for now, and she's still pretty sick from the cure, but she's dropping some pretty broad hints. Says she spent a lot of time with Frederico. Lived with him, talked with him, even drove him to his meetings."

"For God's sake, Barry. When can we get her to testify?"

"I'm meeting her again tonight. We'll have to promise her something, that much I know. She's weak as a kitten, but she's no bunny."

"What's her status on the solicitation charge?"

"Guilty and awaiting sentence."

"Good. Get the sentencing postponed. Do it now, before we go back. Then tonight you tell her she's facing time on the misdemeanors, time for the bail violation, and five to ten for solicitation. Twenty years in total. Give her the hard sell, Barry. Make her come around."

Ten Eyck looked to Gelb, who grinned. "Tell her you'll marry her."

"Whatever you do," Tom said, poking Ten Eyck's chest with the rolled-up witness statement, "close the deal tonight. We just lost half our case against Luciano. Use good judgment, but for God's sake, do whatever it takes!"

Thirty-Six

The Hard Sell

May 1936

IT WAS SOME BIG shot's office where we met, with wicker chairs and a comfortable leather couch and a carved wooden desk. On the desk were pictures I couldn't see in heavy silver frames, and a fancy inkwell in some kind of greenish jade or marble. More important, there was a half-full bottle of brandy standing open next to the inkwell.

That's why I was laying down as I talked, resting a coffee mug on my stomach, and why Mr. Ten Eyck, who said to call him Barry, was pacing back and forth, back and forth, on the other side of the desk.

"So that's how I come to meet Jimmy," I said, finishing my story. "Charlie Spinach was there, and they gave me their spiel on the bonding, and I agreed to play along."

"But really you just wanted to meet Frederico?"

"I guess. I mean, I knew I had to bond if I wanted to stay in the business. But yeah, I wanted to meet this Jimmy Fredericks everybody was talking about. I figured if he was the muscle, then he was the guy I should get to know."

"And then what happened? You actually fell for him?"

I shrugged. "I guess you could say I fell for Jimmy. He was a hardluck story, just like me. We were both a couple of mutts. Turns out we had a lot in common."

"And since Jimmy didn't drive, you chauffeured him around?"

"Sometimes. Like if it was late, and if his pal Danny wasn't around, and if taxis were hard to come by."

"So you must have driven him to some of his meetings with the other combination guys—Tommy the Bull and Little Davie and Charlie Lucky."

It was funny, lying on the couch like that and talking to the ceiling. Like visiting a headshrinker. It made you really focus on what you were saying. And the brandy didn't hurt one bit. In fact, it was the best I'd felt in over a week.

"There you go again with Charlie Lucky," I said to the ceiling, which had a wicker fan with a pull chain. "If that's what you're after, then why don't you say so?"

"I'm only after the truth."

"Yeah, sure. You're like that old man with the lantern."

"I'm certainly not going to put words in your mouth."

"Relax, Barry, you don't have to. I get the picture. Dewey's the monkey, and Charlie Lucky's the weasel. But just out of curiosity, what does that make you?"

I snuck a peek at Ten Eyck. When he wasn't pacing, he was bent over the desk, scribbling notes on a pad. Only this time he was just standing there, watching me where I lay. Even checking out my legs.

"I guess you could say this monkey has coattails."

"Let's hope so, for both our sakes."

"So about Charlie Lucky . . ."

"I read the newspapers. For example, I read where your boss called him public enemy number one."

"But you know him, right? You know what he looks like?"

"Sure I know Lucky. He's tall, but he's kinda short. Thin, but a bit on the heavy side."

"You've seen his picture, haven't you?"

"I said I read the newspapers."

"Do you think you could pick him out of a lineup?"

"I know I could."

"How about a crowded courtroom?"

I propped myself on an elbow and took another sip of the brandy.

"I don't know about a courtroom. I suppose that depends."

"Depends on what?"

"On what kind of a deal I was offered. My memory is fuzzy these days. Sometimes I remember things, and sometimes I don't."

"Look, Flo. All the girls who've testified have gotten the same deal. You'll receive immunity from prosecution for whatever you say on the witness stand. As far as the pending charges go, we'll do everything in our lawful power to get them dismissed. On the prostitution conviction, we'll appear at your sentencing and inform the court that you've been a cooperating witness. We can't guarantee it, but that usually means a suspended sentence."

He was a funny bird, this Ten Eyck. Tall and thin, and though he didn't look that old, he was already losing his hair. Attractive, if you go for the type that looks like he's just stepped down from his sailing yacht. Fair-haired, I guess you might call him, with a long nose and a pointy chin and rimless eyeglasses. He looked a little like Violet's brother Ralph.

"I heard a different story, Barry. I heard girls got out of jail and got taken places."

"Yes, but they're being held as material witnesses, whereas you've been convicted and remanded into custody. I'm afraid there's only so much we can do in your case."

254

"And I'm afraid my memory is starting to fade again."

"Come on, Flo, you're a smart girl. Maybe the smartest of the bunch. Why don't you quit chewing gum and put your cards on the table?"

I half rolled on the couch to look at him.

"You want cards? Okay, here's a card. Like I said, I read the newspapers. So far as I can tell, you and your pal Dewey ain't had a single witness who could put Lucky in a room with any of them other guys."

"We've got witnesses. We just haven't called them yet."

"Oh yeah, who? Nancy Presser? Thelma Jordan? Good luck with them. A couple of dumb Doras. Either one would sell her own sister for a half cube of morphine."

"Sure, like you wouldn't."

I relaxed onto my back again, the coffee mug resting on my stomach like a whispered promise.

"Oh, Barry. You think I'm just some two-dollar bag, but I got news for you. When you were learning your algebra, I was running my own speak. When you were pinning your first girlfriend, I was fucking two of the biggest gangsters in Chicago. I been around the block, honey, and I learned some things."

"We were talking about cards."

"Okay then, here's another. A little birdy told me that Nancy and Thelma are getting a trip to Europe after the trial. Me, I could use a vacation. Especially if Lucky and Little Davie walk, which it sounds like they might. And if that happens, we'll all need to disappear. Maybe even you. Maybe even your boss."

"What you've heard is nothing but gossip and rumor. Nobody's getting any trips. And if you're worried about reprisals, we can protect you."

"Yeah, right. But you know what worries me most? How I'm gonna live when this thing is over. Times are hard, in case you ain't noticed. Oh, I can type all right, but who's gonna hire me? I don't suppose Mr. Dewey is looking for a secretary?"

Barry stopped his pacing and sat. He screwed the cap onto his pen and set it down next to the pad.

"All right, Flo, we don't have all night. What did you have in mind?"

"That's more like it."

I sat up and swung my feet to the floor. I had to wait for a second until the room quit spinning around.

"I know you can't write me a check or anything, so I got to thinking about all those reporters over at the courthouse, all scrapping over the same lousy story like dogs over a bone. And then it came to me that the girl who sends Charlie Lucky to prison is gonna have her name in every newspaper in the country. Maybe even in newsreels and magazines. She could be bigger than Mae West if she plays her cards right."

"Funny you should say that."

"Why?"

"Never mind. Go on, I'm listening."

"So what I figured is, that's gotta be worth something, right? Her life story, I mean. Her exclusive life story should be worth a pretty penny to a magazine or even a movie studio. Especially if someone with coattails were to put in a word to someplace like, say, *Liberty* magazine."

Barry didn't say anything at first. He just sat there with his mouth tight, spinning his pen around like a propeller. And then:

"You understand I can't make any promises. If I did, and the defense were to ask you what we talked about, then you'd have to tell them the truth. So let's speak hypothetically for a second, just you and me."

"That's what I thought we were doing."

"You're right that Mr. Dewey knows a lot of important people, and you're also right that the magazines and the studios have been pestering us, looking for the inside dope."

"There you go. Now you're on the trolley."

"From everything I've heard so far, yours is exactly the kind of story that a magazine might pay good money for. But it needs the right ending, Flo, and it won't have the right ending unless Charlie Lucky is convicted. And that means you taking the stand and tying him directly to the others in the combination."

"I understand."

"Good. Now we're both on the trolley. So go ahead and tell me a story. If I think it's any good, then we'll get a stenographer in here and we'll put it down on paper. After that, I'll take it to Mr. Dewey. He'll want to question you himself, which means that the story you tell now and the story you tell Mr. Dewey have got to jibe. That means no loose ends and no contradictions. Then if he gives the okay, you'll get to tell that story on the witness stand."

"In front of Jimmy and Charlie Lucky."

"And all those hungry reporters. And it better match exactly the story you told in writing, because their lawyers will be getting a copy of the transcript, and they'll turn you upside down looking for inconsistencies. If you do all of that, then after the trial is over, we'll talk again about magazines and movie studios."

"But you can't make any promises."

He didn't answer, so I just sat there for a minute, studying the angles. For something like the twentieth time.

"You really think you can nail Charlie Lucky?"

"We *will* nail Lucky, with or without your help."

"Which means you've got somebody else besides me who'll testify against him?"

"We have several witnesses, only one of whom you've even mentioned."

"And how much do you think a magazine or a movie studio might pay for the exclusive rights to a story like mine? Hypothetically speaking, of course."

"I can't say for certain. I would think a few grand at least."

"At the very least?"

"At the very least."

I nodded. I was feeling tired all of a sudden, and brandy or no brandy, the shakes were coming on.

"Can I have a night or two to think it over and give you my answer then?"

He stood and began gathering up his things.

"You can have one night. After tomorrow, all bets are off. With the bail violation and now the solicitation conviction, that means twenty years, Flo, and Mr. Dewey will see that you serve every day of your sentence. And believe me, when you hear that iron door slam shut behind you, you'll rue the day you let this opportunity pass."

I believed him all right, and I knew he knew I believed him.

"Okay, Barry. You'll have my answer tomorrow."

"That's a smart girl. And just to be clear, I've made no promises about any magazine or movie deal, or about anything else for that matter. I'm going out on a limb for you, Flo, so don't saw it off and leave me hanging."

"I understand. I'd never do that."

"Okay, then. Now the ball's in your court."

Thirty-Seven

What Goes Around

May 1936

LUCKY HAS BEEN counting the witnesses on a yellow legal pad, marking with a series of vertical lines and slashes their halting procession from the side doorway of the courtroom to the elevated witness chair—five witnesses to a group, seven groups in total, the marks evoking ordered sheaves of wheat, or maybe pencils brimming from a row of beggars' cups.

Thirty-six pencils so far, and not a single witness who has directly tied Lucky to the so-called bonding combination.

Some, it is true, have mentioned his name. Bookers Dave Miller, Danny Brooks, and Pete Harris have all testified to conversations they'd supposedly had with others—Fredericks, for example, or Wahrman—in which each had been convinced of the combination's legitimacy on the ground that it was backed by Charlie Lucky. While distressing to hear, these statements, or so Lucky has been assured by both Polakoff and Levy, are not enough to support a conviction.

"We knew there'd be hearsay linking you to the others," Levy tells Lucky after another day of testimony, "and it's unfortunate that the judge is letting it in. But it's meaningless without corroboration from an actual eyewitness who wasn't part of the conspiracy. That means one of the prostitutes, or else maybe a third party. That's what we need to worry about."

"What witnesses? I'm fallin asleep out there, listenin to them whores pile dirt on these other guys' coffins."

"Don't worry," Levy says, "they're coming. If they weren't, you wouldn't have been indicted in the first place."

Then, just as Levy has predicted, the first of them finally appears. It is Thursday morning, the ninth day of the trial, and the witness in question is a recidivist hotel burglar named Joe Bendix.

Under direct questioning by Dewey, Bendix claims to have known Lucky for eight or nine years, and says he was looking for work as a collector for the combination in May or June of 1935 when he was introduced to Jimmy Fredericks by a man named Charlie the Barber. Fredericks supposedly told Bendix that he'd have to run the matter past Lucky Luciano. A few days later, Bendix was instructed to come to the Villanova Restaurant on West 46th Street to meet with Lucky in person. Bendix arrived with his fiancée and found Fredericks and Lucky sitting at a table. After a few minutes, Lucky came over and sat with Bendix, telling him, "If you're willing to work for forty dollars a week, that's okay with me. I'll tell Little Davie to put you on."

Two weeks later, according to Bendix, he again met with Lucky at the Villanova, where Bendix reiterated his interest in the job. Lucky instructed Bendix to report to a man named Binge at the Hotel Wolcott, saying, "He'll take care of you." He then added cryptically, "When you go around to collect, once you get wise to things, you can make yourself a little extra on the side, from the madams."

Bendix concludes his testimony by stating that he'd never managed to connect with Binge, that he'd found other work instead, and therefore that he'd never actually gone to work for the combination.

Dewey then tenders the witness.

"This bastard is so fulla shit his eyes are brown," Lucky whispers to Levy, a vise grip on the lawyer's arm. "Not one fuckin word of what he said is true!"

Lucky's hands, at first balled under the table in rage, begin to loosen once Levy rises and steps to the lectern and begins his gentle cross-examination of Joe Bendix.

He starts with Bendix's criminal history. It is an exhausting recitation of burglaries, arrests, convictions, and incarcerations that begins at the Bridgeport, Connecticut, city jail at age seventeen, ends at Sing Sing prison at age thirty-eight, and includes intermediate stops at the Elmira Reformatory, Sing Sing, the Welfare Island Workhouse, the Ohio State Prison at Columbus, three more visits to Sing Sing, and a penultimate incarceration at the Welfare Island Penitentiary. With Levy's seamless repertoire of questions, asides, vocal inflections, and facial expressions, Bendix is gradually transformed from an earnest volunteer witness into an unrepentant and calculating thief who might very well steal the judge's gavel should the bailiff make the mistake of turning his head.

With the stage thus set, Levy next probes Bendix's claim to have known Lucky for many years. Bendix says he was first introduced to Lucky by a man named Captain Dutton at the Club Richman back in 1928. Only Bendix cannot describe this Captain Dutton—Tall or short? Fat or thin?—and further cannot describe the mutual friend, a Mrs. Casner, who allegedly introduced them. Then Bendix makes his first critical mistake.

Q: How old a man was Captain Dutton, about?

A: A man about 38 or 39 years old.

Q: Give us a good description, will you please, of Captain Dutton?

261

A: I don't recall. I met the man—that is almost eight years ago, and I met him for a half hour.

Q: Yes. But you remember Luciano in great detail, don't you?

A: I know him longer than I know Captain Dutton.

Q: What is that?

A: I know him longer than I know Captain Dutton.

The witness, clearly rattled by Levy's probing, is soon stumbling over other aspects of his story.

Q: Were some extra chairs brought up to the table?

A: There were chairs at the table.

Q: Did you expect somebody?

A: No, that is the way the table was situated.

Q: I beg your pardon?

A: That is the amount of chairs that were at the table. There were four or five chairs at the table.

Q: Just a moment. Richman's Club is a pretty crowded club, is it not?

A: That is right.

Q: And you were sitting at Richman's Club with a party of three and you have got five chairs at the table, have you?

A: The only table available.

. . .

Q: About how many extra chairs were there?

A: There were four or five. The place was not crowded.

Lucky is watching the jury, watching their faith in Joe Bendix evaporate like dew on a hot summer sidewalk. Watching Dewey's face redden, like that of a cartoon thermometer on the verge of exploding. Watching Bendix, shifting and fidgeting in the witness chair, growing ever more combative and insolent as Levy peels his story apart like an onion.

Then, as Levy is examining Bendix about his failed second marriage, Dewey finally does explode, bursting the bubble of cool confidence that had theretofore enveloped the special prosecutor, and for the first time in the course of the trial, Dewey is gently admonished by Judge McCook.

Q: And how long before January first, 1935, were you giving your wife and child nothing?

A: I didn't have much time to give her anything; a short time—

Q: How long before January first, 1935 were you giving her nothing?

A: Will you let me answer that question the way you wanted it?

Q: How long? That calls for time, please.

A: I was only out of prison a short while, and the woman had left me while I was in prison. What do you expect me to do, support her during the time I was in prison and she left me?

MR. LEVY: I am sorry I cannot answer that, but the Court does not permit it, you see.

THE WITNESS: Well then, you asked for it and you got it.

THE COURT: I think instead you had better answer the counsel's question.

Q: You like to volunteer, do you not?

A: In what way?

MR. DEWEY: I object to that, because the witness has been amazingly free from that.

THE COURT: Sustained.

MR. LEVY: I object to the characterization of Mr. Dewey. The witness has been just to the contrary, I maintain, and

MR. DEWEY: Just as I object to counsel's voluntary statements.

MR. LEVY: Will you kindly show the courtesy of listening for once, until counsel is finished? And remember you are not running this courtroom?

C. Joseph Greaves

MR. DEWEY: I have listened for long, and I am tired of being bullied by counsel for Luciano, just because he is counsel for Luciano.

MR. LEVY: Now may it please the Court, I resent that statement, I except to it, and I ask your Honor to rebuke the learned Special Prosecutor for the remarks he made.

THE COURT: That is a little too much like what was said the other day, Mr. Dewey. I do not think you ought to say it. Proceed.

MR. LEVY: I thank your Honor.

Levy next moves to the first of the two alleged meetings, in May or June of 1935, at the Villanova Restaurant. He begins by establishing the presence of Bendix's soon-to-be third wife, a woman named Joy Dixon, at the first of those meetings.

Q: Were you standing up at this particular time?
A: Sitting down.
Q: You remained sitting down?
A: That is right.
Q: At a table with your wife?
A: Yes, not when Luciano walked over.
Q: Wait a minute. What did you do with your wife?
A: I asked her to excuse me when Fredericks came over to the table.
Q: And then she left the table?
A: That is right.
Q: Where did she go?
A: She sat at another table a few tables away.

Then Levy moves to the second meeting and to Bendix's decision to take the job that he, in the final analysis, never performed.

Q: Had you made up your mind at that time whether you wanted to go into the whorehouse business?

A: Yes, sir.

Q: You had made up your mind you wanted to go in the business?

A: Yes, sir.

Q: So the second time you met Charlie Lucky, you were ready to become a collector for whorehouses, is that right?

A: That is right.

Finally, Levy moves to Bendix's last arrest and the circumstances under which he became a witness for the prosecution.

Q: Did you start your sentence in Sing Sing before you wrote to anybody in connection with any crime?

A: I wrote before I got my sentence.

Q: You wrote before you got your sentence. And whom did you write to then?

A: I wrote a letter to Mr. Dewey.

Q: You wrote a letter to Mr. Dewey. Had you previously written a letter to Mr. Dodge, the District Attorney of New York County?

A: I did.

. . .

Q: Where were you when you wrote Mr. Dewey a letter?

A: Tombs Prison.

Q: New York City?

A: That is right.

Q: You wrote and indicated to Mr. Dewey you might know something about this case, is that right?

A: I did.

. . .

Q: What hotel did you operate in the last time?

A: Hotel Madison.

Q: New York City?

A: Right.

Q: Do you remember the room that you got into?

A: I do.

Q: Do you remember the name of the man?

A: I do.

Q: What was his name?

A: Sackett.

Q: Mr. Sackett, the hotel manager?

A: That is right.

Q: And you entered his room, did you not?

A: That is right.

Q: And nobody was there when you got in, was there?

A: That is right.

Q: And you robbed the room of certain things, certain possessions, did you not?

A: That is right.

Q: And that was the last case in which you were involved?

A: That is right.

Q: I will return to that in a moment. What was the last sentence in connection with that crime?

A: Fifteen years to life.

Q: Life is what is called for under the Baumes Act, is it not?

A: No, not life. Fifteen years to life.

Q: Fifteen years to life. That is your final conviction; is that true?

A: That is true . . .

Q: Did Mr. Dewey promise you that if you told the truth as he thought the truth was, that he would try to help you in connection with your troubles?

A: He did, yes.

Q: He did tell you that much?

A: Yes.

Q: And you believed him, did you not?

A: I did . . .

Q: And you were reading the newspapers pretty carefully at that time, were you not?

A: I was.

Q: And you knew about this alleged charge of prostitution at that time, did you not?

A: I did.

Q: And you read in the papers that Charlie Lucky was supposedly the head of it, did you not?

A: I did.

Levy passes the witness. He sits and confers with his client while Sam Siegel takes over the lectern.

"That was fuckin beautiful," Lucky whispers, peering over Levy's shoulder. "The jury ain't buyin a single thing this lousy crumb is sellin. And for that matter, neither is the judge."

"I hope you're right. But we need to find this Captain Dutton, and we need to find Bendix's wife."

"If this guy claims to know me for so many years, then how come he had to go through Fredericks to ask me for a fuckin job?"

"Exactly. A job he decided to take, yet somehow never got around to performing. The whole thing reeks to high heaven."

Lucky nods to the prosecution table, where Dewey, still red-faced, huddles with his assistants.

"Get a load of the Boy Scout. He looks like a kid who just lost his birthday balloon."

" 'They have sown the wind,' " Levy quotes from Scripture, " 'and they shall reap the whirlwind.' "

"You mean what goes around comes around?"

"Just a moment," Levy says, laying a hand on Lucky's arm. Siegel has concluded his questioning, and Levy now stands to address the judge before Bendix can be excused.

"May I also say this? We shall make an effort to locate this man's wife, and if we do—I do not know with what success—we would like to have the opportunity of recalling this man as a witness."

"You want me to reserve your right in case you do?" McCook asks Levy.

"That is right."

"Very well," the judge says, bending forward and making a note.

Thirty-Eight

Wondering

May 1936

GEORGE KNEW THAT his client had dodged a bullet. Only an exceptionally bright and personable witness can get away with back-talking and wisecracking on cross-examination, and Bendix was neither bright nor personable. As a result, he'd alienated both the judge and the jury and had, for the first time since the trial had begun, even rubbed a little tarnish onto the sterling-silver facade of the learned special prosecutor.

All of which raised the question of what, exactly, Dewey had been thinking. Surely he'd known that the testimony of an eight-time loser desperate to avoid life in Sing Sing would carry little weight to begin with. Add to that the man's improbable story, which, not incidentally, contradicted the entire prosecution narrative of Luciano as a hands-off overlord working only through layers of intermediaries. Lastly, Bendix had made the mistake of including at least three eyewitnesses in his story—his wife, Mrs. Casner, and Captain Dutton—and if any of them could be located, then he'd opened himself up to devastating collateral impeachment.

Was that Dewey's best punch? If so, then what did it say about the rest of his case against Luciano? As an experienced trial lawyer, Dewey surely knew the cardinal rules of primacy and recency—that you start strong and you finish strong if you want to have the maximum impact on a jury. If Bendix was, in fact, the prosecution's biggest weapon against Luciano, then what was left in Dewey's arsenal?

Not all George's thoughts, however, were so upbeat. As he'd turned from the podium after cross-examining Bendix, George had noticed Luciano sharing a look with Tommy Pennochio. In fact, George had noted over the course of the trial's first week a disquieting familiarity between Luciano and some of his co-defendants—particularly Betillo, Pennochio, and Liguori. It could, of course, be a simple matter of ethnic affinity. But the ease with which Pennochio and Liguori seemed to greet Luciano each morning and their tendency to huddle and whisper at the end of each day's testimony were ringing familiar bells inside George's head—bells he knew from experience he could ignore only at his peril.

These and other thoughts were racing through George's mind as Dewey assistant Harry Cole led yet another young prostitute—this one a pretty little girl named Shirley Mason—through a direct examination that appeared to be aimed at Jack Eller. Eller was the client of Maurice Cantor, and was the only one of the booker-defendants who hadn't yet taken a guilty plea. George had tuned out the witness and was focused instead on Dewey, watching him slip out of the courtroom and return again through the side door that led to the witness room.

The jurors, too, were watching. If George had learned anything in his twenty-plus years before the bar, it was to never underestimate the observational powers of jurors. For example, George had always worn a wedding band in court, even when between marriages. Once, in the middle of a lengthy jury trial, he'd been running late for court and had slipped the wrong band—a similar one, but the one from his first marriage—onto his finger. The trial had lasted for over two weeks, and once it was finished and George was speaking with the jurors about their verdict, one of them had said to him, "Mr. Levy, we were all wondering why you wore a different wedding ring to court last Thursday."

George was also wondering. Wondering what was so special about the next witness that she merited the personal attention of the special prosecutor. Wondering why Dewey and Gelb were huddling again, their conversation animated, both of them ignoring Cole as he droned on about Shirley Mason's finances, and her stolen wristwatch, and her positive Wasserman test. Wondering why the spring seemed to have returned to the special prosecutor's step.

Moe Polakoff also returned to the courtroom, interrupting George's reverie as he eased into his seat on the other side of their client. After a moment, Polakoff passed a folded slip of paper to George, who, after checking that none of the jurors was watching, held it under the table as he read.

George Paul Dutton
State Police Captain

It was six thirty P.M., and Shirley Mason was just stepping down from the witness chair when Dewey rose to his feet, his gaze pausing on the jury before turning to the bailiff who guarded the side door of the courtroom.

"Flo Brown!" he announced with a flourish.

Thirty-Nine

First Impressions

SHE ENTERED THE COURTROOM in a baggy blue dress and a tilted hat with a veil. Her gait was shuffling, her body caved to one side, and she used the rail of the jury box to steady herself as she walked. As she laid her hand on the Bible, Tom half turned to the door through which Eunice Carter and Barry Ten Eyck had quietly entered behind her. Mrs. Carter nodded. Ten Eyck, poker-faced, moved to his place beside Sol Gelb at the prosecution table.

Still standing, Tom cleared his throat and took a long drink of water. This, he recognized, was the trial's critical moment. It was George Medalie's ruby-red nose. It was the cadenza to the final aria that would evoke either jeers or bravos from the special prosecutor's captive audience of blue-ribbon jurors.

Good-Time Charlie had been a run-out, and Joe Bendix had laid a sulfurous egg whose stench still permeated the highest corners of the courtroom. All of which had left but two crooked arrows in the witness quiver Tom held in reserve for Lucky Luciano: the call-girl Nancy Presser and Mildred Balitzer, the blowsy wife of booker Pete Harris.

Both women were prostitutes, and both were heroin addicts. Neither was what you'd call Phi Beta Kappa material. And then, as if by some golden miracle of providence, Cokey Flo Brown had appeared in his office like Venus in a clamshell, thanks to Barry Ten Eyck's nightly forays into the Women's House of Detention.

Thank God, Tom thought, for Barry Ten Eyck.

Tom watched as the wraithlike figure—his unlikely diva—settled into the witness chair. Cokey Flo was dirty blonde and hazel-eyed and, despite her medical condition, actually looked younger than her given age of twenty-nine years. Best of all, her dissipated appearance, Tom could tell, was already arousing the paternal sympathies of the gray-haired gentlemen of the jury.

Sympathy was exactly what Tom had been hoping for, while its corollary—that Cokey Flo would be unable to withstand the grueling rigors of direct and cross-examination—remained his greatest fear. That she would break down or, worse yet, recant her story under the menacing gaze of Charlie Lucky, or the pleading eyes of Jimmy Fredericks, or the exhaustive, surgical probing of George Morton Levy.

If you'd asked him that morning, Tom would have set the odds of his calling Florence Brown to the witness stand at no better than even money. Although she'd seemed credible last night, when Tom had grilled her for two solid hours, there was still the possibility—as Sol Gelb had repeatedly cautioned—that Cokey Flo was a Trojan horse: a time bomb planted by Luciano to detonate inside the courtroom, blowing what remained of their case against him to smithereens.

And this wasn't the only cautionary note sounded by little Sol. "What if Mildred Balitzer and Nancy Presser are bald-faced liars?" he'd asked Tom in private. "What if they're fingering Luciano just to save their own skins? And what if Cokey Flo is doing the same?"

"You don't really believe that, I hope."

"I don't know, chief. It's gotten to the point where I don't know what to believe."

Tom had maintained an even keel, but Sol's words—his fretful skepticism—had hit him like a tidal wave. If his own men were starting to doubt the case's merits, then what did that say about the prospects for a guilty verdict?

Doubt was like a slow drip that, if left unchecked, could undermine a foundation and bring down an entire building. What if there'd been no downtown meeting as described by Good-Time Charlie, and no job interview at the Villanova as Joe Bendix had testified? What if they and the other key witnesses were simply inserting Luciano into their own life stories, like one of those novelty photos you could take on Coney Island that showed you sparring with Jack Dempsey?

Had Tom and his men leaned too heavily on the witnesses? Had they promised too much for their cooperation? A week ago, Tom would have dismissed such questions out of hand. Of course Lucky was behind the combination! Nearly a dozen witnesses had said as much. But now, after Bendix and Good Time Charlie . . .

They'd had no time to investigate Cokey Flo's story, and they had no eyewitnesses to corroborate it. Worse, they had no grand jury transcript with which to impeach her should she pull a double-cross. Her very appearance in the case was anathema to every guiding principle of the special prosecutor's office—Tom's consecrated temple of meticulous preparation, exhaustive fact-checking, and scrupulous background investigation.

He was, in short, taking a huge gamble. But any qualms he'd felt that morning had been erased by Levy's slashing cross-examination of Bendix. So poor was the hotel thief on the stand that Tom had hastily scrapped his plan to call Joy Dixon, Bendix's wife, who'd been waiting in the adjoining room, as his next witness. Instead, he'd had Mrs. Carter spirit her out of the building—let Levy find her himself, he'd whispered to Sol—forcing Cokey Flo, with whom they'd hoped to share at least one more night of preparation, into the witness box with only half an hour left in the day.

In practice we learn how to weld, Tom reminded himself. There was no room for doubts, and now that Cokey Flo was on the witness stand, there was no turning back.

Q: Is Florence Brown your right name?

A: Yes, it is.

Q: Have you sometimes been referred to as Cokey Flo?

A: Yes.

Q: A name which you very much disliked, as I understand it?

A: That is right.

Q: You are now in the House of Detention?

A: I am.

Q: How long have you been there?

A: Twelve days.

Q: Do you know the defendant Charles Luciano in this case?

A: I do.

Tom paused for a moment, allowing the jurors to glance at Charlie Lucky. Letting them see his icy stare and appreciate the courage it must be taking for this feeble young woman to face down the most fearsome mobster in America.

Cokey Flo actually seemed weaker than she'd been last night, her voice lost in the *whoosh* of rush-hour traffic flooding through the open windows of the courtroom. The judge admonished her to speak up. Defense counsel, like jackals scenting her frailty, eagerly joined in the request.

Tom kept one eye on the clock. Court adjourned at seven, which meant he could cover some background information that evening, end with a modest cliff-hanger, and use the overnight hours to regroup. After preemptively eliciting Cokey Flo's criminal record, her various drug addictions, and her first meeting with Jimmy Fredericks and Charlie Spinach, he moved to his improvised ending.

Q: Now did you, after this event concerning which you have testified, become the mistress of Jimmy Fredericks?
A: Yes.
Q: Did you live with him?
A: I did.
Q: When did you first start living with Jimmy Fredericks?
A: Two years ago.
Q: And you continued to live with Jimmy Fredericks until the time of his arrest on February first of this year?
A: Yes.

Seven o'clock. Tom breathed a quiet sigh, now that the die had been cast. Better still, he sensed that the appearance of Cokey Flo, and the high drama it portended, had rinsed from the jurors' mouths, at least in small measure, the lingering bad taste left by the smirking, smarmy testimony of Joe goddamned Bendix.

Forty

Cokey Flo

May 1936

YOU SHOULD'VE SEEN the look on Mrs. Calvit's face when she opened the door and saw me standing in the hallway with a hunky detective on either arm. Her jaw practically hit the floor, and the cigarette she was smoking *did* hit the floor, and she had to bend over in her ratty bathrobe to pick it up quick before one of the dogs tried to eat it.

"Where's Pearlie?" was the first question I asked her, and even before she could answer, I knew that little Pearlie wasn't there, and that her promise to look after my dog had lasted about as long as it took her to get home from the courthouse and put an ad in the newspaper. At least that's what she claimed she'd done, but for all I knew, she'd just shoved little Pearlie out the door in the middle of the night and left her to fend for herself.

I could've strangled her right then and there, and probably would have except for the detectives and the fact that we were on a tight schedule and had only enough time to grab a couple of dresses and hats, which, thank goodness, were still in the closet and hadn't yet been tossed out in the gutter along with my dog, and then only because Mrs. Calvit, the little cheapskate, was probably planning to sell them.

Life had been one big blur ever since my meeting with Barry Ten Eyck on Tuesday night. First came my formal statement on Wednesday, followed by a grilling from Mr. Dewey and a bunch of his assistants—Sol Gelb, Harry Cole, Frank Hogan, and a nice Negro lady named Mrs. Carter—which had lasted over two hours and had been every bit as tough as Barry said it would be. After that, we'd gone to the Hotel Alamac for my things, then back to the House of Detention for a couple hours of sleep, then over to the Woolworth Building again on Thursday afternoon.

The plan, or so I was told, was to have me testify on Friday morning. But then all of a sudden there was a schedule change and I was rushed to the courthouse in a squad car with the lights flashing and the siren screaming and I was parked in a room with Barry and Mrs. Carter, who'd arranged to have a cot there for me to lie on. I was visited by Mr. Dewey, who told me that I shouldn't be nervous and who handed me yet another copy of my statement and told me I should read it over again for what must have been the fourth or fifth time in the last twelve hours.

I shouldn't be nervous! I was weaker than a day-old kitten, and I was about to see Jimmy for the first time in nearly four months, not to mention go eye-to-eye with Lucky Luciano, and he says I shouldn't be nervous! I asked Mr. Dewey if I couldn't at least have a little brandy, but he said he'd have to ask the judge first, and that it wouldn't be today, so I'd just have to tough it out for the half hour or so that I'd be in the witness chair before the evening recess.

Then, just as Mr. Dewey was leaving he said, "You're a brave girl, Flo, and you're doing the right thing." To which I told him, "I'm counting on you, Mr. Dewey. If Jimmy and Charlie Lucky go free,

278

my life won't be worth a plugged nickel." He didn't respond to that, and he left the room with kind of a queer look on his face that told me maybe he wasn't as confident about his case as Barry said he was, and that made me feel even worse than I already did. And that was saying a lot, believe you me.

It was exactly six thirty when they finally called my name. I sat up on the cot and waited for my head to stop swimming. Then I stood, and with Mrs. Carter's help I walked through the door next to the jury box and into the courtroom.

Everything was silent, like I'd walked in on a funeral. I tried not to look at Jimmy, but I could feel his eyes and Lucky's eyes and the rest of the eyes in the courtroom burning holes in my back as I wobbled past the jury to the witness chair.

Like I was walking to the electric chair, that's what it felt like. Like I was the one on trial, and it was my life that hung in the balance, and whether I lived or died depended entirely on whether the jury believed what it was I was about to tell them. Which, as a matter of fact, it probably did.

I barely remember that first half hour on the stand. All's I know is that Mr. Dewey was asking me questions and the judge and the other lawyers kept telling me to speak up. I tried not to look directly at Jimmy, but of course I couldn't help myself, and anyway I had to find Charlie Lucky so I could point him out when the time came. Then when I finally recognized him sitting between his lawyers at one of the tables, this chill ran down my spine and into my legs, and I swear I almost wet myself right there in the courtroom, that's how scared I was to see that beetle brow with that one droopy eye glowering at me with nothing but pure and perfect hatred.

Then, just like that, the day was over. All the jurors were standing, and the reporters were shouting questions, and that's when I finally allowed myself a good, long look at Jimmy, who was staring straight back at me and shaking his head in little back-and-forth movements, as if to say that he couldn't believe I'd actually done this to him, or maybe to warn me that I was making the biggest mistake of my life.

It was Barry Ten Eyck who came and got me and led me by the elbow past the defendants, who were almost all of them leaning over and whispering to their lawyers. He led me back to the witness room, where Mrs. Carter was waiting, and then together they helped me down a staircase to that same squad car that was parked out back of the courthouse.

Back at the Woolworth Building, Barry got me a glass of brandy and made me promise not to tell anybody, especially Mr. Dewey. I was told to wait in Mr. Dewey's private office, which also had a couch and comfortable chairs and its own private elevator. I laid down on the couch for a minute, and I must've fallen asleep, because when I woke up again, it was dark outside and Mr. Dewey and some of his other assistants—Gelb, and Cole, and Charlie Grimes—were just returning from court, and pretty soon all of them were congratulating me for doing such a great job.

"I was scared out of my wits," I told them, but they said that was okay, and was to be expected, and generally tried to make out like I'd hit a home run when I knew the truth was that I'd barely even stepped up to the plate.

"That worked out perfectly," Mr. Dewey said as he took a cigarette and fitted it into a holder like he was President Roosevelt. "You got your feet wet, and you got the lay of the courtroom. Now it won't feel so foreign tomorrow morning."

"I'm sorry about keeping my voice up," I told him. "It's hard with me being so weak and with all that noise outside and all those people trying to hear me."

He waved it off as he lit his cigarette. He didn't offer me one, but that was okay. I realized that for the first time I could remember, I was actually feeling hungry. The enthusiasm and the confidence those men all seemed to share was rubbing off on me. It felt good to be part of their team—the prosecution team—meeting after hours to plan our next move. Like I was their equal, and like I was finally doing something good for a change, something positive to make the world a better place.

I didn't feel like a rat at all. More like I was walking the right side of the street for maybe the first time in my life.

Mr. Dewey took me through my testimony again, then at around ten o'clock they drove me back to the House of Detention, stopping on the way for tea and a small bite to eat. It was hot that night, but I got a few good hours of sleep, and in the morning actually ate a whole bowl of cereal for breakfast. I was nervous, sure, but like Mr. Dewey had said, it was all familiar to me now, which made it okay. Lots of things in life are scary just because they're unfamiliar, but once you do them and they don't kill you, then all of a sudden you realize they're not so scary anymore.

We got to court at nine thirty, and by ten o'clock I was back in the witness chair. Only this time I was able to look both Jimmy and Charlie Lucky straight in the eye. Siegel was there as well, and I gave him a look that said maybe you should of been a little nicer to me when you had the chance, you fat little prick. And then Mr. Dewey stood up and walked to the little podium and his booming voice brought me back to the present.

"In the spring of nineteen thirty-four," he said, "do you remember going up to some Chinese restaurant uptown with Jimmy Fredericks?"

This was it—the moment we'd been rehearsing for two days straight, and that I'd been practicing on my own even before that. I took one last look at Jimmy and swallowed hard.

"Yes, I do."

Forty-One

Flo's Story

May 1936

COKEY FLO BROWN, who couldn't have weighed more than ninety pounds in her shoes and silly hat, looks more to Lucky like a schoolgirl playing dress-up than the hard-boiled madam she claims to have been. But Lucky could tell from her appearance yesterday that there was steel behind those blinking eyes, and that the blade is aimed straight at Charlie Lucky's heart.

Siegel warned them as much, predicting that whatever loyalty Cokey Flo might once have owed Jimmy Fredericks would have been forgotten ten minutes after her arrest. According to Siegel, Cokey Flo is brassy and shrewd, with a wharf rat's instinct for self-preservation. Too wised up to be testifying without some deal with the special prosecutor, but too crafty to have left her fingerprints on whatever that deal might be. Her only vulnerability, Fredericks had confided to Siegel, was the junk she either shot in her legs or snorted up her nose.

Levy and Polakoff have arranged for a doctor to be standing by in the hope of disqualifying Cokey Flo as a witness on the ground that she's still using dope. If not disqualify her, then at least expose her as a liar right out of the gate, since she has already testified to having been clean for over a week. Also, Levy has asked Maurice Cantor to track down the lawyer whom Cantor recalls having once represented Dorothy Russell Calvit, the daughter of Lillian Russell and the woman who'd testified at Cokey Flo's solicitation trial in general sessions.

According to Levy, the fact that Cokey Flo never appeared before the grand jury makes her dangerous for both the defense and the prosecution, because, unlike the other madams and prostitutes who've been in custody for nearly four months now, her story hasn't been rehearsed and vetted and was reduced to writing only on Wednesday, with the ink barely dry on the paper. Also, Levy said, the fact that she was the girlfriend of Jimmy Fredericks and may still try to protect him means that she might contradict some of the other witnesses, and that that alone could be enough to cast doubt over whatever story she's come to tell about Charlie Lucky.

Now, at the start of her second day in the witness chair, Cokey Flo's story begins with a four A.M. meeting at some Chinese restaurant uptown in the spring of 1934, where she claims that she and Fredericks arrived to find Little Davie, Tommy the Bull, and Charlie Lucky all seated at a table eating noodles. Fredericks introduced her to the others as his girlfriend. The dinner conversation that followed was in Italian, but once they'd all piled into a car to head downtown, the discussion had shifted to English.

Q: Now as best you can, tell us who said what, will you do that?
A: Well, Jimmy spoke up and said, "Gee, I think some of the bookies are holding out joints on us." And Charlie spoke up and said, "Well, can't you get them all together?" And Davie answered, "Well, yes, we can get them all together; naturally it takes a little time." And Jimmy said, "If the bookies wouldn't

hold out the addresses, then we could get more of the joints
together." And Charlie says, "Well, I'll tell you what you do.
Bring all the bookies downtown tomorrow, I will put them on
the carpet, and we will see that that doesn't happen again."
And Jimmy said, "Well, Nick is the worst offender; he collects
bond and keeps it, and then when the places get pinched they
run to me, and I don't know anything about it, I am not able to
take the girls out, because I didn't know they had been paying
bond." And Charlie said, "Well, have them all come down and
we will straighten the matter out." And then they started
talking in Italian, and that was about all at that time.

Lucky has to restrain himself from laughing out loud. As if anyone
would believe he'd incriminate himself like that in the presence of a
total stranger, and a junkie no less, and would conveniently switch
from Italian to English to do it. But as Lucky turns to the jury box,
his smile dissolves at the sight of thirteen stone-faced jurors scribbling
in their notepads.

Q: Now do you recall after that occasion, Jimmy told you about
the meeting which was referred to in that conversation?

A: Yes, he did.

Q: What did he tell you about it?

A: He told me that they had all the bookies down and bawled the
devil out of them for holding out, and that they would be fined
if they were caught holding out any places; and that Nick
Montana thought he was smart, because he had a brother that
was supposed to be a big shot, and he thought he could get
away with things like that, gypping people; and they told him
he couldn't do a thing like that.

Again Lucky is watching the jury, looking for skepticism, searching for some acknowledgment that of all the cooperating bookers

who've testified in the trial thus far—Al Weiner, Dave Miller, Danny Brooks, and Pete Harris—not one of them has mentioned such a meeting. Looking for recognition that if such a meeting had actually happened, it would have been the centerpiece of Dewey's case from day one. But all Lucky sees in the jury box are the same attentive and sympathetic faces, the same furious note-taking.

Q: Now do you recall driving with Jimmy Fredericks and Benny Spiller down to a garage on one occasion in the fall?

A: I do.

Q: Do you recall now where that garage was?

MR. BARRA: Will you fix the date a little bit? The fall of what year?

Q: I said the fall. We have been talking about 1934, haven't we?

A: Yes.

Q: Do you recall now where that garage was?

A: It was on the Lower East Side.

Q: Do you remember the street?

A: No, I don't. I don't know much about the East Side.

Q: When you got there, where did you go, when you got to the garage; where did you go?

A: Well, I sat in the car, I didn't go in.

Q: And did Jimmy Fredericks and Benny Spiller go inside the garage?

A: They did.

Q: Did you wait outside?

A: Yes, I did, for a while.

Q: Then what did you do?

A: Well, I got tired of sitting in the car, and I got out and started walking around a little, and wondered what they had to say inside, and I thought I would listen for a while; and I listened, and all I could hear was—

Q: Now, as I understand, you cannot tell us whose voices you heard?

A: No.

Q: Well, then you cannot tell us what you heard.

A: All right.

Q: After the meeting was over, who came out?

A: Jimmy came out and Charlie and Davie and Tommy, and Jimmy and I got in the car and drove away.

Q: Where was Benny Spiller?

A: He must have still been inside. I didn't see him come out.

Q: He did not come out?

A: No.

Q: Although he went in with Jimmy Fredericks?

A: Yes, he did.

Q: Whom did you drive away with?

A: Just with Jimmy.

Q: Just with Jimmy?

A: Yes.

Q: Do you recall sometime around Easter of 1935 going down to that garage again?

A: Yes, I do.

Q: Whom did you go down with that time?

A: Well, I went down with Jimmy alone.

Q: And when you got there, did you see anybody immediately?

A: No, I didn't.

Q: Where did Jimmy go when you got there?

A: Into the garage.

Q: I beg your pardon?

A: Into the garage.

Q: Where did you stay that time?

A: In the car for a while.

Q: And then did you wander around again?

A: I did.

Q: You heard voices, but you cannot identify who was speaking, can you?

A: No, I can't.

Q: After the meeting was over, who came out of that meeting?

A: The same people.

THE COURT: Tell us the people.

A: Davie, Jimmy, Charlie, and Tommy.

Lucky has stopped watching the jury and is instead now focused on Levy, who is scribbling notes on a legal pad. Lucky leans over to read. Levy has written ADDRESS?? and TWO VISITS! and OWNER? and WHY HASN'T HE TAKEN HER THERE?

Q: Some time last summer did you go down with Jimmy to a restaurant in Chinatown?

A: I did.

Q: Do you recall the address?

A: It is 21, and it is in the Chinatown district, but I don't know the exact name of the street.

Q: You know that there was a street number 21 on the place?

A: Yes, I do.

Q: Do you remember which of several streets it was?

A: I think it was either Pell or Mott. I know they called the place "Twenty-One" anyway.

Q: "Twenty-One" was the name of it?

A: It was also the number.

Q: Oh, I see. Whom did you find when you got down there with Jimmy Fredericks?

A: I found Charlie and Davie and Tommy sitting at a table eating.

Q: And did you go up and join them, you and Jimmy?

A: Well, we walked in, and they asked us to join them.

Q: And were they talking in English or Italian on this occasion?

A: Italian.

Q: Did they at any time talk in English?

A: Yes, they did.

Q: Do you remember any conversation in English about—I withdraw that. When they talked in English, did they talk about anything other than prostitution?

A: No, they didn't.

Q: They switched to English when they talked about prostitution?

A: Yes.

. . .

Q: What did you hear about the subject of prostitution?

A: Well, I heard Charlie say that he was disgusted and didn't like the idea of it at all; that there wasn't much money in it; and they were speaking of—it was getting tough.

Q: All right. Go ahead.

A: It was getting tough, and the joints were getting difficult to manage. A lot of the women—

Q: Will you tell us who it was that was speaking, as best you can?

MR. LEVY: Pardon me, Mr. Dewey. I am sitting a few feet away and cannot get answers. May we have that read, your Honor?

(Answer read.)

Q: "A lot of the women?"

A: (Continuing)—didn't want to pay the bond. Jimmy mentioned that Peggy Wild was being very difficult; that he had sent—

THE COURT: Who besides Peggy Wild did he say?

MR. DEWEY: Nobody, your Honor.

A: (Continuing) No one—that he had sent a collector up to collect the bond, and she wouldn't—she would open the door on a chain and tell him she wasn't doing anything, and he found out later that she was in an apartment across the hall from the apartment that she claimed not to be running in.

Q: Did anybody make any comment on that?

A: Charlie said, "Oh, I suppose she is a wise guy." So Davie said, "Well, we will take care of it; don't worry."

Q: Did Charlie Lucky say anything about what they should do?

A: He said, "Why don't you"—oh, yes, he said, "Why don't you get the madams together, Jimmy?" He said, "You know, I told you before that being nice to them isn't any good." And Jimmy said, "Well, you know how it is; it is tough now, and I thought that if I could talk to them, it might be better."

Q: What did Charlie Lucky say to that?

A: He said, "Well, you can't talk to them; they are too stubborn anyway." He said, "Get after them; step on them a little bit." And Davie said, "We will take care of it. We will see."

By now Lucky has stopped watching the jury and stopped watching Levy and is focused instead on the witness, this Cokey Flo Brown. Although her voice remains weak, her entire demeanor has changed from yesterday's fear and timidity to today's confident self-possession. While yesterday she was unwilling to take her eyes off Dewey, today she is half turning toward the jury during her answers, as if drawing them into her confidence. And the jurors are responding in kind, leaning forward and hanging on every word.

Q: Do you remember an occasion when you went down with Jimmy to another or the same restaurant on the Lower East Side?

A: The same restaurant.

Q: The same restaurant?

A: Yes.

Q: Do you remember about when that was?

A: That was in about October.

Q: Of what year?

A: '35.

Q: Last October?

A: Yes.

Q: And whom did you see when you got there?

A: There was just Charlie and Davie.

Q: And Jimmy Fredericks?

A: And Jimmy Fredericks.

Q: Tommy Bull was not present at that time?

A: Not present at that time.

Q: And what conversation was there at that occasion about prostitution?

A: Well, Charlie said that he was disgusted, and he wanted to have the bonding combination stop bonding altogether. He said there wasn't any money in it, and it was all a big headache, and his name was getting mentioned in it quite a bit, and he didn't like it; and Davie said, "Well, why don't you give it a chance a while? We will see that we straighten things out."

THE COURT: Who said that?

A: Davie. And Charlie said, "Well, I don't know; this Dewey investigation is coming on and it may get tough, and I think we ought to fold up for a while."

MR. LEVY: Pardon me. This is October, Mr. Dewey?

MR. DEWEY: Yes. What else was said as you recall it?

A: He said—so Davie argued for it. He said, "Well, why don't you let it go a while and see how things go? It might pick up. I admit it is slow now because there were quite a few pinches, and naturally that takes money out of the combination, but it may quiet down and get better." Well, Charlie said, "Well, it would be better if we quit a while, and started over again at some other time when things were quiet." He said, "We could even syndicate all the places like they do in Chicago, and instead of three or four combinations having the syndicates, as they do in Chicago, there would be only one in New York, us." So Davie said, "Well, why don't you let it go for a while? I don't think it will be very tough. Even if the Dewey investigation does start on us, they will only pick on phony bonding, that is all. They will probably grab two or three of the bondsmen, and that is all there will be to it." So Charlie said, "Well, all right, then let it go. I will let it go for a couple of more months, and if things are the same, you will have to let it drop."

Q: Was there any mention by—I withdraw that. Do you recall Charlie Lucky saying anything about the A&P?

A: He meant syndicate the places on a large scale, the same as the A&P stores are a large syndicate.

The clock reads ten forty-five when Dewey finally sits. Cokey Flo Brown, her voice now barely a whisper, has finished casting her spell over the courtroom.

Forty-Two

In Chambers

May 1936

"THE WORST OF it is, they believe her."

George patted his pockets as he paced, wishing he could light a cigar. Behind a screen that had been set up in the judge's chambers, two doctors—Milton Bridges for the defense, and Peter Amoroso for the prosecution—were examining Cokey Flo Brown for evidence of recent narcotics use. Eunice Carter stood with Dewey in the opposite corner of the room, both of them chatting with lowered voices, while Judge McCook read the newspaper as he ate a sandwich at his desk.

Polakoff turned his back on Dewey and spoke to George in a whisper.

"Siegel says that she came to his office a couple of times, looking for ways she might help Frederico. He gave her a copy of the indictment, and she sat with it for over an hour, making notes. When he asked her about Luciano, about why his name had been added, she said she'd never heard of him."

"I wish he'd hurry up and get to that. All this business about drugs is trying the jury's patience."

"Siegel and Kopp want you to keep her on the stand as long as possible, to see if she breaks down. I told them I'd run it past you."

George frowned. "That runs the risk that the jury will tire of me before she does."

"Have you got a better idea?"

"I have ideas, but I wouldn't say they're any better. For example, why would the learned special prosecutor put Miss Brown in the witness chair without first driving her to that East Side garage in search of at least one corroborating witness? That would have taken an hour at most—less time than it took to fetch her pretty blue frock. The answer is, he doesn't believe her story any more than we do."

George paused to glance over Polakoff's shoulder.

"He prefers an unknown garage and no corroboration to a real establishment with a real owner staffed by real mechanics who've never laid eyes on Luciano. The same goes for these damned Chinese restaurants. He's learned a lesson, Mr. Dewey has, from our friend Mr. Bendix. The hazier the details and the fewer the eyewitnesses, the less vulnerable a story is to impeachment."

The matron stepped from behind the curtain, followed by the two physicians. Dr. Bridges caught George's eye, giving his head an imperceptible shake.

The judge set down his sandwich. "Gentlemen? We await your verdict."

"Doctor Amoroso and I are in accord," Bridges said, returning a stethoscope to his satchel. "The witness presents as being in the late-middle stages of opiate withdrawal. We can't say for certain, of course, without a blood test, but it appears unlikely she's ingested any narcotic substances in at least the past seventy-two hours."

"Just like I told you," chimed a voice from behind the screen.

"As did I," Dewey said, crossing the room to McCook's desk. "This whole examination has been a cheap circus stunt with no purpose other than to unnerve and intimidate the witness."

"The witness," McCook said, folding his newspaper, "appears to be doing just fine. Wouldn't you agree, Mr. Levy?"

"It's been my experience that most prosecution witnesses do well on direct."

"Yes. Speaking of which, you know I hate to limit your cross-examination, Mr. Levy, but I do hope you'll be more expeditious with this witness. We're down to our last alternate, and I know you feel as I do that we don't want to risk a mistrial."

"Perhaps if the learned special prosecutor tried looking elsewhere than the state's jails and prisons for his witnesses, there'd be less material for defense counsel to cover."

Cokey Flo emerged from behind the screen and was working a pin in her hat.

"Be that as it may," the judge said, "let's try to keep things moving, shall we? Mr. Dewey, is there anything further we need to discuss?"

"There is, Your Honor. Miss Brown, as we all know, is in somewhat fragile condition due to the reduction cure about which she's already testified. I'm told, however, that a small measure of brandy sometimes helps to fortify women in her state, and I of course wouldn't dream of administering same without the court's permission and supervision."

"You've got to be joking," Polakoff said. "You want to let her *drink* on the witness stand?"

"I'm simply proposing that at appropriate intervals throughout the day, the court might wish to allow the young lady a small sip of brandy here in chambers. To keep her strength up, that's all. We can barely hear her as it is, and this constant rereading of her answers is slowing matters to a crawl."

"Yes, I agree with Mr. Dewey," the judge said, standing and brushing bread crumbs from his vest. "Anything to speed matters along. Are there any objections?"

"That is a most unusual request from my learned friend," George said.

"You've seen how they drag out their questioning, Judge, trying to wear down our witnesses. Trying to turn the trial into some kind of a dance marathon. If Miss Brown is too weak to continue, we'll have no choice but to request a recess, and possibly an adjournment. I want to get her on and off the stand as quickly as possible, that's all."

"An occasional sip of brandy seems perfectly reasonable, Mr. Levy. I suppose I could, as an alternative, place a time limit on cross-examination, although I'm loath to do it. But I'll leave that to your discretion."

George could see where this was heading, but he also sensed an opportunity. If he acceded to Dewey's proposal, then the judge would be less likely to sustain an objection to the length of George's cross. It was a trade-off worth considering.

"Might I have a moment to confer with my colleague?"

"By all means," said McCook.

George and Moses Polakoff retired to the corner for privacy while Dewey shared a silent look with McCook, who raised a bushy eyebrow. After a minute of hushed discussion, the huddle finally broke.

"Under the circumstances," George said, "the defense has no objection to our friend's suggestion. Miss Brown has proved herself to be a liar on opium, to be a liar on morphine, and to be a liar on heroin. We shudder to think of the strain she must be under, attempting to lie while totally sober."

"Go chase yourself," said Cokey Flo.

"I have other intentions, Miss Brown. What I propose to pursue is the truth."

Forty-Three

The Letter

May 1936

IT WAS LIKE a hot coal burning a hole in Tom Dewey's pocket.

Albert Unger, an assistant district attorney under William Copeland Dodge, had appeared during the lunch break and had left behind a letter written by Joe Bendix to his wife, Joy Dixon. The letter was dated April 21 and had somehow been misdelivered to Morris Panger, another assistant district attorney with whom Bendix was negotiating for clemency. Scripted in what Tom recognized as the hotel thief's florid hand, the letter urged Dixon to "think up some real clever story" by which to gain the confidence of the special prosecutor's office.

The letter was an explosive piece of exculpatory evidence that, if it found its way into Levy's hands, would destroy whatever remained of Bendix's credibility. The first question confronting Tom was whether Panger had taken the time to make photostats of the letter. The second, of course, was the extent of Tom's obligations as an officer of the court now that he knew of the letter's existence.

Although he was known colloquially as the special prosecutor, Tom's official title was actually deputy assistant district attorney of New York County. That title—the lowest possible rank in the D.A.'s office—was itself a pointed barb from Dodge. But as an assistant D.A. himself, Panger and Tom were theoretical colleagues—partners in the Luciano prosecution—even if, in reality, Dodge and his Tammany Hall cronies were Tom's greatest antagonists.

So where, exactly, did Panger's loyalties lie? If not with the defense, then had he shared the letter with Dodge? Would he? If so, would Dodge use the letter to sabotage the prosecution? Would he take it to the press? Or was this all some kind of a setup—a test to see what the special prosecutor would do of his own accord?

Tom needed time to consider both his options and their ramifications. Thank God he hadn't called Dixon as a witness! But first there was the not-so-small matter of Cokey Flo's cross-examination, which had already resumed.

It had been Siegel and Kopp asking the questions before the lunch recess, each of them like roadside crows, strutting and pecking at the rawer aspects of Cokey Flo's testimony—her drug addictions, her hypodermic injections, her reduction cure. These were, Tom knew, mere pinpricks. Because Cokey Flo's direct testimony had been aimed at Luciano, it would be Levy wielding the carving knife on cross.

Thank God the brandy seemed to be helping. When she'd returned to the witness chair, Cokey Flo's color was better and her voice, as she parried Sam Siegel's final thrusts, was stronger and clearer than Tom had ever before heard it.

Q: How many times were you at my office?
A: Twice.
Q: How many times?
A: Twice.

Q: Twice. It was three times, wasn't it?

A: Yes, three times, that is right.

Q: Three times. You haven't got a very good memory, have you?

A: Yes, I have.

Q: You came to my office without any solicitation from me, didn't you?

A: That is right.

Q: Yes. You came to my office and you told my telephone operator to announce you to me as Flo, didn't you?

A: Yes.

Q: Yes. And when you came in, I asked you who you were, didn't I?

A: Yes.

Q: And you wanted to know what James Frederico was charged with, didn't you?

A: That is right.

Q: Didn't you tell me that the only thing Frederico has to do with this whole matter was in connection with bonding the girls?

A: That is right.

Q: That's right. And that was the truth, wasn't it?

A: It was the truth.

Q: Yes. You were trying to tell Frederico's attorney the truth, to help Frederico, weren't you?

A: Yes.

Q: Yes or no?

A: Yes.

Q: When I showed you that indictment, the last indictment containing ninety counts, it was very late in the evening, wasn't it?

A: Yes, it was.

Q: Yes. I didn't talk to you until you started to go home, isn't that so?

A: That is right.

Q: Didn't I put you in my library and tell you I didn't have time to talk to you, and that you could look at the indictment and make yourself comfortable and make notes from it?

A: Yes.

Q: Yes; and you sat there for how long in that library?

A: Quite a long time.

Q: Over an hour, wasn't it?

A: I didn't measure the time.

Q: Well, you didn't leave until around 6:30, did you?

A: No.

Q: No. And as you left I talked with you, I walked with you a distance of about ten feet from the library to the elevator, didn't I?

A: Yes.

Q: Yes. That is, the elevator opens directly into my law offices, doesn't it?

A: It does.

Q: The elevators of the building?

A: Yes, it does.

Q: And I stood there waiting, signaling the elevator and waiting until it would stop and let you go downstairs?

A: Yes.

Q: Yes. Now you tell me what was said about any of these defendants at that time by you.

A: Nothing was said about any of the defendants.

Q: You don't recall saying anything about Luciano?

A: No, I don't.

Q: Do you remember anything I said about a man named Luciano?

A: No.

Q: Didn't you tell me you had never heard of him, and I wanted to know from you how he was connected in this case, and how he came to be indicted with the others in this last indictment?

A: No, you never spoke of Luciano at all.

Tom knew enough not to smirk at Gelb or Ten Eyck, but was having a hard time restraining himself. So far, at least, Flo Brown had been a perfect witness—smart, poised, and always two steps ahead of her questioner. How a girl with her looks and intellect had ended up in the gutter was one of life's little mysteries.

Siegel was angry now, having effectively been called a liar, and Tom decided to goad him a little as Siegel returned to the subject of Dorothy Russell Calvit, Cokey Flo's last employer.

Q: When did you ask her to get in touch with me after your conviction here about a week or ten days ago?

MR. DEWEY: Objected to. I think we have gone so far afield, your Honor, as to be utterly useless in this cross-examination.

THE COURT: I will not say so yet. I do not know what is in counsel's mind.

MR. SAMUEL SIEGEL: If your Honor please—

THE COURT: I said I will not say so yet. I do not know what is in counsel's mind.

MR. SAMUEL SIEGEL: But I do object to the district attorney making an objection on the ground that the question is utterly useless. I do not know what he is talking about, but he should know that that is not a proper objection.

MR. DEWEY: I consider it—

MR. SAMUEL SIEGEL: If he wants to sum up while he is objecting, I would ask your Honor to tell him not to.

MR. DEWEY: If I did as much summation as my friends, we would never get anywhere.

THE COURT: I suggest you go on, since I have sustained your objection, Mr. Siegel.

MR. SAMUEL SIEGEL: Could I wait until Mr. Dewey takes a glass of water, your Honor?

THE COURT: You may always do that.

MR. SAMUEL SIEGEL: I find it terribly disconcerting when he walks up and down there.

THE COURT: You may always do that. You will not be disconcerted.

MR. SAMUEL SIEGEL: If he thinks he is disconcerting me by doing that, he can lay off his ears.

MR. DEWEY: What a lot of silly nonsense. If he cannot examine when I get a drink of water, then counsel ought not to be at the Bar.

THE COURT: You have intimated that it was and that it was not disconcerting. So please go on.

MR. SAMUEL SIEGEL: What was the last question after Mr. Dewey's remark?

Siegel's cross-examination limped to a close with a parting shot at Cokey Flo's motives.

Q: I ask you, what was the day you were convicted of prostitution?

A: I was convicted May 13th.

Q: What day of the week was that?

A: On a Wednesday.

Q: Wednesday. Did you see Mrs. Calvit that day?

A: Yes.

Q: What?

A: Yes.

Q: Was that the day you asked her to get in touch with me?

A: I do believe I wrote her a letter to that effect.

Q: When?

A: That evening.

Q: Wednesday evening?

A: Yes.

Q: Wednesday evening you wrote her a letter to get in touch with me to help you when you came up for sentence on Tuesday following?

A: Yes.

Q: And two nights later, Friday, you became disgusted with everything and wrote the letter to Mr. Ten Eyck?

301

A: Yes.

Q: What happened between Wednesday night, can you tell us, and Friday night to cause you to become disgusted with everything?

A: Well, it was something that had been going on a long time in my mind.

Q: What?

A: I said it was something—

THE COURT: Read that, please. We will have it read. There was a little noise at that time.

(Answer read.)

Q: That is, rehabilitation?

A: That is it.

Q: Your desire to go straight?

A: That is it.

Q: It culminated in your mind, and induced you to write a letter to Mr. Dewey on Friday night?

A: That is it.

Q: You thought that "now is the time, two charges pending against me, and I am now coming up for sentence," that this would be a grand and glorious time to go straight?

A: No; I thought I might—as long as I was going to be punished, I might as well be punished and clear my conscience, and when I left the House of Detention, be free.

Once Siegel, still visibly agitated, had returned to his place at the defense table, it was Levy's turn at the podium. Tom braced himself. The jurors, who'd come to view the clash between Tom's punctilious direct and Levy's gentlemanly cross as a kind of grand spectator sport, all shifted forward in their seats.

Forty-Four

Cross

May 1936

HE DIDN'T LOOK like much, the little Jew with the rimless eyeglasses and the sleeves pushed up to his elbows to expose his hairy forearms. But he was the one to look out for—both Barry and Mr. Dewey had warned me as much—and he was the one they'd pretended to be when they'd cross-examined me in Mr. Dewey's office, saying things like, "Don't let him lull you to sleep," and "Don't let him get you talking."

He seemed like a kindly uncle when he first started out in this soft and reassuring voice, like we were having a fireside chat over tea, him asking me about my background, like he was concerned for my well-being. But I knew better. I could see right through his little act, and the barbed insinuations he was making. Like that I'd have to be pretty hard-boiled to run a speakeasy when I was fifteen, and that I'd have to be a damned good liar to keep three guys on the string in

Chicago. Of course, knowing what he was doing and stopping him from doing it were two different things.

The problem with cross-examination was that you couldn't explain anything. He'd ask questions like "Isn't it so that—" and "You did so-and-so, did you not?" And if I tried to answer with anything other than a simple yes or no, he'd cut me off with his next question and make it look like I was arguing with him in front of the jury. It was frustrating, I'll tell you that, and after a while I started to feel faint again and asked the judge for a recess. The judge had a matron accompany me into his office, where they gave me another small sip of the brandy. Afterward—this was around three forty-five or so—Mr. Dewey had to tell the jurors that I'd had my little drink, and of course Levy made a big show of how he didn't object, like he was the one who was worried about my fragile condition.

Levy resumed with a bunch of questions about my drug habit, and how I ran my houses, and after a while I got the impression that maybe he was stalling, either to run out the clock or to tire me out before he moved in for the kill. It was weird having thoughts like those, right there in the witness chair, like you were standing outside yourself and analyzing what was happening to you even when you were answering questions and trying to make a good impression on the jury. It wasn't easy, I'll tell you that, and I was getting fuzzier and fuzzier as the afternoon wore on and my side started hurting again, and when I looked over at Mr. Dewey, which he warned me I shouldn't do, I had a pained expression on my face.

Levy, meanwhile would make these little jabs, and then he'd kind of half-turn to the jury and raise his eyebrows, as if to say, "Can you believe this woman?" Like when he was asking me about the effects of opium, trying to imply that it impaired my memory, and when I wouldn't admit that, he'd turn it around against me.

Q: Didn't find any change in your memory at all?
A: None at all.

Q: When you awakened in the morning you would have a clear-cut recollection of what took place the night before, would you?

A: I had to; I had to remember over three thousand customers by name and face.

Q: You had three thousand customers?

A: Yes.

Q: In your house of prostitution?

A: Yes.

Q: And when they called up, you had to remember their voices?

A: Their voice, name and the face.

Q: I see. This is by the year 1933?

A: Yes.

Q: Your memory was sufficiently acute that you could remember three thousand customers?

A: Yes.

Q: By name, voice, and some by telephone number?

A: Yes.

Q: Well then, really—

A: Not by telephone number.

Q: No?

A: By voice over the phone.

Q: And then when they came in, by appearance, isn't that true?

A: That is true.

Q: Three thousand different people you kept in mind?

A: Yes.

Q: And really, Miss Brown, the problem of remembering the details of the story you told today is very small compared to what you needed in your own business; isn't that true?

After sparring like that for over an hour, Levy finally moved to the real issues in the case, and he started out with Jimmy's role in the combination. Again, like I was standing outside myself, I thought, this guy is awfully clever because he knows I'm not gonna dump all over Jimmy. I could see his strategy plain as day, getting me to defend Jimmy and in the process contradict the testimony of the other girls. And while I was happy for Jimmy that someone was finally asking the questions Siegel should have asked, I knew Levy didn't care a rat's ass about Jimmy, and that all he cared about was undermining my story about Charlie Lucky by making me out as a liar.

But like I said, what choice did I have? As angry as I'd been with Jimmy, I wasn't about to hammer another nail in his coffin like that bitch June Gary had done and paint him as some kind of a goon running around with a blackjack threatening to shoot people's dogs.

> Q: At that time you were paying—during the year 1934—you were paying bonding fees, were you not?
> A: Yes, I was.
> Q: Entirely with your satisfaction?
> A: Yes.
> Q: You were only too glad to do it, weren't you?
> A: Yes, I was.
> Q: You realized from your standpoint it was very necessary in your prostitution business, did you not?
> A: Yes, it was.
> Q: And you could not see any reason why any madam in the City of New York should have any objection to paying the small sum of ten dollars to bond; isn't that true?
> A: That is true.
> Q: And Jimmy would tell you that some madams did not want to bond; isn't that true?
> A: Yes.
> Q: And didn't he tell you if they did not want to bond, he tried to coax them, but he never wanted to use any force?
> A: That is true.
> Q: That Jimmy never wanted to hurt anybody?
> A: That is true.

Q: That Jimmy never had a gun, as far as you saw, did he?

A: No.

Q: Or never carried any weapon, as far as you saw, did he?

A: No.

Once he'd got me to contradict what the other girls had been saying about Jimmy, Levy then started in on the Chinese restaurants, and on the fact that I couldn't describe where they were, and the fact that none of Mr. Dewey's men had taken me there so that I could identify them better. I could see that Mr. Dewey and Barry were starting to fidget, and so I got a little rattled, and when Mr. Dewey saw I was getting rattled, he tried to come to my rescue.

Q: Can you give us any better address of this so-called Chinese restaurant, except that it is near Mott Street and near Pell Street in an old dilapidated building?

A: No, that is the number of the restaurant, twenty-one.

Q: And the number of the restaurant is twenty-one?

A: Yes.

Q: When were you last in that particular restaurant?

A: In October.

Q: Of what year?

A: 1935.

Q: And since you told Mr. Dewey's assistant that story, did they ask you to point out that restaurant in any way to them?

A: No, they did not.

Q: Did you go back to look over that restaurant in any way at all?

A: No.

Q: At the time you claimed you last saw Charlie Lucky there, can you tell us who ran the place?

A: No.

Q: Was it a Chinaman or an American?

A: I have no idea.

Q: You have no idea. Don't you know who waited on you at that time?

A: A Chinaman.

Q: A Chinaman. Did you know that Chinaman before?

A: No.

Q: Is that all there is on the outside of it, the word twenty-one or the number twenty-one?

A: Well, I didn't pay much attention to it.

Q: You had been there before, you say, had you not?

A: Yes, I had been there twice.

Q: Yes.

A: I don't take notice of every detail of every restaurant I go into.

Q: Oh, you are getting a little angry now?

A: And I don't think anyone ever does.

MR. DEWEY: I object to counsel's remark.

THE COURT: Sustained.

MR. LEVY: It is a question, your Honor, not a remark. I say, are you getting a little angry?

MR. DEWEY: I object to it as a question.

THE WITNESS: No, I am not getting angry.

MR. DEWEY: Excuse me. I object to counsel badgering the witness.

MR. LEVY: And I object to you trying to badger me.

THE COURT: I overrule the objection. She has answered anyhow, so it is all water over the dam.

Q: Now you say on that occasion that you went in, what month did you put it in?

A: I put it in October.

Q: What month are you talking about that you were in this Chinese restaurant, twenty-one?

A: October.

Q: When in October were you there?

A: 1935.

Q: 1935?

A: Yes.

Q: And that is the last time you saw Charlie Lucky?

A: Right.

Q: How many times before that in your life do you claim that you saw him?

A: I saw him twice in that restaurant.

Q: Yes, any other place?

A: Twice coming out of the garage.

Q: I beg your pardon?

A: Twice coming out of the garage.

Q: Twice coming out of the garage; that is five times?

A: Yes; once uptown.

Q: Up where, uptown?

A: In a restaurant uptown.

Q: Just give us the name of the restaurant uptown.

A: That is also a Chinese restaurant. I couldn't give you the name of it.

Q: Also Chinese, located where?

A: Around One Thirtieth or Fortieth Street and Broadway.

Q: You know that is a big territory, Miss Brown, don't you?

A: Yes, but I could point the place out.

Q: You could?

A: Yes.

Q: Have you tried to with any of Mr. Dewey's assistants?

A: No, I have not.

It got to the point where I felt like Levy was making fun of me, like the story I was telling was so unbelievable that it amazed even him, who thought he'd heard everything. But unlike the other lawyers, Levy never smirked or rolled his eyes. He was always the perfect gentleman, even when he was signaling to the jury by his tone of voice that he thought everything I was saying was a load of hooey.

Q: Now what time did you leave the restaurant at Broadway and One Thirtieth or thereabouts?

A: Well, we left there about quarter of five.

Q: Yes. And you drove without any stop, right on downtown, is that true?

A: Yes.

Q: And during the time you were riding in the car you were listening to the conversation, were you?

A: I was listening—

Q: Is that true now? Kindly answer.

A: Yes.

Q: All right. You had met Charlie Lucky for the first time in your life?

A: Yes.

Q: And on your direct testimony, and on your cross, you have been telling the Court and jury what Davie Betillo supposedly said, what Charlie supposedly said, and what Jimmy Fredericks said, have you not?

A: Yes.

Q: Do you mean to tell the Court and jury that, meeting two strange men or three strange men for the first time, with your attention directed toward driving the car, you could tell the respective voices of the people in the backseat?

A: There was a mirror in front.

Q: Yes.

A: And I could see these three men in back through this mirror.

Q: See through the mirror?

A: Yes, I could see their lips moving.

Q: And through the mirror you could notice their lips moving?

A: Yes, sir.

Q: And you watched them very keenly through that mirror, in order to know which one said which, is that right? Is that true or not?

A : Well, now and again I would glance into the mirror and see them.

Q : You were not inquisitive as to what they were talking about, were you?

A : Well, it was interesting.

Q : Oh, it was, I see. And being interested, you watched them very keenly through that mirror, in order to know which one said which, is that right? Is that true or not?

A : Yes, I watched them.

Q : Now, was it dark around quarter of five in the morning or thereabouts, when you left this place?

A : It was dawning.

Q : I beg your pardon?

A : It was just dawning, just starting to break daylight.

Q : Just starting to break daylight?

A : Yes.

Q : But you could see clearly enough through that mirror the different lips moving, could you?

A : Yes, I could.

I stole a peek at the clock, even though I knew better. Court recessed at seven, and I was dying to get out of there and have another drink and even return to my cell if that's what it took to get away from Levy and all his questions. I'd long ago quit looking at the jury, like Mr. Dewey had told me I should on direct, because Levy kept my answers so short that there wasn't any time to do it, and it would've looked phony-baloney if I tried. But just the one time, after he'd asked me about the backseat voices and I'd said that I could see their lips moving in the mirror—that one time I peeked over to check how my story was going over.

God, I couldn't wait for seven o'clock.

Forty-Five

Reasonable Doubt

May 1936

LUCKY IS DYING a slow death, sitting and listening to the testimony of Cokey Flo Brown. Even on cross-examination, even when Levy is batting her around like a cat with a wounded mouse, Lucky can see that the jury is sympathetic. See that they care about her, and feel sorry for her, and want to protect her from the clutches of Charlie Lucky and his swarthy gang of downtown thugs who've bullied and threatened and reduced this poor, wayward girl to the shivering shell that sits before them in the witness chair.

It's all Lucky can do to control his temper. But a flash of anger, a sudden outburst, is exactly what Dewey is hoping for. Betillo had exploded during the testimony of Danny Brooks, forcing his lawyer, Caesar Barra, to physically restrain him. It had looked bad—like Little Davie was the frightening, hair-trigger thug of Dewey's

312

narrative. Lucky understands this, and Polakoff and Levy have already warned him about it.

The problem, Lucky thinks, is that Levy is taking too damned long with his cross-examination, dwelling on things he's already covered over and over again. Probing for inconsistencies, Lucky supposes, but finding few and boring the jurors in the process. Plus he's burying the good points he's already made and giving Cokey Flo too many chances to repeat her ridiculous story. Worse, he's overlooking all kinds of opportunities to paint her as the dirty rotten liar she obviously is.

Take the fact that she seems to use a different name every time she appears in a courtroom. That should have been central to Levy's cross, but instead of hitting her with it, Levy's passed right over it, even though Cokey Flo herself has said that she'd never commit perjury for anyone.

Or take the fact that she claims to remember everything she'd ordered, right down to what she'd had for drinks and dessert, at some Chinese restaurant where she'd eaten dinner over two years earlier. And yet here she is five minutes later, claiming to have spent hours parked in front of some East Side garage—not once but twice—but still can't describe where the hell it's located.

It's easy, Lucky knows, to watch from the front row and criticize the guys in the ring. But still, Levy is supposed to be a pro. He should be knocking this girl senseless, not treating her with kid gloves. And if his strategy is to wear her down by keeping her on the witness stand, it clearly isn't working. If anything, Levy himself seems to be wearing down, and getting punchy, and putting the judge and the jury to sleep.

Lucky can't wait for the recess, so he can read Levy the riot act. Tell him to make his points and get out again, like a boxer throwing a jab. That's all he has to do—in and out—not spend hours going over every last detail of the direct examination.

And the jury, what are they thinking, sitting there like men around a campfire, hanging on every word and gesture from this lying little hophead? Talk about receiving money from the proceeds of a woman engaged in prostitution! This Cokey Flo is the one who ought to be on trial, not Charlie Lucky.

This whole case, in fact, is ass-backward, with the whores and the pimps and the bookers—the real offenders of public morals—throwing stones at the bondsmen and the shylocks for taking a small piece of their action in order to keep the girls off the city's streets and out of the city's jails. For performing a public service, for Christ sake! Come to think of it, this whole trial seems to be geared toward freeing the whores and madams while cutting their overhead and making their business more profitable.

That's some use of public money!

Finally, thank God, seven o'clock rolls around, and the judge puts Lucky out of his misery. The jurors stand and stretch, and the other defendants hunch to huddle with their lawyers. Lucky waits, ignoring the reporters who shout questions to him over the railing while Levy and Polakoff and Polakoff's kid Mezansky have a powwow by the lectern. Dewey, meanwhile, sits cool as a cucumber as his man Ten Eyck helps Cokey Flo from the witness chair and leads her like the father of the bride through the side door next to the jury box.

Heading straight for the brandy bottle, Lucky figures, or maybe the needle, and soon it's just the defendants and the lawyers left in the courtroom, plus the omnipresent guards, who busy themselves with their shotguns and handcuffs.

"We need to talk!" Lucky calls to Levy, who nods and seeks out the captain of the guard.

Once the four men are alone in the privacy of the wood-paneled jury room, Lucky lets them have it. Too long, too soft, and too goddamned boring! In and out, like throwing a jab. Get the crowd behind you. Bring some electricity into the arena!

"You've got to step on her a little," he tells Levy, knowing even as he speaks them that his words make him sound exactly like the Charlie Lucky of Dewey's narrative—the callous overlord ordering Jimmy Fredericks to beat the madams bloody.

Surprised by his client's outburst, Levy says, "I thought you were the one who said Carlino and Siegel were being too hard on the girls."

"Yeah, but that was before."

"Before they were talking about you, you mean."

"I mean before they started lying, goddamn it!"

"I think you're overreacting, Charlie," Polakoff intercedes in a soothing voice. "In fact, I think it's going rather well. What about you, Sam?"

The Mezansky kid shrugs. "I only caught the tail end, but I'm not buying a word she says."

"What about the jury?" Levy asks him. "Could you get a read—"

"Listen you guys," Lucky interrupts, again raising his voice. "I got ringside tickets to the Louis-Schmeling fight, and the way things are goin out there, I might as well give 'em away. We need to quit dancin around and knock this broad on her ass."

Neither Polakoff nor Levy responds.

"What's the story with this Captain Dutton?" Lucky turns on the kid, who seems to shrink under his gaze.

"We talked to him. He says he's never met Bendix in his life. But here's the best part. He says he knows the wife, Joy Dixon, which is probably why Bendix pulled Dutton's name out of his hat."

"Subpoena?"

Mezansky nods to Polakoff. "He said he'll be available whenever we need him."

A knock sounds at the door. Maurice Cantor, counsel for Jack Eller, sticks his head into the room.

"Sorry to interrupt, George, but I thought you'd like to know. Dorothy Calvit's lawyer is named Samuel Kornbluth. He's got an office in the Continental Building on Broadway."

"Can we talk to her?"

"I haven't called him yet, but I have his number. I figured you'd want to be in on that conversation."

315

Forty-Six

Kornbluth

May 1936

IT WASN'T UNTIL midnight that George and Maurice Cantor were
able to repair to Cantor's office and place the telephone call. Samuel
Kornbluth's voice, thick with sleep, answered on the second ring.

"Hello?"

"Mr. Kornbluth? This is attorney Maurice Cantor calling. I'm
terribly sorry to disturb you at home, and at such a late hour, but I'm
wondering whether you're still counsel for Dorothy Calvit, Lillian
Russell's daughter?"

"Is something wrong with Dorothy?"

"No, nothing like that. But I have an associate here, Mr. George
Morton Levy, and he'd like to have a word with you."

Cantor passed the receiver to George.

"Mr. Kornbluth? George Levy here, counsel for Charlie Luciano
in the Dewey vice trial. First of all, let me join in my colleague's

apology for the lateness of the hour, but I'm afraid it couldn't be helped."

"What is it, Mr. Levy? What can I do for you?"

"Well, Sam—may I call you Sam?—we have a witness on the stand right now who claims she used to work for Mrs. Calvit, and that Mrs. Calvit came to court not long ago to testify on her behalf. This witness, who goes by the name Cokey Flo Brown, claims that she knows my client, Mr. Luciano. My client says she's lying, and we were hoping that your client could help us shed some light on the situation."

"But why would you need to bother Dorothy—"

"Because they lived together, as we understand it, at the Hotel Alamac. We haven't attempted to contact Mrs. Calvit directly, since she'd only refer us to you, so we thought it prudent to contact you in the first instance and try to speed matters along. This is extremely important, as I hope you'll understand, and tomorrow is our last chance to cross-examine this witness. That means we need to know by tonight anything that Mrs. Calvit can tell us about her."

George held the receiver from his ear so that Cantor, leaning across his desk, could hear the sounds of squeaking bedsprings and rustling fabric. When Kornbluth's voice returned, it was louder than before.

"I understand your problem, gentlemen, but my goodness. You don't expect me to call her up and interrogate her at this late hour, do you?"

"Actually, Sam, we were hoping you could meet with her in person. I've taken a room at the Waldorf tonight, and Mr. Cantor and I are heading there in a moment. We'd like you to meet us in Peacock Alley so that we can give you all the details. Then we'd like you to visit Mrs. Calvit and ask her a few questions on our behalf, all within the purview of the attorney-client privilege. Then we'd like you to return to the Waldorf and fill us in. That means you'll have to call her now, as soon as we hang up, to make the necessary arrangements."

"Now hold on a minute—"

317

"Please understand that there's nothing untoward that we're asking you to do. The only thing out of the ordinary is the lateness of the hour and the urgency required."

"Yes, but—"

"I can't overemphasize how important this is, Sam. An innocent man's freedom is at stake."

"I understand, but—"

"And needless to say, you'll be compensated for your time."

The line fell silent as George held Cantor's gaze.

"Compensated how?"

Smiling, Cantor swung his feet onto the desk.

It was nine A.M. on Saturday morning when George descended to the Waldorf's lobby. He'd stopped only at the cigar counter on his way to the Park Avenue entrance, where Samuel Kornbluth, looking rumpled in blue seersucker, waited by the stairs.

"Thank you for being so punctual," George said as he offered the lawyer his hand and continued down the steps to the street. "I'm sorry about last night, but I simply had to get some sleep."

"Of course," Kornbluth said, hurrying to keep up. "I understand perfectly."

The traffic on Park Avenue was light. The bellman blew his whistle, hailing an approaching cab.

"As I told Mr. Cantor last evening—"

"Yes, we spoke on the phone. I hope you don't mind riding with me to the courthouse. I want to hear Mrs. Calvit's story firsthand, as it were."

"Foley Square," George told the cabbie as the men settled, shoulder to shoulder, in the roomy backseat, each with a briefcase in his lap.

"I understand you took notes."

"Yes, of course." Kornbluth unlatched his satchel and rummaged inside. He removed a yellow legal tablet and flipped to a page that

George could see was covered with hasty scrawl. "I'm sorry she can't be of more help to Mr. Luciano."

The cabbie's eyes jumped in the rearview mirror.

"Why not let me be the judge of that? If you would, just tell me what she said."

Kornbluth reclined into the seatback, balancing the tablet on his satchel.

"First of all, she's never heard the name Cokey Flo Brown. But she did read the newspaper last evening, and was quite surprised to learn that her name had been mentioned in connection with the Luciano trial, which she found quite disturbing, as you might imagine. She assumes this Brown person is actually Mildred Nelson, the young lady she hired to act as her personal typist back in February. Miss Nelson had been recommended to Mrs. Calvit by her physician, Dr. Gardener, who happened to treat Miss Nelson for a gall bladder condition."

"Gall bladder condition?"

"That's what Dr. Gardener said. Miss Nelson seemed pleasant enough, and she confided in Mrs. Calvit up to a point, telling her that she was sweethearts with a man named Frederico, who was one of the defendants being held in the Dewey vice case. She said she loved him and wanted very badly to help him. Mrs. Calvit didn't pry, of course, but one day she was reading in the newspaper that Luciano had been arrested out west somewhere, and she commented on that fact to Miss Nelson. Well, Miss Nelson grabbed the newspaper right out of Dorothy's hands and said the photo in the paper didn't look like Luciano. Dorothy asked whether she'd ever met this Luciano before, and Miss Nelson said that she'd seen him, but that the photo didn't look like him."

"Seen him? Not that she'd actually met him?"

Kornbluth shrugged. "Seen him. That's what my notes say."

"All right, go on."

"Having completed the typing work for which she'd been hired, Miss Nelson began looking for her own apartment. On May the seventh, at approximately four thirty P.M., Miss Nelson returned to the Hotel Alamac and told Dorothy that she'd found a room at 140 West Seventy-Fifth Street, and that she'd be moving there shortly. Dorothy wrote down the address. Miss Nelson also mentioned that she'd been picking up extra money in dance studios."

"Dance studios?"

"Yes, exactly. Then two days later at around noon, Dorothy received a telegram from Miss Nelson stating that she'd been arrested for prostitution and was being held under the name Fay Marston on a three-hundred-dollar bond. She asked if Dorothy would communicate that fact to an attorney named Samuel Siegel, which Dorothy did. When the case came up for trial, Dorothy agreed to testify that she'd been Miss Nelson's previous employer, which she also did, but Miss Nelson was convicted anyway. And I'm afraid that's all there is to it."

"No more communications after the conviction?"

"Not until Thursday of this week, when Miss Nelson returned to the apartment with a pair of detectives to pick up some clothes. Dorothy said that Miss Nelson was railing against Frederico and his associates for letting her rot in jail for twelve days."

"And that's it?"

"I'm afraid so. Dorothy is not a well woman, Mr. Levy, and as the daughter of Lillian Russell, she's something of a public figure. I don't think it would be in her best interests to be caught up in this Luciano business. For one thing, it might affect the salability of the book she's working on. And frankly, given the state of her knowledge, I don't see how her testimony would be of any help to anyone."

The taxi had stopped at the courthouse mall. A handful of reporters and photographers approached the vehicle as George leaned to reach into his pocket.

"All right, Sam. I think I agree with your assessment, but give me some time to consider it. Out of curiosity, what's this book Mrs. Calvit is writing?"

"It's her mother's biography. But now that you mention it . . ."

"What is it? What's the matter?"

"Oh, it's nothing, I'm sure. I just remembered that Dorothy said she'd written a story once based on something Miss Nelson had told her. About her life, I presume. Dorothy submitted it to Macfadden Publications, but it was rejected as being too much like fiction. Miss Nelson apparently asked about the story when she came to the apartment on Thursday. Wanted to know if it was going to be published. Dorothy thought it was odd, but Miss Nelson seemed pleased to learn it had been rejected."

Forty-Seven

Missed Connections

May 1936

LEVY OPENED THE Saturday morning session with what struck Tom as a very unusual question.

Q: Miss Brown, did you ever go under the name of Florence Nelson?

A: No, I never did.

Q: Did you ever give your name as Florence Nelson to anyone?

A: No, I never did.

Q: What is the name of the lady that you claimed you worked for up at the Hotel Alamac?

A: Mrs. Calvit.

Q: Calvit?

A: Yes.

Q: And did you tell her that your name was Florence Nelson?

A: No, I didn't.

Tom looked at Sol Gelb, seated to his right. Gelb scribbled something on his pad. It was a question mark.

Q: And when you read about the arrest of Fredericks, did you tell anybody that you were very much in love with him, and that you would do anything in the world to help him?
A: If I did, I don't recall it.
Q: Did you tell the lady you were working for up at the Hotel Alamac, either in the month of February or March, anything to that effect?
A: No, I don't think so.

Gelb was scribbling again. This time his entry read, *They've talked to the Calvit woman!*

Q: You wrote Jimmy Fredericks over in the jail, did you not?
A: I did not.
Q: At no time?
A: No.
Q: Never wrote him a letter?
A: An inmate of one institution cannot write to another inmate.
Q: No, I don't mean that. Before you got into jail, did you write him a letter?
A: Yes.
Q: Write him more than one?
A: A number of letters.
Q: You use the typewriter, do you not?
A: Yes, I do.
Q: May I show you this letter and ask you if you wrote that to Jimmy Fredericks on or about April twenty-third of this year?
(Examines letter.)
A: I don't believe I wrote this letter.

Q: You don't believe you wrote that letter. Now look at it very carefully.

A: I don't believe I wrote it. I would not make that many mistakes on it.

Q: You would not make them? Well then, your statement to this Court and jury is, then, is it, that you did not write that letter?

A: I did write a typewritten letter.

Q: Did you write that particular letter you are now looking at, please, yes or no?

A: I will say yes, because it looks a good deal like it.

Q: Well, a moment ago you didn't think you wrote it, isn't that right?

A: I don't think it is the same letter I wrote.

Q: Well then, which is it? Do you think it is the letter you wrote, or do you think it is not? Please, look at it again if you wish.

(Again examines letter.)

A: I always signed the letters. There is no signature to this.

Q: Yes, that is right. And it is also addressed "Dear Cousin," is it not?

A: Yes, it is.

Q: And that is the customary way you wrote to Jimmy Fredericks, is it not?

A: Yes.

Q: You knew the mail was censored over at the prison, did you not?

A: Yes.

Q: And so therefore you were trying to create the impression that you were his cousin, were you not?

A: Well, I was not trying to create any impression.

Q: Well, you wrote that way, didn't you?

A: Yes.

Q: And you knew when you wrote that way and addressed him as "Dear Cousin," that some of the jail officials would examine the letter, did you not?

A: Yes.

Q: Now look at it again, please, and tell us, one way or another, did you write it or didn't you?

A. Well, I will say I wrote it.

Q: Just a moment. What do you mean, "I will say I wrote it," if you don't think you did?

A: Well, I couldn't say I wrote this letter for sure.

Q: Well, look. Read the contents of that letter, if you will, and see if they do not refresh your recollection that that is your type of language.

(Again examines letter.)

A: All right, I wrote it.

Cokey Flo was dithering, Tom thought, and losing her composure. It was futile to deny that she'd once loved Frederico and had written of her willingness to help him. Why would she even try?

Levy would argue that her willingness extended to perjuring herself to assist the special prosecutor. So be it. Tom would simply counter that her ardor for Fredericks had cooled as she'd cooled her heels in jail. That was a wash at worst, leaving her important testimony—the five in-person meetings with Luciano—intact. What vexed Tom was that they'd already covered the Dear Cousin letters in her preparation sessions. More than once, in fact. She was a silly girl for letting it rattle her.

Having made his point, Levy then moved in a new and unexpected direction.

Q: You knew at the time that you wrote that letter to Mr. Ten Eyck that no defense lawyer intended using you as a witness, did you not?

A: Yes, I did.

Q: There is no question about that in your mind?

A: No, there is not.

Q: And you had read of this sensational case, had you not?

A: I had read of it, yes.

Q: Did you have any desire to get any notoriety out of this case?

A: None at all.

Q: Did you have in your mind that you might get some notoriety which you might be able to commercialize in some way later on?

A: I don't see how I could commercialize that.

Q: Did you, yes or no, please?

A: No.

Levy, Tom thought, was grasping at straws. A bid for publicity? Could he really be serious? What kind of an idiot would want the notoriety that comes with admitting she's a drug addict and a madam, a prostitute and a fugitive? Why, it was laughable on its face. Tom, his eyebrows raised, turned away from the jury toward Ten Eyck.

Who looked like he'd just seen a ghost.

Forty-Eight

Judas

May 1936

AND JUST LIKE that, it was over.

First Levy sat down, then two of the other lawyers—Barra and Paley—asked a few questions each, and then Mr. Dewey stood up and said, "No questions," and the judge said, "You can step down from the stand."

At first I just sat there, still kind of dazed, waiting for the next lawyer, kind of the way that guys in a bar fight wait for the next broken bottle. Then I realized that no more were coming, and that the fight was finally over, and only then did the judge's words finally sink in.

I was a free woman!

Mrs. Carter was waiting for me in the witness room, and she patted my arm and said I was a hero. Some hero! My knees were practically knocking, that's how weak I felt, or how relieved, I

327

couldn't tell which. All's I knew was that it was over, and that I'd survived, and that I wanted out of that building like I'd never wanted anything in my life.

We left by the back staircase again, and again I was driven directly to the Woolworth Building. It was almost noon when we arrived, and this time I was led not into Mr. Dewey's private office but to a larger room with desks and chairs that was used, I think, by the detectives. When I stepped into the room, a dozen heads turned to face me, and some of the people started clapping.

"Here she is, ladies and gentlemen!"

It was Frank Hogan, one of Dewey's men who the girls called Father Frank. He crossed the room to greet me, and then he led me by the arm to an empty swivel chair.

"Just sit back and relax, Flo, this won't take very long."

There were others in the room I recognized, like Dopey Al Weiner—Cockeyed Louis's kid—and Andy Coco. They were all listening to what I thought at first was a radio program, from a loudspeaker sitting on a desk, until I recognized Mr. Dewey's voice.

Pete Harris's wife, Millie, was there, and I changed seats to take the chair next to hers.

"What's going on?" I whispered.

"We're listening to the trial. This is some bath maid from the Waldorf."

"Bath maid at the Waldorf?"

"Where Lucky lived. She says Little Abie and Davie and Meyer Berkman used to come to Lucky's apartment all the time."

"So what?"

"So Levy, Lucky's lawyer, told the jury that Lucky didn't know any of those guys from Adam. So either the maid's lying or he is."

"Shhh!"

Hogan had turned with a finger to his lips, and so I sat back with Millie and just listened. It occurred to me that if Millie knew what Levy had said to the jury, probably in his opening statement, then she must've been listening to the whole trial from the beginning, like it was some kind of radio drama.

It was weird, sitting around like that, listening to what was happening in the very same courtroom where I'd just spent three days spilling my guts. And then I realized that all the people in that room had probably been listening to me the whole time I was on the stand, and I started replaying that testimony in my head: all the lousy things I'd had to say about shooting dope and jumping bail and getting pinched for streetwalking. Sounding like a dumbbell for not remembering the places I said I'd met Charlie Lucky. Sounding like a rat for putting the finger on Charlie and Tommy and Little Davie.

I'm no dumbbell, I wanted to tell them—I'm smarter than you'll ever know. If I'd mentioned exact locations, then people could've gone there and asked questions. And I'm no rat either, because I owed nothing to Charlie Lucky or Little Davie or Tommy the Bull, and I tried my level best to take care of the only man in New York who'd ever taken care of me.

Poor Jimmy, I thought, still sitting in the courtroom with that dazed look on his face, acting like I'd sold him up the river. But I hadn't, had I? I said he'd handled the bonding, and there was no denying that, but I'd made it perfectly clear that he'd never got rough with the madams and that he'd had nothing to do with the booking. I'd done him a favor, the big oaf, even if doing it had made me look like a liar.

Someday Jimmy would understand that, and maybe he'd even thank me. But even if he didn't, then what of it? I had myself to look out for, and my own future to think of, with no combination muscle or fancy lawyers to help me out when I needed it.

I was on my own now, and what was done was done. But I'd been on my own ever since I was fourteen, and you know what? I liked it that way. I always did and I always would, with no man underfoot telling me how to act or what to think. So screw Jimmy, I thought—I didn't need his approval or anyone else's. I was plenty smart, and

I was plenty tough, and I was the one who was gonna be famous when this thing was over. More famous than Mae West even, and who'd be laughing then? I would, that's who. Laughing all the way to the bank.

"Geez, honey," Millie whispered, pressing a handkerchief into my hand. "Don't start bawlin on us."

Forty-Nine

Golem

May 1936

ON FRIDAY, MAY 29, the prosecution finally rests. Dewey moves to dismiss twenty-six of the ninety counts in the indictment, stating that proof as to those matters would be redundant. He has called sixty-eight witnesses, forty of them prostitutes or madams, but only a handful who really matter to the question of Lucky's guilt or innocence.

Joe Bendix was a joke, of course, but Cokey Flo was no laughing matter. Then, perhaps smelling the blood in the water, Dewey followed Cokey Flo with seven employees from the Waldorf and Barbizon-Plaza Hotels who each identified, with varying degrees of certainty, the co-defendants they claimed to have seen visiting Charlie Lucky's apartment.

Next came Nancy Presser, the former girlfriend of defendant Ralph Liguori. A higher class of call girl before her withering descent into

331

heroin addiction, Presser was the third of Dewey's bombshell eye-witnesses, but, as with Joe Bendix before her, the bomb went off in the special prosecutor's face. After testifying to over a dozen professional liaisons with Lucky at both the Barbizon-Plaza and the Waldorf Towers—visits at which she claimed to have overheard Lucky discussing the bonding combination—Presser was eviscerated by Levy on cross-examination when she proved unable to describe Lucky's Waldorf apartment—Was there a piano? Was there a fire-place?—or how to reach it from the hotel lobby, or even whether it had twin or double beds. So flustered was Presser that at one point, claiming sudden illness, she attempted to bolt from the witness chair.

The implosion of Nancy Presser revived Lucky's spirits after the staggering one-two punch of Cokey Flo and the hotel employees. But Lucky was soon back on the canvas with the appearance of Mildred Balitzer, the wife of booker Pete Harris, whom Dewey was saving to deliver his final knockout.

Big and buxom, with the hardboiled demeanor of the prostitute, madam, and drug addict she long had been, Balitzer testified to pleas she'd allegedly made to Lucky, both in Miami and New York, that Pete be allowed out of the combination. As with Cokey Flo's before her, Balitzer's testimony proved difficult to impeach, its impact depending entirely on her credibility with the jury. The only silver lining after her nine hours in the witness chair was Balitzer's admission to a night of revelry at Leon and Eddie's nightclub in the company of Sol Gelb, Dewey's right-hand man—testimony that finally gave flesh to Levy's frequent insinuations of undue witness influence.

Now Memorial Day weekend would mark a sea change in the trial—a shift from the prosecution's case to that of the defense. It would be a time to lick wounds, and take stock, and prepare for what lay ahead.

"Between Cokey Flo and them hotel people," Lucky tells his lawyers after court adjourns on Friday, "this jury's got me fitted for striped pajamas. It ain't a question of whether I testify anymore; it's only a question of when."

"Now hold on a minute," Polakoff tells him. "There's no cause for panic. We've still got Captain Dutton, and now we've got this mis-delivered letter from Bendix to his wife."

"You ain't listenin, Moe. Fuck Bendix. Nobody believed a word he said anyhow. You got a witness who can answer Cokey Flo?"

"Sam Siegel said he'd testify."

"Yeah, well good luck with that. He practically testified already, and them jurors believed every stinkin lie she told 'em. The same with that Balitzer bitch."

"We've got police officers coming from Pittsburg to say that Davey Miller lied when he denied running a disorderly house. Then Gus Franco will testify that he never introduced Mildred to Tommy or Davie like she claimed. Liguori will testify that Dewey's men threatened to indict him unless he fingered you, and that they gave your photo to Nancy Presser and Thelma Jordan to memorize. He'll also say that Dewey promised to send him and Nancy to Europe as a reward for their cooperation. Then Chappie will testify that Gay Orlova's your girl, and that he's never laid eyes on Presser or any of the others before in his life. Plus we've got a dozen witnesses lined up to testify as to your gambling history and habits. In short, we've got more than enough evidence to raise a reasonable doubt in the minds of these jurors."

"But nothin that puts the lie to Cokey Flo."

Polakoff turns to Levy, his look imploring. Levy removes a cigar from his pocket and studies it as he speaks.

"Look, Charlie, I understand how you feel, I really do. But it kills me to put a client on the witness stand, even in the best of circumstances. Here there's no telling what McCook will let Dewey get away with. If you think all the hearsay he's allowed into evidence has been damaging, wait until he lets Dewey examine you about your arrest record, and your income sources, and all your business associations."

"I already told you. I'm a gambler, and I can prove it."

"You also told me that except for Betillo, you'd never laid eyes on any of your co-defendants. And I told that to the jury."

Lucky shifts in his chair, a hand mopping his face. He, at least, can see where this thing is heading, even if Polakoff and Levy can't. Or else they can, but don't want to admit it. But it isn't their necks in the noose. They'll get paid whatever happens to Charlie Lucky, and they'll be out playing golf while he sweats in the prison laundry.

"So maybe I seen Tommy and Ralph around town now and again. So what? That don't mean we done any business together. But if I admitted that to Dewey, he'd make it out like we're peas in a pod."

"If you'd leveled with me, I could have fronted the issue and minimized its impact."

"You fuckin lawyers," he tells them. "You live in your ivory tower and you can't even see what's goin on right in front of your fuckin noses. 'May it please the court, my learned friend for the prosecution.' This ain't the church social, boys. This is a carny, and the game's been rigged from day one. Only a sucker plays fair in a rigged game, and Charlie Lucky is nobody's sucker."

"I'd say this is more like a turkey shoot," Levy counters, pointing his cigar for emphasis, "and you're the one wearing the feathers. We don't want to give them a clear shot at you unless it absolutely can't be helped. We've already given Cokey Flo a black eye, and Mildred Balitzer as well. And we'll argue that by the time the hotel employees were finished looking at Dewey's photographs, they'd have said Santa Claus was in your apartment. Like Moe said, now is no time to panic."

"Listen to him," Polakoff urges.

"Plus I've been talking with some of the reporters," Levy says, trying a change of tack. "We were odds-on for acquittal before Cokey Flo and the bath maid, and now we're back to even money. Given all we've been up against, those are still pretty good odds. Now is no time to put a joker in the deck."

Lucky stands and runs a hand through his hair as he paces a tight circle.

"Okay, here's what I think. First of all, I'm sorry for losin my temper just now. I got nothin but respect for the job you guys done, so let's get that off the table. Second, if you think I'm runnin scared, then you don't know me very well. I ain't afraid of Dewey, and I ain't afraid of what he'll do to me if I testify. So if you think I'm just gonna sit there and let that cocksucker put me in a frame and not do nothin about it, then you got another think comin."

Lucky stops pacing and faces Levy head-on.

"If there's one thing I learned from Arnold Rothstein, it's that scared money can't win. You and me, George, we both know all that innocent-until-proven-guilty stuff is a bunch of bullshit. Only the guilty don't testify, and everybody knows it."

"I knew Rothstein as well, Charlie. And the most important lesson he ever taught me was to quit while you're ahead."

"Only we ain't ahead. You just said so yourself. No, I been givin this thing a lot of thought, and unless you've got an ace up that sleeve of yours, I'm takin the stand and that's all there is to it."

"Then you'll be making a big mistake," Levy tells him. "Believe me, I've seen it before. You have very little to gain by testifying. The jury already knows you deny the allegations. I've told them once, and I'll tell them again. But you have everything to lose by opening the door to your past. In fact, that's exactly what Dewey's been hoping for. Right now, Charlie, I think you beat this thing. But once you get in that witness chair, then all bets are off."

"I'm sorry, George, but I can't let that cunt get away with it. And the old lady's out of the picture, right?"

"If you mean Dorothy Calvit, she's been threatened with arrest if she even talks to us. Sam Kornbluth, her lawyer, has already been arrested for attempted subornation of perjury."

"See what I mean about a rigged game? So look at it this way. If I don't testify, and I get convicted, I'll spend my whole stretch kickin myself in the head for not takin the stand. But if I testify and go down in flames, then what the hell, at least I'll know I gave it my best shot."

Lucky rests both hands on the chair back where he stands.

"I get one chance to look them jurors in the eye and tell 'em the honest truth. I done a lot of bad things in my life, but takin money from whores ain't one of 'em. I gave, sure, but I never took. And if Dewey calls me a crook and says I'm public enemy number one, then so be it. That ain't what I'm on trial for, right?"

"You're wrong about one thing," Levy tells him. "The presumption of innocence is not so lightly dismissed. It's the bedrock of our legal system, and the lynchpin of the closing argument I'd planned to make on your behalf. Right now there are four eyewitnesses against you, and two of them have been thoroughly discredited. Or will be, by the time we rest. Their lies have hurt Dewey's case and hurt his credibility. But if you take the stand and let him bring Al Capone and Dutch Schultz into this courtroom, the jury will forget all of that. Trust me, I've seen it before. They won't give a hang about Bendix or Presser or the charges in the indictment. All they'll want to do is slay the golem Dewey will have created."

"Slay the what?"

"The golem. Like Dr. Frankenstein's monster."

Lucky lays a hand on the older man's shoulder.

"Look, George. I'm sorry if I haven't always played straight with you. But even you've gotta see that Dewey's already made me out a fuckin monster. Now it's up to me to show them jurors I'm human."

Fifty

Faceoff

UNDER THE PERTINENT rules of evidence, proof of a defendant's bad character—for example, that he is dishonest, or violent, or has committed crimes in the past—is inadmissible to show that the defendant is more likely to have committed the crime with which he is presently charged. Only if the defendant himself places his character in issue by offering evidence of his good reputation—his honesty, for example, or his peaceful nature—may contrary evidence be offered by the prosecution.

When an accused chooses to testify in his own defense, however, the evidentiary landscape changes. In that case, evidence of prior crimes or misconduct, and especially crimes involving moral turpitude, is admissible to attack his character for truthfulness. But this rule of automatic admissibility is subject to a very important limitation. Where the prior crime is only collateral to the matter on trial—where, for example, it is offered for the sole purpose of impeaching the defendant's credibility—then the prosecutor is bound by the answers given by the witness, and may not waste time or confuse the issues at trial by offering extrinsic proof as to the prior crime or misconduct.

George, of course, explained these rules to his client. If Lucky took the witness stand, then Dewey could question him as to the facts and circumstances of every crime he'd ever committed. This, George told him, would inject a litany of otherwise irrelevant and highly prejudicial material into the case, all to Lucky's detriment. And George concluded his lecture with a final warning:

"The trial court has broad discretion in determining the admissibility of prior bad acts. That means if you do take the witness stand, you're all but putting yourself at the mercy of Judge McCook."

And the quality of McCook's mercy, George was certain, would be strained indeed, dropping more like a steel hammer than any gentle rain from heaven.

The defense presentation had begun well enough, with twenty-one of Lucky's scheduled twenty-five witnesses having already testified. These included the ephemeral Captain Dutton and assistant district attorney Morris Panger. They included Lorenzo "Chappie" Brescio, and Gus Franco, and the police contingent from Pittsburgh. And they soon would include NYPD patrol officer George Heidt, who would provide a damning eyewitness account of Sol Gelb's and Mildred Balitzer's night of drunken revelry at Leon and Eddie's nightclub.

George tried one last time to dissuade his client from taking the witness stand, only to find himself talking to stone. If anything, Luciano had been energized by the defense witnesses and was more eager than ever to testify.

"Don't worry about me," Lucky told his lawyers when the fateful day arrived. "I can handle that little prick."

Thus was the stage set for the moment that the jury, and the reporters, and most of the American public, had been so breathlessly waiting. The moment that George had so thoroughly dreaded. The moment when, in the trial's fourth week—on Tuesday afternoon, June 2, 1936—Lucky Luciano crossed to the witness chair and raised his hand to be sworn.

George's direct examination was short and to the point. Lucky denied the allegations of the indictment, and he denied any involvement in the business of prostitution. He was a professional gambler and bookmaker, Lucky testified, whose only prior convictions had been for selling narcotics in New York in 1916 and for maintaining a gambling establishment in Miami in 1930. Specifically, Lucky denied ever meeting any of the eyewitnesses—Joe Bendix, Cokey Flo Brown, Nancy Presser, or Mildred Balitzer—who had testified otherwise. With the exception of the hotel employees, he said, "There has not been a witness that got on this stand of Mr. Dewey's that I ever saw in my life." And with that firm denial finally on the record, George sat and braced himself for the coming onslaught.

He didn't have long to wait.

Q: How old were you when you were convicted of selling narcotics?
A: Eighteen, around eighteen.
Q: How long were you selling narcotics before you got caught?
A: Oh, around three weeks or a month.
Q: It was not the first transaction, however, was it?
A: What?
Q: You did not get caught on the very first ounce of morphine that you handled?
A: No.
Q: Was it the second, perchance?
A: No.
Q: Was it the third?
A: I told you, about three weeks after.
Q: I am asking you, how many transactions had you before you got caught?

A: That I can't remember.

Q: Had you as many as a hundred, or just two or three?

A: I didn't have no hundred, and I had more than three.

Dewey then shifted his focus to Lucky's driving record. Reading from a stack of official documents, the special prosecutor reviewed a dozen citations Lucky had received between 1922 and 1931, in each case quizzing the witness as to the story he'd told the arresting officer. While George had instructed his client that on such collateral matters, Dewey would have to accept Lucky's answers and could not impeach him with the written records, Lucky either forgot what he'd been told or else was determined to answer the questions truthfully.

Yes, he might have told patrolman Clay in August of 1922 that he was a chauffeur. Yes, he might have told patrolman Harris in August of 1924 that he was a salesman. While he could not recall telling patrolman Hunt in December of 1924 that he was a fruit vendor, he may have told patrolman Carter in June of 1925 that he was a salesman.

And so it went. All of these answers, of course, belied Lucky's claim to having been employed only as a gambler, a point that Dewey hammered home in a single question:

Q: You lied about things, didn't you?

A: Yes. I probably told them that I had an occupation and I didn't have it.

Dewey then segued from white lies told at a traffic stop to ever more serious falsehoods.

Q: On how many occasions did you perjure yourself when you were trying to get a pistol to carry around?

MR. LEVY: That is objected to, if it please the Court. The word "perjury" under the law is ambiguous.

THE COURT: It may be so.

MR. LEVY: It depends on a great many situations.

THE COURT: Better be more specific. I have heard of such things.

Q: On how many occasions did you lie under oath in order to get a gun to carry around the streets of New York?

A: Once, I think.

Q: Only once?

A: I think so, yes.

Q: Did you get the gun?

A: Yes.

Dewey, George saw, was sketching a picture of the younger Luciano as a bodyguard and gunman, rather than a gentleman gambler. And with his next series of questions, he added color to that portrait.

Q: On July 27, 1926, were you with a man named Joseph Scalise?

MR. LEVY: Again objected to as irrelevant, immaterial, incompetent.

THE COURT: Overruled.

MR. LEVY: Exception.

Q: Were you?

A: That is right.

Q: And did you have two guns and a shotgun and forty-five rounds of ammunition in the car between you?

MR. LEVY: Just a moment. That is objected to as irrelevant, immaterial, incompetent, and improper cross-examination.

THE COURT: Overruled.

MR. LEVY: Exception.

Q: Did you or didn't you?

A: I just come back from the country, and I had a hunting outfit in there.

Q: Yes?

A: Yes.

Q: You had two revolvers?

A: Yes.

Q: And a shotgun?

A: Yes.

Q: And forty-five rounds of ammunition?

A: And a couple of boxes of cartridges.

Q: Yes, and what were you shooting on that day?

A: What?

Q: What were you shooting on that day in the country?

A: On that day, I wasn't shooting nothing.

Q: What were you doing out in the country?

A: I wasn't up the country. I just come in.

Q: Come in from where?

A: From the country.

Q: What had you been doing in the country that day?

A: Shooting.

Q: Shooting what?

A: Birds.

Q: What kind of birds?

MR. LEVY: That is objected to.

A: Pheasants.

Lucky pronounced the word "peasants," and the courtroom erupted in laughter.

MR. LEVY: This is back ten years.

THE COURT: Overruled.

MR. LEVY: Irrelevant, immaterial, incompetent. Exception.

Q: Shooting pheasants?

A: Yes.

Q: In the middle of July?

A: That is right.

Q: Shooting pheasants in the middle of July?

A: Yes, that is right.

Q: Is that your answer?

A: That is right.

Dewey then moved to another occasion on which Lucky had been arrested but never prosecuted.

Q: Do you recall a little incident on June 6, 1923? Does that mean anything in your life?

A: I don't remember what you mean.

Q: No recollection at all?

A: No.

Q: All right. Do you remember first, on June 2, 1923, selling a two-ounce box of narcotics to John Lyons, an informer for the federal Secret Service?

MR. LEVY: Objected to as irrelevant, immaterial, and incompetent.

THE COURT: Overruled.

MR. LEVY: Exception.

A: Nineteen twenty-three?

Q: Yes, sir.

A: I was arrested—

MR. LEVY: Now I object.

Q: I did not ask you that. I asked you whether on June 2, 1923, you did not sell a two-ounce box of narcotics to John Lyons, an informer in the Secret Service.

A: I was arrested, but I never sold anything like that.

Q: I am asking you whether you did not on June 2—I ask you for a third time.

MR. LEVY: I submit it has been answered, if it pleases the Court.

THE COURT: He answered him something else. He may have included that, but I will allow it again so that we get a sole answer to that.

MR. LEVY: Exception.

Q: I want to know whether—

THE COURT: Yes or no is the answer.

Q: —whether on June 2, 1923, you did not sell a two-ounce box—

THE COURT: If you will take the negative out of it, it will be a little better, Mr. Dewey. Then we can get an answer yes or no.

Q: Isn't it a fact that on June 2, 1923, you sold a two-ounce box of narcotics known as diacetyl morphine hydrochloride to John Lyons, an informer for the Secret Service of the United States?

A: I don't know who they were, but I was arrested, and if I was charged with them, that I didn't do.

Q: I did not ask you anything except: Didn't you sell the dope to John Lyons on that date?

A: No.

Q: You deny it?

A: No.

Q: Flatly?

A: I don't deny that I was arrested.

Q: I did not ask you anything except whether you did not sell dope on that day.

A: I didn't sell it to him.

MR. LEVY: It has been answered, your Honor, that he did not.

THE COURT: We finally got an answer.

Q: Your answer is no?

A: No.

Q: Positive? Isn't it a fact that, three days later, on June 5, 1923, you again sold one ounce of heroin to informer John Lyons of the Secret Service of the United States?

A: No, sir.

Q: You did not sell him anything?

A: No, sir.

Q: Isn't it a fact that at 133 East Fourteenth Street in the city of New York, narcotics agent Coyle saw you sell narcotics to John Lyons?

MR. LEVY: That is objected to.

THE COURT: Sustained.

Q: Isn't it a fact that on that date your apartment was searched?

MR. LEVY: Objected to as irrelevant, immaterial, and incompetent.

THE COURT: Overruled.

MR. LEVY: Exception.

Q: Was it or was it not?

A: It might have been.

Q: Was it or was it not?

A: Yes.

Q: Why did you say "might have been?"

A: I wasn't there when they searched it.

Q: You are not quite sure about whether it was searched or not, is that it?

A: That is right.

Q: Isn't it a fact that in your apartment were found two one-half ounce packages of morphine, and two ounces of heroin, and some opium?

A: No, sir.

Q: Absolutely false?

A: Absolutely.

Q: Isn't it a fact that, thereafter, you gave to Joseph Van Bransky, narcotics agent in charge of New York City, a statement that at 163 Mulberry Street they would find a whole trunk of narcotics?

MR. LEVY: That is objected to as irrelevant, immaterial, and incompetent.

THE COURT: Overruled.

MR. LEVY: Exception.

Q: Didn't you give such a statement to Mr. Van Bransky?

A: Yes, I did.

Q: And isn't it a fact that, thereafter, a whole trunk of narcotics was found by the Secret Service at 163 Mulberry Street, New York City?

A: Yes, sir.

. . .

Q: And you still testify under oath before this Court and jury that you have not dealt in narcotics since the year 1919?

A: That is right.

Q: And that is your testimony now?

A: That is right.

Q: That is all on the subject. What were you—a stool pigeon?

A: I told him what I knew.

Q: Were you a stool pigeon?

A: I says, I told him what I knew.

Dewey had struck a nerve, and Lucky was squirming in the witness chair. Changing subjects, Dewey then produced telephone records from the Waldorf Towers switchboard. Why had Lucky made calls to Moe Ducore's drugstore, where Joe Bendix claimed to have visited him? Why had he made calls to Celano's Gardens, where combination meetings were allegedly held, and to Dave's Blue Room, where Nancy Presser said she had met him? Why had he called notorious mobsters like Louis "Lepke" Buchalter, Jacob "Gurrah" Shapiro, Ciro "the Artichoke King" Terranova, and Benjamin "Bugsy" Siegel? And apropos of the testimony of Cokey Flo Brown, why had he made several calls to the Standard Garage on the Lower East Side?

Dewey then returned to the subject of perjury, in the form of statements Lucky had made to the authorities following his 1929 kidnapping.

Q: Do you recall that you were found on Staten Island?

A: That is right.

Q: By a police officer?

A: That is right.

Q: You had been pretty badly beaten up and cut up?

A: That is right.

Q: Tape over your eyes and mouth?

A: That is right.

Q: And you told the police officers you did not want to give any information; that you would take care of that your own way?

MR. LEVY: That is objected to—

A: I did not.

MR. LEVY: —as irrelevant, immaterial, and incompetent.

THE COURT: Overruled.

MR. LEVY: Exception.

A: I gave them all the information I knew about it.

. . .

Q: Isn't it a fact that on or about October 18, 1929, you told Detective Gustav Schley of the New York police force to forget about it, and you would take care of it yourself?

A: I did not. I gave him all the details, how I got picked up, how they grabbed me, and everything.

Q: You were questioned before the grand jury, weren't you?

A: Yes.

Q: Under oath?

A: That is right.

Q: Do you still want to say the only times you lie under oath are when you are getting pistol permits?

A: Yes.

Dewey closed with Lucky's tax returns—a subject dear to the special prosecutor's heart—and specifically with the fact that Lucky had filed his federal returns for the years 1929 through 1934 as a group only eighteen days after Dewey's investigation had begun.

Q: Six years is the statute of limitations on indictments, isn't it?

A: Yes.

. . .

Q: Your rush of conscience is only with respect to the federal government, isn't it?

MR. LEVY: That is objected to.

THE COURT: Read that question again.

(Question read.)

THE COURT: Sustained.

Q: You have not paid a dime to the state government in income taxes yet, have you?

A: That is right.

MR. LEVY: Objected to as irrelevant, immaterial, and incompetent.

THE COURT: Overruled.

MR. LEVY: Exception.

. . .

Q: Your answer was, you have not paid a dime to the state government yet, right?

A: That is right.

Q: And that is because the federal government prosecutes big gangsters and the state does not, by income tax, isn't that so?

MR. LEVY: That is objected to.

THE COURT: Overruled.

MR. LEVY: Exception.

Q: Isn't that so?

A: I don't know.

Q: You do not know?

A: No.

Q: That is all.

And so it was. Over the course of four tension-filled hours, Dewey had managed, with an assist from Judge McCook, to depict George's client as a gunman, a dope peddler, a perjurer, and a tax cheat. What he'd failed to do, however, was connect Lucky in any way to the so-called bonding combination that was the subject of the prosecution.

Which, George knew from experience, didn't matter a whit.

Fifty-One

Verdict

June 1936

THE JURY CAME back on Sunday.

Tom, exhausted by his seven hours of closing argument, had retired to the judges' dining room on the fifth floor of the courthouse shortly after midnight, searching for an empty couch on which to collapse and close his eyes. To rehearse, perhaps, what he soon might say to the press. And what he hoped he'd not have to say.

That was his plan, at least. But what instead confronted him in the silent darkness were a month's worth of regrets and recriminations. Over witnesses lost, and gaffes committed, and opportunities badly squandered. If Luciano were to walk because a dolt like Joe Bendix or a conniving syphilitic like Nancy Presser had been caught in a lie, or because Tom had failed to deliver on the promised testimony of Good-Time Charlie Burke, or because Sol Gelb had foolishly bought a drink or two for a witness who needed them, then what was the

349

point of all the hours, all the effort and energy, that had gone into staging what amounted to the most complex and meticulous criminal prosecution in New York history?

The jury *had* to have seen the truth, he told himself. Seen how the other defendants and even their lawyers had fallen on their swords for the Boss. Seen how policemen from jurisdictions both within and beyond the subpoena power of the court had flocked to Foley Square on Luciano's behalf. Seen the terror in the faces of the witnesses who'd been brave enough to take the stand and meet his baleful stare.

The combination men were only using Luciano's name, Levy had argued in his closing, to achieve their nefarious ends. But if Luciano were simply a gentleman gambler, as he'd tried to portray himself on direct, then what were the Jimmy Fredericos and the Benny Spillers and the Pete Harrises of the underworld hoping to achieve by invoking his name? Why would a recalcitrant madam or a reluctant booker of women find fear or succor under the shadow of a mere gambler? Surely the jurors, each experienced as such, had to see the logic of that. See that Luciano was no mere gambler. See that he was and is precisely what Tom had labeled him: the greatest gangster in America.

And what of Marjorie Brown from the Waldorf-Astoria, the young girl who'd stood in the hotel hallway five afternoons per week, waiting to clean Charlie Ross's room? Little Molly, they called her, who'd stepped bravely from the witness chair to touch the shoulders of Wahrman, Betillo, Berkman, and Frederico. And why would a two-bit thug like Frederico have visited Lucky's apartment twenty or more times, as Molly had attested, if not to discuss the bonding combination that was Frederico's only possible connection to the Boss?

And then there was Cokey Flo. Sick, frail, and yet brave beyond measure, she had answered every disgusting question, endured every leering insinuation the defense had hurled in her face. But never once, despite nine hours of the most grueling cross-examination Tom had ever witnessed, had she given an inch of ground in her depiction of Luciano as the heartless mastermind of the combination, ordering that houses be wrecked and madams beaten. If there had been no other testimony in the case—no Mildred Balitzer or Molly the bath maid—surely that of Florence Brown alone should have been enough to win conviction on all counts.

But wait. Levy had cajoled Cokey Flo into admitting that she'd voluntarily bonded, and had been only too happy to do so. Tom had thought nothing of that testimony when given, but now he realized its import. If the jurors considered Cokey Flo to be an accomplice or co-conspirator, then her testimony would require independent corroboration. If so, and if the jury disbelieved Bendix and Presser, then they would need both to believe Mildred Balitzer's testimony and to categorize her as a victim . . .

Confounded by these ruminations, vacillating between glorious victory and crushing defeat, Tom finally dozed. Dozed while the defendants played pinochle in the witness room downstairs. While bleary-eyed reporters, chatting and smoking, clustered in the courthouse stairwell. While the wives of the defendants sought fitful sleep on folded newspapers in the hallway outside the courtroom. While over a thousand anxious spectators—mostly neighborhood Italians— stood candlelight vigil in nearby Mulberry Park.

All of them waiting for the jury's verdict.

A poll of the reporters, taken just after closing arguments, had Luciano acquitted by a vote of thirteen to one. Inside the witness room, the atmosphere was similarly optimistic, even ebullient. The defendants joked and wagered and roared with laughter when Ralph Liguori gave Jimmy Fredericks, stamping and cursing, a hotfoot. Reflecting the upbeat mood of their clients, the defense attorneys had gathered at an all-night restaurant across the square, where, like soldiers after a battle, they recounted each sortie and skirmish of their righteous campaign with hyperbolic bravado.

Only George Morton Levy, still brooding over his client's testimony, was absent from the celebration. Once McCook had completed his charge to the jury at approximately nine thirty on Saturday evening, Levy had slipped quietly through the hallway crowds and down the staircase and out into the square, where, ignoring the flashbulbs and the shouted questions that had followed him onto the courthouse steps, he'd lit a cigar and melted into the crowd.

Meanwhile, inside the jury room, a ballot was taken. And then a second.

Philip McCook switched off his desk lamp and removed his glasses and pinched the fatigue from his eyes. He pushed up from his chair and crossed to the little bathroom, where a new shaving kit, purchased for the occasion, had been laid out on the shelf above his sink. He ran the tap and, while waiting for the water to warm, removed his tie and collar.

Outside the bathroom, where the thin light of dawn was just filtering through the curtained windows of his chambers, a buzzer sounded three short bursts.

Tom woke with a start, as though heeding some silent alarm. It was Sunday, he realized, the seventh of June. It was five o'clock in the morning. He sat upright on the couch and ran a hand through his hair before swinging his feet to the floor. He stood and straightened his clothes and started for the hallway door, where he was met by a breathless court attendant.

"Mr. Dewey," the young man said, "the jury's returning!"

Judge McCook was already on the bench when Tom arrived in the courtroom, and the jurors, looking tense and exhausted, were waiting in the box. Tom sought their eyes as he walked down the aisle and passed through the gate and took his usual chair, but none found his in return. That fact, combined with the relative speed of the verdict, weighed heavily in his stomach.

There followed agonizing minutes of delay and confusion as first the defendants and then their various lawyers returned to the courtroom. The scene was an incoherent jostling of bodies and briefcases, knees and elbows, made doubly strange by the total absence of conversation—as though all present had been summoned to some solemn and hastily called requiem.

Finally, as the last of the newspaper reporters took his seat beyond the railing, the hallway doors were locked and a sepulchral silence settled over the courtroom.

Mr. McNamara, the head clerk, stood and cleared his throat.

"Edwin Aderer," he began, reading the roll of jurors.

"Present."

"Theodore A. Isert . . . "

The wait was interminable. Tom glanced over at Levy, who was studying the jurors with focused intensity, and took small comfort from the fact that the veteran trial attorney appeared to be just as anxious as he was.

The roll completed, the clerk set down his roster. He then intoned, "The foreman will please rise."

Mr. Aderer, Juror No. 1, stood.

"Gentlemen of the jury, have you agreed upon a verdict?"

"We have," the foreman said, unfolding a paper from his pocket.

"How say you, gentlemen of the jury? Do you find the defendant Luciano guilty or not guilty on count one?"

Tom held his breath as the foreman, his face without expression, half turned to Luciano, who was gripping the edge of the table.

"Guilty," he said.

The word sang like a bullet, its twin syllables the entrance and exit wounds that felled Luciano where he sat.

A communal gasp had sucked the air from the courtroom. Tom lowered his head. A hand was slapping his back. To his right, somewhere at the defense table, he heard a pencil snap.

The rest of the verdict took forty-five minutes to read. Forty-five minutes of liturgical call and response punctuated by murmurs from within the courtroom and muffled screams from without.

By the time the entire verdict was read, the word "guilty" had been pronounced 558 times.

Fifty-Two

Aftershocks

June 1936

I KNEW THIS girl from California once, her name was Jean, and she told me all about earthquakes. About how they happen all of a sudden, with no warning or anything, and how they can knock your plates off the shelf and your food right out of the icebox. And just when you think they're over and you've cleaned up the mess, how another one comes along and does it all over again.

The verdict in the Dewey vice trial was kind of like that. We got the news during Sunday breakfast at the House of Detention. It was a great win for the prosecution, the warden announced, with all the defendants found guilty on all counts. That shook the ground, believe you me, and for a lot of the girls at our table it called into question the basic laws of nature.

The ones who'd cooperated were relieved, as you might expect, and the ones who hadn't probably felt like saps. I wouldn't know.

I was too busy making plans for what I was gonna do once the dust finally settled.

Then around two weeks after the verdict came the first aftershock. Twenty-five years for Tommy the Bull. Twenty-five to forty for Little Davie. Thirty to fifty for Charlie Lucky! Even the bookers who'd cooperated got knocked off their pins. Pete Harris and Dopey Al Weiner each got two to four years, and Davey Miller three to six.

But the worst aftershock came when I heard about Jimmy's sentence. Because this was his third felony conviction, Judge McCook had thrown the book at poor Jimmy and given him twenty-five years in prison. Twenty-five years! For a low-level schnook who'd been earning all of thirty-five dollars a week!

I have to admit, I cried when I heard that bit of news. But I didn't cry for very long.

He could've turned state's evidence, I told myself, and cooperated like I did. Or he could at least have taken the stand and testified in his own defense. But no, not Jimmy. Instead he just sat there like a puppy dog and let Siegel run the show for him, never understanding that his lawyer was more concerned about saving Charlie Lucky's skin than he was about saving Jimmy's.

I'd tried to warn Jimmy about Siegel, but would he ever listen to me? No, of course not. And now look where it had landed him.

After the verdict, but before the sentences had been handed down, Judge McCook had ordered all the girls who'd testified back to the courthouse and then, one by one, into his office. There, right in front of Dewey or one of his assistants, he'd made them all swear on the record that their trial testimony had been true and voluntarily given.

In my case, he and Barry Ten Eyck and a court stenographer made a special trip to the House of Detention. That was on Monday, the day after the verdict. The judge, when I saw him, seemed almost sheepish, like he was asking me for a favor. He wanted to know if I'd told the truth on the witness stand, and whether I'd been coerced in any way, and even whether I'd been "plied with liquor," as he put it.

No sir, Judge! Now can I get my stuff and go home?

But where was home, exactly? Technically speaking I was still awaiting sentencing on the solicitation charge, not to mention trial on the other charges from back in January. What was worse, I realized then, was that all I had to show for my cooperation with Dewey was a handshake agreement with Barry Ten Eyck that nobody else had witnessed. So now it was my turn to put my trust—my faith, my future—in the hands of somebody else's lawyer.

Say what you will about Dewey, but as far as I'm concerned, he was a man of his word. First Mrs. Carter took me to court in general sessions, where she told the judge how I'd cooperated with the big vice investigation and where I was given a suspended sentence on my solicitation conviction. Then Barry Ten Eyck himself came with me to special sessions and had a word with the judges in private, after which I pled guilty to the earlier charges and received another suspended sentence.

That could've been you, Jimmy. Hell, that could've been both of us, together.

When I was down at the Woolworth Building that last time before going to court in special sessions, Barry explained to Mr. Dewey that I'd lost my job on account of Mrs. Calvit being sore at me for dragging her name into the trial. Then Barry told Mr. Dewey that he wanted to include me in that magazine and film deal that he and Dewey were negotiating for Mildred Balitzer. Well, that was the first I'd heard anything about Millie being part of the deal, but it was okay with me on account of I liked Millie and figured there'd be more than enough green to go around. Besides, Millie had had it pretty rough—she'd had a miscarriage while in custody—and what with Pete heading for at least two years in the slammer, she'd need some help getting back on her feet.

So one day this man named Doherty, Edward Doherty from *Liberty* magazine, came and met with me and Millie at the House of Detention. We talked for over an hour about the kinds of stories we could write—about running a house, and shooting dope, and living with wise guys like Jimmy and Pete. I have to admit, we laid it on pretty thick. Then, just before I got sprung, Millie and me went with Barry to the Macfadden Publications offices in the Chanin Building and met with the head honcho there, a man named Fulton Oursaler, who said that while the movie deal hadn't come through just yet, we shouldn't worry about it because he knew the business and thought that once the articles got published starting in December, we'd have the studios begging us for the exclusive rights to our stories.

The actual deal Barry cut with Macfadden was that Millie and me would each get fifty bucks a week for ten weeks, as an advance against a total payout of $1,250 each. And while that wasn't quite as much money as Barry had promised, it was still okay with me on account of Millie getting her share and the movie deal being just around the corner. Plus it meant that Mrs. Calvit would see my name in the magazine every week for two or three months running while she, a so-called professional writer, couldn't sell her pathetic stories or her stupid book proposal for love or money.

I only wished I could be there to see the look on her face when she opened her precious *Liberty* magazine and saw my name in black and white. But I planned to be in Hollywood by then, lounging at poolside and sipping daiquiris under a palm tree. Hoping there wasn't an earthquake that might shake a coconut loose!

Things were happening so fast by then my head was practically spinning. It was only that first weekend after I'd been sprung from jail that I finally had a moment's peace and quiet to put my feet up and think about all that had happened. About how I'd gone from being carried to solitary sick and crying, abandoned by Jimmy and suffering from the five-day cure, to sitting in a plush leather chair in the editor's office at *Liberty* magazine. And all of it happening in the space of just five crazy weeks!

Only in America. If you used your noggin and played your cards right, it really was the land of opportunity.

Or so I thought at the time.

Fifty-Three

True Colors

"YOUR HONOR, I have nothing to say outside of that—I want to say it again—that I am innocent."

Simple and straightforward, these are the last words Lucky will ever speak to Judge McCook, although they're not the exact words he personally would have chosen. What he wanted to say—what he *would* say if Levy and Polakoff would only let him—is more along the lines of "Judge, you're crookeder than I'll ever be, you sorry fucking hypocrite. First you let the whores and the madams go free—which makes you the patron saint of New York prostitution—and then you railroad me into jail for what's probably the only crime on the books I ain't never committed. And the worst of it is, you know goddamn well that I'm innocent, and that your boy Dewey would never have laid a glove on me if you'd refereed a fair fight. So fuck you, Judge, and fuck the mayor and the governor too. And if I was all of you, I'd start watching my backs from now on."

This is what Lucky aches to say, but with sentencing imminent and post-trial motions yet to be made, there is no profit to be had in antagonizing the old man. Or at least that's what Levy and Polakoff have told him. So Lucky says what he does—defiant, yet measured—then waits for the hammer to fall.

While Lucky is livid at McCook, and even more so at Dewey, he recognizes that the weight of the sentence, whatever it is, will rest squarely on his own shoulders. Levy and Polakoff had warned him—had all but begged him—not to testify, but rather to let the lies and the slanders wash over him like so much rain on a stone. To place instead his trust in Levy's high-minded notions of reasonable doubt and presumed innocence. But Lucky was never one for trusting the law, let alone its fictions and constructs, and he'd vowed to himself that if he did testify and rolled snake-eyes, he'd at least leave the game with his head held high.

And that's what he plans to do.

McCook, for his part, has shed his veneer of judicial politesse and offers instead a scathing pronouncement before imposing sentence.

"The crimes of which you stand convicted are of placing females in houses of prostitution, receiving money for such placing, and knowingly accepting money from their earnings without considera-tion. An intelligent, courageous, and discriminating jury has found you guilty of heading a conspiracy or combination to commit these crimes, which operated widely in New York and extended into neighboring counties. This makes you responsible, in law and morals, for every foul and cruel deed, with accompanying elements of extor-tion, performed by the band of co-defendants whose records and characters will shortly be discussed, or some of them. I am not here to reproach you but, since there appears to be no excuse for your conduct or hope for your rehabilitation, to extend adequate punishment."

And then the hammer falls.

Afterward, on the steps of the courthouse, the special prosecutor joins the judge in abandoning pretenses.

"This, of course, was not a vice trial," Dewey tells the throng of waiting reporters. "It was a racket prosecution. The control of all organized prostitution in New York by the convicted defendants was one of their lesser rackets. The prostitution racket was merely the vehicle by which these men were convicted. It is my understanding that certain of the top-ranking defendants in this case, together with other criminals under Lucania, have gradually absorbed control of the narcotics, policy, loan-shark, and Italian lottery syndicates, the receipt of stolen goods, and certain industrial rackets . . . "

When Lucky reads Dewey's remarks in the evening papers, he is livid all over again. This is precisely the point that Levy had tried to make, first to the jury and then to the judge when objecting to Dewey's closing argument: That Lucky has been prosecuted not for the crimes charged in the indictment, but for his suspected associations and his criminal reputation.

With Lucky's stay request having already been denied, he is soon to be moved: first to Sing Sing for processing and then farther up the river to Dannemora. But first he holds a series of private meetings with selected visitors to the Raymond Street Jail.

With his brother Bartolo, Lucky plans for the future of his family. With Moe Polakoff, he makes arrangements both for Gay Orlova and for the new legal team that will soon be handling his appeal. Finally, with his old friend Meyer Lansky, he weighs the fate of his newly uncertain empire.

"It was a rotten business from the get-go," the little man says, settling into his chair in the visitor's room, where he and Lucky face each other through a screen of wire mesh.

Lucky shrugs. "Not much you can do when the fix is in. Or maybe it's just that Dewey's Jews were better than my Jews."

Meyer smiles at this. "That's what you get for listening to Frank. You wanted the best Jews, you should have come to me."

"And you wanna know the funny thing? Four fuckin weeks I sat there lookin at them broads, maybe fifty of 'em, one whore after another, and not one of 'em you'd screw without a bag over her head. Two bags, in case the first one fell off. I mean, gettin convicted is one thing, but my rep with the ladies may never recover from this."

"I must say, Charlie, you're in better spirits than I expected under the circumstances."

Lucky checks to be sure that no guards are within earshot before leaning forward in his chair.

"That's because we got new evidence that all of Dewey's witnesses were lyin through their teeth."

"What evidence?"

"It ain't important. The point is, I'm hopin this jail thing is only temporary. Meanwhile I got motions and appeals and appeals from my motions, so it looks like I'll be inside for a few months at least, no matter what happens. Plus they're sendin me to Siberia, so communication won't be easy. What I need to know is that somebody's got my back down here and is takin care of my end. And by that I mean someone I trust."

"Relax, Charlie. I've already talked it over with Frank and Joey and Vito. They send their regards, and they want you to know that everything will be business as usual. It'll be just like you were still at the Waldorf. If you want, I'll personally move everything that's yours to Zurich, so it'll be waiting for you when you get out, which we all hope will be very soon. Meanwhile, I'll handle your day-to-day banking like I already do for Benny."

"Like you already do for Batista."

Meyer shrugs. "Like I would for all my good friends. You'll have to sign a few papers, that's all. I'll send them up with Moe. Now what about your family?"

"That's already taken care of. If Bart needs money, you see that he gets it. Moe too. I'm figurin on a hundred grand for the appeal. Jesus Christ, Meyer, you shoulda been a lawyer. I was just thinkin this morning, I could've put every whore in Manhattan on my payroll, had all of 'em waitin for me when I got home at night, maybe eight or ten girls to a shift, and still come out ahead. Instead what I got was this."

Lucky gestures to his surroundings. To the industrial gray walls and the cold iron bars.

"We've got people at Dannemora, Charlie. They'll take good care of you. However long it is, it'll be easy time. Only I can't promise any showgirls."

"Jesus Christ, Meyer. And here I thought you was connected."

Lucky is smiling again when he stands and places a hand on the screen. Meyer mirrors the gesture, so that their palms are pressed together.

"We had a helluva run."

"That we did."

"With your brains and my balls, we nearly took every trick."

"If only for that damn wild card."

"Hey, what was that guy's name again, the one with the wings made of wax?"

"You mean Icarus?"

"Yeah, that guy. You watch yourself, Meyer. Especially down in Cuba, you keep your wings out of the sun."

"I will, Charlie."

"And one last thing. Tell Bennie if he wants to bake me one of them cakes of his, to be sure to put a hacksaw inside."

"We'll do better than that. We'll have a cake waiting for you at the Waldorf, with Gay Orlova inside."

"Good thing we both know a guy in the sugar business."

"That we do, Charlie. Only don't keep her waiting too long, you hear me? Even sugar won't sit on the shelf forever."

Fifty-Four

Wild Card

July 1936

ON TUESDAY, THE ninth day of June, just two days after the Luciano verdict, the intercom buzzed in George Morton Levy's Mineola office. It was lunchtime, and George hesitated before lifting the receiver, fearing yet another reporter or, worse, another publicity-seeking crank.

"Who is it this time?"

"He won't give his name, Mr. Levy, but he says he has important information about the Luciano trial."

"Take a message, Miss Dooley. I don't think I can take another—"

"I think you'd better take this one, Mr. Levy. He seems on the up-and-up."

George looked at the clock. He was due at his club in twenty minutes.

"All right, put him through."

George could hear voices in the background, and the musical clatter of dishes and glassware. A restaurant, he thought, or a maybe a tavern.

"Mr. Levy?"

"This is George Levy."

"My name is Marr, Mr. Levy. I've got a letter for you, a very important letter from one of the witnesses in that Luciano trial."

"What witness?"

"I don't know, some broad. All's I'm doin is a favor for somebody else, that's all. You want the letter or not?"

"Yes, I want the letter. Where are you now? Can you deliver it here?"

"I'm in the city. At the Villanova, on West Forty-Sixth. Can you come here?"

"No, I'm afraid that isn't possible."

There was silence on the line as a hand covered the mouthpiece.

"Okay, look. I'll come as far as Jamaica. We can meet at the station."

George again eyed the clock.

"I have a lunch engagement I can't get out of, but I can send someone from my office. And forget the station. There's a lawyer named Vollmer, Henry Vollmer, who has an office at one sixty-one Jamaica Avenue. Why don't you wait there, or better yet, why don't you just leave the letter there and—"

"No can do. I'm supposed deliver it personally."

"Deliver it for whom, exactly?"

"Never mind that. Who should I be lookin for?"

"A young man by the name of Weil, Harold Weil. He works for me, and you can trust him to bring the letter straight here."

"Henry Vollmer. One sixty-one Jamaica Avenue. Harold Weil. How about we say one o'clock?"

"That will be fine. And listen, where can I reach you in case something goes wrong? Is there an address or a telephone—"

"Look, I don't want nothin to do with this, okay? Like I said, I'm just doin a favor for a friend."

George went ahead to his meeting, and when he returned to his office at two thirty, an envelope bearing his name was waiting on his desk. He opened the envelope carefully. Inside were two handwritten notes, one folded inside the other. The outer message was written on a sheet torn from a legal pad, and while it was not signed, George recognized Harry Weil's neat, slanting hand.

Mr. Levy:

A Mr. Mar gave me this note at Vollmer's. He said it was given by Helen Kelly to the wife of the owner of Monroe's Tavern on 76th St. in N.Y.C. Helen Kelly was escorted by a cop and somehow managed to slip this note to the woman. Mar received it yesterday. The girl will try to phone you today between 5 and 6, but he does not know if she has your office number, and she will have to slip away from the cop to phone. He will try to call you today around six o'clock, and will see you tomorrow if he does not call.

The second note appeared to have been hastily scrawled. It covered the entire front and back of a plain white envelope.

My name is Helen Kelly. I am a Dewey witness. I have some important information which I believe could help to clear C. Lucky. The evidence against him from N. Presser + T. Jordan + M. Harris was perjured. I can swear to that. I should be glad to testify for him at the appeal if it could be held over until the case against Gypsy Tom Petrovich is over and I am released. I shall call Geo. Morton Levy's office Tuesday evening about 5 or 6 P.M. Please believe I am sincere in trying to help Charlie Luciana. I can't stand seeing a man go to jail on perjured evidence without a fair trial.

For Charlie's sake please don't tell Dewey about this. I'd do time if he found out I got in touch with you people.

> *Sincerely,*
>
> *Helen Kelly*

Please don't notify Dewey. It would mean big trouble for me.

George was standing by his desk as he read the letter. He looked at the clock. And then he sat down.

He remembered Kelly, but only vaguely, and so had to consult his notes from the trial. She was a prostitute who'd been called by the prosecution early on, right before Joe Bendix. Harry Cole had examined her, and Cantor and Murray had crossed. George hadn't paid her much mind and had made no notes of any substance during her testimony.

George dug the city phone book from the bottom drawer of his desk. He dialed the number for the Villanova restaurant. It was the same restaurant, he recalled, at which both Bendix and Mildred Harris claimed to have met Charlie Lucky.

It took a while, but George finally spoke with the owner, a Mr. Joe Carroll. Yes, he was the one who'd asked Marr to deliver the letter. No, it was all on the level. The Kelly girl, Carroll explained, had written the letter there, in the ladies' room at the Villanova, and had wanted to pass it to Carroll but hadn't the chance and instead had slipped it to the bartender at Monroe's Tavern. She knew plenty, she'd told Carroll, and wanted to talk to George. Carroll didn't know all the details, but he thought it involved Dewey's men taking the girls out and getting them drunk.

After he hung up with Carroll, George phoned Moe Polakoff and alerted him to the letter's existence. Then he sat watching the telephone, which, to his growing consternation, never rang again.

At seven o'clock, George put the letter in his office safe and went home for the night.

There were several phone calls over the next two weeks: cryptic and furtive messages that, in each case, had caught George out of the office. Then the sentences were handed down, and the calls stopped altogether. Polakoff, who seemed conversant with the inner workings of Dewey's office, said that the Kelly girl was still being held as a material witness in respect of this Petrovich character, a notorious pimp. He said he would monitor her status and advise George when and if she was ever released from custody.

Another week passed. Then on a Friday afternoon, the third day of July, George was stuffing his briefcase for the Independence Day weekend when the intercom buzzed. The woman's voice when it came over the wire sounded young yet surprisingly poised.

"Mr. Levy? My name is Helen Kelly. I'm terribly sorry it's taken this long for us to finally talk."

Fifty-Five

Risk Management

July 1936

IT HAD BEEN McCook's idea to bring the girls back to the courthouse in order to refer them out to various social service agencies. But
it was Tom who'd suggested that the judge put them under oath again
and make all of them reaffirm their trial testimony. Winning a verdict
was one thing, Tom knew, but keeping it was another story. And
when it came to protecting this particular verdict, the judge and the
special prosecutor needed to be singing from exactly the same hymnal.

Given the nature of the prosecution, Tom recognized that the case
had certain vulnerabilities on appeal. Did the joinder law, for example,
really apply retroactively? Were the defendants entitled to know who
had testified before the grand jury? Did failure to charge a conspiracy
vitiate the wholesale introduction of hearsay evidence?

But the biggest vulnerabilities by far were the witnesses themselves, for the simple reasons that few were educated, most had been

drug addicts, and all would soon need money on which to live outside of jail. For many, despite their heartfelt vows of sobriety and chastity, that would mean a quick return to drugs and prostitution. And if a girl was willing to sell her body for a couple of greasy dollars or a shot of heroin, then how cheaply might she be willing to sell her word?

Tom knew that the moment the girls were released from the House of Detention, Luciano's minions would descend on them like gnats on an open wound. Beyond the protective custody of the court, and with the sword of prosecution gone from over their heads, the girls were liable to say or do just about anything. Which meant that, whether the inducement took the form of money, drugs, or simple threats, many were likely to recant.

Such was the gossamer of which the prosecution had been woven.

Compounding this dilemma was the inconvenient fact that none of the girls had cooperated when first arrested. Since it had been the practice of the special prosecutor's office to make a stenographic record of every witness interview, that meant most of the girls had already given at least one sworn statement denying any knowledge of the bonding combination or, ipso facto, the involvement of Charlie Lucky.

Thus the fact of a girl's recanted testimony, combined with her initial denials, gave at least a numerical advantage to the appellants in urging reversal of the verdict. This was the edge that Tom, with McCook's cooperation, was hoping to neutralize.

"Think of it as a firewall," Tom had told the judge. "A way to contain flare-ups before they burn down the entire house."

"What about the defense?"

"We just want statements, Judge. We don't want to retry the case."

It was no coincidence, therefore, that the first witness to be interviewed, in her case at the House of Detention, was Cokey Flo Brown. It was important to question her, Tom had urged McCook, before Frederico was sentenced, and while her own charges were still

pending. And so, with Barent Ten Eyck at his side and a court stenographer seated between them, McCook settled into the warden's
chair and again faced the slender young woman who had all but
single-handedly slammed the prison door on Lucky Luciano.

Q: May I congratulate you on looking better than you did in
   court?
A: Thank you.
Q: And I congratulate you also on the way that you seemed to be
   able to stand the strain of the court. I heard you testify. Did you
   tell the truth?
A: I did.
Q: If you had to go on the stand again—which I don't think you
   will, certainly not before me—you would tell the same story,
   except perhaps add something more that you might remember
   or something less that you might forget, you would tell the
   same?
A: I would.
Q: Were you ever intimidated or threatened or frightened or
   anything of that kind?
A: No.
Q: By either District Attorneys or anyone here?
A: Never.

. . .

Q: Did they say what they would do for you if you did tell the
   truth? Did they say anything of that sort to you?
A: No; they said that they would help me as much as legally
   possible.
Q: In the troubles that you were already in?
A: Already in.
Q: Were you properly treated by them at the Woolworth Building
   and here?
A: I was.

Q: And you have no complaints to make; nothing you think that could help other people who get into trouble here, or jacking them up and make them do different?

A: Not at all.

Q: All right as far as you know?

A: All right.

Q: And you have no criticism of the District Attorney's office either?

A: None at all.

Q: Did you see anybody plied with liquor, or were you plied with liquor yourself or anything of that kind?

A: No.

Q: All that happened to you was that when you were sick once or twice, they gave you liquor by my directions?

A: Yes, that is right.

Q: That is all you know about it?

A: That is right.

Q: Did anyone ever make improper advances to you anywhere, either there or here?

A: No, sir. Absolutely not.

Q: I realize that your situation is quite different from that of the others here, a good many of them, most of them, and all I can say is that I believe the District Attorney will continue to help you by keeping his promises to you in every way that he can, and if anything goes wrong or you think that it is not being done right for you, send for me, will you?

A: I will, thank you.

And so the process began, and before it was over, all seventy-seven of the women still in custody as material witnesses faced the same obsequious jurist conducting the same gently solicitous interrogation— all without the knowledge, consent, or participation of counsel for the defense.

The girls for the most part affirmed the truth of their trial testimony while denying any coercion or undue influence by the office of the special prosecutor. All, that is, until a breathless Stanley Fuld, the chief legal scholar on Tom's staff of all-star assistants, returned to the Woolworth Building on Saturday morning, June 20, and made a beeline for his boss's office.

He entered without waiting for an answer to his knock.

"Stanley? What's going on?"

"It's the Kelly girl, Helen Horvath. I just came from McCook's chambers."

Tom closed his file and set it aside. Helen Horvath, or Helen Kelly as she was known in the trade, had been a minor witness for the prosecution who was fast becoming a major pain in the neck. She'd lived with several of the key witnesses before the trial, including both Mildred Harris and Nancy Presser, and she'd told Paul Lockwood after the verdict that both Mildred and Nancy had perjured themselves, and thus that Luciano had been convicted on what she'd called "a pack of lies." Alarmed by her allegations, Lockwood and Jake Rosenblum had immediately put her under oath and taken yet another detailed statement.

"You look as though you ran the whole way here, Stanley. Please, sit down. Here, have a glass of water. I thought Harry was the one handling those things."

"He was, but he had a conflict this morning, so I agreed to pinch-hit."

Fuld dragged a chair directly opposite Tom's desk while Tom, his pulse quickening, struggled to hide his irritation at Harry Cole for delegating what was probably the most sensitive of all the post-verdict interviews to poor, bookish Stanley.

"Okay," Tom said. "Tell me exactly what happened."

"I met with McCook beforehand to explain the situation, and I showed him the witness statement she'd given to Jake and Paul. He read it through, then asked if that was still the girl's position. I said it was. He said not to worry, and that he'd try to finesse it as best he could. He also said that Petrovich, the girl's boyfriend, was coming up for sentencing, and that he'd remind her of that fact."

"And? For God's sake, man, what did she say?"

Fuld unfolded a document from an inside jacket pocket and slid it across the desk. Tom recognized it as a "daily"—a rough transcript of the morning's interview prepared by the court stenographer but not yet proofed or certified. Tom tore through the pages, looking for the relevant passage, and he found it starting on page five.

Q: These various things that you say that you discussed with the women that were with you around in different places and hotels—I suppose you don't know why they said to you the different things they said to you?

A: No.

Q: You have no way of knowing whether they said various things to you by the instructions of the office or some other way?

A: No, your Honor.

Q: And therefore, you have no way of knowing whether these women knew any of the people who were on trial before me; that is, you have no way of knowing of your own knowledge.

A: No.

Q: How did they go about questioning you, in respect to your knowledge of various individuals, at the District Attorney's office? Some of these girls testified that pictures were shown them. Were pictures shown you?

A: Yes.

Q: And what was said to you when you were shown pictures?

A: Mr. Lockwood asked me to look through a bunch of pictures and see if I could identify anyone.

Q: Did he give you any names, or indicate to you whom he wanted you to select?

A: No, I selected—

Q: Did Mr. Rosenblum either?

A: No.

Q: Did anybody?

A: No, nobody.

Q: All they did was to show you about how many pictures?

A: Oh, I don't know; I must have looked through several hundred on different occasions.

Q: And out of those, you selected some of the people that you knew?

A: Yes.

Q: And you testified about those or some of them before me, I suppose, and my jury?

A: Yes.

Q: Who were some of the people that you picked out as looking like people that you had seen, do you remember? Did you find out afterwards who some of those people were?

A: Yes.

Q: And who were some of the people that you afterwards found out the names of that you picked out at trial as people that you had seen?

A: Jo Jo Weintraub, Jack Eller, Jesse Jacobs. I thought I knew Davie Betillo, but I wasn't sure, and I picked out Charlie Luciano's picture, but I didn't know his name at the time. I thought I had—

Q: What did you tell him about the person whose name you afterwards found out was Lucky? Where did you say you had seen him, and in whose company?

A: I met him in Gypsy Tom's company two years ago, before I became a prostitute.

Q: Did you hear Gypsy Tom and him talk?

A: No, there wasn't any conversation between them.

Q: Did you hear any name used?

A: I just heard him referred to as Lucky.

Q: By Tom?

A: By Tom, but, your Honor, I am not sure it was that man.

Q: I did not ask you whether you were sure; that is, I did not ask you whether you were sure.

A: Yes.

Q: Did anybody at that office ask you whether you were sure?

A: Yes; they asked me if I was sure, and I said I couldn't be sure; he just merely looked like a man that I had seen two years before.

Q: Yes, exactly. And that the name called was Lucky?

A: Yes.

Q: You saw a man in the court—you saw plenty of men in the court?

A: I did.

Q: Did you recognize one of them as the same man that you heard called Lucky?

A: The man that I saw was heavier; he had the same sort of an eye, a drooping eye, but he seemed to be a little bit heavier-set.

Q: Is there any more difference in weight than would naturally result from a month or two in jail?

A: Well, I don't know.

Q: You realize, I suppose, that Gypsy Tom has pleaded guilty before me?

A: Yes.

Q: And I am going to sentence him later on . . .

Tom leaned back and relaxed. The old man, he thought, could still cross-examine. He slid the transcript across his desk.

"Well, Stanley, now that the judge has covered these matters in such detail, I suppose we can destroy that last witness statement, wouldn't you agree?"

Fifty-Six

California

December 1936

WE SPENT THE rest of that summer up in New Rochelle, Millie and me, living in a hotel and writing down stories and meeting with Mr. Doherty, who lived nearby in Larchmont. According to Barry Ten Eyck, Judge McCook had warned the defendants that if any harm came to any of the witnesses, he'd personally make sure that each defendant served every last day of his sentence. So while we weren't afraid of getting bumped off or anything like that, we were still being pretty careful, keeping our eyes open and our ears to the ground.

We went into the city once a week to pick up our paychecks, which were mailed to Barry's office at the Woolworth Building, and to get a read on the situation. We'd been warned by both Barry and Mr. Dewey that Lucky's people might come looking for us, pestering us to change our testimony, and so we used phony names and colored our hair and generally snuck around like thieves in the night, avoiding the old hangouts and always checking to make sure we weren't being followed.

It was actually kind of fun in a way, or maybe it was just silly, us acting like spies or lamsters when all we were really doing was going to the drugstore or visiting the hairdresser.

Come fall, once the writing was finished, Millie and me moved back to the city full-time and took a room together at the Park Crescent Hotel. I was Gloria Moore, and she was Norma Gordon. We tried to visit Barry a few times, but it seemed like he was always too busy to see us, and that maybe he was giving us the brush-off. Pete was up in Sing Sing, but they were holding him in solitary for what they said was his own protection and they wouldn't even let Millie visit. We were still avoiding the people and places we'd known before, and we were trying to watch our money, so when we weren't out to the movies, we'd spend most nights in the hotel just reading magazines or playing cards or listening to the radio.

Pretty soon we were bored stiff, and I knew that if we kept on going like we were, we'd wind up in trouble again. Since there wasn't any more dough coming in from Macfadden, and since I had my bail money back and still had a little nest egg stashed away from before I'd been pinched, me and Millie decided to buy ourselves a car, a used Chrysler, and head out to California to wait for the *Liberty* articles to appear. That way, we figured, when opportunity knocked, we'd be right there to answer the door.

Neither of us had ever driven that far before, so we made a vacation of it. We took the southern route, stopping for three days in Hot Springs, which is where Charlie Lucky had been arrested, and from there we sent a letter to Barry Ten Eyck letting him know that we'd blown town.

Millie was good company. We talked about buying ourselves a little business when we got to California, like maybe a millenary or a lingerie shop, but then as we put the miles behind us, we got an even better idea. There was money to be made, we decided, in the tourist court business, and it seemed like something we could afford. And when I say "we," I really mean me, because Millie had only her *Liberty* money and her witness fees, most of which she'd already blown by the time we left New York.

We arrived in Los Angeles the week of Thanksgiving, and by that time we'd watched carefully and asked questions and learned how to pump our own gas and check our own oil and tires. So we looked in the L.A. newspapers and found a small filling station for lease with an attached motor court called White's Auto Camp in Pomona, which is around thirty miles east of Los Angeles proper.

They had orange and lemon groves in the Pomona Valley, and palm trees, and daytime temperatures that were still in the upper eighties at a time when New Yorkers were already wearing their furs. You could wear short pants and sandals practically year-round, and you could walk down the street and pick an orange right off of some-body's tree and eat it on your way to the post office. I must've eaten a crate of oranges that first week we were there, and except for the dry desert air taking all the curl out of my hair, I hadn't felt or looked better in years.

We told Mr. White, the owner of White's Auto Camp, that we were Gloria Moore and Norma Gordon, magazine writers who'd been working for Macfadden Publications but had left New York in search of warmer weather and a steadier paycheck. We listed Barent Ten Eyck, Esq., as our lawyer and financial manager, which was practically true, and then we sent Barry a telegram letting him in on the gag.

I ended up putting five hundred down for the station, plus another hundred for stock and sixty bucks to improve the lighting. We renamed it the Rooster, on account of a hot dog stand next door that was called the White Hen and was shaped like a giant chicken. I'm not kidding, they had some crazy buildings in California.

Once word got around that a couple of girls were running a filling station, well, people started coming by just to see for themselves.

Millie would top off the gas while I'd look under the hood and check the oil and water and clean the windshield. We had business cards printed up, and we flirted shamelessly with the cops and the truck drivers, making sure everyone got a card and sometimes a peck on the cheek before they left. As far as the locals went, we told 'em we were new in town and just getting started, and that we'd sure appreciate it if they'd keep buying their gas from us. And it worked too, because pretty soon we were selling more gas than both of the other stations in town put together.

I wrote a few letters to Barry, always as Gloria Moore, updating him on our progress and pestering him for news about the movie deal. Warner Bros. had passed, he finally wrote us, but there was still hope that one of the other studios might be interested. But then the first article appeared in *Liberty* in early December under the title "Underworld Nights," and I for one thought it was a real stinker, and so did Millie. No wonder the studios weren't interested!

Around mid-December we got hit with a double dose of bad news, in the form of two letters from Barry that arrived on the same day. The first said that the movie deal was probably kaput because none of the other studios seemed to be interested, although there was one that might be willing to buy the title "Underworld Nights," for all the good that did us. The second letter said that Addie, my former housemaid, had just contacted Dewey's office claiming she wanted my address so she could send me a fur coat that I'd left at Dorothy Calvit's.

What made the movie news so lousy wasn't just that we weren't going to be rich and famous—that was bad enough—but that Millie, who by then was flat as a flitter, couldn't pay back any of the money I'd been fronting for the business. I mean, it was one thing to help her get back on her feet and all, but that didn't mean I had to carry her for the rest of my life, did it? And to make matters worse, Mil was a real city gal who'd never liked getting her hands dirty in the first place, and now she was all the time bellyaching about this crummy job, and this two-bit town, and how her clothes were always smelling of gasoline.

But all of that was peanuts compared to the other news, because there was no way that Mrs. Calvit would have tracked Addie down on her own, and certainly not to return a fur to the likes of me. No, someone had put Addie up to it—someone who wanted to know where Millie and me were hiding out—and I wrote Barry right away to tell him so.

By around Christmastime the situation with Millie had finally come to a head. We were barely talking by then, even when she bothered to show up for work, which wasn't very often, and the business was suffering. Then I got another letter from Barry, this one telling me that Millie had sent him a telegram, and couldn't we work something out to keep the business running and keep Millie happy in California? Well, that tore it as far as I was concerned, her whining to Barry behind my back, and so I really let her have it, telling her she either had to straighten up or else hit the bricks.

It was the very next morning that a truck driver walked over from the White Hen to talk to Millie, telling her that he'd overheard some guy at a Texaco station down the road asking the attendant if he knew anything about two women from back east who'd come out here to go straight and were running a filling station. I'd seen Millie and the trucker talking, so I asked her what was up, and she told me what he'd said. She was all matter-of-fact about it, but I said maybe we ought to buy ourselves a gun. She said that was crazy, and that I needed to calm down because it was probably nothing, and I was left with a nagging feeling that Millie knew more about the situation than she was letting on.

So I slept on that, tossing and turning, and the very next day I sat Millie down again over breakfast. I told her this was no time for secrets, and that whatever had happened between the two of us was water under the bridge, and that what we needed now more than anything was to stick together, because we were in a jam, and how! And that's when it all came out—the tears, the confessions, the truth.

It turned out that even before we'd left New York, Millie had been in touch with a private dick named Dunn who'd been hired by Moses Polakoff, one of Charlie Lucky's lawyers. Dunn was out visiting from Los Angeles, but he'd told Millie he was working with another shamus from New York named McCarthy. Millie said she'd admitted to this Dunn that all of her trial testimony about Charlie Lucky had been a lie to help Pete, but she'd also told Dunn that she wasn't ready to do anything about it just yet, and then she'd skipped town with me and had never gotten back to him.

But that was only the beginning. Millie then confessed that when the movie deal fell through and things had started to go sour between the two of us, she'd wired Jo Jo Weintraub in New York to ask for Dunn's address in Los Angeles, and in the process might have told Jo Jo where it was we were hiding out.

Let me tell you, it was a good thing I hadn't bought that gun, because if I had, I'd have shot Millie right between the eyes! And when I asked her how she could possibly be so stupid, she started bawling again and finally admitted what I'd come to suspect; namely that she'd scored some junk off a trucker a couple of weeks back, and that she was using again. She said she had no money now and no husband and nowhere else to go, and that she'd figured she could maybe sell her story to Dunn or, if not that, then at least get a train ticket back to New York, where she knew people and wouldn't feel like such a stranger in a strange land.

"I know what I done was wrong," she said between sobs, "and that I should've told you before. But I'm lonely and homesick, Flo, and I was afraid you'd think I was a no-good rat and toss me out in the street."

"So you think the guy who's been poking around is this Dunn character?"

She nodded. "He's on the level, Flo, I swear he is. He used to be a G-man. He just wants our statements, that's all."

"*Our* statements? You think I'm gonna stab Barry in the back after all he's done for us?"

"Oh, yeah?" she said, smearing her face with a wrist. "What's Barry done for us that was so great? He got us a few lousy bucks for a whole summer of work, and then when it came time for the big payoff, all's we got was the air. Face it, Flo—they played us for suckers. Look at poor Pete. He cooperated, and what did he get? And all so Dewey could be a big man and get his picture in the newspapers. Some deal that was! And never mind what happened to Charlie Lucky."

I went to the bathroom and brought her some tissue paper.

"It's always the same old story," she said when I came back. "The high-hats get the cake, and we get the crumbs. We're holed up in Podunk, while they're strolling down Park Avenue. They're gonna make Dewey the next governor, and we can't get ourselves arrested. As far as I'm concerned, your pal Barry can kiss my ass, and that goes double for his boss."

She blew her nose and put the tissues aside and took hold of my hands.

"Tell me I'm wrong, Flo. Go ahead. Tell me we wouldn't be better off cooperating with Dunn and going back to New York. There's nobody gunning for us there. In fact, it's just the opposite. Think about it. They need us more than ever. Lucky's lawyers, I mean. We're their only hope. If Hollywood won't pay for our stories, then why shouldn't we sell them to Dunn and McCarthy?"

She got up and went to a drawer in the kitchen and came back with a great big lump of Mexican brown.

"New York, Flo. New Years in Times Square. Champagne at the Stork Club. A couple of months and we'll be back on our feet again, with gowns and furs and clean fingernails."

"And what are we supposed to do for money?"

"What we've always done! With the girls all free and the combination guys in jail, it'll be just like old times. We can run a house and hire our own girls and never have to worry about bookers or bonding or any of that bullshit. The town is wide open, honey!"

I picked up the lump and studied it. I held it under my nose.

"What have we got to look forward to here?" Millie said as she stood again and crossed to the kitchen and came back with an old cigar box. "Selling more fan belts? Maybe someday buying the White Hen? Whoopee! You may call that living, honey, but I'd rather wake up tomorrow in a pine box. At least that way I wouldn't stink like gasoline."

Fifty-Seven

Siberia

December 1936

INMATE 24806 OF the Clinton Correctional Facility spends most of
his days in the prison library, where he finds respite from the swelter-
ing heat or the teeth-chattering cold that seasonally afflicts
Dannemora, New York, only ten short miles from the Canadian
border. It is there that he sits and quietly reads—his lips moving, a
stubby finger tracing the words—cloistered from the stink and noise,
the squalor and brutishness that are the lot of the ordinary prisoner.

He is no ordinary prisoner. He does not, for example, wait in line at
the mess hall, or at the barber shop, and when he enters the communal
shower, the other inmates quietly depart. When he approaches a group
of men playing at cards or checkers, they all stand to greet him. He is
on a first-name basis with the warden, and when the guards—those
burly French-Canadians with their steel-tipped canes and perpetual
scowls—see him coming, they step aside and solemnly nod.

His privilege, however, comes at a price. He makes no trouble, and sees to it that no trouble occurs. At exercise time he is besieged by inmates seeking his advice, his opinions, his personal benediction. He serves as a counselor, and a conciliator, and as the final arbiter of all disputes within both the Italian and Jewish populations. And as an inmate's discharge date approaches, he even acts as a kind of referral agent, sending written recommendations 320 miles south to Manhattan, where the word of Charlie Lucky still carries the weight of a papal edict.

He receives visitors. Meyer Lansky and Frank Costello, or Vito Genovese and Joe Adonis. Men whose mere presence within the prison walls sends whispers down the hallways, through the units, and into the cell blocks. Usually it is Moses Polakoff who accompanies these visitors, according them the privacy of attorney-client conferences at which Polakoff sits in the corner while Lucky conducts the clandestine commerce of the Broadway Mob or the Unione Siciliana.

But all this is background, just as the hum of the laundry or the din of the mess hall is background to the daily life of the prison. For what concerns Lucky most—what commands his attention from sunup until sundown—is getting out of Dannemora and returning to the bright lights of the city after five long months behind bars.

And on that score, at least, things are looking up.

The first break comes when one of the prostitutes still in police custody, a girl named Helen Kelly, kites a note to George Morton Levy. Kelly then meets with Levy in person, providing an affidavit that not only blows the lid off the inner workings of the special prosecutor's office but also obliterates the trial testimony of Nancy Presser and Mildred Balitzer.

And this, Polakoff reports, is only the beginning. In mid-November, Joe McCarthy, a private detective hired by Polakoff, lured Nancy Presser and Thelma Jordan—both recently returned from Dewey's European junket—to the Hotel Belvedere, where he'd planted a Dictaphone and recorded Jordan's admissions that she'd never even heard of Charlie Lucky before her arrest, that Lucky had nothing whatsoever to do with the bonding combination, and that she'd lied on the witness stand when testifying to the contrary.

The dominos, Polakoff tells Lucky, are starting to fall.

The next to topple is Nancy Presser, who, again thanks to McCarthy, agrees in early December to provide Frank Adams and Martin Conboy—the heads of Lucky's new appellate team—with an affidavit recanting her trial testimony.

"That's two down," Polakoff says, snapping his briefcase closed, "and two left to go."

Then, in what looks to be the biggest break so far, McCarthy receives a visit from Jo Jo Weintraub—the erstwhile errand boy for booker Pete Harris—who reports that Harris's wife Mildred has wired him from California and is apparently ready to talk. That, Polakoff tells Lucky, means that Cokey Flo herself might be in play, and if Cokey Flo recants, then there's nothing left of Dewey's case but hot air and yesterday's headlines. And very possibly—once the Kelly affidavit hits the courtroom—a state ethics investigation into prosecutorial misconduct.

"But we need to proceed with caution," Polakoff warns his client. "Remember what the judge said. If either Mildred or Cokey Flo spooks, and if word gets back to McCook, you could be stuck up here until doomsday."

"Caution? Fuck caution! I just turned thirty-nine in this shithole! Whether I do thirty years or fifty years, I still walk out of here an old man, and that's if I walk out at all. No, you tell Adams and his boys I want those affidavits, no matter what it takes to get 'em."

"All right, but don't forget—"

"And here's another thing! You tell Jo Jo there's a payday for him if he delivers. Then tell him you got a private message, straight from me. Tell him Charlie Lucky says he should go after them two broads as though his life depended on it."

Fifty-Eight

Helen's Story

March 1937

HER REAL NAME, it turned out, wasn't Kelly at all, but Helen
Horvath. She was a comely girl in a big-boned sort of way, and she
wore the same floral dress that George remembered from the trial. If
she was at all nervous, she certainly didn't show it, but rather entered
George's office with an air of self-possession that seemed preternat-
ural for a girl of nineteen, accepting George's proffered hand with a
grip that was firm and warm.

She'd arrived in the company of Luciano's brother Bartolo and a
man from Monroe's Tavern, both of whom, at George's insistence,
were made to wait outside in reception. George introduced her first
to the stenographer he'd hired for the occasion, and then to Edward
Thompson, a local attorney and notary whom George had asked to
act as a witness.

"Can I offer you anything, Miss . . . "

"Horvath, please."

"Horvath. Coffee, for instance?"

"No thank you, Mr. Levy. If it's all the same with you, I'd just as soon get this over with. I'm afraid it's a rather long story."

The story began in Kentucky, where Helen was born the youngest of four children to a couple named Nemeth. Her mother died when she was two, Helen said, at which point her father moved the family to New York and boarded her with a family here, then promptly stopped paying the board and disappeared from her life altogether. Helen entered foster care and was eventually placed with John and Anna Horvath, who raised her from ages three through fifteen—by which time she'd completed two years of high school—and then took her with them to Europe in 1932.

Her foster parents settled in Hungary, in Vesperin, but she became pregnant there and returned to the United States, alone, in October of 1933. She'd found work as a hostess in New York at a restaurant on St. Mark's Place, when she was raped by a co-worker and pressed charges against her assailant. She was held in the Florence Crittenden Home for two months as a material witness until, after the trial—a conviction—she entered the Guild of the Infant Savior, a home for pregnant girls. Her daughter Margaret was born in April of 1934, at City Hospital on Welfare Island, and was placed with the Godmothers' League in July of that year, when Helen was just seventeen years old.

With her baby in foster care, Helen was able to work a succession of menial jobs that included stints as a pantry maid and a waitress. Then, in October of 1934, she met Gypsy Tom Petrovich, a handsome Yugoslavian, who soon put her to work as a prostitute. She became ill after several weeks on the job, which engendered a severe beating from Gypsy Tom, and she found herself back on the streets again, homeless and destitute.

She soon met a man named Jack Kelly and became his live-in girlfriend. She returned to restaurant hostessing and taxi dancing, at which she earned up to twelve dollars per week in salary and tips.

Then Kelly became ill, forcing Helen to return to prostitution, again through the dubious offices of Gypsy Tom.

In November of 1935, while working at the house of a madam called Hungarian Helen, she was arrested for prostitution and advised by bondsman Jesse Jacobs to jump her bail, as there was no defense to the charge. This she did, becoming a fugitive from justice. She then contacted Pete Harris, who began booking her into various houses around the city, including those of Cokey Flo and Jenny the Factory, where she earned two dollars per assignation. This lasted for approximately nine weeks, until she again switched bookers. Under Jack Eller she began earning three dollars per customer at houses run by Gussie Silver, Morris Stein, and Jimmy Nusso.

She wasn't picked up in the great raid of February 1, 1936, but, upon learning that Mr. Dewey was offering immunity for cooperating witnesses, voluntarily appeared at the special prosecutor's office, where she was interviewed by Dewey assistants Paul Lockwood and Jake Rosenblum. She gave a sworn statement that day, and another a few days later, following which she was formally arrested as a material witness and brought to Judge McCook's home on 57th Street, where her bail was set at twenty-five thousand dollars.

She spent two weeks at the House of Detention, in a cell opposite that of Mildred Harris, before complaining to Lockwood about her treatment. She was soon released from jail and moved to the Hotel Albert, at 10th Street and University Place, on February 21, 1936. She lived there with another witness named Irene Smith for approximately one week, whereupon both were moved to the Concourse Plaza in the Bronx, where they remained for another week before moving again, this time to the Hotel Margaret in Brooklyn. Irene Smith was then released from custody altogether, and Helen was moved to the home of a policewoman named Margaret O'Dell on Staten Island for a few days while the special prosecutor's office awaited an infusion of fresh funding from the Department of Finance.

Helen said she was under the direct supervision of one police-woman or another throughout this entire period, was earning $21 per week as a material witness, and was taken out to dinner and to the movies on an almost nightly basis. Cigarettes, newspapers, magazines, and taxis were all provided to her free of charge.

After several more moves, Helen was joined by witness Nancy Presser at the Casa Blanca apartments in Bay Ridge on a Saturday in late March of 1936, approximately one week before Luciano's arrest in Arkansas. Helen was first introduced to Nancy at the Woolworth Building the previous night, a Friday, where Dewey assistants Cole, Ten Eyck, and Lockwood all asked Helen for help in convincing Nancy to cooperate. On Saturday evening, their first night together, Nancy told Helen that Cole and Ten Eyck were "trying to get her to implicate someone she didn't even know."

Since Nancy was being interviewed at Dewey's office on a daily basis, Helen would accompany her to the Woolworth Building and would usually wait in the press room while Nancy was privately questioned by Ten Eyck and Cole. Nancy and some combination of Ten Eyck, Cole, Lockwood, and Gelb would go out for lunch and dinner every day while Helen stayed behind. The dinners would last from approximately seven to nine P.M., and Nancy would invariably return drunk. On the first such night, a Monday, Nancy was so intoxicated that Ten Eyck and Gelb had to physically support her, with Ten Eyck telling Helen that Nancy "could drink more Old Fashioneds than anyone I've ever seen."

On the last day of their week together in Bay Ridge, Nancy told Helen that she'd finally agreed to cooperate with the prosecution, stating, "I have nothing to lose and a lot to gain." Nancy showed Helen a newspaper photo they'd given her of Charlie Lucky's arrest, and Nancy told Helen she was trying to memorize Lucky's face.

In early April, Helen was moved to an apartment in Jackson Heights, where she joined witnesses Mildred Harris, Peggy Wild, and Jenny "the Factory" Fischer. It was while they were living together in Jackson Heights that Mildred told Helen it had taken her six weeks before she'd finally agreed to cooperate, that she didn't know Charlie Lucky "any more than I knew Thomas E. Dewey," and that she was cooperating solely to help her husband, Pete. Since Peggy Wild actually *did* know Lucky, who'd been an occasional customer, Mildred would pepper Peggy with questions—How old is Lucky? How tall? How much does he weigh? Does he limp? Does he have a gold tooth?—to which Peggy tartly replied, "I never opened his mouth to look at his teeth!" Peggy Wild—one of New York's more notorious madams—also confirmed to Helen that, as far as she knew, Lucky had nothing whatsoever to do with the prostitution racket.

Helen and Mildred lived together at three different locations over the course of the last three months leading up to the trial. Mildred repeatedly told Helen that she'd never met Charlie Lucky in her life. Like Nancy Presser before her, Mildred would visit the Woolworth Building on an almost daily basis and return to the apartment drunk. On one occasion, Helen accompanied Mildred and NYPD officer William Grant to Joe Conway's Tavern at 95th Street and Amsterdam Avenue, where they'd stayed until seven A.M. with Mildred getting so drunk that she refused to climb the stairs at the apartment, making them all wait until the elevator operator reported for work.

As the trial date approached, Mildred told Helen, "I have them where I want them—I do what they say, and they're going to do something for me," and "I won't be given money directly, but I'll be given ways to get it." When pressed, Mildred explained that she was going to write the story of her life and that Dewey's people were going to help her sell the movie rights. Mildred also told Helen that Nancy Presser and Thelma Jordan were being given a cruise in exchange for their cooperation.

Helen's own trial preparation consisted of mock direct and cross-examinations conducted by Harry Cole, who would coach her on how to respond, telling her, "When I ask how you came to be a voluntary witness, come out proudly and say you wanted to salvage the remains of your self-respect. Lay it on good and thick." It was Cole, in fact, who suggested—she presumed at Mildred's urging—that Helen should testify that Pete Harris told her, "You're too nice a girl to be in this line of business."

Helen was shown photos and asked if she recognized Charlie Lucky. She remarked that the photo of Lucky resembled a man she'd once seen while in the company of Gypsy Tom. Cole and Gelb both pressed her to say that the man in the photo was Charlie Lucky, and that he was mixed up somehow with Gypsy Tom. She refused, stating only that she thought she'd once seen the man in the photo, but that she didn't know his name, and knew of no connection between the man in the photo and Gypsy Tom.

On the day of her testimony—Wednesday, May 20—Helen finally saw Charlie Lucky in the flesh and knew immediately that the man in the courtroom was not the man she'd seen that night she was with Gypsy Tom. She said as much to Gelb, who nonetheless spent an hour with her in the witness room trying to convince her to testify otherwise before finally giving up.

A few days later, after both she and Nancy Presser had testified, Helen saw Nancy again at the Woolworth Building while the trial was still in progress. Nancy was sitting in the investigator's office as part of a crowd that included Pete and Mildred Harris, Cokey Flo Brown, Danny Brooks, Al Weiner, and several others whom Helen did not recognize. All of them—a group that included both witnesses who had testified and those who had not—were listening to the trial on a direct wire that had been run from the courtroom to the office of the special prosecutor.

Nancy Presser was reviewing the transcript of her trial testimony when Barent Ten Eyck entered the room and asked, "How do you like your testimony?" to which Nancy replied, "Gee, I did pretty well, didn't I?" Helen later asked Nancy when she and Thelma were leaving on their cruise, to which Nancy replied, "As soon as they release me."

The day after the verdict, Helen found herself back in the Woolworth Building, where the atmosphere was celebratory. Paul Lockwood asked her, "What do you think of our success?" to which Helen replied, "I'm afraid you won't like my answer." She told Lockwood that the verdict was the result of perjured testimony, reciting what she'd been told by Nancy Presser, Mildred Harris, and Peggy Wild. "Luciano," Helen concluded, "was convicted on a pack of lies."

Lockwood huddled with Rosenblum, and together they hustled Helen into an office where, before a stenographer, they took yet another lengthy statement in which Helen repeated exactly the story that she'd just finished telling to Lockwood.

Shortly after the sentencing, Helen was taken back to the courthouse in Foley Square to get, she thought, her release papers signed. Instead she was told to wait in the courtroom while Stanley Fuld, one of Dewey's assistants, met privately with Judge McCook. After around five minutes, Helen was ushered into McCook's chambers. A stenographer was present, and McCook was reading the transcript of the latest statement Helen had given to Lockwood and Rosenblum. The judge then questioned Helen angrily about the statement, trying to establish that she had no firsthand knowledge as to whether the testimony of Nancy Presser and Mildred Harris had been truthful. Helen had to concede that she did not, and was relying solely on what she had been repeatedly told by Nancy, Mildred, and Peggy.

Helen concluded her statement in George's office by describing her efforts to make contact while still in police custody, and the note that she'd slipped to the bartender at Monroe's Tavern, and her motive in now coming forward, which was to help correct what she believed to be, in her words, an "unjust conviction."

From the stenographic transcript of Helen's statement, George prepared a detailed, twenty-three-page affidavit. Helen returned to George's office the next day—Wednesday, July 8, 1936—and signed the affidavit after making only a few minor corrections on both the original and the carbon. George made sure that Helen initialed every page of both documents before thanking her for her candor and watching through the open doorway as she left his office in the same way that she'd come, with her head held high.

His interview with Helen Horvath was, for all intents and purposes, George's last involvement in the defense of Lucky Luciano. He would deliver the Horvath affidavit to Polakoff, and then it would fall to others to pursue Charlie Lucky's post-trial remedies. These, George knew, would include a motion for a new trial and, failing that, a series of appeals.

George continued to follow the case, of course, and soon learned through the grapevine that Nancy Presser, Mildred Balitzer, and Cokey Flo Brown had all recanted their trial testimony in sworn affidavits, effectively corroborating the allegations of young Helen Horvath.

George wasn't so much elated or even surprised by these events as he was profoundly saddened. If the Horvath girl's story was to be credited—and George was convinced that it should—then Thomas E. Dewey, aided by an overzealous cadre of white-shoe assistants and Justice Philip J. McCook himself, had perpetrated what amounted to one of the greatest miscarriages in the history of American justice.

And now, George was relieved to know, the truth would finally come out.

Fifty-Nine

Going to Towns

March 1937

CHARLES LUCIANO'S MOTION for a new trial based on newly discovered evidence—which included the affidavits of Helen Horvath and Nancy Presser, as well as affidavits and post-trial interview transcripts from Mildred Balitzer and Cokey Flo Brown—had landed like a bomb on the fourteenth floor of the Woolworth Building, and like a bomb it had left its intended targets both stunned and covered with dirt.

Three days later—on Sunday, March 14—the still-smoldering ordinance sat before Tom Dewey as he surveyed his inner circle of assistants from the head of a long conference table. The group, which included Sol Gelb, Barry Ten Eyck, Bill Herlands, Paul Lockwood, Jake Rosenblum, Harry Cole, and Frank Hogan, had assembled at Tom's summons on what would otherwise have been a rare morning off from their ongoing restaurant rackets case, then in its ninth week of trial before Judge McCook.

The mood in the room was gloomy, with a possibility of thunder.

"This motion," Tom began with a tremor in his voice, "represents nothing less than an assault on the integrity, reputation, and career of every man in this room. It accuses this office not only of suborning perjured testimony but also of outright bribery, and, by logical extension, of conspiracy to obstruct justice. It goes without saying, therefore, that every resource at the disposal of this office must be mobilized to oppose and defeat this disgusting and libelous work of fiction!"

Tom stood and pressed his fists into the tabletop.

"I want affidavits from every man in this room! I want an affidavit from every police officer whose name appears in that Horvath declaration! I want affidavits from every officer who ever guarded, transported, or spoke with any of these women! I want affidavits from every social worker who interacted with them, and from every employee who worked where they lived while still in custody. I want the certified transcript of every contrary statement these women ever gave, and an affidavit from the stenographer who took it. And for God's sake, don't forget those one-on-one sessions they each had with McCook after the verdict was rendered. Bill!"

Herlands jumped in his chair.

"We need to delay the hearing on this motion for as long as possible. Use the pending trial as an excuse. We need time to assemble an opposition so thorough and so convincing that it leaves no room for even the slightest doubt as to the integrity of this verdict, not to mention the integrity of this office. Remember, gentlemen, our audience isn't just McCook, but also the press and the Court of Appeals. What is it, Sol?"

Gelb lowered the hand that he'd raised.

"I've read the motion twice now. If you look at the transcript of the interview that Mildred Balitzer gave in New York, which is attached to the McCarthy affidavit, you'll notice she says that she stopped taking dope a year earlier, just after the raid on February first, and she swears she's been clean ever since. Also, both Mildred and

Cokey Flo swear they received nothing of value in exchange for their recanted testimony."

"What of it?"

"Well, I was talking to one of my sources up in Sing Sing yesterday, and he told me that Pete Harris had dropped a stray remark to the effect that Mildred and Cokey Flo took a cure together at some private hospital in New York. Recently, was the impression I got. If that's true—"

"If that's true," Tom interrupted, his fist pounding the table, "then we've caught her in a bald-faced lie! Sol, get up to Sing Sing and talk to Harris. And I mean now, this afternoon. Harry, I want every available detective working on this, even if it means double overtime. We need to find this hospital and subpoena their patient records. Make that our number-one priority."

"But is it really that important, Chief? Who cares if Mildred's on dope or she isn't?"

Tom sat again. The tremor, they all noticed, was gone from his voice.

"You don't get it now, Harry, but you will. Trust me on this. As George Medalie used to say, the smallest fact is a window through which the infinite may be seen."

Tom returned to his rackets trial, but his mind was never far from the Luciano verdict. It was his greatest achievement in a career of outsize achievements, not to mention the source of his national reputation, and he wasn't about to let a pair of drug-addled prostitutes snatch it from under his nose.

The break came a few days later, when police detectives visited the Towns Hospital on Central Park West. Towns was a private sanitarium that specialized in the treatment of drug and alcohol addiction—a drug mill, Tom had no doubt—and while no records reflected the treatment of either a Flo Brown or a Mildred Balitzer, both women were known to change their names about as often as Tom changed his socks. So it wasn't until the detectives flashed booking photos of Mildred and Cokey Flo that they finally hit the jackpot.

"They were admitted on February twenty-fifth under the names Marion Wilson and Florence Stern." Barry Ten Eyck tossed a folder onto the special prosecutor's desk. "The rate was a hundred dollars per week per patient, with payment coming from a 'Mr. Stern.' We showed them a few more photos, and just like we figured, 'Mr. Stern' turns out to be Jo Jo Weintraub, Pete Harris's lobbygow, which explains how Pete knew all about it. And get a load of this."

Ten Eyck laid another Photostat atop the hospital records.

"The Sing Sing visitor's log. It seems our friend Jo Jo tried to visit Pete on September eleventh, but was refused entry. He then returned as Simon Balitzer and visited Pete fourteen different times between October of last year and February of this. The last time in the company of Maurice Cantor."

"Cantor? That makes Jo Jo an agent of the defense attorneys." Tom leaned forward, a finger stroking his mustache. "First Jo Jo steers Mildred and Cokey Flo to this Dunn character in Los Angeles, then the next thing you know he's checking them into a hospital in New York. All on Luciano's dime, I'm sure of it. By God, I'd love to put Polakoff and Adams under oath."

"Wait till you hear the best part. Mildred and Cokey Flo were signed up for a three-week cure, but they both checked out a week early. On Monday, March the eighth to be exact. And what's the significance of March the eighth? Why, it's the same day they signed their recanting affidavits."

Tom slammed his fist on the records.

"It's perjury, plain and simple! Worse, it's a deliberate fraud on the court! Knowing Mildred, she's been doping since the day we cut her loose. Then she and Flo go out to California, where Mildred runs out of money. The film deal stalls, so she wires Jo Jo and offers to sell her story to Luciano's boys in exchange for God-knows-what. Money, or dope, or maybe Pete's safety in Sing Sing. In any event, she gets a trip back to New York and a paid stint in the hospital. Then they rush her straight from the hospital to Adams's office to sign an affidavit in which she swears she hasn't taken drugs for over a year!"

"And that neither received anything of value for her testimony."

"By God, when we bring this to McCook's attention, he'll bounce them right out of the courtroom. Maybe straight into a holding cell."

"I assume you'll want an affidavit from this Dr. Towns who owns the hospital?"

"I want affidavits from every doctor, nurse, receptionist, orderly, and janitor who ever saw them there. Don't you get it, Barry? This is our ruby-red nose. Instead of a she-said-then, she-says-now contest between a couple of hopheads, we'll put the lawyers on trial for suborning perjured testimony!"

Tom grabbed his cigarettes and leaned back in his chair, propping his feet on the desk.

"McCook won't even *read* the recanting affidavits once he hears how they were obtained. In fact, here's a better idea. What do you say we submit our opposition in camera and not even serve it on the defense? We'll ask McCook to hold a preliminary hearing into whether Polakoff and Adams are trying to perpetrate a fraud. Then we'll invite the press to the hearing and cross-examine the lawyers in open court. Just sandbag the hell out of them. Instead of recanted testimony, the headlines will read 'Lawyers Lie for Luciano.' "

"I like it, Chief. I like it a lot."

Tom lit his cigarette.

"Silver medals are nice in track and field, but inside the courtroom, all that matters is who takes home the gold. You remember that, my boy, and the world will be your oyster."

Sixty

Marked Woman

November 1937

IT WAS BARELY sunrise when I reached El Paso and stopped at the first open hash house I could find. Two rusted-out trucks sat in the parking lot along with a skinny brown dog that stood and raised its hackles as I stepped onto the broken asphalt.

"Get! Go on, shoo!"

A bell tinkled over the door as I entered, and the four cowboys at the counter all looked up just in time to watch me trip over the threshold and nearly fall flat on my face.

"What're you gawkin at?"

They all returned to their coffees. I slumped into a booth by the window where I could keep an eye on my car and watch the highway beyond. There was a late-model Buick I thought had been tailing me ever since Las Cruces, but then again, maybe it was just my nerves.

My car had steam drifting up from the radiator, and now the dog was circling it, sniffing at the air. I rubbed my eyes and was looking over the menu when the waitress came from around the counter with a pad in one hand and a coffee pot in the other.

"Just scrambled eggs and toast," I told her.

I sat watching the highway, and the odd passing car, and the sun climbing cold and white over the bare treetops. One by one the old cowboys finished their coffees and dipped into their pockets and slid some coins onto the counter. They mumbled goodbyes to the waitress, and shrugged into their coats, and then the last of them tipped his hat in my direction as the door swung closed behind him.

The joint was empty then, and after another minute of sputtering engines and belching smoke, so was the parking lot. Even the dog was gone. As the sun rose higher, it shone through the window like a spotlight casting shadows across the tabletop—the ketchup bottle and the creamer and the salt and pepper shakers. I pawed through my bag and put my sunglasses on. I finished my coffee and raised my cup to the waitress.

I'd started thinking by then—daydreaming, you might call it— like I always did when things got too quiet. And like always, what I thought about first was the trial. Not just the courtroom part of it— I'd already worn that memory bare—but that whole crazy year that began with me running my own house and living with Jimmy Fredericks and ended with me being, well, whatever it was I'd become.

Joe Sussman used to say that you can't really understand a thing until you've put it far behind you. But I think Suss was wrong about that, because the more time and the more miles I put between me and that goddamn trial, the more I realize I'll never fully understand what it was that actually happened.

Take how it ended. Here were me, and Millie and Nancy Presser, all of us swearing that what we'd said on the witness stand was a lie, and here was Helen Kelly giving the judge chapter and verse about the boozing and the coaching and all the promises that had been made to me and Millie and Nancy and Thelma. And yet with all that evidence going for him, what was the iceberg that sunk Lucky's ship?

Millie, telling a little white lie about dope.

Like it mattered whether we were using or not, or when we'd started or stopped. And that, I guess, was the part I'll never understand. When I was Dewey's witness, it was okay that I'd just taken the cure and could barely see the nose in front of my face, let alone that I needed a belt or two just to keep from falling out of the witness chair. Same thing with Millie. But once we were Lucky's witnesses, then all of a sudden we couldn't be trusted anymore? All of a sudden we were hopheads and therefore vulnerable to what the judge called "undue influence?"

Gee, Judge. What do you call being threatened with twenty years in state prison?

And who, for that matter, was the one who shouldn't be trusted? Dewey swore up and down that he'd never promised Nancy or Thelma a cruise, yet when it turned out he gave 'em one, that was okay. Dewey swore he'd never promised a magazine deal for Millie or me, but when it turned out we both got one, well, that was okay too. Dewey swore that his men had never taken the girls out drinking, but when a cop no less finally testified that they did, that was just hunky-dory. But let Mildred Balitzer tell a tiny fib about dope and all of a sudden our affidavits "reek with perjury" and we're not even allowed to get on the stand and tell the world what really happened?

So here's how I look at it now. Lucky and Dewey, they were like two heavyweights battling their way up the ranks and knocking out every opponent they faced. Then fate played matchmaker and put them both on the same card. Neither had seen the other fight, but each thought he had his man measured. Dewey, he figured Lucky for a barroom brawler with a horseshoe hidden inside his glove. And Lucky, he figured Dewey for a gentleman boxer who fought by the Queensberry rules.

Except that one of them figured wrong, and a whole lot of people got spattered at ringside.

But the world turned, and people moved on, and after a week or two nobody gave a hang about what did or didn't go down on the fourteenth floor of the Woolworth Building because now there was a civil war in Spain, and the Japs had invaded the Chinks, and that cute Amelia Earhart was still missing somewhere in the Pacific.

So Charlie Lucky rots in a prison cell, thanks to the testimony of four or five witnesses who were either proven to be liars or who came right out and admitted it. And Dewey, the little crumb, is hailed by the press as some kind of great and incorruptible crime-buster and gets portrayed on film by Humphrey Bogart and then gets himself elected district attorney, all while climbing over the backs of guys like Lucky and Jimmy and Pete.

Then again, maybe I was just sore. Sore at Dewey and McCook for what they done to Jimmy. Sore about the lousy deal Ten Eyck had cut with Macfadden, letting them sell our stories to Warner Bros. and gyp us out of our cut. Sore that I had to buy a ticket like all the other suckers just to watch Bette Davis play me—me, Flo Brown!—up on the silver screen. Sore that when I told the guy sitting next to me in the theater that I was the girl who the picture was really about, he moved over a seat, like I had two heads or something.

All of which explains why I'm broke now, and on the move, and down to my last quarter cube. But don't get me wrong, I ain't complaining. I've got hot grub in my belly and just enough gas to get me where I'm heading—to where this girl in L.A. told me the dope was cheap and the houses were legal and the action was hot and heavy twenty-four hours a day.

So you see, I can take care of myself. Hell, I been taking care of myself ever since I was fourteen. I don't need any Ralph or Big Joe, any Jack Zuta or Joe Sussman, any Jimmy Fredericks or Barry Ten Eyck to be holding my hand. I'm like that cat who, no matter which way you drop her, she always lands on her feet. And like that cat, I've got a few more lives left to live.

I signaled for the check, and with my very last dime bought a pack of cigarettes for the road.

"Which way to Juárez?" I asked the waitress, tapping out a smoke.

She pointed south.

Author's Note

On October 27, 1907, Salvatore Lucania, the nine-year-old son of an impoverished Sicilian sulfur miner, arrived in New York City. By 1931, he'd grown to become Charles Luciano, a.k.a. Charlie Lucky, the most powerful gangster in New York and the reputed head of organized crime in America.

In June of 1935, Governor Herbert H. Lehman, under pressure to combat organized crime and its corrupting influence on New York politics, chose as his weapon a politically ambitious, thirty-three-year-old former assistant U.S. attorney named Thomas E. Dewey. Appointed special prosecutor for New York County and armed with expansive new legal powers, Dewey set out to do what many considered impossible: bring down the nation's most powerful mobster.

On a Friday afternoon in May of 1936, a forty-eight-year-old Long Island defense attorney named George Morton Levy received an unexpected telephone call. Moses Polakoff, counsel for Lucky Luciano, needed a trial lawyer of unimpeachable reputation to handle his client's defense against ninety counts of compulsory prostitution.

"How much time would I have to prepare?" Levy asked, to which Polakoff replied, "The trial opens Monday."

Florence Newman left Pittsburgh at age fourteen, quickly embarking on a downward spiral of crime, drugs, and prostitution. By the time she settled in New York at age twenty-two, she was Cokey Flo Brown, an addict and a madam and, as the Luciano trial commenced, a pseudonymous inmate suffering through agonizing heroin withdrawal on the fourth floor of the Women's House of Detention.

Four colorful lives, each on its own incandescent trajectory. Dewey would go on to become governor of New York, would nearly become president of the United States, and would ultimately lead one of the world's largest and most powerful law firms.

Levy would retire from practice to found Roosevelt Raceway in 1940, briefly returning to the national spotlight as the first witness called before the U.S. Senate's 1951 Kefauver Committee hearings in New York, famously depicted in *The Godfather, Part II*.

Luciano would serve ten years in Dannemora before winning a pardon from then-governor Dewey for his role in assisting the U.S. war effort in Europe. Deported to Italy, he would briefly reside in Havana, Cuba, from which he—along with boyhood chums Benjamin "Bugsy" Siegel and Meyer Lansky—would finance construction of the famous Flamingo hotel-casino in Las Vegas.

For her part, Cokey Flo Brown would move to California, would see herself portrayed on screen by Bette Davis, and would ultimately disappear into obscurity and addiction in the brothels of Ciudad Juárez, Mexico.

But for four short weeks in the spring of 1936, the intersection of these four lives—in their respective roles as defendant, prosecution attorney, defense attorney, and star witness—enthralled the nation, introducing America to the violent and darkly glamorous world of organized crime and leaving our culture, laws, and politics forever changed.

★   ★   ★

For thirty-five years, the definitive account of the Luciano vice trial was Hickman Powell's *Ninety Times Guilty*, first published in 1939 and later reprinted under various titles. An investigative reporter for the New York *Herald Tribune*, Powell covered the trial as it occurred and personally interviewed many of its key participants. Described by his colleague Charles Grutzner of the *New York Times* as "an admirer and close friend and confidante" of Thomas E. Dewey, Powell went on to serve as a staff assistant to Governor Dewey and as a speechwriter for both of Dewey's presidential campaigns. Dewey also appointed Powell to positions on the New York State Power Authority, the Legislative Commission on Industrial and Labor Conditions, and the Joint Legislative Committee on Wiretapping.

Given his close personal relationship with the special prosecutor, it is perhaps not surprising that *Ninety Times Guilty* reads as a sycophantic paean to Dewey, depicting him as an intrepid and incorruptible reformer battling the dark forces of moral corruption personified by Luciano, a sinister whoremaster. Then in 1974, Doubleday posthumously published the first of a planned two-volume Dewey memoir titled *Twenty Against the Underworld*, which, for the most part, embraced and affirmed the Powell version of history. That same year, however, another, more remarkable book was published, shining a new and very different light on Luciano the man and on the vice trial that ended his criminal reign.

The Last Testament of Lucky Luciano was written by *New York Times* reporter Richard Hammer from notes provided by Martin A. Gosch, a modestly credited Hollywood producer who claimed to have collaborated with Luciano, then living in exile, on a film version of Luciano's life. When that project was abandoned, Luciano instead proposed that Gosch turn the notes of their meetings into a definitive biography, but with one important proviso: The book was not to be published until ten years after Luciano's death.

Luciano died on January 26, 1962, of an apparent heart attack at Capodichino Airport in Naples, Italy. Gosch, tantalizingly, was at

Luciano's side when he died. Gosch himself, however, died on October 20, 1973, before *The Last Testament* was published. Hammer, the book's author, never met Luciano. Moreover, the notes from which the book was purportedly written were subsequently lost by Gosch's widow.

Given *The Last Testament*'s murky provenance, it is only natural that its authenticity has been questioned. Further complicating matters are the numerous instances in which events described in the book conflict with demonstrable historical fact. (For an excellent analysis of these conflicts, I direct readers to Richard N. Warner's "The Last Word on 'The Last Testament,' " which appeared in the April 2012 issue of *Informer* magazine.) On the other hand, *The Last Testament* is rich in intimate life details that preclude its facile dismissal as a clumsy fabrication.

Is *The Last Testament* a hoax, as some suggest, or is it a genuine oral memoir whose defects are fairly attributable to the frailties of human memory and to Gosch and/or Hammer's sometimes clumsy efforts to fill in the narrative gaps? While I don't purport to know the answer, I do know that the book provides a compelling counterweight to the Powell and Dewey portraits of Luciano as imperial overlord of the 1930s New York prostitution bonding combination.

Other books, of course—not to mention films, television series, articles, essays, websites, and blog posts, all seemingly without number—have been written about Luciano, his trial, and the milieu in which it occurred. These include *Five Families* by Selwyn Raab, *The Luciano Story* by Sid Feder and Joachim Joesten, *The Case Against Lucky Luciano* by Ellen Poulsen, and *Boardwalk Gangster* by Tim Newark, to name a few. All were influential in my confection of *Tom & Lucky (and George & Cokey Flo)*, as were *My Partner-in-Law*, Martin Littleton and Kyle Crichton's 1957 biography of George Morton Levy; *Thomas E. Dewey and His Times*, Richard Norton Smith's exhaustive 1982 Dewey biography; and *Little Man*, Robert Lacey's immensely readable biography of Luciano friend and confidante Meyer Lansky.

Author's Note

★ ★ ★

My own interest in the demimonde of New York organized crime can be traced to two extraordinary conversations to which I was a party, almost twenty years apart. The first occurred in the mid-1980s when a friend told me the story of a strange little man who had lived in their rural upstate community near Interlaken, New York. "Danny King" was a virtual hermit who was notably evasive about his origins and personal history. When King was hospitalized in the late 1960s, he gave my friend's father a box for safekeeping that contained what King described as his "most prized possession." Following his neighbor's death, my friend's father opened the box and found that it contained a book, *Women for Sale* by Chile Acuna, which had been published in 1931.

Acuna, it turns out, was the star witness in Judge Samuel Seabury's 1930 investigation into New York public corruption, and the book is a memoir of Acuna's role as chief stool pigeon in a Kafkaesque scheme by which vice officers, bondsmen, paid informants, lawyers, and judges all conspired to free the guilty, jail the innocent, and generally subvert justice in the New York Magistrate's Court. It was these shocking revelations of the Seabury Committee that led to the resignation of Mayor Jimmy Walker and, indirectly, to the appointment of Thomas E. Dewey as special prosecutor for New York County. Acuna himself, who lived under heavy police guard after the trial and who legally changed his name to Charles Mason, was alleged to have died during routine surgery at a Brooklyn hospital in 1932—a death that some regarded as too convenient by half.

I first met Elise "CeCe" Levy, the daughter of George Morton Levy, in Los Angeles in the late 1990s. At the time, I'd never heard of CeCe's father, although I later came to appreciate that he was one of the best-respected trial lawyers of his day. One afternoon in 2004, CeCe casually mentioned that after her father's death in 1977, she'd packed up fifteen locked file cabinets from his law office and moved them to a friend's barn in upstate New York. Intrigued, I asked if she would allow me to review the files. She agreed, and I immediately hopped a plane to JFK.

The file cabinets were there, as advertised, rusting under a moldering tarp. My brother and I spent an entire day combing through every drawer, every file, until we found what we were looking for: George Morton Levy's sixty-eight-year-old case file in the matter of *People v. Charles Luciano.* Inside the file were Levy's correspondence, his trial notes, his annotated motions and briefs, and a whole assortment of original, never-before-seen documents from one of the most notorious criminal trials in American history. With CeCe's permission, I took possession of the file, vowing that if ever I were to trade my own law practice for the writing life—which I finally did in 2006—I would one day devote myself to the Luciano trial.

Was Lucky Luciano really guilty of the crimes of which he was convicted on June 7, 1936? It's a question that's been debated to one degree or another ever since the day the verdict was rendered. Powell and Dewey present strenuous arguments for the affirmative, while *The Last Testament* paints a starkly different picture—of another kind of conspiracy, in which an overzealous, politically ambitious young prosecutor and a compliant judge worked hand in glove using the unlimited resources of the state to achieve a preordained result.

The gist of the case against Luciano was that he actively oversaw and profited from a criminal conspiracy that sought to organize the previously independent purveyors of New York prostitution. That such a conspiracy existed, that it was overseen by Luciano co-defendants Little Davie Betillo and Tommy the Bull Pennochio, and that its edicts were enforced by co-defendants James Frederico and Abraham Wahrman are beyond reasonable dispute. But was the Boss of Bosses himself—a man whose multimillion-dollar empire encompassed liquor, drugs, and gambling—really stooping so low as to skim the meager earnings of two-dollar prostitutes?

One thing that becomes clear to any who study the trial and appellate records is that it was Cokey Flo Brown's eleventh-hour appearance in the proceedings that turned the tide for the prosecution, breathing new life into what had been a moribund case against Luciano and forcing a reluctant George Morton Levy to put his notorious client on the witness stand, with foreseeably disastrous results.

Prior to the advent of Cokey Flo, the only direct evidence linking Luciano to the so-called bonding combination were (a) the testimony of hotel thief Joe Bendix, (b) the expected testimony of prostitutes Nancy Presser and Mildred (Balitzer) Harris, and (c) the identification testimony of a half-dozen hotel employees. Indeed, Justice McCook ultimately instructed the jury:

> As a matter of law, if the jury disbelieve the testimony of the witnesses Bendix, Nancy Presser, Cokey Flo and Mildred Harris, they must return a verdict of not guilty for the defendant Luciano on all counts charged in the indictment.

For a number of reasons, however, this eyewitness testimony was deeply suspect, particularly when viewed in the context of all that transpired both before and after the verdict was rendered.

Let's start with Genevieve Flesher, a.k.a. Nancy Presser. Nancy was a prostitute, a heroin addict, and the former girlfriend of defendant Ralph Liguori, the alleged holdup man for the combination. Once she'd been arrested in Dewey's vice raid on February 1, 1936, Nancy was held as a material witness on a bond of ten thousand dollars. At first she denied any knowledge of the man called Charlie Lucky. Then, after two months in the Women's House of Detention, she asked to meet personally with Dewey. Shortly after that meeting, she was moved to a hotel and, like the other cooperating witnesses, was allowed to visit movie theaters, restaurants, and even nightclubs, all on the government's dime.

In her trial testimony, Nancy claimed to have first met Luciano in 1928, and to have visited him professionally on numerous occasions at both the Barbizon-Plaza and the Waldorf Towers. She testified to several incriminating statements allegedly made by Lucky in or near her presence, all pertaining to the bonding combination. But Nancy's credibility was eviscerated by Levy on cross-examination when Nancy was unable to describe Lucky's hotel rooms—even, for example, whether they had twin beds or double beds—or the way in which a visiting guest must gain access to the Waldorf Tower from the lobby of the hotel.

Next came Mildred Balitzer, a.k.a. Millie Harris. Mildred was a prostitute, an addict, a madam, and the wife of booker Pete Balitzer, a.k.a. Pete Harris, a Luciano co-defendant who'd pleaded guilty and who, in a package deal with Mildred, had agreed to testify for Dewey in exchange for leniency in his sentencing. Once moved from the House of Detention to a comfortable hotel, Mildred was allowed to visit restaurants and nightclubs multiple times in the company of police officers and, on at least one verified occasion, assistant prosecutor Sol Gelb, a particularly embarrassing fact that NYPD officer George Heidt would later confirm on the witness stand at trial.

Mildred testified that she went to Florida in January of 1935 and there saw Luciano at the Paddock Bar and Grill. She allegedly asked Lucky to allow Pete to quit the bonding combination, a plea that Lucky rebuffed. She also testified to a second, similar conversation with Lucky outside New York's Villanova Restaurant in May of 1935.

On cross-examination, Mildred repeatedly denied having received a promise of immunity from prosecution for her trial testimony:

Q: I was referring to any promise concerning immunity or a reward to you for your testimony. Did you receive any such promise in writing?
A: No.
Q: Did you receive any such letter to that effect?
A: No.

Like Nancy Presser before her, Mildred was badly impeached at trial, both by a written statement she'd given on March 5, 1936, in which she'd denied ever having met Charlie Lucky, and later by the testimony of her former boyfriend, Gus Franco, who described a conversation in which Mildred admitted she "didn't know Lucky from beans," but that she "had to back up Pete." Then, after the trial had concluded, her credibility was further damaged by the disclosure of a pre-trial, handwritten letter of immunity signed by Dewey assistants Tom Hogan and Sol Gelb—the latter of whom was present in court but had sat mute even as Mildred denied the letter's existence.

The third and final witness to directly link Luciano to the combination—and the first to so testify—was Joe Bendix, a serial stool pigeon, who, following his eighth hotel-burglary conviction, was about to begin serving a prison sentence of fifteen years to life. When Bendix learned of the big vice trial, he wrote to Dewey's staff and offered to testify against Lucky in exchange for a recommendation of executive clemency. Bendix claimed to have known Lucky for more than seven years, having first been introduced to him by a man named Captain Dutton, and to have been personally hired by Lucky as a collector for the bonding combination—a job he admitted he never performed. Bendix then testified to several incriminating statements allegedly made by his new employer.

As with the other purported eyewitnesses, Bendix was impeached in myriad ways, both before and after he'd left the witness chair. First and foremost, the premise that Jimmy Fredericks had to take Bendix to meet Charlie Lucky before Bendix could be hired on as a forty-dollar-per-week collector both beggars the imagination and contradicts the entire prosecution theme of Lucky as the hands-off mastermind of the bonding combination.

Second, if Bendix really had known Lucky for so long—the unstated implication being that Lucky acted as a fence for items Bendix had stolen—then why did Bendix need to go through Fredericks to gain an interview with Lucky?

Third, once the defense finally located Captain George Paul Dutton—in charge of regulating nightclubs for the state police—Dutton testified that he'd never met Bendix in his life, but that he did know Bendix's third wife, a showgirl named Joy Dixon, which might explain why Bendix had invoked his name.

Finally, Joy Dixon herself, whose real name was Muriel Weiss, and whom Bendix repeatedly claimed was present at the Villanova Restaurant when Bendix met with Lucky about the combination job, later denied having attended any such meeting and even proved by her own passport that she'd been out of the country at the time the alleged meeting occurred.

The final nail in the testimonial coffin of Joe Bendix came when a letter he'd written to Joy from the Tombs prison was mistakenly delivered to the office of Assistant District Attorney Morris Panger, with whom Bendix had also been negotiating for executive clemency by offering to testify for the prosecution in a different high-profile case. In that letter, Bendix stressed the importance of gaining Dewey's cooperation and urged his wife to "think up some real clever story" to tell. Dewey, not incidentally, had the Bendix letter in his possession for over a week before it finally came to the attention of the defense via Morris Panger.

It is also worth noting that at the time Bendix was testifying for the prosecution, Joy Dixon was, unbeknownst to the defense, waiting in the adjoining room and was scheduled to be Dewey's next witness. Levy, in open court, stated to McCook, "We shall make an effort to locate this man's wife, and if we do—I do not know with what success—we would like to have the opportunity of recalling this man." Yet Dewey and Gelb sat silently at the prosecution table, even though Dewey assistant Eunice Carter was sitting in a room with Dixon not fifty feet from where Levy stood.

There were other instances, it should be noted, in which perjured testimony was either presented by Dewey or allowed to go uncorrected into the record. One example of this was the testimony of

David Marcus, a.k.a. Davey Miller, one of the bookers who'd begun the case as a co-defendant before turning state's evidence. On cross-examination, Miller—a former Pittsburgh police constable—denied having ever run a disorderly house, thus forcing the defense to call detectives from Pittsburgh to prove that both Miller and his wife had, in fact, previously been convicted of doing precisely that—a fact that Dewey's team, ever scrupulous in their due diligence, almost certainly knew.

As for the hotel employees who were called by Dewey as identification witnesses—that is, neutral corroborating witnesses able to place Lucky in the company of co-defendants Betillo, Pennochio, Wahrman, and Fredericks—all were brought to Dewey's office and shown photographs of the thirteen defendants on multiple occasions before testifying. Marjorie Brown, for example—a bath maid at the Waldorf—testified that she'd spent no fewer than five sessions with the photographs before being called to the witness stand, which naturally raises the question: If she was able to recognize the defendants from their photos the first time, then why were four additional sessions necessary?

Despite these serial rehearsals, the hotel witnesses actually performed rather poorly in court. Frank Brown, an assistant manager at the Barbizon-Plaza, took the witness stand and failed to identify a single person in the courtroom. Marjorie Brown identified George Levy as a visitor to the Waldorf before correcting herself. Waldorf employee Henry Woelfle misidentified attorney Moses Polakoff as defendant Abie Wahrman. William McGrath, a night bellboy at the Barbizon-Plaza, identified attorney Maurice Cantor as having visited Lucky. Barbizon-Plaza elevator operator Lawrence Overdriver first identified defendant Jack Eller from his photo, then switched in court and identified Jimmy Fredericks as the man he'd once taken to Lucky's room.

Between the dubious testimony of Nancy Presser, Mildred Balitzer/Harris, and Joe Bendix and the shaky identification testimony of the various hotel employees, Dewey had to have known that his case against Luciano—which he was required to prove beyond a reasonable doubt—was headed for serious trouble. And thus the eleventh-hour appearance of an intelligent, attractive eyewitness who claimed she could personally tie Lucky to the others in the vice combination must have seemed like manna from prosecutorial heaven.

So what are we to make of the testimony of Cokey Flo Brown?

Cokey Flo—also known as Florence Newman, Frances Martin, Mildred Nelson, Fay Marston, Gloria Moore, and Florence Stern—first testified to a meeting that occurred in the spring of 1934 at four A.M. in a Chinese restaurant on Broadway near 130th Street. The restaurant, the name of which she could never seem to recall, was some seventy blocks from her apartment at 333 West End Avenue. She and Jimmy Fredericks had left her apartment at approximately three A.M. with the stated intention of going to meet Luciano. Cokey Flo drove, as Fredericks did not have a license. Present when they arrived at the restaurant were Lucky, Tommy Pennochio, and Davie Betillo. Fredericks introduced Cokey Flo to the others as "a girlfriend of mine."

After some nonsubstantive dinner conversation in the restaurant, conducted mostly in Italian (which she—unlike the others present—neither spoke nor understood), Cokey Flo then drove Fredericks, Lucky, Betillo, and Pennochio to 121 Mulberry Street, an address she somehow remembered clearly. Again, the men spoke mostly in Italian. It was during this drive downtown that Cokey Flo claimed that the bonding combination was discussed, in English, with Fredericks complaining about bookers withholding addresses and with Lucky telling Fredericks, "Bring all the bookies downtown tomorrow, I will put them on the carpet, and we will see that that doesn't happen again," and then, "Have them all come down and we'll straighten the matter out."

The second event to which Cokey Flo testified is alleged to have occurred in the fall of 1934. She claimed on that occasion to have driven Fredericks and a loan shark named Benny Spiller to a garage somewhere on the Lower East Side, where she parked on the street and waited while Fredericks and Spiller went inside. Growing bored, she left her car and entered the garage, where she overheard the men's voices. Fredericks later emerged with Lucky, Betillo, and Pennochio, at which point she drove Fredericks home.

The third event occurred around Easter of 1935, when she again drove Fredericks to the same garage, again grew bored and entered the garage, and again saw Fredericks exit in the company of Lucky, Betillo, and Pennochio.

The penultimate event occurred in the summer of 1935, when she and Fredericks went to a restaurant in Chinatown that bore the street number "21." There they encountered Lucky, Betillo, and Pennochio at a table eating, and were invited to join them. As at the previous restaurant meeting, the conversation took place mostly in Italian, with Cokey Flo testifying that "the conversation switched to English when they talked about prostitution." Lucky is alleged to have complained to Fredericks that the racket wasn't producing sufficient income to continue because the houses were too difficult to manage and the madams too resistant to bonding. When Fredericks urged patience, Lucky is alleged to have said, "Why don't you get the madams together, Jimmy? You know, I told you before that being nice to them isn't any good."

The fifth and final event occurred in October of 1935, at the same Chinatown restaurant, where Lucky is alleged to have again complained about the problems with the bonding racket, and also complained that his name was being mentioned too frequently in connection with its operation. "This Dewey investigation is coming on," Lucky is alleged to have said, "and it may get tough. I think we ought to fold up for a while." Ultimately, after listening to Betillo, Lucky decided, "I'll let it go for a couple more months, and if things are the same, you'll have to let it drop."

Now let's analyze Cokey Flo's testimony in light of other facts adduced both during and after the trial.

First, we must consider the extent to which Cokey Flo's various addictions must have affected her ability to recall the alleged events and conversations to which she testified in such detail. By her own admission, she began smoking opium in 1931, with her habit growing from four or five pills per month to five or six pills per day. She began injecting morphine in January of 1935 at the rate of one-quarter grain, three times per day. This gradually increased to one and a quarter grains per day. Then, in mid-February of 1936, she switched from morphine to heroin, which she used at the rate of one ounce per week until her arrest for solicitation on May 8, 1936.

They didn't call her "Cokey Flo" for nothing, and all her testimony must be viewed through the compound lens of narcotic impairment, addiction, and withdrawal.

Dewey contended in his opening statement—before he knew of Cokey Flo's existence—that Lucky Luciano was the secret mastermind behind the vice racket, that Lucky took great pains to insulate himself from those who actually booked, bonded, and operated the so-called disorderly houses, and that Lucky was careful to limit knowledge of his involvement to only a small handful of trusted lieutenants.

This characterization is significant because, at the first meeting about which she testified, Cokey Flo was a total stranger to Lucky. Is it credible that Fredericks would have felt it appropriate to bring his girlfriend to such a meeting, or that Lucky would have allowed it? That Lucky would discuss intimate details of the vice racket in her presence? Or that when the others present all spoke Italian, he would switch to English for that part of the conversation, and for that part only?

This incriminating conversation, moreover, took place in a car not her own that Cokey Flo was driving, with her back turned to Lucky, Betillo, and Pennochio—three people whom she'd only just met. When asked how she could distinguish the voices of these three strangers, Cokey Flo testified that, despite the pre-dawn hour and the absence of any artificial light in the car, she could see their lips moving in the small rearview mirror.

Substantively, Lucky is alleged to have instructed Fredericks to bring all the bookers downtown to be called on the carpet. Cokey Flo testified that, according to Fredericks, this had indeed happened shortly after the conversation in the car. Yet despite their plea bargains and agreements to cooperate with Dewey, not a single one of the booker defendants—Dave Miller, Al Weiner, Jack Eller, or Pete Harris—ever corroborated such an occurrence. Indeed, none of them claimed to have ever met Luciano in person.

The other two restaurant meetings about which Cokey Flo testi-fied carry the same fishy taint. Would Lucky, in English, really discuss incriminating matters in front of a woman who, if no longer a stranger to him, was by then well known to be an unreliable drug addict?

Cokey Flo's testimony regarding the two meetings alleged to have taken place in a Lower East Side garage is similarly suspect. While she was able to remember verbatim conversations from the restaurant meeting in the spring of 1934—not to mention the exact time of her arrival, and even the food that she'd ordered and eaten—as well as the specific address to which she allegedly drove the men after the meal, she was somehow unable to describe the location of a garage she'd more recently visited not once but twice, having parked there long enough on both occasions to grow bored and exit the vehicle to wander.

Dewey assistant Barent Ten Eyck had been in negotiations for Cokey Flo's testimony since May 16, and after multiple meetings had finally obtained her signed witness statement on May 20, at a time when no fewer than twenty-eight prosecution witnesses were still scheduled to testify. With his army of attorneys and detectives, Dewey had ample opportunity to undertake an investigation to corroborate some of what he knew Cokey Flo would say. He could, for example, have sent detectives to drive with her to find this alleged garage and in the process might have talked to the owner and his employees and perhaps have located other valuable eyewitnesses.

Given Dewey's meticulous nature and his penchant of leaving no stone unturned, this was an opportunity he could scarcely have resisted. His failure to do so suggests either that he knew Cokey Flo was lying, making such an expedition pointless, or that he suspected as much and didn't wish to provide the defense with an address at which exculpatory witnesses might be found and subpoenaed.

Cokey Flo's selective memory is perhaps the most damning of all her shortcomings as a witness. So shaky was her appearance on the witness stand that Justice McCook—incredibly—allowed her to take periodic sips of brandy during breaks from her testimony. When asked the day on which she first communicated with Dewey's staff only a week before her testimony, she first said that it was on Friday, then later that it was on Saturday. When asked how much of her own money she'd put up for bail when she was arrested in January of 1936, she first said $900, then later said "over $2,000." When asked to identify the bank account from which the funds were drawn, she said "Central something or other" at Broadway and 94th Street, where no bank existed. Yet when asked on cross-examination to repeat the incriminating conversations she claimed to have overheard, she did so almost perfectly, with a rehearsed, word-for-word precision.

Which brings us to the blandishments Dewey offered to obtain the testimony of Cokey Flo and the other key prosecution witnesses. Defendant Ralph Liguori, the former boyfriend of witness Nancy Presser, testified that Dewey's office had offered him an expense-paid trip to Europe with Nancy in exchange for his cooperation in testifying against Luciano—an offer he'd refused. Affronted, Dewey ridiculed the very idea, and in his closing argument stated:

Oh, and the trip to Europe? That invention was just a little too funny. I mean, some of these lies you cannot analyze, but some of them—who in heaven's name is going to pay for a trip to Europe?

I, on the City's salary? My assistants, or the City of New York? When you get through with this case, gentlemen, I would like to have you look at my appropriation. I would like to have you analyze it, and the contingency fund. Trips to Europe! How utterly impossible and ridiculous! And that is the kind of things they invent in desperation.

Yet at the trial's conclusion, Nancy Presser and fellow cooperating witness Thelma Jordan did find themselves first-class passengers aboard the S.S. *Samaria*, en route to a three-month European tour, all compliments of Dewey and his assistants.

Helen Horvath, a.k.a. Helen Kelly, was a prostitute who, while being held as a material witness for the prosecution, lived in hotels and apartments with both Nancy Presser and Mildred Balitzer. In a detailed, exceptionally compelling post-trial affidavit, Helen adverts to a conversation she'd had with Mildred in April of 1936, before the trial had begun, in which Mildred bragged that in exchange for giving false testimony against Luciano, "she would not be given money directly, but would be given ways to get it," and specifically that "she was going to be given a chance to write a story of her life and they were going to obtain movie rights for her story."

After the trial, Cokey Flo and Mildred Balitzer did, in fact, sell their life stories to Bernarr Macfadden, the publisher of *Liberty* magazine, in a deal brokered by Dewey and Ten Eyck. The articles appeared in serial form during 1936 and 1937, whereupon Warner Bros. purchased the movie rights. In the 1937 film *Marked Woman*, Humphrey Bogart plays a crime-busting Manhattan prosecutor who persuades a reluctant "nightclub hostess" played by Bette Davis to testify against the city's biggest gangster.

Helen Kelly first attempted to contact George Morton Levy on June 9, two days after the verdict, while she was still in police custody. They finally met on July 6, when, in the presence of witness and notary Edward Thompson and a court stenographer, Helen gave a lengthy statement that Levy then reduced to a twenty-three-page affidavit, which Helen corrected, initialed, and signed on July 8, 1936. This affidavit was never filed with the court because Moses Polakoff, wary of further antagonizing Justice McCook, felt its contents were too inflammatory. Instead he prepared a sanitized version of the affidavit, which he eventually filed along with his motion for a new trial.

Helen's original affidavit—a copy of which (together with several other never-before-seen case documents) can be viewed on my website, www.chuckgreaves.com—describes a sorority-house atmosphere in which the arrested prostitutes, once they'd signaled some willingness to cooperate with the special prosecutor, were released from custody, moved to various hotels around the city, and taken to movies, restaurants, and nightclubs. Nancy Presser is described as getting drunk on a regular basis with Dewey assistants Harry Cole, Sol Gelb, and Barent Ten Eyck, while Mildred Balitzer is reported drinking with Gelb and her various police escorts.

Dewey, again, took umbrage at these allegations and offered rebuttal affidavits from various police officers who'd been assigned to guard the three women. NYPD officer William Grant, for example (with whom Mildred was later alleged to be having an affair), submitted an affidavit that is almost comical in its attempt to rebut the charge that Mildred—a recovering addict—was repeatedly plied with liquor:

> At no time was any one of the witnesses above named, while in my custody, in an intoxicated or other condition which necessitated assistance to said witness . . . On many occasions at meals Mildred Balitzer would partake of drinks of liquor, sometimes as many as five or six, but in no instance was she so affected by those drinks of liquor as to lose control of herself or be incapable of conducting herself with usual and normal facility . . . My attention has further been directed to a portion of said Helen Horvath's affidavit on page 15 thereof in which it is stated that I went with Helen Kelly

and Mildred Balitzer to Joe Conway's Tavern, 95th Street and Amsterdam Avenue, remaining there until 7 o'clock in the morning, and with the result that Mildred Balitzer became extremely drunk. There was one occasion when I, Helen Kelly and Mildred Balitzer went to Joe Conway's Tavern at the address stated. We remained there until 4 o'clock in the morning, approximately. Mildred Balitzer had about six drinks and she was the only one who drank as much as that. She did not show in any apparent manner that she was drunk, intoxicated or otherwise seriously affected by the liquor. We then left Joe Conway's Tavern and went to a Child's Restaurant nearby for some food. Thereafter we returned to the house. It is true that Mildred Balitzer insisted upon waiting for the elevator operator who was not on duty at that time, and finally consented to walk up, but this was an invariable practice and routine of Mildred Balitzer's.

Justice Philip J. McCook merits special attention for his role in Luciano's conviction. McCook was a political animal—a sponsor of the New York Young Republicans and a close friend and ally of Fiorello La Guardia's, with whom he'd run for public office in 1919. It was McCook, in fact, who'd administered the oath of office at La Guardia's mayoral inauguration in 1934. While ostensibly acting as a neutral referee of the Luciano vice case, the judge's actions in many respects more closely resembled those of a co-prosecutor. Here are but a few illustrative examples:

The U.S. Constitution prohibits "excessive" bail, meaning bail in a sum that is punitive, and the typical bond for a charge of prostitution in 1936 New York was approximately three hundred dollars. Dewey, frustrated by the arrested prostitutes' initial unwillingness to cooperate, asked McCook to come to the Woolworth Building and arraign them all as material witnesses and to impose bonds in unprecedented sums ranging from ten thousand to twenty-five thousand dollars, effectively guaranteeing that none of the women would ever go free. The judge agreed, and the women were held incommunicado in the House of Detention while Dewey and his assistants worked for several months to turn them into cooperating witnesses.

Before the trial commenced, McCook issued a standard pre-trial order barring witnesses from the courtroom lest they collude or conform their testimony. But he'd already given Dewey permission to run a direct wire from the courtroom to the special prosecutor's office at the Woolworth Building, where, unbeknownst to the defense, Dewey had assembled many of the prosecution witnesses—both those who'd already testified and those waiting to do so—to provide a running commentary to Dewey's assistants, who would then relay any insights or ideas to Dewey by telephone during breaks in the trial.

When Norbert Gagnon, one of the sequestered jurors, learned from his wife that "Italian-looking" strangers had appeared at their apartment building while the trial was in progress, he reported the incident to McCook, who assured him that all steps would be taken to protect his family. McCook then assigned a police detective to guard the juror's home—an inflammatory fact that was known to and discussed at length among the other jurors. The defense, however, was never apprised of either the incident itself or the judge's actions.

The record is replete with instances in which Dewey and his assistants had ex parte communications with the judge. A telling example of this occurred when attorney Samuel Kornbluth—counsel for Cokey Flo's former employer Dorothy Russell Calvit—agreed to meet with George Levy following the second day of Cokey Flo's testimony. When Dewey's detective team got wind of Kornbluth's cooperation with Levy, they arrested Kornbluth in his home. On the evening of May 26, with the trial still in progress, Dewey assistant Thurston Greene accompanied Kornbluth and the arresting officers to McCook's apartment at 57th Street and First Avenue, where McCook anointed himself a "committing magistrate" and, with no notice to the defense, charged Kornbluth with "attempting to suborn perjury" and ordered him jailed. The next day's banner headline in the evening edition of the New York Post screamed LAWYER HELD AS VICE RING PLOTTER, and Samuel Kornbluth, an attorney of twenty-five years' standing with an otherwise impeccable reputation, saw his life and his livelihood ruined.

After the trial, and despite knowing that post-trial motions and appeals would be pursued, McCook nonetheless called all the women who'd testified as prosecution witnesses back onto chambers and quizzed them, under oath and in the presence of one or more prosecuting attorneys, as to the veracity of their trial testimony. This was an obvious effort to insulate the verdict on appeal and was undertaken, once again, without the knowledge, consent, or participation of the defense.

Later, once the key trial witnesses had all recanted, the defense filed a motion for a new trial with the recanting affidavits attached. Dewey prepared a 450-page opposition but, rather than serving it on the defense, he submitted it to the court in camera with a request that McCook conduct a "preliminary inquiry" into whether the recanting affidavits constituted "a fraud upon the court." McCook acceded to Dewey's request and summoned attorneys Moses Polakoff and Lorenzo Carlino to court on April 20, 1937, placed Polakoff under oath, and, over his strenuous objections, allowed Dewey to cross-examine him as to the affidavits he'd filed and the manner of their preparation.

Despite repeated pleas from the defense, McCook never allowed any of the recanting witnesses to give live testimony in support of the motion for a new trial, which he "heard" on April 23, 1937—after giving the defense less than three days to reply to Dewey's opposition—and which he denied on May 7, 1937.

Finally, at the conclusion of the trial, McCook approved the payment of approximately $450, or $3 per day, to each material witness who'd fully cooperated with Dewey's staff. Those whose cooperation was less than total received $1.50 per day. Those who'd refused to cooperate received nothing.

The post-trial recantations of Mildred Balitzer/Harris, Nancy Presser, and Cokey Flo Brown completed a disturbing pattern in which these three witnesses, whose testimony had effectively slammed the prison door on Lucky Luciano, seemed willing to swear to whatever facts best suited their present interests. Immediately following the raid of February 1, 1936, when both thought a return to business as usual was imminent, Nancy and Mildred claimed ignorance of Lucky's involvement in the vice combination. Once it became clear that the combination had been broken and that their own liberty was at stake, both women changed their tunes and implicated Lucky. Once the emoluments of their testimony ran dry, however, all three witnesses returned to their original positions. Each contradictory version was, of course, offered under penalty of perjury.

At the end of the day we are left with two competing but equally compelling narratives that underlie the trial and conviction of Lucky Luciano. In one, an intrepid prosecutor's dogged persistence overcomes fears of mob reprisal to expose the sordid truth. In the other, a zealous prosecutor and a sycophantic judge mount a reckless crusade to win conviction at any cost.

In rendering its verdict, the jury made its choice. With this novel, I invite readers, and historians, to make their own.

A word or two on methodology. In undertaking to write *Tom & Lucky*, I tried to adhere to the true historical record in all material respects. All of the testimonial excerpts that appear in the book, for example, are taken verbatim from the official court record, with only a few minor corrections for punctuation or spelling. As for the careers of Thomas E. Dewey and George Morton Levy, each unfolds along an accurate timeline, even if the individual scenes employed to depict them—the authorial devices of setting, dialogue, and internal monologue—are fictionalized. And while little is actually known about the woman who became known as Cokey Flo Brown, I've employed scattered clues from her testimony and her few extant writings to construct what I hope is a plausible, albeit largely fictitious, life story.

With a character like Lucky Luciano, however, fact and fiction have an unhappy proclivity to blend. Take, for example, the events of October 16, 1929, when Staten Island police officers found a beaten and bloody Salvatore Lucania staggering along Hylan Boulevard. That Luciano survived being "taken for a ride" is such an integral part of his personal legend that no biographer can possibly avoid it. But why did it happen? And who, exactly, was responsible?

There are at least five different versions of this story, three of which are attributed to Luciano himself. The first, which he told to police at the time, was that three unknown assailants had kidnapped him from a Manhattan street corner, taped his mouth shut, then beat and stabbed him before dumping him, unconscious, near Huguenot Beach. Years later, Luciano told a different version of the story to an undercover narcotics officer. In that iteration, it was the police who had kidnapped him, seeking to learn the whereabouts of the fugitive Legs Diamond.

Other versions followed. In *The Last Testament*, Luciano tells Martin Gosch that his assailant was none other than Salvatore Maranzano, who ordered him strung up and tortured for refusing to kill Joe the Boss Masseria. An even more colorful variant of this story appears in Hank Messick's 1971 biography of Meyer Lansky and features Lansky and Bugsy Siegel shooting it out with Maranzano's henchmen to rescue Lucky. Then there's the story told by a former FBI agent in which Lucky is kidnapped by different police officers for the crime of dating one of their daughters.

What's a writer to do? I went with the Legs Diamond version of the story, both because it seems the most plausible—Diamond was, after all, the object of an intensive manhunt at the time—and because it was corroborated by Frank Costello in George Wolf and Joseph DiMona's 1974 biography, *Frank Costello: Prime Minister of the Underworld.*

Here's another example. There are many different versions of the events of April 15, 1931, when Giuseppe Masseria was gunned down at Nuova Villa Tammaro, ending the Castellammarese war and installing Salvatore Maranzano, however briefly, as the Mafia's undisputed Boss of Bosses. And while it is generally agreed that Lucky was the man behind that murder, some versions have him actually pulling the trigger, while others have him hidden in the men's restroom when the shooting occurs. Still others have him many miles away.

Nearly all versions of the story, however, agree on one aspect: that the murder occurred during a card game that had followed a sumptuous multicourse meal. After all, Joe the Boss was a legendary glutton, the murder occurred at approximately three twenty P.M., and Nuova Villa Tammaro was reputed to be one of his favorite restaurants. In *The Last Testament*, the meal was "antipasto, spaghetti with red clam sauce, lobster Fra Diavolo, [and] a quart of Chianti." *The Luciano Story* tells us that "from antipasto to zabaglione, everything had been as delicious as the Old Country." In *Boardwalk Gangster*—billed as "the true story" of "the real Lucky Luciano"—the meal was "spaghetti with red clam sauce and lobster, all washed down with some Tuscan red wine."

There's only one problem with each of these accounts. In Masseria's autopsy report, dated April 16, 1931, medical examiner G. W. Ruger confirms that the victim's stomach was "practically empty," containing "about 2 ounces of thin, greenish bile."

You get the point. The fact is, Luciano's was a life lived mostly in secret and chronicled mostly in hindsight. Where the truth ends and the myths begin, none can honestly say. And while I've tried my best to sift the chaff from the wheat, even I couldn't resist that damned lobster Fra Diavolo.

★ ★ ★

I'll conclude with some well-deserved thanks. First, to all the authors whose work I've previously mentioned, and especially to Littleton and Crichton, from whose Levy biography certain quotations appearing in chapters 14 and 26 of *Tom & Lucky*—those of Saul Rogers, Arthur Hendrickson, Margaret Levy, and Martin Littleton—are taken. Second, to Elise "CeCe" Levy, not only for allowing me access to her father's files but also for sharing with me an invaluable series of autobiographical essays that George Morton Levy dictated during his lifetime. Third, to Sally Dickinson of the Watkinson Library at Trinity College in Hartford, Connecticut, for facilitating my access to the *People v. Luciano* trial and appellate records, which were gifts to the college by Trinity alumnus Philip J. McCook. Fourth, to L.A. super-lawyer Steven G. Madison for his guidance on certain questions of criminal procedure. Fifth, to Darienne Oaks—the granddaughter of George Morton Levy—for her assistance with a few odd matters of Levy family history. Sixth, to my wife, Lynda Larsen; my brother Dan Greaves, and my niece Katie Thomas Greaves for reading *Tom & Lucky* while still in manuscript and providing much-valued feedback.

Finally, I would like to thank my literary agent (and Sicilian translator), Antonella Iannarino of the David Black Agency, and my intrepid editor, Anton Mueller of Bloomsbury USA—along with Rachel Mannheimer, Marie Coolman, Laura Phillips, Helen Garnons-Williams, Maureen Klier, and the rest of the Bloomsbury team, both here and abroad—for their input and their ongoing faith and support, without which this book would not have been possible.

Grazie a tutti.

C. Joseph Greaves
Cortez, Colorado

A Note on the Author

C. Joseph Greaves is a former LA trial lawyer now living in Colorado. His first novel, *Hard Twisted*, was a finalist for the Oklahoma Book Award in Fiction and was named Best Historical Novel in the SouthWest Writers' International Writing Contest, in which Greaves was also honoured with the grand prize Storyteller Award. Writing as Chuck Greaves, he is a Shamus Award finalist for his Jack MacTaggart series of legal/detective mysteries.